P9-BVB-999

A Lady's Revenge

TRACEY DEVLYN

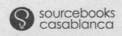

sourcebooks
casablanca

Published by Sourcebooks Casablanca, an imprint of Sourcebooks, Inc.
P.O. Box 4410, Naperville, Illinois 60567-4410
(630) 961-3900
FAX: (630) 961-2168
www.sourcebooks.com

Printed and bound in Canada
WC 10 9 8 7 6 5 4 3 2 1

*To my husband, Tim. You're the man,
you're the man, you're the man.
Thank you—for everything.
HILWY,
Tracey*

One

1804
Near Honfleur, France

GUY TREVELYAN, EARL OF HELSFORD, STOPPED SHORT
at the sharp smell of burning flesh. The caustic odor
melded with the dungeon's thick, moldy air, stinging his
eyes and seizing his lungs. His watery gaze slashed to the
cell's open door, and he cocked his head, listening.

There.

A sudden scrape of metal against metal. A faint sizzling
sound followed by a muffled scream.

He stepped forward to put an end to the prisoner's
obvious suffering but was yanked back and forced up
against the dungeon's cold stone wall, a solid forearm
pressed against the base of his throat.

Danforth.

Guy thrust his knee into the bastard's stomach,
enjoying the sound of air hissing between his assailant's
lips, but the man didn't release his hold. Nearly the same
size as Guy, the Viscount Danforth wasn't an easy man to
dislodge. Guy knew that fact well. For many years they
had tested each other's strength.

"What the hell is wrong with you?" the viscount
whispered near his ear. "We're here for the Raven. No
one else."

Guy stared into Danforth's shadowed face, surprised and thankful for his friend's quick reflexes. What would have happened had he stormed into the cell to save a prisoner he knew nothing about, against odds he hadn't taken time to calculate? Something in the prisoner's cry of pain struck deep into his gut. His reaction had been swift and instinctual, more in line with Danforth's reckless tendencies than his own carefully considered decisions.

"Leave off," Guy hissed, furious with himself. He pushed against Danforth's hold, and the other man's arm dropped away.

He had to concentrate on their assignment, or none of them would leave this French nightmare alive. The mission: retrieve the Raven, a female spy credited with saving hundreds of British lives by infiltrating the newly appointed emperor's intimate circle and relaying information back to the Alien Office.

Guy shook his head, unable to fathom the courage needed to pull off such an ill-fated assignment. The ever-changing landscape of the French government ensured no one was safe—not the former king, the *Ancien Régime*, the bourgeoisie, or the commoner. And, most especially, not an English secret service agent.

Although Napoleon's manipulation of the weak and floundering Consulate stabilized a country on the brink of civil destruction, the revered general-turned-dictator wasn't content to reign over just one country. He wanted to rule all of Europe, possibly the entire world. And, if his enemies didn't unite under one solid coalition soon, he might achieve his goal.

Another muffled, gut-twisting cry from the cell drew his attention. He clenched his teeth, staring at the faint light spilling out of the room, alert for movement or any signs of what he might find within.

Sweet Jesus, he hoped the individual being tortured

by one of Valère's henchmen wasn't the Raven. In his years with the Alien Office, he had witnessed a lot of disturbing scenes, some of his creation. But to witness the mangled countenance of a woman... The notion struck too close to the fear that had boiled in his chest for months—*years*—giving him no respite.

On second thought, he hoped the prisoner was the Raven. Then he wouldn't have to make the decision to leave the poor, unfortunate soul behind, and they could get the hell out of this underground crypt posthaste.

"Are you well?" Danforth asked, eyeing him as if he didn't recognize his oldest friend.

Guy shoved away from the stone wall, shrugging off the chill that had settled like ice in his bones. Devil take it, what did the chief of the Alien Office expect him to do? Walk up to the prisoner and say, "Hello, are you the Raven? No? What a shame. Well, have a nice evening." Only one person knew what the agent looked like, and Somerton did not offer up those details before ushering them off to France. *Why?* he wondered for the thousandth time. It was an answer he intended to find as soon as they got back to London, assuming they survived this mission.

"I'm fine." He jabbed his thumb over his shoulder. "Now cease with the mothering and get behind me."

He barely noticed the fist connecting with his arm, having already braced himself for Danforth's retaliation. Some things never change. Inching toward the cell door, he tilted his head and concentrated on the low rumble of voices until he was close enough to make out individual words.

"Why do you force me to be so cruel?" a plaintive voice from inside the chamber asked. The Frenchman spoke slowly, as if talking to a child, which allowed Guy to quickly translate the man's unctuous words. The gaoler continued, "All you have to do is provide my master with the information he seeks."

A chain rattled. "Go to the devil, Boucher," a guttural voice whispered.

Guy's jaw hardened. The prisoner's words were so low and distorted that it was impossible to distinguish the speaker's gender. Every second they spent trying to solve the prisoner's identity was a second closer to discovery.

The interrogator let out a deep, exaggerated sigh. "The branding iron seems to have lost its effect on you. Let me see if I have something more persuasive."

An animal-like growl preceded the prisoner's broken whisper. "Your black soul will burn for this."

Boucher chuckled low, controlled. "But not tonight, little spy. As you have come to discover, I do not have the same aversion to seeing you suffer as my master does."

Something eerily familiar about the prisoner's voice caught Guy's attention. His gaze sliced back to Danforth to find puzzlement etched deeply between his friend's brows.

Guy turned back, the ferocity of his heartbeat pumping in his ears. His stomach churned with the certain knowledge that what he found in this room of despair would change his life forever. He steadied his hand against the rough surface of the dungeon wall, leaned forward to peer into the cell, and was struck by a sudden wave of fetid air. The smell was so foul that it sucked the breath from his lungs, and he nearly coughed to expel the sickening taste from his mouth and throat.

The cell was twice the size of the others they had searched. Heaps of filthy straw littered the floor caked with human waste and God knew what else. Several strategically placed candles illuminated a small, circular area, leaving the room's corners steeped in darkness. In the center stood a long wooden table with a young man strapped to its surface by thick iron manacles.

A young man. Disappointment spiraled through him. He glanced at Danforth and shook his head, and then evaluated their situation. The corridor beyond the candlelit chamber loomed like a great, impenetrable abyss.

The intelligence Danforth had seduced from Valère's maid suggested the chateau's dungeon held twelve cells. If the maid's information was correct, that left four more chambers to search. Would they, like all the others, be strangely empty?

Guy narrowed his gaze, fighting to see something—anything—down the darkened passage. It yawned eerily silent. Too damned silent. The lack of movement, guards, and other prisoners scraped his nerves raw. That and the realization they would not be able to slide past the nearby cell without drawing attention from its occupants.

Dammit.

He ignored Danforth's warning tap on his shoulder and peered into the young man's cell again. The prisoner's filthy legs and arms splayed in a perfect X across the table's bloodstained surface. A few feet away, with his back to the prisoner, stood a slender man dressed in the clothes of a gentleman, his unusual white-capped head bent in concentration over an assortment of spine-chilling instruments. *Boucher.*

Guy watched the man assess each device with the careful attention of an enraptured lover, masterfully prolonging the young man's terror. Give a victim long enough, and he'll create plenty of painful scenes in his own mind that the interrogator need only touch his weapon to the prisoner's skin to elicit a full, babbling confession.

He couldn't walk away from the poor soul struggling on the table, nor could he cold-bloodedly put an end to his misery. The young man was a countryman, not his enemy, and he would never leave one of his own in Valère's hands.

With great care, he withdrew a six-inch hunting knife from his boot. He heard Danforth curse softly, violently, behind him, and then a rustle of movement. His hand shot out to stay his friend, and a short struggle ensued. Their roles now reversed, Guy whispered in Danforth's ear, "There's no way around, and I'm not leaving him here."

"We don't have time—"

"I'm. Not. Leaving. Him."

After a moment, Danforth gave a sharp nod and settled into the rear support position once more, anger dripping off him in waves.

He couldn't blame his friend for wanting to press on. Evil penetrated every crack and hollow of this place. Even with his vast experience with the darker side of human nature, Guy felt trapped and edgy and unusually desperate.

Guy shifted his attention to the prisoner just as the young man's head swiveled toward the open doorway. Bleakness and terror etched his swollen, blood-encrusted face, but something more blazed behind the young man's steady gaze—strength, fortitude, and a hint of hope.

He was a fighter, a warrior entombed in a rapidly weakening young man's body. A rush of fury mixed with a healthy dose of respect surged through Guy. How did one so young get involved with the likes of Valère?

The prisoner's chest rose high with each deep, agonized breath. As his torturer intended, the young man knew Boucher's next attempt at pulling information from him would be far worse than the last.

Candlelight flickered over his youthful features. When the prisoner focused in on Guy's position, his terrified blue-green eyes—or eye, as one was little more than a bloated slit—opened wide.

Guy's heart jolted, fearing the young man would call

out. With an index finger to his lips, he motioned for the prisoner to remain quiet.

Familiarity washed over Guy again. His gaze cleaved to the prisoner's; his focus sharpened.

Blue-green eyes. An unusual color Guy had seen only once before. His muscles contracted. A wave of frigid heat swept across every inch of his skin, and nausea twisted in his gut.

He knew those eyes.

The young man wasn't a man at all. But a goddamned woman.

Cora.

Two

CORA DEBEAU'S HEART GROUND AGAINST THE WALL OF her chest. She peeled her blurry gaze away from Boucher, unable to watch her gaoler touch each instrument as if he were selecting the perfect snuffbox for his waist-coat pocket. Her keeper was a strange combination of depraved villain and thoughtful philosopher. She had initially thought him French, but she had isolated another, more subtle accent during the times he was caught up in the excitement of his "little experiments."

As he was now.

In an attempt to bolster what meager courage she had left, she concentrated on the rusty metal hook near the cell's door.

Her gaoler enjoyed prolonging her anticipation of what was to come and relished her building fear, her struggle to be brave. Her inevitable failure.

He fed off her pain, of which there had been a great deal.

Constant. Never ending. Nearly unbearable.

Cora knew with profound sadness—and utter relief—that she would soon break. The endless dark days and stifling black nights, the vicious rats, and the limitations of her female body would lead to her compromise.

As Valère knew it would. His legendary patience

would see Cora crumble to the ground like a marionette discarded by its unforgiving owner.

Soon she would be forced to rattle off every bit of intelligence she knew about the Nexus, a group of international spies who worked so diligently, so stealthily toward containing Napoleon's ambitions. Then Valère would kill her and all the other agents of the Nexus. Her three-year sojourn in this country would end abruptly, and the man responsible for killing her parents would forever run free.

Agony of a different sort tore through her chest. Ten years of preparation and three years of searching snuffed out in a matter of days by a Frenchman in a full pout. When Valère had learned of her betrayal, his fury had known no bounds. None.

She hadn't reached her breaking point. Not yet. By now, Dinks, her maid and sometime messenger, would have notified Lord Somerton of her capture. Even now, her former guardian could have men on the way.

In the public eye, Somerton was known as chief of the Alien Office, a small division within the Home Office originally created to monitor the influx of French émigrés after the Terror. But secretly, as head of the Nexus, Somerton commanded a contingent of highly skilled and highly intelligent secret service agents. Because of the group's international reach, the Nexus was actually under the auspices of the Foreign Office.

An image of Guy flashed through her mind, and her heart soared with another infusion of determination. The thought of Guy rescuing her strengthened her mind and numbed her body for what was to come. She could hold on, for a little while longer. She must, if only to see his face one last time.

Then she realized Somerton would never send an administrator on a rescue mission, especially one who could botch the mission from the weight of his emotion alone. Fear for her safety would drive him to brash action, endangering them all in the process. No, Somerton would not be so foolhardy as to send Guy to her. On the tail of this realization, her body suddenly felt anchored in exhaustion. The hours to her possible rescue seemed an eternity to wait.

Her gaze flicked to the open doorway. Something had shifted in the shadows. A mere disturbance of air. She squinted, trying to penetrate the gloom.

Had Valère returned again? He'd made a habit of standing unobtrusively in the darkened corner to watch Boucher practice his art of persuasion. When the torture became too much and she could no longer hold back her screams, he would scurry from the chamber, taking with him any hope of release.

A face pressed through the darkness. Her empty stomach tightened, and tears swarmed her eyes when Guy Trevelyan's features materialized. Familiar and beloved.

And, oh, so out of place.

She blinked several times, thinking he was one of those desert mirages she had read about. But his image never wavered.

She shook her head, wanting desperately to warn him off without drawing Boucher's attention. What was Somerton thinking? Not only was Guy a newly belted earl, but he had no experience with this sort of thing. At least not that she knew of. His particular talents lay in assisting Somerton with the administration of the Nexus, not traipsing through a French dungeon where he could get his bloody self killed.

The darkness behind him remained unruffled; she could detect no other presence. Surely the idiot did not come to Valère's stronghold without a swarm of reinforcements. A shout of warning welled in her throat. She could not bear to watch Guy suffer the same fate she had endured these many days. If they came out of this rescue alive, she was going to kill him. Right after she showered his bloody handsome face with a thousand kisses.

Bloody handsome? She had obviously been spending too much time in Dinks's company. The outrageous maid was rubbing off on her.

A shiny, long object in Guy's hand caught her attention before it disappeared behind his back. He held his finger against his lips, silencing her. She hadn't realized her breaths sawed in and out of her lungs like a spent racehorse.

"Yes, my dear," Boucher said, noticing her distress. A disturbing satisfaction edged his words. "I will join you in a moment. I cannot seem to find an instructional tool that I haven't used on you before."

Instructional tool?

Her interrogator seemed especially cruel and deliberate tonight. He always enjoyed toying with her, but rather than his normal cool detachment, a strange excitement laced his words. It was almost as if all his earlier sessions were nothing more than preparation for this one awful moment.

Panic spasmed through her muscles, and she jerked against her shackles, splitting open old wounds. She forgot all about her savior in the shadows. For days she had been careful not to show her fear, careful not to incite Boucher's baser instincts. But it all had suddenly become too much.

Freedom. Its scent had filled the air seconds ago, making her reckless like a starving caged beast. All she wanted to do was run headlong into its warm embrace.

"Ah, here we go," Boucher whispered.

Cora whipped her head around to watch her tormentor slide his freakishly pale fingers down a long clamp with four sharp, curved prongs that looked like they could wrap around something the size of a man's fist.

Boucher approached her left side, slowly, admiring his weapon with the same worshipful eyes as a child holding a Gunter's chocolate cream ice on a hot summer day. She swallowed hard. Her muscles grew taut, and her body began to shake.

He ran the bloodcurdling device along her breast, and she knew then what he meant to do with his newest toy. A vivid image of the prongs closing around her breast, squeezing until the blood pounded hotly against the strained surface—she bit down hard to stop an involuntary scream of terror.

Through her fear, she managed to remember Guy. She needed to keep Boucher's attention on her. Given her interrogator's current fascination, she didn't think it would be a problem. If she could distract Boucher long enough, Guy could make his move.

Part of her longed for Guy to slip away undetected, return to England and remember her the way she had been before traveling to this godforsaken country. And another part of her, the selfish and frightened part, prayed he would be the savior she so desperately needed.

Various schemes flashed through her fevered mind until one settled in place like the aftermath of a violent storm. Calm and surreal. And oddly sunny.

She grabbed hold of it like a rope to salvation and dragged in a fortifying breath. There would be no second chances.

"No," she whimpered, having no problem dropping her mask of courage.

He skimmed the breast-ripper over her chest again. "Tell me what my master wants to know," he said, "and this time, I promise to stop before you scream."

"Very well." She kept her voice low. Too low. "Please, no more pain."

Triumph lifted his placid features. "Go on. Speak up."

She licked her swollen, cracked lips. "Hurts."

He placed the well-cared-for clamp over her right breast. A warning. "You can have all the water you desire *after* you give me the names. Every single one. Leave no one out."

She forced a cough, a hard, rattling cough that scoured her throat and vibrated through her chest.

"Tell me." His knuckles slashed across her cheekbone, breaking skin already swollen with blood. His calm command stood out stark against the swift delivery of his fist. Warm liquid oozed from her cheek and slid into her hair. Black spots blanketed her vision. It was the incentive she needed to get the words around the mountain lodged in her throat.

After nearly a fortnight of isolation and torture, Cora submitted.

As expected, Boucher leaned close, listening greedily to a long list of coveted names. Her restraints made him bold, unconcerned for his own welfare. She spoke slowly, pronouncing each syllable with precise measure. Careful to keep his attention locked on her words.

Through the whiteness of his hair, she could see his scalp, a pale pink that looked far too delicate on such a monster. Such an odd thing to notice when her existence could be counted in seconds rather than years. She had no doubt that Boucher would kill her once she spoke the last syllables of the final name.

When she shifted her attention to the doorway, it was empty. Her voice staggered for the merest second. Had Guy come to his senses? Or had someone attacked him from behind? So focused was she on keeping

Boucher's attention that she couldn't recall hearing any signs of an altercation.

Closing her eyes, she forced down her alarm, only to have it push to the surface again. Sweet heaven, she wasn't ready to die. Exhaustion and a deep sense of failure penetrated her every muscle and thought. Had her incompetence killed Guy? She had become too confident, too complacent around Valère. One misstep was all it took to land her in a pit beneath his country chateau.

She covertly searched the cell for Guy's solid presence one more time. But with Boucher's body angled over her the way it was, much of her field of view was blocked. *Dammit. Where was he?* She couldn't bear the thought of his death on her hands, too. Her parents were enough. More than enough. Not Guy. Never Guy.

When she pulled the last name from her lockbox, she knew her time had come to an end, and her body gave up the fight. It melted against the bloody table, boneless and beaten.

Boucher's body crashed into her, heavy and rigid. Pain shot through her ribs like a piece of jagged glass ripping through muscle. Air wheezed between her lips, and her eyes shot open.

That's when she saw the mahogany-and-pearl-handled knife protruding from his back. Boucher's knees buckled, and Guy grabbed a handful of his collar and lifted him away.

For a moment, Boucher stared at her with his pale, cruel eyes, glassy now with pain. His natural skin color provided a perfect mask for death. "You will still die." His threat was delivered with a frail wheeze, but Cora felt his words sink into her bones.

Guy whirled her tormenter around and slammed him to the stone floor. Boucher's newest toy clattered uselessly to his side.

A whip of silence cracked through the room. She and Guy stared at Boucher's unmoving body as if waiting for him to miraculously rise. He didn't.

Then Guy's burning gaze slashed to hers, and three years sifted away. They were once again in Mrs. Lancaster's sitting room, standing face-to-face, aching for the other's touch but unable to breach the line of friendship.

"Guy," she choked out.

Two swift steps brought him to her side. He cradled her face, and she felt a pang of embarrassment at what he must see.

"What are you doing here—?"

"Shhh," he interrupted, bending to test her restraints.

"Helsford, what the devil are you doing?" another man whispered, skidding to a halt beside Guy. "We don't have time for this."

Guy's eyes softened, although his features remained harsh, savage even. "I'm saving Cora's life, man."

Danforth's incredulous gaze sliced to hers. "Cora?"

She peered through rapidly swelling flesh to see the Viscount Danforth. She tried to send him a welcoming smile, but she managed only to rip open the weeping slit on her bottom lip. She settled for a simple, tear-clogged greeting.

"Hello, Brother."

Three

GUY CRACKED THE BUTT OF HIS PISTOL AGAINST THE guard's temple and dragged him inside the last of the empty cells. He glanced back at Danforth, who hovered in the shadows, holding a precious bundle of feminine skin and bones in his arms. As he stared at the two deBeaus, a heavy weight of dread pressed down on his shoulders.

What if he couldn't get them to safety? What if one of them died during their escape? He closed his eyes briefly, pushing back the pain. For as far back as he could remember, the deBeaus had been a part of his life. Every time his parents had found some new pleasure, they had readily abandoned their only son to unsuspecting family and friends, or they simply left him at Eton and made him the headmaster's problem.

The boisterous and unconventional deBeaus had given him more than a place to stay for a few weeks. They had given him a glimpse of what a real family could be, *should* be. They had given him a home.

He set his jaw and motioned Danforth forward. No one was going to bloody die. No one.

Then he caught a glimpse of Cora's wide-eyed countenance as Danforth strode by and felt another volley slam into his chest.

Sweet Jesus, she was a mess. And frightened as hell.

He wished he could sweep away her time in Valère's dungeon like a broom swipes cobwebs from a darkened corner. But he couldn't, and the realization nearly destroyed him.

How long had she been held captive? How long had she suffered? Questions without answers ricocheted through his mind in an endless, haphazard circle.

Getting Cora to safety was his only clear thought. The mystery of the empty cells, the absence of the Raven, and the reason for Cora's presence in Valère's dungeon all paled in comparison to getting out of this warren of dank passages that teemed with squealing rodents and rotting refuse.

Guy bent to retrieve the guard's lantern and then led the way toward the secret portal they had used to enter the Frenchman's lair. "This way."

Every corridor he turned down looked the same as the last. The same musty smell, the same abysmal darkness. There were no chambers here, only unbroken stone wall. Even the floors were more primitive, nothing but hard-packed dirt.

None of it mattered, though. Guy had memorized every turn in direction and every change in elevation. Had ticked off each alteration in his head, one by one, storing them in a compartment until it came time to use the information. The underground system of passages proved no challenge for his near-perfect memory.

"Helsford, wait," Danforth said.

Guy came to an abrupt halt and swiveled to look at his friend, who had his ear cocked toward the unlit tunnel behind them. "What is it?"

"I'm not sure."

Mimicking Danforth's stance, he strained to isolate the noise that had caught the viscount's attention. Nothing but the sound of his own breathing penetrated the silence.

Could he have missed a chamber somehow? Had Danforth picked up the distinctive rattle of a prisoner's chains or someone's moan of distress? Cora's frail hand clutched the lapel of her brother's coat with a desperation that tore at Guy's heart. In that moment, he no longer cared about the consequences of leaving England's most valuable spy behind. Whatever punishment Somerton and his conscience dealt out later, he would accept.

Right now, he had two friends to protect, and his world narrowed down to that singular, inviolable goal.

"Danforth," he warned, eager to be away. Then he heard the sounds of pursuit. Masculine shouting and pounding feet echoed through the dungeon, pulsing down a multitude of passages, making it difficult to gauge their enemy's location. He locked eyes with his friend and found the same feral determination to survive this night that pumped hotly through his own veins.

"Go," Danforth urged. "Run."

Guy was already turning away. No longer concerned with stealth, they bolted the final distance, nearly missing the portal leading to the outside. The flush surface of the door blended with the dungeon's wall in both color and texture, giving the illusion of another unbroken corridor.

He stood to the right of the door, waving the lantern in a systematic pattern, searching for the small, rectangular protrusion. When he found it, he handed the lantern to Cora so he could use every bit of strength at his disposal.

With only the blunt tips of his fingers, he pulled and tugged at the stone device until he heard a distinctive click. The door cracked open and was followed swiftly by a suction of air. Now for the hard part. After three fortifying breaths, he braced one foot against the wall, curled his fingers around the door, and pulled.

"Hurry, Helsford."

"I am," he gritted out.

Nestled inside the stone façade sat a heavy iron door. The slab must have weighed as much as a horse, for his muscles stretched and groaned and strained. Earlier in the evening, with the two of them pushing it wide, the barrier had challenged his strength, but not like this gut-ripping test of pulling the damned thing open unassisted.

After what seemed like an eternity, he straightened and then squeezed through the twelve-inch gap. "Hand her to me."

Silent until now, Cora shoved against her brother's shoulders. "You needn't toss me from one pair of hands to the next like a sack of grain. I can walk."

Guy glanced at the stubborn set to her jaw, so familiar and dear. She never liked feeling weaker than them and would always push herself to try and match their strength, sometimes beyond what her body could bear. As she was now. Unfortunately, they didn't have time for his usual cajoling methods to soften her hard head. He held out his arms. "The burns on the soles of your feet tell me otherwise."

She turned her head away while Danforth maneuvered her through the narrow opening and handed her off to Guy.

When she stiffened in his arms and a soft whimper escaped past her lips, sweat broke out on his forehead.

"I'm sorry, sweetheart," he whispered against her burning temple.

Another shout from behind reached them, this time closer. Much closer.

"Go on," Danforth said. "I'll get the door."

Guy wasted no more time. The narrow tunnel opened on the far side of the stables, a clever escape route built hundreds of years ago during one of France's many religious wars. Whatever the reason for its existence, he was thankful for it.

And he was glad to be partnered with Danforth on this particular mission. The viscount's special talent lay in his ability to charm secrets from the most skittish female, a trait Somerton had put to good use over the years.

Every powerful, self-serving man generally aligned himself with one of three types of women—a submissive woman, an embittered woman, or a stronger, more intelligent woman. Danforth had a way of flushing out a wife's hidden desires and turning them to his advantage. The women divulged their husbands' secrets, and Danforth satisfied their craving for a handsome, virile, attentive man's devotion. His talent was both ruthless and effective.

Cora pressed her insubstantial weight against his arm, straightening her back. "How much farther?" she whispered.

Even in the dim light, he could see the battle she waged against an unseen foe. Had she sustained some type of internal injury? Broken rib? Punctured organ? Could she even now be bleeding to death? "Where are you hurt?"

She started to laugh, but it was cut short by a swift intake of breath. After a moment, she managed, "An easier question might be—where am I not?"

Unable to share her humor, he said, "Be specific."

She sent him a cross look. "Ribs. Broken or bruised, I'm not sure which."

Pausing midstride, he adjusted his hold. "Better?"

She nodded, releasing a breath. "Thank you."

"The draught grows stronger, warmer—a good indication we're nearing the entrance to the tunnel." He resumed his ground-eating pace, terror prodding him to greater speeds. The sound of metal against rusted metal reached his ears, indicating Danforth was making progress. Incapable of completely setting aside his original mission, he asked, "Have you seen other Englishwomen here?"

The ends of her butchered hair brushed the underside of his chin. "No."

He grew more and more weary of this damn espionage business. The out-and-out lies, the half-truths, the realities that were distasteful but necessary. Not knowing friend from foe. The life no longer held the glamour it once had. If not for a pair of anguished blue-green eyes, he would have moved on a few years ago.

He shook off the thought. His reasons for becoming a cryptographer for the Nexus no longer mattered. Over the past year, he had worked with Danforth on several cases and was grateful for the added distraction. His restlessness had increased over the last few months when Cora's society reports to Somerton had become scarcer.

A few feet before the overgrown opening, Danforth overtook Guy and pushed the tangled vines aside.

Guy dragged in a deep breath. The cool night air washed away the oppressive stench of the dungeon. But the horrific image of Cora fettered like a rabid animal would stay with him forever.

Cora's brother blew out the lantern and led the way to their awaiting horses.

Guy pressed his lips to Cora's ear. "Almost there."

Her head jerked once in acknowledgment.

He couldn't help but notice the foul odor coming from her weightless body. Rage burned anew. When Guy returned to retrieve the Raven, he would make sure Valère paid for the atrocities he had forced on Cora.

They picked their way around protruding boulders, low-hanging limbs, and thorny bushes until they approached the area where their horses were tethered. Anxiety drove through Guy at the thought of Cora being jounced around on horseback at full gallop with a rib injury.

He glanced down and found her gaze probing the darkness.

Alert.

Tense.

Expectant.

She appeared so vulnerable wrapped in her brother's coat, but her brutalized face revealed nothing but an unflinching resolve. Guy had always been protective of her as a child, but seeing her in this state, stripped of all vitality, heightened his natural instincts.

What the hell was she doing in Valère's dungeon? The question continued to echo through his mind. The last he had heard she was still in Paris with her great-aunt, Lady Kavanagh, feeding *on-dits* of Parisian intrigue to Somerton.

Jesus.

The deep quiet of the forest was his first clue they were not alone. No insects chirped. No small animals scurried for cover. No wind whistled through the leaves.

The second clue came in the form of a hushed yet heated conversation beyond the low rise ahead.

Where they had left their horses.

A cold wave of anxious fury swept through Guy's body. He crouched low, peering into the distance. Danforth followed suit.

Escape was impossible without their mounts. One hour before sunrise they had a rendezvous with a fishing boat that would take them to their awaiting ship.

The waning moon seemed to mock them with its steady descent to the horizon.

He backed up a dozen feet and deposited Cora inside a shrubby alcove. Her fingers dug into his arm with unexpected strength. She looked up at him with fretful, swollen eyes. "What are you doing?"

Bending close, he whispered in her ear. "Getting our horses. I'll be right back."

She gave him a short nod before shrinking into the shadows. Guy chafed at the meager protection, but it would have to do.

He rejoined Danforth and, with a few hand signals, they set out in opposite directions, intent on surrounding their quarry.

As they closed in, Guy began to decipher the intruders' whispered argument.

"We must do something, you old fool," one intruder said.

"They'll return, don't ye worry," said a rougher but equally low voice.

Guy knelt down. He located the two dark silhouettes huddled against a large tree trunk about twenty feet away. To his left, he spotted Danforth, who nodded his readiness, but his assessing gaze lingered on Guy.

He set his jaw and waited for Danforth to turn away before swiping the moisture from his forehead. *Backbone, Helsford,* he chided himself. *Don't turn into a piss-in-your-pants cub like last time.* Make the kill; retrieve the horses; get out of France. His chest rose high and then folded down on a long exhalation.

Danforth looked back at him, waiting for the signal. He gave it, and they both pulled lethal knives from hidden sleeves in their boots and stepped forward as one. Silent. Intent. Deadly.

"I'll never forgive you if my little mite dies in there," the smaller but no less sturdy silhouette muttered.

Guy and Danforth halted.

Little mite? Cora's brother mouthed to Guy.

A memory flashed so swiftly through Guy's mind that he couldn't latch on. It hovered teasingly out of his reach.

He frowned and motioned to Danforth for them to move closer.

"Stop your blathering, woman," the other silhouette grumbled. "The two gents will take care of them toad-eaters, if Miss Cora hasn't already."

Guy eyed the two until recognition dawned. The hard knot of tension eased from his shoulders, and a smile danced across his lips. Danforth stared at the silhouettes, shaking his head in disgust or amazement; Guy couldn't be sure which.

He and Danforth stood less than five feet behind the bickering couple. Near enough to lunge forward and dispatch them with a single slice of their blades. His blood beat in thick waves at how close they had come to eliminating Cora's beloved servants.

They put away their weapons. The rush of energy that always prepared him for a kill took much longer to sheath.

An amused smile cut across Danforth's face. "Listen to him, Dinks."

The maid yelped and lost her balance. She would have landed on her bum had it not been for her companion's quick reaction.

"Unhand me, you old goat," Dinks sputtered, righting her tangled cloak.

"Bah," Bingham said. "Next time I won't save your contrary woman's pride."

"Quiet," Guy warned, his gaze skimming their surroundings.

Dinks crossed her arms over her broad chest and carried on in a lower voice, "As if you've never been caught unawares."

The coachman shuffled from foot to foot, eyeing his counterpart with anger and a hint of chagrin. "Ye just won't let it go, will ye?"

Guy shook his head. The servants' familiar

squabbling—something he hadn't heard in a long time—washed over him and tightened his chest.

"Never mind about that." Dinks sent the coachman a dismissive wave and rushed toward Guy, urgency lacing her words. "Did you find Miss Cora, my lord?"

"We have her, Dinks," Danforth interjected. "We stashed her in the woods when we heard your whispering." He looked to Guy. "I'll get her."

Guy nodded, his attention fixed on Cora's servants. Something about this entire situation left a hollow feeling in his gut as if someone had removed a vital organ and failed to tell him.

"Would either of you care to explain why I found your mistress in Valère's dungeon?"

"Dungeon?" Dinks whispered, her face crumpling.

Bingham slipped a massive arm around the maid's hunched shoulders.

Guy steeled himself against their distress. "Yes. I overheard Valère's man asking her for information. Did he find out she had been feeding society intelligence to Somerton?"

Bingham's lips disappeared inside his mouth, and Dinks averted her watery gaze.

Their refusal to answer his question reminded him of their unfailing loyalty toward their mistress. It had always been thus, even when their role was more caretaker than protector.

Guy had always found their devotion endearing. Until now.

"Never mind," Guy said. "Why don't you tell me what the two of you are doing here? Is Jack with you?" Guy peered into the gloom, looking for Cora's lanky footman.

"Jack went for help. We kept watch," Bingham said.

Dinks sniffed and straightened her shoulders, forcing Bingham's supportive arm to fall.

The coachman scowled.

"It took us a few days to pick up that Frenchie's trail," Dinks said. "Once we knew where he'd taken Miss Cora, we sent word to Lord Somerton straight away."

Bingham scowled. "Didn't I just say that?"

Before Guy could question Dinks further, Danforth emerged from the dense undergrowth, carrying Cora in his arms.

Dinks ran forward. "Miss Cora!" she exclaimed in a rough whisper.

Cora's head lolled against Danforth's shoulder. Her dry, cracked lips turned up in a reassuring smile.

A tear ran down Dinks's once beautiful face. After a decade of service to the deBeaus, she had allowed her trim, svelte lines to expand into a more fulsome figure. "Oh, no." She tentatively touched Cora's arm. "What did that rat-bastard do to our little mite?"

Danforth cleared his throat. "She'll be fine, Dinks."

Cora's thin, trembling hand slid over Dinks's larger one. "Don't fret, dear Dinks."

Guy's vision blurred. Leave it to Cora to try to comfort others at a time like this.

"We have only a few hours to make the coast," Danforth cut in. "We need our horses."

"They're safe, m'lord," Bingham answered with a slight bow of deference. "The black and chestnut were restless and wouldn't calm down, so Jack took them to the creek bed not far from here. The mare you brought is tied up with our horses just beyond the tree line."

Guy clapped the older man on the shoulder. "Thank you, Bingham."

Red faced, the coachman glanced at his mistress and mumbled, "Miss Cora would have my hide if I neglected my duties."

Guy looked back toward Valère's chateau. Apprehension

crawled beneath his skin. Instead of escaping with one prisoner, they now had four innocents to get to safety. Given the exact set of circumstances, he would have made the same decision, yet leaving their original target behind scraped against his conscience.

Cora drew his gaze for the hundredth time. The fact that Somerton had sent him and Danforth here to retrieve a female spy, and the only female in Valère's dungeon happened to be Cora, struck him as entirely too coincidental. However, he found it hard to reconcile his childhood friend with the elusive Raven, known for her ability to seduce secrets from the most reticent of French agents.

As he watched, Cora's eyelids finally gave up their exhausted battle and lowered shut. Guy released a relieved breath and shut out the mystery of Cora's imprisonment. God willing, she would sleep through the grueling ride back to the coast.

A hound bayed in the distance.

Everyone froze; no one breathed.

Another howl rent the air.

Then another.

Dammit. Men they could elude for a time, but trained dogs would lead Valère right to this misfit group. "To the horses," Guy quietly ordered.

They scrambled toward the three horses tied up nearby. Once Guy was seated, Danforth lifted Cora up into his arms.

She stirred, tensed. "What's wrong?"

Guy accepted a wrap from Dinks and draped it around Cora. His heart pounded, but he spoke with calm reassurance. "Nothing, sweetheart. But we have a hard ride ahead of us."

The hounds bayed again, and her fingers dug into his shoulder. She buried her face in his neck. "I'm ready."

Guy glanced back to make sure the others had mounted and then kicked his steed into a fury of swirling leaves and flying dirt.

Four

A FEW DAYS LATER, CORA FOUND HERSELF ENSCONCED in Somerton's library at his spacious London town house. She sat in the corner of the soft leather sofa with a kersey-mere lap rug over her legs and a pretty lemon-colored shawl draped around her shoulders.

The bandage covering her right eye was still an annoyance, but she had finally become accustomed to viewing the world through her one-eyed perspective. Although she was looking forward to removing the bandage in a few days, she wasn't anxious to reveal her disfigurement. Her hair would grow back, and the burns and bruises would heal, but the scar would remain forever etched upon her face—a constant reminder of her imprudent arrogance.

Peering around the familiar room, she adjusted the sling securing her left arm to her chest and ignored the three large men strategically stationed around her. She could feel their curious stares and imagined she could hear the interrogating questions lining up in their heads.

Although she had prepared herself for this meeting, she had no wish to begin. Pulling in a calming breath, she tunneled her finger beneath the bothersome turban to scratch her itchy scalp. She hated wearing the ridiculous adornment, but Dinks insisted, since they hadn't yet cleaned up Boucher's handiwork.

Her reluctant gaze shifted to Guy, the Earl of Helsford, as he was now called after his father's passing last year. With his broad back facing the room, she got a good look at his unfashionably long black hair trailing from a leather thong at his nape. She toyed with the blunt ends of her own hair peeking from beneath her turban and experienced a momentary pang of envy.

Their years apart had wrought compelling changes in his physique. On the few occasions he had visited her sick room, she hadn't been able stop herself from drinking in his sheer masculinity. Then, as now, power radiated off his body in disturbing waves that both attracted and rebuffed. The angular set of his jaw, the tempting fullness of his mouth, and the stillness of his warrior stance left her feeling awkward and ugly and completely enthralled.

But she also recognized the hollowness hovering behind his watchful eyes. Something horrid lurked in the dark cavern of his gaze, something strong enough to rattle the cage he had carefully erected around his emotions. What past event drew him so completely from the present that she had to prod him several times to return?

She sighed softly, frustrated that time and distance hadn't dampened her curiosity about him. As with many times in the past, she would either uncover the answers she sought or banish the question from her thoughts. The option she took depended entirely on how it affected her primary goal of finding the man who killed her parents.

Her hand slid to the pendant hanging from her neck. *I haven't given up, Mama.*

"Thank you for meeting with us," Somerton said, interrupting her thoughts.

Her former guardian's commanding crystalline gaze settled on her, as disquieting as always. She had never feared him, but the intensity of his study had an unnerving effect on her.

Somerton continued, "Would it not have been better for us to come to you?"

Cora smoothed her hand over the lap blanket. "I needed a change of scenery." How did one explain the feeling of walls closing in on oneself? She had wanted, needed to come to the library. Her chest rose high, and she took in the peaceful smell of old tomes and burning coals that tinged the air. The library had always been her favorite place in the house.

Soon after their parents' deaths, she and her brother Ethan had been conveyed to their new home at 35 Charles Street. During those first few months, she would sneak downstairs at night and curl up in Somerton's large overstuffed chair near the fireplace.

Sometimes she would read until the wee hours of the morning; sometimes she would cry herself to sleep. And sometimes she would stare listlessly into the dying embers of the fire and wonder what awful deed she had done to make God punish her so.

Cora shrugged off her old demons and angled her head toward the room's occupants. Across from where she sat, Ethan balanced on the edge of her old favorite chair. Restlessness vibrated off her brother in thick, tense waves. His striking resemblance to their father comforted and unsettled her in the same breath.

In vivid contrast, Somerton, watchful and silent, anchored himself in front of the grate filled with burning coals. His broad shoulders and thickly muscled body made him an imposing figure. Many who did not know her former guardian would label him cold and unfeeling. Cora knew better. Somerton had honored his best friend's request to look after his two young children when it would have been easier to ship them off to a distant relative. He had given her everything she had needed and more, including the resources to avenge her parents' murders.

Somerton moved to stand before her, his hands clasped behind his back. "We will take this as slowly as you wish. But I need to know how you came to be in Valère's dungeon."

And with a single question, the interrogation began. Cora had given careful consideration as to how much of her eleven-day imprisonment she should reveal to these men whom she loved beyond measure. There were pieces of her tale that must remain locked away, events she daren't relive, sacrifices best not disclosed to loved ones.

Her gaze fell on her immobile hand, noticed her thumb tucked between her first two fingers. She gritted her teeth. For many years, she had controlled the telltale sign of her unease. Not once while she was in prison had the weakness appeared. Why did it surface now?

She unlocked her fingers and allowed the blood to stream back into her thumb. She glanced at Guy to make sure he hadn't noticed her reversion to old habits, and released a breath when only his back met her gaze.

Cora raised her chin before addressing Somerton. "I would prefer to get this over with as quickly as possible." Even with dread tingling through her body, culminating in damp pockets on her palms, she somehow managed to hide the growing anxiety caused by her inquisitors' stares.

"As you wish, Cora." He resumed his place by the fire.

Cora began emptying her mind of past, present, and future doubts. She wrestled her thoughts into a logical—and safe—pattern of events, and then inhaled three deep breaths. The familiar exercise, one she had used many times since arriving at Charles Street, steadied her fragile nerves.

Still, she hesitated. Her gaze flicked to the unmoving figure by the window.

Noting her concern, her brother said, "Cora, you may speak freely in front of Helsford. He's been privy to our family's secrets for years. You know he is more like a brother than friend."

For you, perhaps.

For her, brotherly feelings toward Guy had ceased during her last summer in England, three years ago. The same summer her guardian and mentor deemed her ready to cross the Channel to find the man who murdered her parents.

The summer her childhood friend became her living hell.

"Remove the mask, Cora."

Cora bit back a sharp retort, unwilling to comply with Guy's demand. The black silk mask she wore to conceal her identity provided a small measure of protection against his dark, probing gaze.

He stalked closer, looking more beautiful and dangerous than she could ever remember. And she remembered everything about him.

"Perhaps you need assistance," he said.

She could tell from the tone of his voice that his protective instincts were fully engaged. Always sensitive to her welfare, he would not understand her attendance at Mrs. Lancaster's masked ball. No one would, really, except Somerton, but then he was not keen on her presence here, either.

Why, tonight of all nights, did Guy have to return to England? Had he already learned of her purpose for coming to the masquerade? She studied his expression and decided he had not. His features reflected determination and a guarded curiosity... and a compulsion to admire the indecent amount of flesh rising above her crimson bodice. No, if he had known why

she was dressed in such a revealing gown and what had caused
the flush across her cheeks, he would be hauling her out of here
like a misbehaving child.

She glanced around the small sitting room she had ducked
into earlier to compose herself. It was free of other guests, and
Guy's broad shoulders blocked the French doors leading out to
the small terrace. She set her jaw, knowing he would not relent
until he had his way. "That won't be necessary, you beast."

She tugged on the ribbon holding the mask in place and
felt a wave of vulnerability wash over her. She, too, had
transformed in the intervening months. Would he like what she
saw? Would she measure up to all the exotic ladies he had met
during his travels?

The mask fell away, and a new intensity sharpened his
features. "You've changed." He stepped closer, his gaze traveling over every square inch of her face. The backs of his fingers
caressed her cheek. "Matured."

His voice—a richer, deeper, more languid version of the one
she recalled—burrowed beneath her skin, causing chill bumps to
cover the surface. The warmth from his hand made her want to
lean into his touch and absorb his strength. She would need it
now—more than ever.

Instead, she tilted her head away the slightest bit to break
contact. "I should hope so." She pulled on her gloves, praying
he did not see her hands tremble. "Is that all you have to say
after spending a year and a half abroad? Have you no 'It's nice
to see you again, Cora'?"

She did not wait for his answer. "Now that I have done
as you have ordered, perhaps you can explain why you were
spying on me."

He blinked. "I wasn't spying on you."

"Oh? Do you normally smash your face against your hostess's
terrace door?"

A light flush colored his cheeks. "Don't be ridiculous."

She raised one brow. "What is it you want, then?" She

hoped he never discovered her true reason for attending tonight's affair. Why hadn't Somerton mentioned Guy's return?

The curiosity in his eyes gave way to something darker, more dangerous. Something normally not shared among friends.

Liquid heat spiraled into the area between her legs, reigniting the slow burn of awareness her earlier activities had aroused. Following Somerton's instructions, Mrs. Lancaster had planned this exclusive masked ball, with all its excesses, for Cora's introduction to the art of seduction. Although Somerton had been initially reluctant to consider her proposal, he had finally conceded the fact that she could not infiltrate France's elite as a missish debutante. With that in mind, Somerton's mistress had made certain Cora knew what it was like to touch a man's warm, naked flesh and be touched in return.

The woman had done her job well, for now Cora's mind sifted through the courtesan's secrets as she met Guy's gaze.

He moved closer. So close that his unique musky scent wrapped around her, melting her defenses. His finger slid beneath her chin, and lifted.

Time slowed. The room disappeared.

She could hear her own pulse, feel the warmth of his breath against her lips.

"What I want," he said in a husky undertone, "is to know why my best friend's little sister is masquerading as a Cyprian? Not that I don't like the view."

Cora blinked away the memory, one that seemed a lifetime ago. Her mortifying introduction to the male form was rather tame compared to all that she had seen and survived while in France. But the courtesan's shrewd instruction on that momentous night had helped Cora navigate the luscious intrigues of Parisian society.

"Besides," her brother said, drawing her attention back, "we all work for the Nexus."

She released a slow, unsteady breath, still feeling the effects of Guy's touch more than three years later.

His continued involvement with Somerton's elaborate system of spies surprised her. When they were younger, the thrill of adventure had guided his actions. However, when his father fell ill, she sensed a shift in his focus, one more committed to the welfare of his family and estates than secrets and deceptions.

She remembered sitting through many lively conversations at the dinner table, where Guy had pelted her guardian with questions about crop rotations, investments, and politics. Conversations that had sent her scurrying back to the training room, for her focus had remained ever constant, ever unswerving.

Ever on revenge.

"Cora?" Somerton asked.

She nodded, knowing she could delay no longer, so she transported herself back to the recent past, to a different kind of living hell. She rubbed her chest, choosing her words carefully.

"The evening of the Bellecôte ball began like any other. Valère escorted me there, giving no hint that he had become suspicious of my activities. It was not until after I delivered my message to our agent that I noticed a reversal in his attitude toward me." Her voice held little emotion, no suggestion of the fear and loathing she still felt toward Valère—and herself.

Cora stared off in the distance. "Normally, he danced with fluid passion, full of touches and innuendo, but after my return from the balcony, his movements became stiff and crushing."

The same sinking feeling in the pit of her stomach she felt then revisited her now. The same paralyzing thought echoed through her reeling mind—*he knows, he knows. Oh, dear God, he knows.*

"Why were you keeping the Frenchman's company?" her brother asked.

"For the same reason you make yourself available to wives of powerful politicians, Brother."

A mixture of anger and chagrin passed over Ethan's face. "What was your mission, Sister?"

Somerton interjected, "To help our office confirm or deny whether Valère was responsible for the disappearance of six British ships."

Cora caught the sharp look Guy sent Somerton over his shoulder.

"Sounds like something the bastard would enjoy," her brother said.

"Language, Danforth," Somerton scolded.

Undeterred, her brother asked, "How did Valère confirm his suspicion that you were a spy?"

Cora loathed that term. The vulgar label reduced their lifesaving work down to something dishonorable and underhanded. As secret service agents, they strove to protect England and all her many interests. They had formed alliances that would hopefully one day destroy France's greatest military leader and would then work to rebuild all the nations Napoleon had desecrated by his arrogant ambitions.

Not until her assignment to Valère had she ever been ashamed of her role in their clandestine war against the new emperor. She wasn't regretful of the intelligence she had gathered and passed on. No, it was the manner in which she had collected the information that left her feeling as if she had wallowed in the dregs of Valère's dungeon for centuries.

Perhaps *spy* was an apt name after all.

"The duc de Bellecôte dabbles in a bit of intelligence gathering," she continued. "The columns along the balcony are hollowed out, large enough for a man to fit inside. Tiny peepholes make it possible for the inhabitant to identify those outside." She turned her lips up into a rueful smile. "Evidently, Valère has made use of these clever contraptions before, and it was my poor luck to have scheduled an exchange that night with my Swiss contact."

Somerton shifted. "You sound as if you admire him."

"Why would I not? Valère's clever, resourceful, and handsome. A perfect agent."

"Not perfect," Guy said, still peering out the window. "He lost you."

Cora stared at Guy's back. Had she detected a note of pride in his quietly uttered words? An unpleasant stinging sensation bit into the backs of her eyes.

"Why would Valère share such a valuable secret with you?" her brother asked.

Guy threw her brother a savage look over his shoulder.

"What?" Danforth asked. No sooner than he uttered the question, deep chagrin replaced her brother's look of confusion.

"Worked it out, did you?" Cora's voice held a trace of amused sympathy. "Obviously, there's no harm in revealing one's secrets to a dead person. As you surmised, Valère did not intend for me to live and, I believe, he relished the opportunity to boast about how he outwitted me."

A deep ache of exhaustion pulled at her body. Time to end their interrogation. "As for my captivity, let me just say your arrival was timely." For the first time since she had entered the library, Guy faced her, his stance wide, his jaw set.

She glanced at Somerton and then her brother. The same uncompromising lines hardened their features; the same questioning look sat in their eyes.

Did she betray her country?

Her disquiet turned to icy rage, even as a heated flush suffused her face. During the night of her rescue, she remembered her desperate need to save Guy, remembered the never-ending pain.

And she remembered whispering names—Aphra Behn, James Bruce, Robert Burton, Mary Wollstonecraft, William Painter, Frances Sheridan, and so on—names of deceased writers whose works she had spent hours reading in this very room. Names that would cause no harm but would distract Boucher long enough for Guy to enter her cell unnoticed.

But Guy knew none of this. He knew only that she had shared information with Boucher. But Boucher was dead. Why would they care about her supposed revelations? Anything she might have revealed lay trapped in the Frenchman's cold corpse. Lost to Valère. So why bother informing Somerton at all?

Maybe it wasn't what they believed she had told a dead man but what they feared she had revealed during the previous ten days. Given her condition, she shouldn't blame them for their caution. But she did.

Their lack of faith—Guy's lack of faith—tore at her insides like a rabid dog. He knew her. Knew what she was capable of—and incapable of. Never had she betrayed his confidence. Not once in all the years of their friendship. They should have trusted her just as she had trusted them to come for her.

Of the three men, Guy was the last one she would have expected this from. The pain of this discovery was worse than any wound Boucher had inflicted.

She turned away from Guy. To Somerton, she said, "Ask your question."

"Cora, you know we must—"

"Silence, Ethan." Her gaze never left Somerton's face. Cora couldn't fathom how it had come to this after all she had done, after all she had sacrificed and *endured* for her country—and for her family.

"Did Valère gain any intelligence from you?" Somerton asked.

Being right about their questioning looks didn't stop the hurt and humiliation from churning like acid in her stomach. "Have I ever let you down, sir?" When Somerton remained silent, she asked again in a voice strangled with emotion. "Have I?"

"No."

"Then why doubt me now?"

Her brother said, "Had we been in your place, we would likely have faltered."

She released a short, bittersweet laugh. "Have I finally bested you in a test of strength, then?" Tossing off the blanket, she struggled to gain the edge of the sofa. Each man made to help, but she blasted them with a *stay-where-you-are* glare, stopping them in their tracks. With agonizing care, she stood on shaking legs. "Other than my innocence, Valère gained nothing from me."

Ethan cursed. Somerton stared, and Guy closed his eyes. The perverse pleasure she took in each of their varied reactions didn't last long. Soon, shame blanketed her features and clogged her throat. She lowered her gaze and took her first painful step toward escape.

Guy moved to stand beside her. "Chin up," he murmured, staying apace with her.

She unconsciously did as he instructed, tears stinging the backs of her eyes. This was the Guy she remembered. Always there. Always believing in her.

She limped toward the door. The raw burns on her feet made it feel as though she were walking on a mass of angry bees. The combination of pain and pent-up emotions caused her body to quiver uncontrollably. The library door became a burning candle at the end of a tunnel, a small glimpse of hope that the torment would soon end.

She had to get out of here.

Somerton crossed the room and opened the door, motioning to someone in the corridor. Dinks and Jack appeared in the doorway. When she drew alongside Somerton, he said. "I'm sorry."

Her throat closed. The last time she had received an apology from him was when he had found her shivering in an attic storage cupboard after the first governess he had employed had locked her in hours earlier.

Her brother chimed in. "You did well, runt."

Fire licked through her veins. "I did a lot better than a mere 'well,' Ethan."

Never one to misinterpret Cora's moods, Dinks grasped Cora's elbow, squeezing it in warning, or support; Cora couldn't be sure which.

She patted her maid's hand and then turned to face the men. "You can take your tepid praise and go to hell." She ignored the feminine groan at her side and leveled her gaze on Guy. "All of you."

Five

GUY WATCHED CORA'S LESS-THAN-GRACEFUL EXIT, longing to lift her into his arms and save her from such foolhardy behavior rather than trail along by her side.

When the footman moved to assist her, Guy experienced an immediate sense of relief, followed swiftly by a dark desire to throw him against the nearest wall. He swiveled around and made his way back to the window until the library door clicked shut.

Her final words and accusing stare had cut through the room like a butcher's cleaver chopping through muscle and bone. He felt her disappointment as keenly as if it were his own. How would they ever earn her forgiveness for that bit of ruthlessness?

The few times he had seen her since their escape to London grew no less shocking than when he found her stretched across Valère's bloodstained table five days ago. The Frenchman had tried to remove every piece of beauty she possessed. Once lustrous brown hair streaked with gold had hung in beautiful straight bands to the middle of her back. Now her shorn locks barely fell below the edges of her headpiece.

Her rose-colored, high-necked gown made an admirable attempt at concealing the manacle of bruises around her throat, but Guy could still detect the outlines of individual fingers. Images of the horrors she must have suffered through began to take root, materializing in a macabre stream of endless flashes. He closed his eyes and forced his mind to focus on her captor.

"Other than my innocence, Valère gained nothing from me."

Cora's revelation, so matter-of-factly uttered, destroyed any hope he had carried that Valère hadn't assaulted her, as well. Her strength humbled him, and he better understood how deeply their questions had hurt her. In his heart, he knew the question had to be asked, but Inquisition-style was not the right way. She deserved better from them. Better from him. He had much to make up for.

And he would start by gelding the bastard Valère with the dullest, filthiest blade he could find. He grabbed the windowsill, longing to lay his forehead against the cool pane to ease the building pressure.

Guy glanced over his shoulder and found the other two men looking equally shaken. "Her lack of detail is telling." The knowledge that she protected them from the grisly aspects of her captivity knotted his stomach.

Danforth held his head in his hands. "Yes."

Guy eyed Somerton. "She would never willingly betray her country."

"Seasoned agents have broken under less intense circumstances than what Cora suffered," Somerton said. "If she had revealed confidential information, I wouldn't have blamed her. I needed to understand what we were up against. What may be coming." He stared into the distance. "Many would like to see us fail in our fight against Napoleon. It's my job to ensure we do not. For the past several months, I've been conducting an investigation within the Foreign Office to uncover an intelligence leak. Someone within our ranks is supplying Valère with sensitive information."

Danforth said, "Any suspects yet?"

Somerton shook his head, his lips thinned. "Only that it's likely someone higher up in the Office. No field agent has access to the information being conveyed to Valère."

"Is that the real reason you assigned Cora to observe Valère?" Guy asked, keeping his tone even.

"Yes."

Danforth's head snapped around to stare at Somerton. "What of the ships?"

"That needed investigating, too," Somerton said.

Danforth shot out of his seat. "I always knew you were a ruthless bastard, Somerton. But I never thought you'd turn that keen mind against those you've sworn to protect." His fingers curled into a tight fist. "Just when did my sister's role turn from observation to whoring?"

Guy stepped forward and clasped his friend's shoulder in a show of comfort and to prevent him from doing anything stupid. No matter the provocation.

Somerton's voice lowered to a lethally low level. "When I received word of our enemy placing Carib women and children in holds of ships and gassing them with sulfur for no other reason than the color of their skin." Somerton's normally cold gray eyes now burned with a volatile intensity, revealing more emotion than Guy could ever recall observing in their leader.

"Good God," Danforth said.

"Napoleon, I presume," Guy said.

Somerton gave him one sharp nod without taking his gaze off Cora's brother.

"Where?" Guy asked in an attempt to remove Somerton's focus from Danforth.

The older man's eyes glazed with a sadness so profound that Guy felt the effect slam into his chest. "Guadeloupe." Somerton turned away, silent as he stared into the fireplace.

The tension in Danforth's shoulder eased, and Guy released his restraining grip.

"Like Napoleon," Somerton said, "I will pay for my sins in the afterlife." When he faced them again, the ice had returned to his gaze. "But I'll be damned if I let that French upstart do to more innocents what he did to the people in the West Indies."

For several seconds, Guy's heart beat in time with the gilt bronze mantel clock. "Did Cora fully understand the complexities of her mission? The dangers involved?"

Somerton aimed his reproachful gaze at Guy. "Of course."

Guy released a slow breath. Although he would have preferred a different agent on the case, he had to admit that Cora had the greatest chance of success of any female agent in the Nexus.

The situation surrounding the agent Raven had plagued him for days. With this new information about Cora, more pieces about their recent attempt to rescue the female agent fell into place.

Somerton's insistence that he and Danforth take the mission, the limited details on the subject's appearance, and the chief's inability to mask the underlying urgency in his every word. One detail had been clear. Rescue the female agent who had appeared on the Continent several months ago, saving hundreds of British lives by gathering crucial information for the Nexus.

For Somerton, to be exact.

"You don't seem concerned that we failed our original assignment, sir," Guy tested.

Somerton's crystalline gaze met Guy's. "You saved Cora. I can hardly call it a botched mission."

Danforth said, "Any word where Valère stashed the elusive Raven?"

Without breaking eye contact with Guy, Somerton answered, "I've heard nothing new."

Guy pressed, "Raven's a rather valuable agent for us to have left behind. I take it a reprimand will be forthcoming?"

Something in Guy's tone must have alerted Danforth to the growing tension. "What's going on?"

"Nothing, Danforth," Somerton said. "Your friend concerns himself with a trivial matter."

"Trivial?" Guy said.

"Yes," Somerton agreed. "It's best to think no more on it."

"Helsford, what the hell is going on?" Danforth growled.

Guy's teeth ground together. He was tired of the game. "Tell him, sir."

Somerton remained unmoved. "Tell him what?"

Danforth looked from one man to the other, his lips pressed together in a thin line.

"Why do you continue with this pretense?" Guy asked, unable to read his mentor's features.

"Goddammit, man," Danforth said. "I've had enough of your bloody innuendos. If you have something to say, just say it."

When Somerton remained silent, Guy came close to hating his mentor in that moment. He understood the chief's caution, shared it, even. If the French ever uncovered and seized the leader of the Nexus, many agents' lives would be in peril.

To Guy's knowledge, Somerton alone held the true names of all the agents working for the Nexus. But in this instance, his friend deserved to know the truth.

He turned to Danforth. "It is my belief that the operative named Raven is none other than Cora deBeau."

Six

THE FOLLOWING AFTERNOON, CORA SAT WITH HER head resting against the side of the bed. Her rapid, shallow breaths echoed through the room, and a fine sheen of sweat covered her brow and back.

Such a fuss to relieve oneself.

Just a few more halting steps and she would have been comfortably ensconced in her downy-soft bed. Instead, she sat on the hardwood floor with quivers of exhaustion wracking her body.

If she hadn't grabbed the bedpost at the last second, she would be suffering a great deal more. As it was, her bruised ribs felt like they had finally cracked and were now piercing one of her lungs.

Cora closed her eyes. She needed a few minutes to catch her breath before beginning the arduous task of pulling herself up, one-handed, onto the bed.

The previous day's abomination spiraled through her mind with dizzying speed, not helping her present condition. How could they have doubted her? Have so little faith in her? If she had come crawling back to them, ravaged but alive, she would have understood their skepticism. It would have been reasonable to suspect that she had given up valuable information to save herself.

Guy had witnessed her resistance. Even though he couldn't hear the words she whispered, surely he realized her tactic. Why hadn't he spoken up on her behalf? His was perhaps the worst betrayal of all.

Cora opened her eye and searched the room for something else to focus her mind on. Even with its limited perspective, her bandaged gaze feasted on the soothing rose-and-light green bed hangings, the satinwood writing desk. She had found peace here, once.

And then her gaze roved over the portrait on the opposite wall, painted only a few years before her family was crippled by tragedy. Her smiling mother and serious father sat on a bench amidst a profusion of multicolored flowers, with a ten-year-old Ethan standing at his father's shoulder and a six-year-old Cora tucked into her mother's side.

Happier times. Simpler times.

She tried to shift into a more comfortable position, but the movement sent a bolt of fire through her midsection. She stared hard at her mother's beautiful face, waiting for the onslaught to recede. She longed to feel her mother's soft, delicately perfumed hands cradling her face once more, to experience the butterfly caress of her thumbs sweeping over her heated cheeks. And to hear her mother's melodic words of reassurance that always bolstered her courage. *My sweet girl. Always so brave and strong. One day we will find you a husband equally courageous.* "Oh, Mama," she whispered, her mother's promise slicing through her battered heart, "I wish you were here."

One of Cora's greatest regrets was how little she remembered of her parents, having lost them both when she was just ten. No matter how hard she tried to ignore it, the image that took precedence over all others was of their last horrific night on earth, when she watched a French assassin murder her father, her mother already sprawled at his feet.

She swallowed hard against the aching sadness and rolled her face into the counterpane, no longer desirous of exploring her old bedchamber.

A perfunctory knock reverberated through the room, and Cora snapped to attention.

"Cora, may I come in?"

Guy. Dear Lord, not now.

She grabbed the counterpane in a desperate bid to save her pride. But her muscles had grown nearly useless during her captivity and could no longer support her weight. She slid back down in a heap of humiliation.

"Cora?" The door opened, and the light from the corridor cast Guy's shadow across her bedchamber floor.

With reluctance, Cora peered around the end of the bed. With the light behind him, she could not make out his features, but his rigid posture spoke volumes.

"What happened?" he demanded, advancing toward her.

"I'm fine." She clawed at the bedcovering again. Valère and the war had stolen most everything dear to her, everything except her dignity. *That* she would not relinquish quite so easily. Her fingernails snagged in the cover, bending back. With a hiss of pain, she released it and slid to the floor.

"What are you trying to do, cause yourself further injury?" Guy asked.

"No," she said, shrinking away as he approached. "I needed to use the water closet. What are you doing here? Come to see if I'm writing missives to the enemy?"

His jaw locked a moment before he scooped her up into his arms. Her body went rigid.

"Is there not a chamber pot beneath your bed?" He placed her gently within the cocoon of bed linens, his body surrounding her, suffocating her, spiraling her mind back to another time and place.

She could not breathe, could not get far enough away. Her

eyes burned with unshed tears as Valère's hands held her immobile. His vile breath fanned her face, making her gag. Convulsions racked her bruised body. She lashed out repeatedly with her fists. No, no, no!

"Cora!"

God, no. Not again.

Never again.

In a whirlwind of movement, Cora found herself on the far side of the room where the darkness closed in around her. Blessed darkness, wretched darkness...

"Cora! It's Guy."

She stilled, forcing away the awful images filling her vision, drenching her mind.

"That's right, sweetheart. Come back to me."

The light. Where was the light?

"You're safe, Cora."

Safe.

No. Valère loved to feed her mind fruitless information in order to gain her cooperation. "Guy?"

"Yes, Cora-bell. It's me."

Cora-bell. Only Guy had ever used the endearment. She closed her eyes and pulled in a shuddering breath. The tension leached from her muscles, leaving behind an empty sort of desolation.

The fog of the past dissipated by slow degrees, muted hues of gray cast a thin shroud over the blurry room before her.

"You have nothing to fear from me, Cora." He gestured toward her right hand. "You never did. You never will."

She glanced down and was surprised to find her fingers wrapped around a silver-plated candlestick. Despite the pain, she had crouched into a familiar stance with her knees bent, her weight balanced on the balls of her feet, and her arm raised into a defensive tilt.

Her head throbbed at the implication. She couldn't remember picking up the candlestick, only the mind-drugging fear. Her makeshift weapon landed on the floor with a heavy *thunk*. Wiping her sweaty palm on her nightdress, she said, "I–I do not wish to be touched."

"I understand." His voice was calm, reassuring. He clasped his hands behind his back.

A shiver rippled through her body, and she stepped sideways, seeking the only ray of light in the room. Warmth cast over her bare feet, bringing with it clarity and control.

And unbearable mortification.

Keeping her gaze on the far window, she said, "Forgive me." How could she have been so out of her mind with fear that she would mistake Guy for Valère? Her mind was breaking, shattering into a thousand pieces of shame and guilt and dread.

"There's nothing to forgive. My apologies for frightening you—I shouldn't have been so rough, but I couldn't stand seeing you in such a position."

With reluctance, she met his concerned gaze. "It would seem I am not quite ready for company, my lord." Cora chafed at the amount of time it was taking her body to heal. After several days of bed rest and regular meals, she should be much stronger.

"Guy," he murmured.

"Excuse me?"

"Before you sneaked away to France, you used to address me by my Christian name. You've stopped. Why is that?"

"I didn't sneak away."

"You never said good-bye either."

"There was no opportunity," she said. "Until I saw you at Mrs. Lancaster's, I had not realized you had returned to England, and I was scheduled to leave the following morning. As for how I address you, you have a title now and—"

"And what?"

"It's been a long time."

"Yet, I still refer to you as Cora."

Rubbing her arm, she relented. "As you wish, *Guy*."

His lips twitched and then thinned into an imposing line. "You're cold." He motioned her forward. "Allow me to help you back to bed."

After what happened a few minutes ago, she didn't trust that she could accept his touch without attacking him again. A disturbing thought, not being in control of one's body. She nodded toward the foot of her bed. "I think I'll stay here for a moment, but, I wouldn't mind having my dressing gown."

He retrieved her cotton wrap and held it out for her to step into. Such a simple, intimate gesture, one she would have welcomed prior to her imprisonment. However, today, the thought of presenting her back to Guy—to anyone—made her stomach swell with nausea.

"Let's take this one step at a time, Cora," he said in a soft undertone. "You know I won't hurt you. Do you recall who kept your head above water when you were learning to float?"

She swallowed, and her eyes began to well with moisture. "You did."

"Do you recall who taught you how to use the heel of your palm to draw a boy's claret should he forget his manners?"

A tear crested her lower lid and trickled down her cheek. She had used the technique on Willie Benton's licentious nose when she was fourteen. "You did."

"Who did?"

"You did… Guy."

The severe planes of his face softened into a gentle smile. "That's right, sweetheart. I won't ever let you falter."

She drew in a shuddering breath and took three shaky steps forward, then turned to face the wall. She closed her eyes and waited for the madness to strike. Waited for the banshee to emerge and disgrace her again.

He eased the dressing gown over her free arm and then settled it around her shoulders. His hands brushed airily down her upper arms before he stepped around to face her again. "I'm going to tie your wrap now."

She nodded, unable to speak. Her skin felt stretched tight across her bones, and her chest felt leaden and knotted. The icy fingers of the dungeon traced down her spine, paralyzing her body and sending her mind into a frenzy of self-preservation. She longed to lean into his warmth, take comfort in his arms, but the banshee had started her low, keening wail.

One more minute. To take her mind off Guy's ministrations, she asked, "Did you have a particular purpose in coming here?"

"Yes." Perhaps sensing her struggle, he made quick work of her sash, and then slowly, carefully, he hooked his finger inside her palm. Of their own volition, her fingers tightened around his. "We'll get through this together, Cora. I swear it."

"I'm almost tempted to believe you." She squeezed his finger once before resuming her place against the wall. The surge of energy that flooded her body was dissipating at a rapid pace.

"You're stronger than you give yourself credit."

She nearly laughed. If he only knew how close she was to collapsing in front of him. "Your reason for being here?"

"I have two. One—I wish to apologize for yesterday."

Why did he have to bring up their meeting? She had

managed to put it out of her mind for a while. She had no wish to revisit the subject, for she feared there was nothing he could say to make up for his silence.

"Apology accepted." Her legs began to quiver in exhaustion. She gauged the distance between her current position and the bed and knew she would never make it without falling. Instead, she leaned her weight against the wall and waited.

For him to finish studying her.

The moment stretched, uncomfortable. As her strength faded, her body pressed farther into the wall, and her knees eased out of their locked position.

"I am truly sorry, Cora."

"Do you believe I betrayed the other agents?" The question emerged before she could pull it back.

"No, I do not."

The sincerity of his words helped soothe the hurt she had difficulty controlling. Her lips lifted into a tight smile. "Well, that's one out of three."

"Cora, your brother—"

"Why did you remain silent?" she asked in a rush. "Why did you allow Somerton to believe I might have divulged the Nexus's secrets?"

"I knew you hadn't. We all knew, Cora, but the question had to be asked."

"Why? Why did the question have to be asked? Why couldn't you have trusted me?"

His jaw hardened, and his eyes closed as if in pain. When he opened them a few seconds later, they burned with a helpless intensity. "Too many lives were at stake, Cora. Somerton couldn't take the chance that you had under torture divulged information. But he should have asked you privately."

Her anger dissipated from one breath to the next, but the hurt remained. No matter Somerton's logic, she wished he'd had more faith in her. But she did not walk in his shoes and could not fathom the level of responsibility he carried for his agents. She had been the recipient of his protection many times and was glad for it. So who was she to question his tactics now?

"Of course," she said, rubbing her temple. She could actually feel her body folding in on itself. "Your other reason for being here?"

"To invite you down for something to eat, but I see your strength is waning. Will you not at least accept my arm to cross over to your bed?"

Cora's hand dropped to her side. She wanted to give in to his strength, allow him to take her burden. But she couldn't. Not now. Not after nearly bashing his head. All she needed was to be alone, to sort things out. To feel warm again.

She took a small step to the left, following the shifting patch of sunlight, away from Guy. "I-I can manage."

"Would you prefer I send Dinks up?"

She shook her head. "No, thank you. Privacy is all I require at the moment."

"Very well, Cora. I'll see you soon."

She steeled herself when he hesitated at the door. *Go*, she silently pleaded. Remaining upright took every morsel of strength she possessed. Her nerve endings prickled beneath her skin, causing her muscles to tense.

"Cora."

"Yes?"

"You're safe. I will see to it that Valère pays for what he has done."

"No." The word ripped from her throat. The thought of Guy facing a man like Valère, especially on her behalf, sent a surge of raw fear through her exhausted body. "You are not to get involved."

His gaze remained steady, resolute. "Too late."

"I mean it, Guy. The man's a cold-blooded killer."

He stared at her for a heart-pounding moment before saying, "We are evenly matched, then."

Cora stilled. "What do you mean?"

His features shuttered, as if he had realized he'd said too much. Instead of explaining his statement, he asked, "Are you sure I can't help you?"

Disappointment sharpened her tone. "Quite."

"Rest well, Cora."

When the door closed, she crumpled against the wall, sliding down its cold, hard surface. The welts on her feet, inflicted by Boucher's branding iron, throbbed with fire.

She closed her eyes. The acrid aroma of burning flesh still stained her nostrils, and her throat felt as though it were lined with shards of glass.

As fatigue overtook her body and clouds rolled across the sun, taking its warmth and light, Cora prayed for a new day to arrive, one that included dainty pastries, flaring candlelight, and Guy's strong arms wrapped around her.

She tilted her head back, reassured by the wall's solid surface, unsurprised when her prayer remained unanswered.

&

Guy was going to be sick.

A few feet from Cora's bedchamber, he braced his hands on the windowsill, his blunt fingernails cutting into the wood. The image of her fleeing his arms and taking up a weapon against him replayed in his mind until hot bile pushed into his throat.

My God, she's afraid of being touched. He smacked the window frame with his hand, barely managing to keep the nausea at bay and his fury leashed.

If she only would have listened to him. His nails bit deeper into the wood.

Before he had left on his first mission, she had confessed her desire to find the Frenchman who had killed her parents. In his youth, he had lacked delicacy and tried to convince her to abandon such a hare-brained notion. She had ignored his pleas, as he would have hers had their roles been reversed. To complicate the situation, years of learning intelligence gathering techniques and self-defense training had fed her savage need for revenge, blinding her to the realities of war.

If only they hadn't thought teaching Danforth's little sister how to pick a lock or how to incapacitate a man twice her size was great fun.

In the beginning, none of them knew why Somerton was teaching them such unique skills. Only later did they learn that their mentor had tested them, followed their progress to see what talents he could mold and sharpen. Only later did they learn they had become weapons.

And Cora had become Somerton's secret weapon.

Guy pulled in a deep breath. Valère had taken much more than her innocence. He had stolen her confidence and plunged her into a well of fear by exploiting all her vulnerabilities. She no longer viewed the world through invincible eyes.

"Are you unwell, my lord?" Dinks asked.

He straightened, startled that he had not heard the maid's approach.

"I have been better, Dinks."

"I'm right sorry to hear that, sir." She stopped in front of him. "Would you like one of my special tonics to help calm your nerves? It involves a wee bit of brandy."

He smiled. Dinks's concoctions always included a dram of the amber liquid. "Thank you, but that won't be necessary."

He studied Cora's door again. "Has Cora spoken to you about her captivity?"

The maid stood silent for a moment, a faraway look in her eyes. "No, my lord."

He stared at the maid, measuring the veracity of her words. Even if Cora had confided in Dinks, the older woman would never disclose any information without Cora's consent. "I suppose it's still too early."

"I'm not sure she will ever speak of it, my lord," Dinks confided. "Miss Cora's a private person and can be overly protective of those she loves."

Guy nodded, remembering Cora's refusal to share the details of her imprisonment yesterday morning. Truth be told, he came here today to coax more information from her.

There was a time when Cora would have shared everything with him. Over the last few years, though, their bond had frayed like the ends of a ship's flag left too long in the sea breeze. He missed their connection and had come to her chamber in the hopes of reestablishing it. She needed someone to lean on, and he wanted to be that person.

"It's up to us to change her mind, then," he said, coming to a decision. "I'll be back tomorrow morning. Please have a breakfast tray for two sent to her room by eight."

Dinks sent him a gap-toothed smile. "That's the way to slay her demons, my lord." Dinks patted her ample hips. "Food's always been dear to my heart."

He winked at the audacious maid and then cast a final look toward Cora's door. "She needs your assistance, Dinks. She's too damn stubborn to admit it, though."

"The little mite's having a bad time of it this morning, is she?"

"Yes, and my clumsy efforts didn't help matters any."

"I'll give her a spot of laudanum to take the edge

off," Dinks said. "She'll fight me some, thinking she'll become dependent on the opiate like her mum and those cowardly society ladies, but I'd as soon cut off my right hand than allow my little mite to wither away like that." Dinks's eyes widened. "Pardon me, sir. I should not have said that about Miss Cora's mother."

"Rest easy, Dinks," Guy said. "You did not say anything that I did not already know." Cora wasn't the only one protective of those she loved. He thought back to an alcohol-induced conversation he'd had years ago with Danforth and knew, as Dinks knew, that Cora worried about something far more insidious than becoming one of those "cowardly society ladies."

"You're a true friend, Dinks. Thank you for taking such good care of her." He bowed and turned to leave. "Don't forget—tomorrow morning at eight."

The maid beamed. "She'll be ready, my lord. Don't you worry."

By slow degrees, the nausea abated. He would spend the rest of the day figuring out the best approach to dealing with Cora's mental wounds. It would take skillful cunning on his part, for she would not welcome his interference. But he knew how to tiptoe around her prickly pride. Had done so for years.

As Guy descended the staircase, Somerton appeared in the doorway of his study.

"Helsford, do you have a moment?" Not waiting for an answer, Somerton turned on his heel and disappeared inside.

Guy stared at the empty space a moment before following in his mentor's wake.

The moment Guy closed the door, Somerton said, "We must move Cora someplace safe."

"Has there been a new development?" Guy asked.

"My sources report a great deal of activity at Valère's

chateau a few days ago. From the sounds of it, he might have been marshaling for an extended journey."

"Can we not wait until you receive something more certain? She can barely walk."

Somerton's lips thinned, unaccustomed to explaining himself. "No. I can't take the chance. He could be here even now. Rather than bringing her here, I should have sent her to a safe house the moment you landed on English soil, but I allowed my emotions to have their sway."

"Do you really think Valère would risk crossing the Channel for her?"

"Yes."

Guy remained focused on Cora's lack of physical strength, ignoring his instincts. "Surely not with the contentious relationship we have with France—"

"Our lack of rapport with France did not stop you from entering the country to save Cora, did it?"

Guy canted his head to the side, eyeing his mentor. "I thought I was there to rescue our agent Raven."

A muscle jumped in Somerton's jaw. The Nexus leader didn't make such greenling mistakes.

"Why do you deny Cora's the Raven?" Guy asked.

"I denied nothing."

"Nor did you confirm my suspicion for Danforth." Guy could still hear Danforth's laughter ringing in his ears after he had declared Cora the Raven.

"I don't reveal my agents' identities." Somerton's gaze turned so hard and frigid that ice crystals seemed to form around their crystalline edges. "Not to anyone."

The muscles in Guy's shoulders bunched into a tight knot. He knew the only reason he, Cora, and Ethan were aware of each other's role in the organization was due to the nature of their upbringing. Had they not trained together as children, they would likely not know each provided a service to the Nexus.

Somerton said, "Shall we get back to Cora's safety?"

Chastened but no less irritated, Guy nodded.

"With her great-aunt's sponsorship, Cora was able to mingle with Parisian society as herself. Valère knows Cora's true identity."

"I know," Guy ground out. Considering Valère's resourcefulness, he probably knew she was the Raven. An English spy who had penetrated France's elite and had cost Napoleon—and Valère—much.

"Good," Somerton said. "Then you understand the situation."

"Indeed. For the record, I agree."

"About what?"

"That you should have put Cora in a safe house the moment she arrived."

His mentor's jaw visibly hardened. "The question still remains—what did Cora tell Valère?"

"Cora said she told him nothing, and I believe her."

"As do I," Somerton murmured. "However, Valère's said to be quite handsome and very charming, especially when he wants something. With the amount of time they spent together—"

"Are you saying she spent intimate time in his company before the kidnapping?"

A charged pause. "Yes."

A gale of jealous rage swept through Guy. Too late, he recalled Cora's description of Valère's dancing ability.

Normally, he danced with fluid passion, full of touches and innuendo, but after my return from the balcony, his movements became stiff and crushing.

Goddammit. How could he have forgotten the rumors of the Raven's ability to seduce secrets from the enemy? Had Valère succumbed like all the others? Or had the Raven fallen prey to a more masterful predator?

"How long?" Guy nearly growled.

"A fortnight, maybe longer."

The pressure in Guy's head grew with each revelation. "Bloody hell."

Somerton moved to stand behind his desk. "Cora might not have revealed British secrets, but it's possible she inadvertently revealed some of her own."

Guy's teeth clamped together so hard his jaw popped. "In which case, Valère might know about you."

"Precisely. And her brother."

Which meant none of their holdings would provide a safe harbor for Cora.

"It's doubtful he knows about me," Guy said without hesitation. "When my aunt Phoebe passed away last fall, she left me a small estate in the country. Few know of it. Perhaps now would be a good time to air out the place."

Somerton tapped his fingertips on his desk, considering Guy's offer. "It could be several weeks before we rout Valère."

"I understand." Guy straightened his shoulders. "She'll be safe with me."

"I don't doubt it." Somerton paced over to the window. After a moment, he faced Guy again. "With Cora protected, I could devote my attention to finding Valère and removing the threat—before he finds her."

Guy's disappointment in Somerton's decisions didn't stop him from warming under his mentor's praise. Somerton had never been an emotionally demonstrative man, but neither was he impossible to please. Quite unlike Guy's father.

"Thank you, sir."

"Take Cora's servants with you," Somerton instructed. "They'll help keep an eye on things and are useful intermediaries for communication purposes."

"Very well. I can be ready to depart for the country

as early as tomorrow afternoon. I've arranged to breakfast with Cora in the morning."

"I will alert her servants," Somerton said, returning to his desk. He shuffled papers around, indicating their meeting had come to an end. "All will be in readiness for your departure."

Guy hesitated.

His mentor glanced up. "Something wrong?"

"I seek only one favor for my intervention."

Somerton eyed him. "Indeed."

"Did the message I deciphered about the British ships aid in your decision to send Cora to Valère?"

The slight lowering of his mentor's eyelids sent Guy's heart crashing into his stomach.

Somerton folded his hands on his desk. "As I mentioned in the library, I assigned Cora to the task of exposing a double spy. Having her keep an ear to the ground for intelligence on the ships, as well, only made sense."

The bile he had wrestled into submission earlier reemerged. He knew better than to challenge Somerton's assertions; the man kept information more securely than any cast-iron safe.

"I take it we will have no further discussion on this matter," Somerton said.

Guy's pulse pounded in his temples. "No, sir." He bowed and turned to leave. His world felt tilted, out of kilter. By deciphering one of Valère's messages, he had provided the door to Cora's imprisonment. Good God, how was he supposed to live with such knowledge?

He thought of their journey tomorrow, made all the more difficult with this bit of treachery between them. The best he could hope for was that she never learned of his involvement. Could he be her friend while hiding such a hideous secret?

For a little while. Enough time for Somerton to

track down the Frenchman and secure Cora's safety. After that…

Cora would no doubt balk at the enforced rustication. As he made his way to the entrance hall, his mind sifted through various schemes on how to mitigate her displeasure.

He rejected them all. She had never abandoned a fight before, and running off to the country would rub raw her natural instinct to meet Valère's threat head-on.

Releasing a resigned breath, he made up his mind to do whatever it took to keep her safe.

Even if it required force.

Seven

VALÈRE SET HIS EMPTY WINE GLASS DOWN NEXT TO THE floral abomination on the small, round table. Rather than an elegant arrangement of blood red roses, Alexander Grillon decorated his lobby with a disorderly assortment of sprays, leaves, and small flower buds. Valère's vision wasn't the only one of his senses assaulted by the bouquet. His nose was equally offended. Why would anyone choose the earthy scent of wildflowers over the exotic fragrance of a velvety rose, or, better yet, jasmine? One would think the former *chef de cuisine* to Lord Crewe would be gifted with a more refined taste.

"Pardon me, sir."

His muscles tightened at the interruption, but he was careful not to reveal such emotion. Instead, he took a moment to retrieve the gold-rimmed spectacles from his pocket and slid them in place. Squinting through the thick layer of glass, he peered up at the tall blond waiter. "Yes?"

"The quiet booth you requested is now open," the waiter said. "Perhaps you would prefer to lounge there, sir?"

"Yes, indeed, young man." He analyzed his response, ensuring no hint of accent had escaped his control. Pleased with the result, he eased himself into a standing position, slowly straightening his back. He began a slow, arduous shuffle across the lobby of Grillon's Hotel, his ivory-handled cane clicking across the tiled floor.

Opened less than a year ago, the hotel still smelled of fresh mortar and new upholstery. The brass fixtures gleamed beneath the flickering lamplight, and every horizontal surface glowed with a scratch-free shine. Selecting Grillon's proved the perfect choice for Valère's business. Situated near Bond Street's fashionable shopping district and St. James's Street's notorious row of gentlemen's clubs, the hotel was a popular choice for London's elite. All manner of *on-dits* could be overheard here, just by sitting quietly. He had gleaned more intelligence in a single afternoon than he would have gathered from Paris in a year's time. *Stupid English, they think they are safe on their little island.*

"Pardon, sir?"

The waiter's question caused a hitch in Valère's step. Had he spoken his thoughts aloud? By the expectant look on the waiter's face, he must assume so. An intolerable mistake. He must be vigilant while on the enemy's territory. Mishaps like that could trap him on this miserable spit of land.

As they approached their destination, he skimmed the half-shielded booth and his lip curled up. "Be so kind as to remove the table decoration," Valère ordered as a means of distraction. "The flowers make me sneeze." Not at all true. But such subterfuge was sometimes necessary to achieve his goal or ensure his comfort, two areas he deemed of the highest priority.

"Apologies, sir." The waiter picked up the arrangement and held it respectfully behind his back. "May I bring you another Burgundy?"

Valère considered the late afternoon gloom and decided to indulge in another glass. "You may."

The waiter pushed back the concealing drape so Valère

could maneuver himself up onto the bench. Once he settled in, the heavy, sapphire-colored material fell back in place, and he was alone. He should have felt a sense of peace or comfort at having escaped the bustle of Grillon's. But he did not. Serenity had visited him only once during his thirty-three years, and that was at the command of a sable-haired English spy.

No other woman had ever been brave enough to seize control of his bed, to demand of him absolute obedience. And to punish him when he failed. He failed often.

The image of a particularly satisfying session pulsed seductively through his mind, his body stirred, and he released a slow, uneven breath.

As he had done so many times since her escape, he pulled a delicately embroidered handkerchief from his coat pocket. Even after weeks of handling, the silk still held the faint scent of jasmine.

Cora. Before he could will them otherwise, his eyes closed so he could absorb the full effect of her exotic scent.

Besides his constant pursuit of power and money, few things held his attention beyond a passing glance. Everything and everyone had their place and use.

Until the English beauty crashed into him at the Comédie Française theater.

From the moment he had peeled her off his chest, she had become an obsession. Her exquisite beauty, unrepentant intelligence, and lack of apparent interest in his position had fueled his unprecedented desire to possess her.

Instead of furthering his ambitions, he had spent hours contemplating how to entice her into his bed, and then he had spent hours entertaining her in said bed. If there were times when she had seemed less than enthusiastic about their entertainments, he had ascribed her feminine sensitivity to inexperience, which he knew how to remedy.

For a blinding moment, a mere second of agonizing time, he had considered ignoring her betrayal. His need for her special skills was that great. He would never forgive her for taking away his finest pleasure or for tempting him to forsake his duty to his emperor. Never.

He crumpled the handkerchief into his hand. His obsession with her had cost him the trust of his superiors and the respect of his men. He could buy more men, but it would take him years to cultivate such powerful allies again. Years he did not have.

Once he had deduced that she was not only a filthy English spy but also the menace Raven, he knew the only way to earn back his superiors' favor was to kill anyone who threatened the expansion of French ideals. If he succeeded, he would be lauded a hero. His actions would catch the notice of the emperor himself, who would no doubt seek Valère's counsel on future campaigns.

Valère released the square of silk and smoothed out the wrinkles. Unfolding it, he slid his forefinger along the silky item inside.

A smile played over his lips when he recalled Boucher's knife severing the first lock of Cora's sable hair. Soon after, handfuls of her thick, lustrous hair fell in cheerless clumps around her feet. She had not uttered a sound of protest or a whimper of distress. Her show of courage made him yearn for her more. So he did what any man in his position would do—he removed every bit of her allure.

The memory released a wave of regret. Before Boucher had alerted him of her perfidy, Valère had begun making plans for a more permanent alliance. Not marriage, of course. He couldn't have his children tainted by such inferior blood.

But a mistress, whose ambition equaled his own and who would prove a powerful ally... and well-trained bedmate.

A shadow cast over the booth. Valère carefully folded the handkerchief over the lock of hair and returned it to his pocket before welcoming the newcomer. "Good afternoon, my lord."

"I do not care to be summoned, Mr. Taylor."

Valère sent his visitor a confident smile. "Sometimes these things cannot be avoided." He motioned to the opposite bench. "Please. Sit."

Unable to do anything else, the other man sat stiffly across from him, balancing his walking stick against the padded bench.

Fitted with a severe black kerseymere coat covering a dark gray patterned waistcoat and topped with an elegant but simply tied neckcloth, his visitor was the epitome of a pompous English aristocrat. With no bright colors, the gentleman looked dressed for a funeral rather than an important business meeting.

"Now that our pleasantries have concluded, what news do you have?" Valère watched his visitor's lips firm in indecision, watched him sift through which falsehood to share. He had seen it a thousand times, to nauseating degrees. All informants who still retained a bit of their morality and patriotism went through the same phases as their brethren before them.

They first assessed Valère's physical strength, his mental fortitude, and finally his inclination toward violence. No matter their skill at such negotiations, they all eventually surrendered. The only question was when. He normally enjoyed the verbal fencing sessions, but this informant held answers that were of personal interest to Valère. He had no wish to wait for the man's answers.

When his informant remained silent, Valère released a regretful breath. "Need I remind you of your current circumstances, my lord?"

"No."

"Then why the delay? You have something I want, and I have something you want, yes?"

The man's jaw tightened so hard Valère feared the bone would crack.

Finally, the informant revealed, "They are removing her to Hampshire."

Valère had expected Lord Somerton to secret her away, but a specific location had eluded him. "Where in Hampshire?"

"Helsford's maiden aunt left him a modest country estate in Yateley."

"At what distance is Yateley from London?"

"A fair day's carriage ride." His informant's hard gaze shifted to the milling crowd.

Valère examined the various minutiae he knew of this high-ranking official until one detail stood out above all others. "Correct me if I'm wrong, my lord, but I believe you own a residence in this Oxfordshire region, do you not?"

The man returned his resigned yet furious gaze back to Valère. "Yes."

"Ah, very good. I have one more favor to ask of you, my lord." He took little pleasure from the starkness of the man's features, for his mind had already turned toward the next level of his plan, which was shaping into a rather stimulating game of chess.

He loved chess. Excelled at it as he did every game of stratagem. The Raven—the Black Queen—was not the only one who could penetrate enemy lines.

Eight

WHILE PEERING INTO THE LOOKING GLASS ABOVE HER dressing table, Cora removed the bandage hiding the right side of her face. When the last strip of linen fell away, cool air pressed against her flesh, and dismay tightened her throat.

Three inches of angry red stitching closed the deep gash made by Valère's ring. The cut began below her temple and curved along her cheekbone.

Even though the doctor had used small, even stitches, a scar would mar her face forever, a constant reminder of her incompetence, of her extreme arrogance. She squeezed the bridge of her nose. How had she so thoroughly failed her country? And her parents?

"Here we are, Miss Cora," Dinks said, carrying a small jar of salve provided by the doctor. "I'll dab a bit of this on your cheek before setting your hair to rights."

"There's little to be done with it, I fear." Cora ran her hand over the back of her head. "Trim up the ends so it doesn't appear as though I just stepped out of Bedlam. A hat and veil will serve to conceal the rest."

As Dinks worked her magic, Cora searched her mind for a way to avoid her impending breakfast with Guy. Humiliation from yesterday's debacle still sat in the pit of her stomach like a mass of uncut gems, sharp and heavy.

She feared her imprisonment had affected something elemental in her mind. What sane person reacted with such virulence after being touched?

Guy's calm patience in the face of her attack left her flabbergasted, even now. She could still envision his dark eyes filled with understanding and a burning desire to help her. Oh, God, how she wanted to accept it, and perhaps she would, but she was the only one who could fix this irrational fear of a man's touch. She was the only one who could conquer the demons that inhabited her mind when a man drew near.

Damn Valère for turning her into this skittish, broken creature. She swallowed, fighting back the tears that threatened her composure. She had to be strong—for her sake and for those around her.

She shifted her attention to the looking glass, where a small breakfast table set for two reflected back. The aspect appeared so welcoming, so normal. But the next hour would be far from normal. With the exception of her captivity, the next sixty minutes would likely be the most interminable of her life.

Anxious flutters beat inside her chest.

Guy would press her for more information about her time in France. She realized his need to know more would eventually win out over his attempt to respect her privacy. The thought of sharing such sordid details with him caused a swell of nausea to bubble into her throat.

How could she reveal such things? Having him look upon her in disgust would tear at her soul. He had been a hero to her from her earliest years, always watching over her, ever her courageous champion.

Even though four years separated them, they had been dear friends, especially after Somerton began her training regime. And, on that long-ago night in a private sitting room, her twenty-year-old heart had recognized something more between them. Something essential. Promising. *Carnal*.

Cora closed her eyes against the bittersweet memory. Much had changed since then. If what Guy said was true and he had become an assassin for the Nexus, then they had both sold their souls for England's cause. She wondered whose was most lost.

She bent closer toward her reflection, at the hideous creature staring back. The bruises on her face were beginning to fade, yet swirls of yellow, green, and deep violet remained stubbornly behind. She examined the tightness surrounding her eye. The swelling had reduced enough that she no longer looked over a mound of purple flesh. When she canted her head to the side, she spied a blood red circle surrounding her iris.

Perfect.

Now she resembled a demonic bedlamite.

Cora dropped her gaze, no longer able to tolerate the sight of her destroyed countenance. She really needn't worry about fending off a man's intimate touch. Valère had made sure no man would ever want her again.

"Now, now, Miss Cora, none of that." Dinks tsked. "We'll have you back to your beautiful self in no time." A few minutes later Dinks patted her shoulder. "There. Let's have a look at you." When Cora hesitated, Dinks coaxed her to lift her gaze. "Haven't I always taken good care of you, Miss Cora?"

"Yes, Dinks. Yes, you have."

"Chin up, little mite. Everything's going to be fine."

Unable to put off the deed any longer, Cora turned back to her reflection and gawked.

Without the weight of her long locks, her hair lay in a halo of soft waves around her head, decorated with an artfully looped pale blue ribbon tied at the back of her neck. Cora couldn't believe the effect. Somehow, Dinks had changed her deranged bedlamite appearance into a sophisticated sprite, although her demon-eye remained.

With the help of Dinks's masterful touch, Cora could rejoin society soon, a notion both welcome and repugnant. She needed her body to be whole again in order to defeat Valère, but the prospect of taking up her former role of seductress sat heavily on her conscience.

Her fingers hovered over the gash near her eye. Even though Valère had been drawn to her looks, she knew he would see her disfigurement as a trophy to his superiority, and a perverse excitement would follow. An excitement she would use to her advantage.

But the irony of her damaged face was not lost on her. The same marks that would help her destroy her enemy would limit her future use to the Nexus. An easily identified secret service agent was a useless agent.

If she came out of this battle alive, what would she do? Continue searching for the man who murdered her parents, surely. That was a certainty. She would not stop until she gazed into the killer's eyes.

Without the Nexus, she had no purpose, no reason to leave the comfort of her bed every day. The Nexus was her life. She knew no other way and, even if she did, it was no longer open to her.

"Do you not like it, Miss Cora?" Dinks asked, her tone uncertain.

Cora shook off her melancholy. As usual, she would do what must be done. For now, she must eliminate Valère as a threat. She would see to the rest later.

She made a show of admiring Dinks's handiwork, for the maid had truly done wonders with her appearance. She stood to embrace her friend. "Thank you," she whispered. "Thank you so very much."

"You're welcome." Tears choked the maid's words. A handkerchief materialized from the depths of Dinks's skirt, and she dabbed Cora's tears away and then her own. "That rat-bastard won't get the best of us."

"Never."

"We must be vigilant."

"Yes. He'll not stop until he finds me."

"We'll be waiting."

"I won't let my arrogance place you, Jack, and Bingham in danger again." Cora clasped Dinks's hands. "I'll take better care of you this time—I swear it."

"Is that what you think? That it's your fault things turned out as they did? Are you daft?"

Cora blinked. "Pardon?"

"Are you a mind reader, now? Perhaps, you're kin to the Almighty and can be in several places at one time?"

"No, of course—"

"Now, you listen here, missy." Dinks's eyes narrowed. "The three of us knew what we were getting into when we followed you to France—Lord Somerton made sure of it. The only people at fault here are that miserable Lord Valère and his toad-eating lackey."

"Dinks, I'm sorry—"

"None of that, now," Dinks said, the heat leaving her voice. She busied herself around the room. "His lordship will be here soon, and I need to tidy up."

Cora's fist pressed against the unexpected lump lodged in her chest. The guilt of her incompetence eased a bit with Dinks's fierce defense. She still blamed herself for the botched mission, but it helped to know that Dinks and the others didn't.

She looked around her childhood room with longing. How nice it would be to go back to those simpler times.

Cora glanced back at her reflection and wondered if Guy would like her hair.

Nine

"Good morning, Dinks," Guy said.

The maid curtsied. "That it is, my lord."

Guy stepped into the bedchamber—and stopped dead in his tracks.

"Oh!" Dinks exclaimed, crashing into his back. "I'm right sorry, my lord. Didn't expect you to be standing in my path like that."

Guy ignored the maid's rebuke. His nostrils flared as the fragrant, moist air of a recent bath reached his nose. But it was the sight of Cora standing near the breakfast table that held him captivated.

A silky blue dressing gown hugged the contours of her body, concealing the effects of her captivity, and a matching ribbon wound through her shorn hair. The effect was stunning in its simplicity. With her regal stance and fading bruises, she reminded him of a wounded angel.

"Your hair."

Turning her damaged cheek away, she lifted her hand to tug on the ends of her hair. "It will grow out... eventually."

"It's beautiful."

She stared into his eyes. "W-what?"

He moved to stand before her and, without thinking,

reached out to touch her rich brown waves. The soft locks slid through his fingers like the downy end of a feather.

Bending forward, he kissed her cheek. "Beautiful."

He heard her sharp intake of breath, saw her stiffen and lean away. "Guy, I—"

His hand fell to his side. "Do not trouble yourself, Cora.

Little by little, touch by touch, he would help her overcome her trepidation. Valère had taken more than her innocence. He had stolen her confidence. "One step at a time, remember?"

She nodded and chanced a glance at him.

Her vulnerability washed over him, and Guy's stomach clenched against the impact. He recovered enough to send her a feigned smile. "I have no doubt cropped hair will soon be all the rage amongst the *ton* ladies once they see you. It's quite becoming, Cora."

"Thank you, but there's no need to say such things. I'm quite aware of what a mess I am." She indicated the table. "Shall we eat?"

Her carefully controlled expression gave nothing away, other than her emotional retreat. Unlike yesterday, when shock over her reaction to his touch left her a little uneasy, she now faced him with protective reserve. As hard as he tried, he could not detect a trace of his former friend or a hint of the easy affection they had once shared.

"Certainly." He pulled out a chair for her and then moved to take his own. "I did not compliment you out of charity, Cora."

"Out of charity or by rote," she said with a dismissive flick of her hand. "Both meaningless and unwelcome."

Guy bit back a sharp rebuttal. She would not believe he thought her more beautiful for having survived an ordeal that would have broken the strongest of men.

She would not believe her beauty encompassed more than the creamy perfection of her skin or the lushness of her sable locks. And she certainly would not believe her beauty lay in the vivid intelligence sparkling behind her blue-green eyes.

Dinks lifted the covers from the serving trays and inhaled deeply. "Ah, Cook out-cooked herself this morning."

"Indeed, she did, Dinks," Guy responded when Cora said nothing.

"Is there anything else you need before I leave you to your meal?"

"No, that will be all," Cora said. "Thank you."

The maid rubbed her stomach and winked at Guy before exiting the room and leaving the door ajar.

Cora stared at the entrance to her bedchamber long after Dinks had left the room.

"Is something wrong?" Guy asked.

"I don't know why she bothers."

He followed her gaze to the open door. "She bothers because she loves you and wishes to protect you."

Cora snorted. "There is nothing left of my reputation to safeguard."

Guy held his tongue. It was true Cora would be ruined if the paragons like the Lady Patronesses of Almack's found out about her work for the government and her time with Valère. Guy was never good at following the dictates of the *ton*, though. Her decision to go to France revealed a depth of character and courage that few in polite society would understand.

"Forgive my sharp tongue, Guy. I-I don't understand what's happening. I—" Without warning, she bent forward and grabbed his hand where it rested on the table. "I want you to know, no matter what I might say or what I might do, I shall never forget that precious moment when you revealed yourself to me in the dungeon. Never. I was so close to giving in to Boucher's demands, so close to giving up. You saved me in more ways than one." Gratitude shimmered in the depths of her unusual eyes. Her final words emerged on a choked whisper. "Thank you, Guy."

He knew her well enough to know that revealing such a perceived weakness was a tremendous concession on her part. At this budding sign of trust, his heart swelled to painful proportions, forcing him to take a moment before he spoke. "You are most welcome, Cora."

Her features lightened into what some might label as a smile before she released her hold and began loading their plates with an array of food. Guy stared at his hand, at the place where she had made her first voluntary contact. Although her action filled his heart with encouraging hope, he experienced a stab of regret when cool air replaced her warmth.

Lifting his coffee cup, he followed the preciseness of her movements. Every time she swallowed, she lowered her eyes as if in concentration. His gaze dipped down to the faint imprint of fingers still evident on her neck.

"How are you feeling today?" he asked, keeping his voice devoid of the helpless anger eating at his gut.

"Better." She raised a rasher of bacon to her mouth. "Any news on Valère's whereabouts?"

He set the cup down on its saucer, and it rattled into place. "Nothing for certain. The likelihood that he would brave England's shores is debatable."

She sipped her tea. "He'll come. Despite Somerton's best efforts to watch the ports and coastline, Valère will find a gap."

Her faith in the Frenchman struck a sensitive chord. This was the second time she had sung the bastard's praises, and Guy liked it not one whit.

"So sure?"

"Quite." She returned her cup to its saucer before meeting his gaze. "Evidently, I have something none other of my ilk possesses. He will come, either to acquire it or to terminate it."

My ilk? What the devil did she mean by that remark? And what did she have that was so valuable to a man like Valère? He ached to ask the questions, but the closed set to her features indicated any attempt to learn the answers would not end in his favor. *Damn stubborn woman.*

As was his wont, Somerton had assessed Cora's situation with blinding accuracy. And Guy was suddenly anxious to be away. He had to keep Cora safe. Keep her away from Valère and out of the bastard's control. No one could survive the Frenchman's style of interrogation a second time. Not even the Raven.

"It is good we won't be here when he arrives, then."

She stared at him, her fork suspended in midair. "Excuse me?"

"This afternoon I will escort you to my country estate."

"Is that so?"

"It's all been arranged." He ignored the cold realization hardening her gaze. "Somerton's notifying your servants as we speak. We'll leave for Herrington Park around luncheon."

"Herrington Park? What of your aunt Phoebe?"

"She passed away last year."

"Oh, Guy. I'm so sorry. The last time I saw your aunt she was as vibrant as ever."

He smiled a little, enjoying this glimpse of his old friend again. "Even with fluid heavy on her lungs, she still managed to harangue me about my bachelor state."

"As she should. The event is long overdue."

He caught her gaze and held it until her eyelids

fluttered with awareness. A flush raced up her neck and
blossomed in her cheeks, and Guy felt an answering pang
in his chest. "Perhaps, you're right."

She dropped her gaze to the food before her. When
she lifted her lids, Raven the Spy had returned. "I don't
appreciate how you and Somerton have reordered my
life without first consulting me."

"Somerton and I agreed that—"

"I don't give a fig about what you and my *former*
guardian have agreed to," she bit out. "I have taken care
of myself for the past three years in a country filled with
vanity, intrigue, and ruthlessness. Not once did I require
a man to do my thinking for me."

His jaw clenched. "And you did an admirable job of
it. However, it is no longer safe for you here."

"That may be, but I'll be no safer at Herrington Park."

"You will. There's no way Valère can know of my
aunt's estate."

Once the meaning behind his words registered, her
expression dulled. "Why is that, Guy?"

Guy remained silent, unwilling to relive the debacle in
the library. He didn't believe she had divulged information that would place her family in jeopardy, but this was
the only foolproof way to guarantee everyone's safety,
including hers.

When he said nothing, her chin rose. "I see."

And she did. Guy caught the flash of hurt before she
masked her emotions again.

"So you are the recipient of unwanted baggage. Do I
have that part right?"

"No. It was my suggestion."

Surprise flickered through her eyes. She tilted her
head back a fraction. "As I said before, I don't want you
involved in this."

An unbidden pang of disappointment bloomed in his

chest. "I became involved the moment I pulled you off that bloody table."

She sucked in a sharp breath.

He regretted delivering the reminder. She had been through so much and didn't need to recall such awful memories. She needed to understand, though, that their lives were irrevocably entwined for as long as Valère lived.

Her eyes narrowed. "In what capacity do you serve Somerton?" she asked, her tone harsh.

Years of forced secrecy caused him to hesitate. Only a select few knew of his gift for breaking French ciphers, and even fewer knew of his ability to go deep inside enemy lines. Secretive barriers that kept not just him breathing, but many others, as well.

He recalled the day she had caught him and Ethan sampling Somerton's finest brandy. They had both expected a visit from Somerton, for they had denied her the grown-up treat. She had stormed away, promising retribution. But the earl never came. No, her idea of reprisal came in the form of pouring a large glass of water over each of their top sheets on a cold winter's night.

Cora could be trusted with his secret. Of this he was certain. If he wanted her to trust him, he must extend her the same courtesy. But how much did she really want to know? Better yet, how much did he want her to know?

He had only to look at the bruises on her face to realize the answers to both questions. "You might recall my affinity for figuring out how things work?"

"I do, indeed." Her features softened. "When we could get you to sit still, you would spend all your time tinkering with things, taking them apart and putting them back together. I remember being in awe of the way your mind worked."

Warmth pierced his heart. "My *tinkering* turned into a useful commodity in our war against Napoleon."

She tilted her head to the side, studying him with her shrewd gaze. "You are a cryptographer."

He nodded, his chest pounding.

"Of course," she said. "I couldn't think of a more perfect position for you. Why would Somerton send a cryptographer on a rescue mission?" She asked the volatile question as if she were inquiring about the weather.

Guy knew his answer held far more importance than the temperature outside.

His grip tightened around the knife and fork he held. "Because breaking ciphers isn't the only commodity I provide."

"You mentioned a penchant for killing," she said in a matter-of-fact voice. "My brother is also multifaceted, I gather."

"Of that, you must speak to Danforth." No longer hungry, he laid his silverware down and wiped his mouth. "We must get you away to safety, Cora. I would prefer to work with you on this, but I'm not above taking whatever steps are necessary to protect you."

"You have made that perfectly clear, my lord," she said. "What you don't understand is that your interference is unnecessary and unwanted. You see, I learn quickly from my mistakes and won't underestimate Valère again."

Unwanted.

Guy's temples pounded with a sudden burst of anger. Who was she to deny his help? By God, if it weren't for him, she would be quite dead by now. The awful thought socked him in the gut. He'd be damned if he would allow her to take foolish chances with her life again.

He rose, allowing his serviette to fall heedlessly to the floor. With dispassion, he watched her eyes widen at his approach. Bracing one hand on the back of her chair and the other on the table, he bent forward until he could feel the heat from her skin and smell the fresh scent of her recent bath.

"If you were so good at taking care of yourself, I would not have had to traipse across the Channel to rescue you. Or shall I say the Raven? After all, it was the Raven I was sent to fetch."

Her eyes widened even more. "Did Somerton tell you?"

"You've been at this too long, old girl, if you think Somerton capable of revealing your alias. Even to me."

"But how—?"

"I'm good at putting the pieces together, remember?" he asked.

All the joy he had felt upon entering her chamber had disintegrated into a pile of half-truths, missed opportunities, and bitter regrets. Tomorrow, during the long ride to his country estate, he would try to reach her again. This morning, he'd had enough.

He leaned closer until the soft curls above her ears grazed his cheek. He lowered his voice. "Depending on others will not weaken you, Cora." He pulled back until their gazes met. "You'll still be the strong and courageous person you've always been." Before he thought better of it, he placed a tender kiss on her lips. He lingered there to make sure she understood the difference between this kiss and the pecks of greeting he used to give her. He wanted her to remember how a man's touch could bring comfort rather than pain and humiliation.

When he straightened, he was relieved to see the dazed look in her eyes. So much better than the terror he witnessed yesterday. Progress.

"Another step, Cora."

He gulped down a final drink of coffee and then pivoted to leave. At the door, he infused as much authority into his tone as possible. "I will return for you after luncheon. Do not keep me waiting."

A half a second after the door clicked shut behind him something crashed against the door. Dinks sat on a chair a few feet away, her wide eyes slanting from him to the door and back. As Guy passed her position, he winked and said, "Progress, Dinks."

The maid smiled. "Slew her demons, did you, sir?"

"Not yet, but I'm working on it."

As he continued down the corridor, he heard Cora's door open, then Dinks's voice. "Now what have we here, Miss Cora?"

Guy couldn't stop the smile from breaking across his face. It had felt so damn good talking with Cora again. She had always been a worthy adversary when it came to opposing opinions. Her skills had merely sharpened in the years they had been apart.

And the kiss. Such a stimulating mixture of poignant exploration and seductive enticement. Her scent, her taste, the exquisite softness of her mouth had pushed his limits of control.

But what had intrigued him most was the fact she hadn't pulled away. He couldn't be sure, but, the fraction of a second before he ended the kiss he felt a shift beneath his lips. Engagement? He could only hope.

He slid his tongue over his bottom lip, tasting a hint of her morning tea.

Progress, indeed.

Ten

"ENOUGH." GUY STRUCK THE ROOF OF THE TOWN coach with the side of his fist, unable to watch any longer.

When the coach slowed to a stop, he leaned out the door and addressed Dinks, who sat in the driver's seat next to Bingham. "Get the laudanum. Now."

"I'll not take it," Cora said from inside.

"You will. Even if I have to pour it down your damn stubborn throat." He would not travel another mile watching her cringe against every rut in the road, big or small.

"Here you are, my lord." Dinks handed him a small bottle and an opened silver flask. "Two drops. No more, mind you."

"Thank you." Guy sniffed the flask's contents. Water. "Dinks, why don't you, Bingham, and Jack take a walk down to the bend in the road and back?"

"Perhaps, I should stay—"

"Yes, sir." Bingham interrupted, tying off the horses. He clambered down and grasped Dinks's elbow. "We'll be back in twenty minutes."

"Stop your manhandling, you old goat. Miss Cora might need me."

Bingham gently but firmly pulled the maid down the hard-packed road. "Her man will take care of this. She don't need you."

"Of all the things to say…" The sparring couple set off on their hike, with a smiling Jack ambling along behind, his hands clasped behind him.

At any other time, the sight of Cora's mismatched servants strolling down the middle of the road—one stocky and slightly stooped, another regal and broad-hipped, and the third lean and dark-haired—would have elicited a smile.

Not today, though. Today, he wanted them to pick up their pace, to get beyond hearing distance, so they wouldn't feel compelled to come to their mistress's defense should she scream.

He waited another full minute before reentering the carriage. Shutting the door, he leveled his most determined gaze on Cora. She glared back with her red-rimmed eye, the one filled with false courage and aching vulnerability. A bead of sweat edged its way over her vivid red scar, and her sheet-white face glowed in the late afternoon light. The sight of her misery stopped the harsh words in his throat.

"Save yourself the trouble," she said. "I'm not taking any more of that poison. And you won't bully me today like you did yesterday."

Ignoring her, he tilted the vial of brown liquid until two drops splashed into the flask of water.

"Have you ever seen a woman who is dependent on laudanum?" she pressed.

"Cora, you won't become an opium eater by taking measured doses for a short period of time. The women you're speaking of have taken the opiate for months, possible years, to stave off severe headaches or unsatisfactory husbands. Neither is the case for you." He held out the flask. "Drink it."

Her hands remained tucked around her middle.

Disquiet pulsed below the surface of his unwavering resolve. They had several hours to go before reaching

Herrington Park. She wouldn't last another quarter hour. Nor would he.

Then something quite unexpected happened. Unshed tears shimmered in her eyes, and her chin wobbled with repressed emotion.

Guy scooted to the edge of his seat. "Cora."

She shook her head, worrying her bottom lip. "My mother"—she cleared her throat—"my mother used to—"

He touched her knee, stopping her difficult confession. "I know, sweetheart."

"You do?" she asked in a shaky voice. "How?"

He rubbed his thumb in large, soothing circles. "Men talk, too."

"Ethan." She stared into space. "I've never spoken of it."

"Many years passed before Danforth revealed your mother's dependence." Guy watched her expression, gauging her reaction. "Heavy drink tends to loosen a man's tongue."

Her gaze focused on his left shoulder. "Until the year before her death, my mother was perfectly normal. She was loving and happy. Bigger than life in some ways."

Guy balanced the flask between his feet and drew one of her hands between his. He waited for her to withdraw, but she never noticed his bold touch. Her thoughts had turned deeply inward.

"During that last year, she alternated between being the mother I had always known to a cruel and sullen creature. It didn't take me long to connect the brown bottle sitting on her bedside table, the one she ripped from my hands when I dared to inquire about it, to the volatile woman who sent me fleeing for the security of my chamber at every turn."

Guy's throat clenched against the image of a young Cora hiding from her beloved mother. He chafed the ice from her fingers. "Hold the good memories of your mother to your heart. Those are the ones she would want you to remember."

She nodded, her gaze falling to their clasped hands.

"You're not your mother, Cora."

"I know." He heard little conviction in her tone.

He picked up the flask and wrapped her fingers around the metal container.

"If you won't do this for you, do it for Dinks." *And me.* "She worries about you."

She closed her tempest-filled eyes. "Not fair."

Relief banished his disquiet. Even as a girl, Cora had been headstrong, but she had always favored others' needs above her own.

When her eyelids finally lifted, he saw resignation in their blue-green depths.

"Trust me, Cora."

Upending the flask, she downed the bitter concoction as if she raced against time, then offered the empty container back to him. "That's vile."

He smiled. "I wondered if it tasted as awful as it smelled."

She sent him a blistering look, then her eyes widened when he took the flask from her with one hand and captured her fingers with the other.

He brushed his thumb over her knuckles. "You'll soon fall asleep."

She glanced around the carriage interior, assessing its close confines and no doubt realizing the trust she would have to place in him while she slept. No doubt thinking of their shared kiss. As was he.

"If I joined you over there," he said, indicating her side of the conveyance, "you could use my lap as a pillow, and I would keep you from sliding off the bench and causing yourself further injury."

A considering look entered her expression. She was fighting. Fighting this new compulsion of hers for flight. Pride swelled inside his chest, tightening his muscles.

"Trying to take care of me again, Guy?"

"Always." He paused. Allowed her time to absorb his remark. "Whether you like it or not."

Her lips thinned. "*Not* would be my current sentiment."

His lips quirked. "May I?"

She gave him a curt nod.

Tossing the flask aside, he maneuvered around and sat beside her, then propped his arm along the back, inviting her to lie down.

With taut, jerky movements, she removed her hat and eased down until her cheek rested on his thigh.

Awareness stabbed through his gut and pulsed in his cock. Guy clenched his teeth, fought the need to grind his desire against something soft and feminine. *Cora.* He clutched his other thigh, and his right hand grasped the seat's back as if it were the only thing holding him in place. Sweat broke out on his brow.

He squeezed his eyes shut and prayed she couldn't hear the chaotic pounding of his heart. He wanted her to draw comfort from his presence, not fear.

"Guy?"

"Yes, Cora." His tone sounded guttural, even to his own ears.

"Thank you."

His throat closed tight, and stinging needles pricked the backs of his eyes. "You're welcome, sweetheart."

They sat in strained silence for ten racking minutes before her body faded into a more relaxed position and her breathing deepened into a soft snore of contentment.

A few minutes later, Dinks's profile appeared at the window. "My lord?"

"We're ready," he whispered.

"Is the little mite resting now?" she asked with concern edging her voice.

"Yes, Dinks. I won this round."

Amusement tinted her words. "Well done, sir."

The coach soon lurched into motion.

Guy braced himself against the gentle swaying motion of Cora's head. The movement matched his body's urgings to a dangerous precision. He pulled in a deep, calming breath. Perhaps if he steadied her head, the torment would lessen. Perhaps.

Whom was he kidding? He'd wanted to weave his fingers through the silky skeins since the moment he became aware of her as a woman. Time, distance, and a belief she was unobtainable had prevented him from assuaging his heart's desire.

His fingers flexed, itching to smooth over her close-cropped hair. Dare he risk waking her? The selfish bastard in him responded with a resounding "Yes!"

He finally gave in to the impulse and ran the back of his forefinger along the snipped end of a soft curl. It sprang back after each pass, determined and buoyant, as its mistress eventually would become once her mental scars healed with time. The new style suited her. It emphasized her high cheekbones, narrow chin, and feline eyes. It symbolized her new journey, a fresh start.

A beginning that must be delayed until Valère was no longer a threat.

The town coach dipped hard into a rut, and Guy held his breath. When she made no move to grab her jarred ribs, when no flash of pain crossed her face, he sighed. He would be bloody glad to have this drive behind them.

Unable to stop himself, he burrowed his fingers farther into her mop of newfound curls and savored their silky texture. Although her new look charmed him, he mourned her long brown locks. Would have loved to have been able to spread them over his pillow, but—

Dammit. What the hell was he thinking?

This was Cora. His friend. Someone he had always thought of as a little sister.

At least, until she turned into a desirable woman when he wasn't looking.

The image of Cora in a black mask and scandalous red dress flashed through his mind. The erotic sensations she had stirred in him at the masquerade were definitely *not* sisterly.

Nor were his thoughts now. Even in her current damaged state, she called to him. He squeezed his eyes shut while his body waged war with his mind. He needed a distraction, something to occupy his hands, if only for a few minutes.

He released the back of the seat and stretched his fingers wide to ease the ache caused by his taut grip. Then he bent forward to find a traveling rug beneath the bench, his chest but a hairsbreadth from her cheek. He glanced down. For some inexplicable reason, he yearned to see the image of her resting peacefully in his lap.

Lingering in such a close position proved fatal.

Perhaps sensing his warmth, Cora angled her head around to nuzzle the side of her face into his chest. Had she done so an hour ago, her butterfly touch would have barely registered through his thick coat. But he had unbuttoned the garment after the last stop, electing comfort over propriety. Now only a fine layer of silk and linen protected him from her siren's call. It wasn't enough.

His muscles locked, and a flush of heat gripped his body and surged into his groin. His cock hardened, lengthened, until it filled the tight folds of his breeches.

Oh, dear God. He swallowed hard, fighting back the desire that was eating away at his good intentions.

Closing his eyes, he indulged the pleasurable sensation a moment longer, suffered its full, glorious effect, and then shifted out from beneath her, replacing his lap with the thick traveling rug.

With rigid movements, he made his way to the other side of the carriage, his heart pounding in his ears and a strange heat blurring his vision. What was happening to him? How could her innocent touch cause such a visceral reaction?

Goddammit, he was supposed to be protecting her, not lusting after her like some ravenous cub at the height of his pubescence. Leaning over his knees, he dropped his face into his hands. What kind of monster lusts after a woman who has been abused and misused?

He peered through his splayed fingers and stared in dismay at the object of his tangled desires; disgust and warmth swirled through his body, neither one gaining the upper hand.

Jesus, what was wrong with him? The chant continued to echo through his mind when no acceptable answer appeared.

He *would* conquer this damned inconvenient attraction. Until Cora could master the panic that gripped her every time she encountered a man's touch, his desire had no place in their lives.

Sliding his face deeper into the palms of his hands until his heels pressed hard into his eye sockets, he began a different chant—*I will conquer my attraction. I will conquer my attraction.* I must.

Eleven

AFTER SLEEPING AWAY MUCH OF THE PREVIOUS DAY, Cora looked forward to exploring Guy's new home and taking in some much-needed fresh air. From her second-floor bedchamber window, she spotted a small, inviting copse of linden and maple trees a short distance away. Far enough from the house to give her neglected muscles a good turn and close enough should she need help. Equipped with a comfortable pair of half boots, she made her way downstairs on slightly shaky legs.

As she journeyed toward the back door, she took in every morsel of her surroundings. The staircase balustrade sported a beautiful barley-twist design, and the drawing room's fireplace surround spoke of restrained elegance with its fluted pilasters and marble inserts. Every room was decorated in warm tones and with comfortable, sturdy furniture. Perfect for the new owner.

While growing up, Guy had visited his elderly aunt quite frequently, always bringing her silk embroidery threads of every hue from his various travels and the latest edition of *The Lady's Magazine* from London. Items she could not easily acquire in remote Yateley. The way Guy had doted on his aunt Phoebe had always touched Cora's soft spot.

His aunt was the only real family he'd had. In all

the years Cora had known Guy, she had met his aunt a handful of occasions but had never met his parents. The earl and countess had seemed uninterested in their only son's whereabouts, for they were always chasing the next house party.

Cora's heart stung. She recalled the flash of hurt that had crossed Guy's features when she ruthlessly stated she didn't want his help. At an early age, she had detected his need for family. For love. If not for his aunt Phoebe and Cora's odd little family, Guy would never have experienced the tender emotion or received instructions on how to be a proper, responsible earl.

Thank God for Somerton. He had patiently answered Guy's many questions and showed him how to keep an eye on his finances and properties. He had taught him how to be a nobleman, a gentleman.

Cora's gaze swept over her surroundings again. Losing his aunt must have been quite devastating. She felt a twinge of regret for not having been there for him.

As she wandered from room to room, poking her head into each, she noted the furnishings and color combinations would indeed appease both male and female tastes. The drawing room held a lovely rose-colored settee that would appeal to any female, although Cora preferred the two dark brown leather chairs that sat in a small vee around the crackling fire. The room's walls also exhibited a wide-ranging combination of hunt scenes and landscapes.

Hearing Guy's and Dinks's voices straight ahead, presumably from the kitchen, she veered left—away from them—and found a rear door that led to the landscaped gardens and beyond. The moment her foot crossed the threshold, two armed men stepped forward.

Cora's training took over. She crouched low, tucked her shoulder and rolled, and came to her feet with a knife in one hand. "Stay where you are!"

"Whoa, my lady." The big blond to her right held his hands out in a sign of peace. "We're here to guard you, not harm you."

Cora eyed the fair-haired man, assessing him from head to toe. Unable to detect an immediate danger, she released a pent-up breath. And that's when the pain of her exertions seeped into her consciousness.

"Under whose orders?" Even as she barked out the question, she remembered Dinks making mention of extra guards being posted.

"Lord Helsford, my lady," the blond-haired man said. "We've been instructed to escort you wherever you wish to go."

Cora eased out of her defensive stance but kept her blade aimed at the two strangers. Anger simmered low in her stomach. Down deep, she knew Guy's precautions were for the best. But she resented them all the same. He could have discussed this with her, or, at the very least, warned her she would be trading one prison for another.

"What are your names?" she demanded of the blond, unable to moderate her tone.

"I'm Neil. That's Samuel."

Cora's gaze flicked back to Neil's partner. A giant displaying a barbarian's naked pate stood facing her, his hands raised, palms up. He presented an odd pairing of submissive warrior.

The last of her initial fear faded, but wariness remained. Walking in the woods with two strange men dogging her steps dampened her enthusiasm for a refreshing stroll.

Cora stashed her knife back in her skirt pocket and turned toward the wooded copse, unable to give up her outing. "Follow me, gentlemen. If you must."

From that point forward, Cora did her best to ignore her protectors. If she allowed herself to be honest, she was secretly comforted by their presence. Valère was out there. Somewhere. Lurking in the shadows, waiting for the perfect moment to reveal himself. He would make her pay first for her betrayal and then for her escape.

And that's why she needed to make the most of today. There might not be a tomorrow.

The trail snaked through a small meadow flaunting an abundance of spindly shrubs and wildflowers of all colors. She inhaled the clearing's fresh scent while her free hand splayed over the tops of the tufted grasses, allowing their feathery heads to tickle her sensitive palm.

Steeped in training for so long, then in deception, many years had passed since Cora was able to simply absorb the outdoors, to release her worries and enjoy nature's beauty.

While in France, she had spent few days outside the bustle of Paris. On those rare occasions that took her outside the city, the French countryside had not endeared itself to Cora's heart as had England's expansive dales, ridges of heather moorland, and ancient stone fences.

Not until this moment, when chattering birds sang overhead and good English soil churned beneath her feet, had she realized the power her country held over her. And she looked forward to the moment when her mind would drift and her senses would blend with all this natural wonder.

She stopped, closed her eyes, and listened.

Her patience was soon rewarded when the rapid flicker of a cicada rent the air, followed by the joyful warble of a robin and the blaring trill of a toad. The sun warmed her face even as the dappled shadows of the nearby forest beckoned her, as a flickering flame tempts a curious moth.

Thirty feet inside the shade the wariness she had not been able to completely shake grew to a fever pitch. She

sought the solid comfort of her knife as she glanced over
her shoulder.

Bolstered by the guards' presence, Cora traipsed
deeper into the maze of maples. The more she ventured
into their depths, the more the serenity of her surroundings ebbed away.

Any sane woman would scurry back to the house and
leave her guards to investigate the source of her unease.
But Cora felt far from sane these days. Although she never
wanted to return to Valère's dungeon, she couldn't bring
herself to run from the bastard.

When the frenzied prattle of birds and insects quieted
and the swirling breeze died, her suspicions were
confirmed.

She was not alone.

The weight of the intruder's stare pressed upon
her from all sides. She slowly turned in a circle,
searching the area, seeing only a tangle of leaves
and branches.

No one—only her guards. Could the laudanum still
be working its way through her body and affecting her
mind? Causing her to sense danger where none existed?

She shook her head, trying to free her mind of the
terror and confusion warring for control.

There's no one there, she chanted to herself, *only the
guards Guy assigned to watch over me. That's all.*

Her reassuring words did little to stem the building
panic, and her grip tightened around the rosewood-
handled blade. Memories intruded, pulling her deeper
into the darkness, to a place where she had been more
animal than human.

*Cora shivered, her torn and bloodied chemise provided little
protection against the cell's frigid dampness, and her muscles
ached from being strapped to the stone slab for so long. And
the darkness. Oh, God, the darkness continued to beat at her*

flagging sanity while the hunger clawed at her empty stomach like a ravenous beast.

A violent shiver convulsed through her body.

Above her, heavy footsteps rapped against the floor. Her gaoler's familiar stride was unhurried, measured. Designed to elicit anticipatory terror in the prisoner below. Each step thundered in her ears like a thousand lightning storms blasting the night sky.

She jerked her hands, and the metal cuffs anchored into the slab held solid. The door leading down to this abysmal place opened, and hours of terrifying darkness gave way to splintering shards of candlelight. She closed her eyes and put every ounce of her weight behind the next pull.

The cuffs' moorings shifted, sending a surge of excited blood pounding through her body. She pulled again. More movement. She gritted her teeth against the cold metal burrowing into the raw wounds that encircled her wrists.

The flickering light grew brighter, closer to her cell.

She yanked one last time with all her strength, and the chain popped free. Stunned, she did nothing for two full seconds before scurrying off the table. She pressed her shivering body against the wall near the cell's open door. Bracing her feet apart, she gripped the heavy irons and waited.

His footsteps slowed.

Blood pounded in her ears. Come on. Come on. *She struggled to even her breathing, to slow her heart rate. But the fear of losing this one opportunity to escape ran high, and she could not control her body's reaction to the forthcoming footsteps.*

"Cora, I brought you a present." *High-pitched squealing punctuated his promise. The toe of his boot crossed the threshold.* "Cora?"

She reared back and whipped the irons at his head.

"Cora!" *another man's voice yelled.*

She stared at the intruder, her gaze unfocused, her

laboring breaths sawing through the air. The dank cell finally disappeared, and Guy's harsh features sharpened into crisp—real—lines.

And pain radiated through her wrist.

Guy held her right hand aloft, far above her head. Her muddled mind could make no sense of the situation until her gaze landed on the four-inch stiletto clasped between her fingers, its gleaming blade pointing down at a deadly angle.

"Oh, no. No." Her gaze raked over him for a spreading patch of crimson. Nothing visible. "Are you injured?" She stepped forward to pat his body, certain she had stabbed him, but his implacable hold on her wrist held firm, stopping her short. "Tell me! Did I hurt you?"

"I'm fine, sweetheart." Guy loosened his grip and nodded to someone behind her. "No harm done."

She dropped the knife and stepped back. Glancing over her shoulder, she saw the guards rapidly retreating.

"Cora. I'm unharmed." Guy's voice was calm, reassuring.

She shook her head, the movement sluggish. The imprint of the knife's carved handle still burned her palm. Without thought, she rubbed her hand against her hip, much the same way she had in her bedchamber a few days ago.

"You don't understand—" Unable to say more past the lump in the back of her throat, Cora bolted in the opposite direction.

"Wait!"

Cora ignored Guy's plea.

She ran until her ribs screamed in protest, until she could no longer smell the decay that permeated the dungeon. She ran until the fiery rods of pain stabbing at the soles of her feet buckled her knees.

Twice now she had lost her sense of time and place and had threatened Guy's life. Nightmares not only savaged her dreams, they were now taking control of her waking hours.

Even before her captivity, she had always traveled with a concealed weapon. The practice had served her well on a few occasions, but today she came close to killing her childhood friend.

Squeezing her eyes shut, Cora drew in deep, measured breaths through her nostrils. She pressed a hand to her rib cage to stem the pulsing ache while she climbed to her poor tormented feet. She stood there, lifeless yet alive. Aware yet devoid of conscious thought.

The world outside intruded upon her vacuous state. She stood at the edge of a small lake where enormous willow trees swayed in the breeze, their leafy fingers trailing along the surface of the dark water. Bare patches of earth near the lake's edge released a pleasant loamy fragrance into the air. Dragonflies darted amongst the reeds, feeding upon small insects, while a swallowtail butterfly flittered drunkenly around the muddy embankment.

The peaceful scene failed to settle the turmoil inside her. How could she have become so immersed in the events of her past and transferred her response to the present? How could she be so stupid as to confuse the two?

Fearing she was about to be sick, she pressed her fingers against her lips. *God, help me. Please, please help me.*

Rapid footsteps approached from behind, soon followed by the ancient, alluring scent of sandalwood.

Guy.

He broke through the undergrowth to reach her. "There you are."

"Are you sure you're unharmed?" she asked over her shoulder.

Strong arms slid around her waist. "I'm fine."

Cora stiffened, but she didn't pull away. She needed to feel his strength, hear his breathing, count his heartbeats.

"Relax," he said. "I'm in need of some comfort after the scare you gave me back there."

"I'm so sorry." Her apology emerged fragmented, nearly inaudible to her own ears.

"Do you wish to discuss it?"

She shook her head and pushed against his hold. "No." *God, no.* How does one explain a total loss of self?

"Then leave off," he whispered near her ear, tightening his hold. "I won't hurt you, and you know it."

In her mind, she knew he was not a threat. He had always protected her. From the moment her ten-year-old feet had tripped up Somerton's front steps to her recent stay in Valère's dungeon, Guy had been there to pick her up. Knowing all of this did not stop the sensation of a thousand worms burrowing beneath the surface of her skin at his restraining embrace.

"Take another step, Cora."

His challenge heated her skin. Something in his tone told her the next step would be the largest one of all.

By slow, controlled increments, she allowed her body to sink against him, to melt into the cradle of his arms. To yearn for the press of his lips.

❧

As Guy brushed a kiss against Cora's silken curls and rested his chin there, the scent of jasmine reached his nose. When her body gave way and molded itself against him, he sighed a relieved breath. Yes, his Cora was a fighter.

He stared across the glade with unseeing eyes. Never would he forget the sight of her standing on that narrow deer path, her terrified eyes dilating at his approach, her

hand frantically searching the depths of her skirt pocket—
locked in a nightmare only she could see. He had called
to her several times with no response. The moment he
reached for her, her hand broke free, and the steel blade
of a knife sliced through the air at him.

His quick reactions not only saved his life but likely
Cora's, as well. She would never have forgiven herself had
she struck him. Her look of self-disgust was proof enough.

"It's beautiful here." Her quiet murmur pulled him
back to the present.

Indeed, it was. A riot of early summer flowers tangled
with short grasses and wispy bushes. In the distance, at
the edge of the lake, a long, yellow-legged heron stalked
some silvery prey that sliced back and forth beneath the
surface of the shimmering water.

The tentative brush of her fingers drew his attention.
Her free hand hovered over his, which were clasped
securely around her waist. He held perfectly still while she
made her decision. When her chilled palm finally covered
his knuckles, his tense muscles relaxed.

His thumb brushed across the sling anchoring her left
wrist against her chest. "Does it hurt terribly?"

"No, not really. It's only sprained, after all. The
swelling has gone down enough that I should be able to
remove it soon."

She spoke as if her injuries were of little consequence.
When in reality, the damage Valère had inflicted upon
her body was the worst he had ever seen. Guy changed
the subject, not wanting her to fall prey to painful
memories again.

"Do you remember when we were children? How
the three of us would sneak off on hot summer after-
noons to cool off in the lake?"

"Mmm-hmm."

"Cora-bell the fish," he teased, remembering one of

the many nicknames he and Ethan had given her. "I'm still amazed at how long you could swim underwater without coming up for air."

She snorted. "A survival technique I was forced to learn in order to escape two boys with constant mischief on their minds."

Guy opened his hand, palm up, in invitation. When her slender fingers slid between his, his pulse leaped.

"We had many great times, did we not?" he said in a low voice.

A small smile crinkled the skin near her good eye. "Yes. Yes, we did."

He held up their entwined hands. "Our past is woven together as tightly as our fingers." The side of his nose rested against her hair. "And I have every reason to believe our future will be, too." He did not disclose how closely he would like to see them entwined.

She ripped free from his embrace and put several feet of distance between them. "Please don't."

Guy cursed this overwhelming need of his to be near her, to comfort her. To bring warmth back to her life. He stared at her rigid back. "Don't what?"

A lifetime passed before she faced him. When she did, her features were composed—cool.

Raven.

She used the persona as a defense mechanism, one where she could remain detached, unemotional. He was beginning to hate that particular cast to her features.

"I appreciate what you're trying to do," she said. "But please don't. I'm willing to work with you on conquering this"—she waved her hand in vicinity of her head—"this weakness of the mind, but I have no interest beyond a few chaste touches."

If he were a gentleman, he would murmur his agreement and assure her that he meant nothing untoward by

his comment: his only goal was to help her overcome her
fear and keep her safe.

He wasn't a gentleman, nor was he a liar. "Does your
aversion exclude kissing, Cora?"

Wariness filled her gaze. "W–what do you mean?"

"I'm merely trying to grasp the rules of our campaign."

She said nothing, but Guy could see her filtering
through the advantages and disadvantages of her response.

He shortened the distance between them. "Is kissing
forbidden, Cora?"

Her gaze dropped to his mouth, and Guy's gut
clenched around an answering surge of anticipation.

"Cora." He was close enough now to feel her rapid
bursts of exhalation. He skimmed his mouth along the
soft swell of her lower lip, mixing his breath with hers.
The feathery sensation tickled and tantalized, teased and
taunted, and Guy locked his arms at his sides to keep
from dragging her into a more satisfying position. "Do
you wish to deny yourself this small comfort?"

Her eyes closed, and she released a slow, trembling
breath. "No."

Desire surged through him, expanding his muscles
and tightening his groin. He reached for her, only to be
stopped by a firm hand to his chest.

"Not yet, Guy. Please. Not yet." Tears choked her
words, and violent tremors racked her body.

He rubbed her bare arms, trying to bring some
warmth back into her chilled body. "Sweetheart, don't."
When she continued to tremble, he made to pull away,
to give her the space she needed to combat the nightmare
overwhelming her mind, but she crashed into his chest
and folded her right arm around his waist. She held onto
him as if she battled gale-force winds.

He held out his arms, not knowing what to do with
them. If he wrapped them around her, would she feel

caged and threatened? If he continued to avoid contact, would she become self-conscious and flee his presence?

Bloody hell.

In the end, he did what any red-blooded man would do in the face of a distressed woman. He patted her back and made shushing noises. He felt like a damned idiot, but after a few agonizing minutes, her shaking dissipated. When the stillness grew awkward, she released her hold and backed away.

Not a single tear stained her cheeks.

He glanced down and noted her first two fingers strangling her thumb in her old telltale sign of anxiety. Slowly, he reached for her hand and pulled her thumb free. He didn't release his hold.

She sent him a wan smile. "Old habits."

He swung her hand back and forth. "I remember how to fix it."

"Will you never grow weary of fixing me, Guy?"

Lifting her hand to his lips, he said, "No. Cryptographers never tire of piecing things together."

Gratitude sparkled in her eyes, and Guy's heart clenched at the sight. He disliked seeing her weighed down by such fragile vulnerability. For a moment, he wished for the return of her Raven mien.

She needed to regain the confidence she had lost during her flight through the woods. "I have something for you."

"For me?"

"Yes." He retrieved her knife from his coat pocket. "I believe you dropped this in the woods."

She reared back. "No. I don't want it."

"You must." He forced her fist open and pressed the handle into her palm.

"I can't be trusted with a weapon. You should know that better than anyone."

"You are safer with it than without it."

"Whether you realize it or not, Guy, I could have done you serious harm back there."

"But you didn't." He closed her fingers around the knife. "I cannot be with you every minute of the day, and I shall rest easier knowing you carry this."

She hesitated a fraction longer, and then with expert ease, she inspected the blade's edge before sliding it back into her skirt pocket. "Thank you." She wrapped her arm around her middle, where her bruised ribs were no doubt protesting her recent exertions. "I think I've had enough fresh air for one day."

"Come." He held out his arm, setting aside his disappointment at having to share her again. "Let me escort you back to Dinks. She'll brew a special tonic that will take the edge off your pain."

Understanding glimmered in her eyes as she accepted his arm. He steeled himself against her light touch. The heat from her fingers penetrated the many layers of cloth and muscles, warming him all the way to his bones.

"Familiar with Dinks's tonics, are you?" she asked.

"I doubt there are many around who have not benefitted from her brandy-laced brews."

"True."

They continued on in easy silence, each deep in their own thoughts. Each wondering what would have happened had they given in to their craving for each other's kiss.

Twelve

Two days later, Cora removed the irritating sling and made for the kitchen. Her appetite had returned in full force, and she longed for something more solid than her current diet of watery soup and clotted-cream porridge. But as her appetite increased, her sleep had fallen victim to nightmares of the past once she had stopped taking the laudanum. As much as she hated the opiate, she longed for a full night's rest.

She rubbed her exhausted head and trudged through the sun-brightened house, experimentally flexing her hand and rotating her wrist. Needles of pain shot up her arm and, after so many days of idleness, her muscles felt leaden and useless.

She performed the exercise a few more times, shrugging off the discomfort. Regaining strength in her arm was just one more obstacle to overcome. She had lost count of how many of those she had encountered since her first introduction to Valère.

As she headed for food that she could actually cut with her teeth, she passed the library door and heard a muffled expletive. Retracing her steps, Cora peered into the room. At first she thought the room empty, until her gaze lowered and was greeted by a man's well-shaped bottom clad in fawn-colored wool.

"Come out from under there you insufferable fur ball." Guy made a quick grab for something beneath the burgundy chaise longue. "Dammit."

Cora raised an eyebrow, amused to see the Earl of Helsford in such an undignified position. "Why don't you try using some of your legendary charm to coax your friend out?"

He jerked up, smacking his head on the chaise. "Ow!" Rubbing his head, he sat back on his heels and sent her a you'll-pay-for-that look, an expression she hadn't seen in a very long time—and one she keenly missed.

"Do not scowl at me," she admonished, ignoring the ache in her heart. "I had nothing to do with your current affliction."

"Sneaking up on me doesn't count for culpability?"

"No."

Cora stepped closer to investigate. What would tempt Guy to get down on his hands and knees? As she bent forward, a delicate gray face with large green eyes peeked out to investigate *her*.

A kitten.

She shifted her attention to Guy. "How on earth did the little creature get in here?"

"How should I know," he grumbled. "But it's going back to wherever it came from."

She watched the poor kitten inch closer. "Don't be silly. If I can't find its mother, I'll care for it."

"The fur ball's not staying in this house."

"Are you afraid the kitten will bother your aunt's birds?" During one of her exploratory circuits, Cora had found a large brass-wired cage sitting atop a pedestal in the far corner of Aunt Phoebe's rose-colored drawing room. Inside, a pair of small yellow birds flapped about their enclosure, tipping their little heads from side to side at her approach. When they realized she wished them no harm, they had extended their feathered throats and began to sing to her... at least that's how Cora interpreted their action.

Guy's jaw firmed. "No, I'm not worried about the birds. If anything, I might let the kitten loose inside the cage just to shut them up."

"You'll do no such thing." She watched the kitten edge closer to Guy's boot. "What's your aversion, then? We harbored many barnyard cats in the past."

His eyes narrowed. "It's a damned ankle-biter."

"A what?"

"You heard me," he said. "The little baggage thinks it's great fun to attack my ankles while I'm sitting here. I now have some very decorative claw and fang marks on my new boots."

Cora waved her hand in the direction of Guy's black Hessians. "Let me see."

Hiking his foot up on the chaise, he pointed to the offending marks around the ankle area. "There."

Sure enough, little gouge marks punctured the expensive soft leather.

She pointed to the top of his high boot. "I suspect your tassel is more temptation than the little one could bear." Her lips twitched.

"You find this amusing, my dear?" He dropped his foot to the floor.

"Not at all." She couldn't remember the last time she had felt unfeigned amusement. But the gouge marks, the kitten, and Guy's expression—

"I don't think you would find it entertaining if it were your poor ankles being attacked by ten tiny needles and a set of butcher-sharpened fangs."

"No. No, you're quite right." She struggled to keep the quiver from her voice.

Picking up a quill from the desk, she knelt down.

Uncomfortable with her nearness, the gray kitten wedged itself deeper into the shadows but kept its unblinking green eyes on her. Kinship for the trapped animal clamped around her heart.

Cora wriggled the quill once, twice, and, on the third time, the kitten pounced on the white feather, biting and slapping it into submission. Inch by inch, she moved the quill out of its reach, coaxing the intent kitten from its hiding spot.

She reached out and smoothed her hand over its delicate back, the plush coat more luxurious than any fur muff she had ever owned. When it showed no sign of attacking her hand, she scooped the wide-eyed kitten into her arms and, before long, a rumbling tempest sprang to life inside its small body. Needles bit into the backs of Cora's eyes at the endearing sound.

"Damnation," Guy said.

Cora tilted her head up and caught Guy's lopsided smile, and then a thoughtful expression transfigured his features.

"It appears you have made a friend."

"Force and intimidation can sometimes have the opposite result of its intended effect. Patience might prove a more effective means of getting one's way."

His midnight eyes bore into hers. "So it would seem."

For several excruciating seconds, he studied her. The intensity of his scrutiny made her feel gauche and exposed. She wanted to pull the curtain of her hair over her eyes. But her long locks were gone, and she had learned long ago not to show such weakness.

He glanced at the kitten, breaking their eye contact. "Be sure to throw that menace outside when you're done coddling it." He turned on his heel and left, his gentle tone belying his harsh words and abrupt exit.

For a long time after his departure, Cora stared at the

open doorway, absently rubbing her thumb along the downy coat under the kitten's neck, wondering what she had revealed to Guy's considering gaze.

Thirteen

THE OCCUPANTS IN THE HOUSE HAD LONG SINCE retired upstairs for the evening, leaving the lower level in eerie silence. With book in hand, Cora curled up on the brocade chaise lounge where Guy had knelt earlier in the day, displaying his fabulous bottom and a hint of something more forbidden.

The boy from her youth had made an appearance this morning. She had enjoyed their interplay, seeing his beautiful, long-lashed eyes narrow, promising retribution if she didn't tread carefully. Memories of her time in France hadn't existed during those precious moments. Cora's heart had gloried at the feeling of freedom. The guilt and shame, her yearning for revenge and justice had slid away, making room for the comfort of an old friendship.

A small, furry paw swatted her arm, startling her from her contemplations. She glanced down to find Guy's ankle-biter hunkering down on the floor. "What are doing down there? I thought Dinks built you a warm nest in her room."

The kitten stared intently at the ribbon hanging from her elbow, a predatory gleam in his green eyes. "In the mood to play, I see. You had best not bother the earl. He'll not be happy that I didn't turn you out."

"What the hell are you wearing?" a shocked voice demanded from the doorway, sending the kitten scurrying for cover.

Cora turned to see Guy eyeing the lower half of her body. Bewildered, she looked down to see one bare foot hooked onto the back of her makeshift bed and the other burrowed beneath a pale yellow woolen coverlet. Nothing to cause such a rumpus, although the pose was less than ladylike. Guy had no doubt seen worse from her over the years.

Cora heaved a sigh. So much for everyone being asleep in their beds. "I believe they're called breeches, my lord. Have you not heard of them?"

His eyes narrowed. "Those are not breeches."

Cora shook her head, exasperated. After all these years, men were still a mystery to her. Her *pai jamahs* covered every inch of her body—except her feet. A pair of ordinary feet, if one ignored the burn marks. By Guy's reaction, one would think she danced around the room naked.

"Yes, they are—just not your typical English style."

"Why are you running around the house with them on?"

"Do go away, Guy." She waved him off. "I'm trying to enjoy my book, and I can't do that with you standing there ogling me."

Instead of leaving, he moved forward, hovering over her like a bird of prey sighting a plump hare.

Her teeth clenched, knowing he wouldn't stop pestering her until she answered. "I came across these a few years ago in an Indian bazaar and have begun wearing them to bed, as I find them to be more comfortable and warmer than a nightdress." He made her feel nine years old again, answering to her father for some minor misdeed.

"Move your feet out of the way."

"Why?"

"Because I'm going to sit down."

"You'll do no such thing—"

Grasping her ankles, he shifted her legs enough for him to slip beneath and then placed her feet on his solid thigh. Cora swallowed, the intimacy of the contact making her heart lodge in her throat.

She tried to pull her feet out of his grasp, not wanting him to see or touch her burns. "If you need a place to sit, I'll be happy to read in my bedchamber." Even though her insides clenched with embarrassment, nervous excitement thundered in her chest.

"As you can see, that's not necessary," he said in an unperturbed tone. "You may continue to read while I help you relax."

"And how exactly are you going to do that?"

He answered by kneading between her toes.

Bliss shot up her leg, and tension locked her muscles. The juxtaposition of the two sensations sent her mind reeling. His strong fingers manipulated the soreness from the pads of her feet, careful not to touch her wounds. Her body wanted to melt into thought-numbing ecstasy, but her mind wouldn't release her.

She waited. Waited in silent horror for him to come to his senses, to pull away in disgust.

"Relax, Cora."

"I can't," she whispered.

"You can. Now, breathe."

She tried and failed.

"Again," he demanded.

His fingers skimmed carefully over the half-dozen circular burns dotting the soles of her feet. She closed her eyes, her body tensing even further.

"That's not helping," she ground out.

He ignored her. "Do these still cause you pain?"

Enough, her mind raged. She pulled at her foot.

"Do be still." He tugged her foot back in place. "Answer my question, if you please."

Jaw clenched, Cora glanced down at where his hands continued their masterful manipulation. "No. Just tender."

When he lifted one savaged sole toward his lips, her eyes rounded in horror, and her body turned into a block of cold, unmovable marble.

"Oh, God," she choked out, her toes curling. "No, Guy, please don't—" His lips pressed against first one burn mark and then the other. Tears threatened. "P-please stop."

With the greatest care, he rested her foot across his thigh and cupped the bottom of her foot with his warm palm. His other hand smoothed over the tops of both her feet. "I will do everything within my power to give you ease, Cora."

Gratitude flooded her body, but she had to struggle to enjoy the sensation. She wanted to follow his lead, allow him to help her through this dark hour. But the emotions were trying to choke her. There were so many of them to grasp and control and to set free.

She gathered her tumultuous thoughts together and focused them on his strong hands, on the exquisite pleasure spiraling up her spine. Nothing else. Only the hedonistic joy of the moment.

He continued his gentle assault, rubbing every muscle and crease of her foot. Within minutes, her eyes fluttered shut and her body melted into the cushions of the chaise. She idled in this half-aware state until an odd throbbing against the side of her foot brought her back to full awareness. She glanced down and noticed her foot now rested against his groin.

His hard, pulsing groin.

"Guy—" She made to sit up, but her chest met his staying hand.

"Ignore it."

It drew her attention again. While she stared down at his lap, *it* lengthened and stretched to an impressive and painful-looking size. "I don't know if that's possible."

"Do your best. I can't control my body's response to your nearness, especially dressed as you are, but I can control how I react to such temptation. So relax and allow me to do this one kindness for you."

Cora searched his eyes for a secret meaning and found nothing save sincerity. When the nightmares remained locked away in her mind, she eased back, giving her silent consent.

Approval shone in his dark eyes, and Cora felt a ridiculous amount of satisfaction at her accomplishment. He began working on her other foot, and then those amazing hands kneaded their way up her calf.

She emitted a low, approving groan, certain there was a special place in heaven for hands as skilled as his. He had a wonderful knack for hitting all the right spots. She thought of all the beautiful women for whom he had mastered the technique, shocked by the stab of jealousy that shot through her heart.

How many feminine calves had it taken for him to learn the exact amount of pressure to exert in order to arch a woman's back? Her mind shied away from such useless questions. *Concentrate on the pleasure*, she chided herself.

She gave it her most valiant effort, but her mind veered back to Guy. In his youth, he had been a handsome lad with a decided bent toward mischief. Even now, in unguarded moments, she could detect a sparkle of the boyish charm that had saved him from numerous lashings. But the glimpse of her old friend wasn't what compelled her to spy on him beneath her lashes.

It was the rugged perfection of his sculpted features. Every line on his striking face seemed carved by the hand of the great Bernini. If not for the end-of-the-day stubble on his chin and the disheveled sweep of his hair, he would be too damned perfect for her taste.

His hair.

Aching to feel the silky texture of his long locks, she twisted her fingers together before she succumbed to such enticement. Thick strands of black hair had escaped his leather thong, making him appear as though he had just stepped off the deck of a two-masted brigantine. Piratical. Dangerous. Seductive.

When she drew in a calming breath, his scent—an exotic combination of sandalwood and musk—filled her nostrils. Her pulse stuttered, and her stomach clenched. Out of sheer torture, she indulged in another deep inhalation. Her body grew languid, her eyelids heavy.

"If you continue to stare at me in such a way, Cora, I may have to rethink my earlier statement about controlling myself."

Her eyes widened, and heat crawled up her chest and into her face. Who would believe that Cora deBeau, British agent and seductress, remembered how to blush? She disliked her loss of control. She had worked hard over the years to mask her emotions. Emotions that could get her—and others—killed. What was it about Guy that made her forget years of training and discipline?

And yet, she was tempted to burrow beneath the Raven's persona and see where things led.

"Is that a challenge I see in your beautiful eyes?" he asked, his tone drenched in male desire.

For a charged moment, she allowed his question to hover in the air between them. Then she dug her foot into his thigh. "Yes, I can see how I would inspire uncontrollable lust in my present state, especially with a man of your experience."

He looked down at his arousal. "I believe my current state of discomfort belies the first part of your comment. As for the latter part... what do you know of my experience?"

She glanced away, her unease returning. Their conversation had crept over the invisible line of what she could tolerate. Her hand rubbed over the area around her heart. It felt like a ball of slithering snakes resided within. She needed to move, needed to escape.

This time when she tried to remove her feet, he released them without comment. Placing a supportive hand against her rib cage, she sat up and planted her damaged feet firmly on the floor. She stared at the worn carpet fibers, fighting the compulsion of her own mind.

He touched her shoulder. "Cora."

The contact pushed her over the edge. She stood.

"Don't run."

Glancing over her shoulder, she said, "More like a strategic retreat."

She wanted to stay but needed to go. She hated this weakness, hated Valère for ruining her chance at love. Hated herself for caring about something she had forsaken years ago.

Squaring her shoulders, she opened her mouth to apologize for her cowardice, for not being strong enough to be his friend. Before she could say a word, a grimace shot across his features, and his eyes widened in pain.

"Damn man-eating tiger," he growled, bending over. "I'm going to turn you into a hand muff."

Before he blocked her view, Cora caught sight of the kitten wrapped around his bootless ankle, claws extended, fangs exposed. He disengaged the kitten and raised him in the air by the scruff of his little neck. The incredulous look on Guy's face and the swatting kitten dangling in midair was too much. A gurgle of amusement started low in her stomach, building steadily until it finally emerged on a snort of laughter.

Guy's stunned gaze locked with hers across the short distance, her laughter having caught them both off guard. A warm smile lit his face, even as he dodged the small beastie's sharp claws.

Cora's heart lodged in her throat at his display of tenderness.

She had revealed too much.

Again.

His upturned lips transformed into a stern, thin line. "It's not funny, Cora. His attacks were bad enough while I wore leather boots, but razor-sharp needles penetrating my stocking-covered ankle ceases to amuse."

Grateful for the distraction, Cora responded, "You're right, of course. Here."—she reached for the kitten—"let me take Scrapper to my bedchamber, so he won't cause you further injury."

"Scrapper? You named the damned cat *Scrapper*?"

"It was either that or Fang, and I think Scrapper has a certain poignancy to it, wouldn't you agree?" She turned to leave.

"Cora, come back here. I'm not through with you yet."

She continued her escape with the kitten hooked over her shoulder. "I believe that's enough comfort for one evening. Good night, my lord."

Cora couldn't contain the huge grin and accompanying chuckle any longer. She dug her fingers into Scrapper's velvety fur and climbed the stairs to her room on feet lighter than when she had descended. She barely felt the pinpricks of pain each step caused.

It wasn't until later, when Cora lay in her bed, staring at the darkened canopy above her and the kitten purring

contentedly atop her chest, that she permitted herself to
bask in the warmth of Guy's smile.

⁓

Guy's attention narrowed on the furry menace draped
over Cora's shoulder as she dashed from the room. Was
that a twinkle he saw in the damned cat's eyes? Before
Cora turned the corner, the little feline baggage stretched
out a paw toward him, claws extended.

How the hell was he supposed to interpret that?
Probably trying to get in a last bloodletting swipe before
being carted off.

Cora's soft chuckle reached his ears. The pure beauty
of the sound left him reeling with joy, his furry nemesis
forgotten. This morning, when she noted *Scrapper's* claw
marks on his Hessians, her smile nearly broke free, and
he had mourned the loss. But tonight... tonight she had
laughed, actually laughed for the first time since they had
retrieved her from France.

His mood darkened.

She had been nothing more than a bundle of bones
when they had found her. Not an ounce of femininity
could be found. If not for her unmistakable eyes, he
might have left her behind. Guy pulled in a ragged breath
to stem his churning stomach.

Thanks to Dinks's encouragement, or rather, her
bullying, the hollows in Cora's cheeks had already begun
to fill in, and the skin stretching across her narrow fingers
no longer looked so stark and colorless. Although her
recent merriment was short-lived, it signaled yet another
area Valère failed to destroy and heralded another step
closer to her recuperation.

The faint scent of jasmine lingered in the air. It pulled
at the tension coursing through his shoulders until they
relaxed by slow degrees. As he reclined on the chaise,

feeling the warmth left behind by Cora's body, he clasped his hands behind his head and began plotting ways to make her laugh again.

Fourteen

AS THE PORCELAIN-AND-ORMOLU CLOCK IN THE drawing room chimed for the eighth time, Guy strode through the kitchen door and circled around the dew-dusted herb garden with its diamond-shaped design full of rosemary, parsley, peppermint, and an assortment of other greenery he couldn't identify. Before long, he found the narrow path that would take him to the small lake nestled on the west side of his property.

For the last two mornings, Cora had hidden in her chamber until Dinks served her luncheon meal, and then she would disappear with her guards in tow. He was certain she had adopted this careful ploy because of their encounter in the library. The unmistakable evidence of his desire had at first flustered her before it reawakened the ever-present terror that refused to release her from its grasp.

His anger fired at the implication evident in her reaction. Valère not only damaged her body, but he had crippled her soul, an injury that could take decades to mend. Guy would devote whatever time he had left in this life—and the next—to her recovery. After all she had sacrificed, she now deserved a bit of happiness. They both did.

Once he had detected Cora's current preference for solitude, he had decided to allow her this small respite from his company. However, on the rare occasions their paths crossed, he would take the opportunity to kiss her hand, cradle her elbow, or stand too close. His decision might prove a difficult setback in his goal to unearth his former friend, but he was willing to risk it, for he needed a reprieve, as well.

The feel of her satiny skin beneath his palm and the weight of her appreciative gaze roaming over his body was an incredible, erotic combination. He couldn't remember ever being so swollen with need for such an extended period of time. Not until the moon had begun its westerly descent had his cock ceased its demand for release. And every time he thought about Cora in those provocative silk *pai jamahs*, the torment would begin all over again.

As it did now. *Bloody hell.*

Guy's ruminations came to an abrupt halt when he noticed a man lounging against a tree, watching something in the distance. The cold heat of danger swept through his body, heightening his awareness of his surroundings. He reached inside his coat to retrieve his gun and crept a few steps to the left for a better look.

The man's profile soon came into view. *Jack.* For some reason, the realization didn't lessen the tension thrumming through his muscles. He peered beyond Jack's shoulder to see what held the footman's attention so thoroughly that he hadn't yet registered Guy's presence.

When he located Cora across the clearing, dressed in manly garments again, his hand tightened around his pistol.

Bloody damn hell.

Fire pounded through his veins, and his gaze flicked to the footman, who still hadn't detected the danger lurking at his back. Had Guy been one of Valère's men, the handsome devil would be dead right now.

Rather than scanning his surroundings, Jack's attention centered on his mistress. Intent and highly disrespectful.

"Enjoying the view?" Guy asked.

The footman started, and he whipped around with his fists raised like a seasoned pugilist. When recognition dawned, the Irishman's familiar cocky grin surfaced.

"Couldn't call myself a man if I didn't, m'lord." The younger man straightened when he noticed Guy did not share his amusement. "Ay, now, it ain't like that, you know. If it weren't for Miss Cora, me and my sis, Grace, would be on the streets. I owe her my life. She's a fine-looking woman, I admit, but I got no designs on her person."

Guy's muscles remained taut, ready. "That's good to hear."

Jack's gaze dropped to the gun in Guy's hand then nervously flicked up to Guy's face. "You got no need for that, m'lord. I swear it."

Guy removed his finger from the trigger. "Watch your back as well as your mistress's," he warned the footman. "The enemy rarely attacks head-on."

"Yes, sir." The footman's expression turned sheepish. "Did you come to relieve one of us, m'lord?"

"Yes." He scanned the wooded edge of the clearing. "Where's your partner?"

Jack jerked his thumb to the left. "Old Bingham is crouched over there, pretending like he's asleep." He snorted. "About as likely as me becoming the king of England, it is."

"I'll take over from here. Go find out what supplies Cook needs from town and keep your ear to the ground for any mention of strangers in the area."

"Will do, m'lord."

Guy waited for the underbrush to swallow the footman's back before stepping to the edge of the tree line.

It took him several minutes to shake off the disquieting feelings brought on by Jack's casual attitude toward his duties. He decided to have a follow-up discussion with the footman when he returned from his errand. They could ill afford such mistakes with the Frenchman at large. Valère's keen intellect would pick up on the slightest misstep.

Putting Jack's odd behavior aside, he ignored the luscious green glade enveloping the small crescent-shaped lake and searched for the woman who had held her long-time servant transfixed. Opposite him, beneath the swaying arms of a giant willow. Cora performed a series of slow, fluid maneuvers. With her body poised in a semicrouch, her arms and legs wove in mesmerizing circles.

The artistry of her movements left him spellbound. Her technique was much more improved, controlled and precise, yet fluid and graceful. She wore a fitted teal tunic over a pair of white silk *pai jamahs*—an outfit that shouldn't be worn outside the bedchamber, in his opinion—and her feet were bare. Again.

When he had asked his men about her activities, they told him she walked, she read, and she stared a lot. They said nothing about this.

It was their mention of her staring at some unknown object for long periods of time that brought him to the lake today. He didn't want her reliving the past, terrorizing her mind over and over. If she must revisit the memories in order to put them behind her, then he wanted to be there to help her through the pain of remembrance.

Following the line of trees, he circled around until he stood ten feet from her. Focused on her maneuvers, she gave no indication of being aware of his existence. That would soon change. Thankfully, he wore a pair of old boots that he easily toed off—his stockings, coat, waistcoat, and cravat followed suit.

Many years had passed since he had last practiced the ancient art of Tai Chi with the deBeau clan. Cora's father, the late Lord Danforth, was first introduced to the stylized martial art during one of his frequent trips to the Orient. Many years ago, Cora had found her father practicing the meditative movements and cajoled him into teaching her. And so he did. Soon after, Guy and her brother had joined them.

His friend's animated sister had always charmed Guy, but he had had little call to spend much time with her until then. Their Tai Chi lessons had changed all of that. For one hour every day, she had focused that incredible mind of hers inward. She became stronger mentally and physically. At the tender age of eight, she had a better understanding of herself than few achieved with decades of training.

He now recalled meeting Somerton during one of their sessions. At the time, he thought nothing of the hawk-like way in which the earl studied them or of the quiet conversations between Somerton and Cora's father as they followed their pupils' progress. Were the two plotting even then to bring the trio into the Nexus?

The disturbing thought curdled his stomach.

Emptying his mind of such troubling musings, he watched Cora for a moment and then slid into place beside her, matching her movements with rusty precision. She didn't miss a step, accepting his company as if she had expected him.

The calming motions were thought to enhance one's physical, mental, and spiritual well-being. As Guy's hands pushed forward from his chest, he knew this to be true. The movements came to him easily, even after so long an absence.

Their budding connection resurfaced, and his body responded to her nearness, despite his meditative state. He set his jaw and continued to match her form to form until she finally brought the session to a close.

Their gazes caught, and held; neither was as relaxed as they should have been after such an exercise. He tried to keep his approach of quick, seemingly meaningless touches in the forefront of his thoughts and failed. His mind warred with the demands of his body. He used guilt and shame and honor to repress his forbidden impulses. He didn't want to ruin the tranquility of the moment, nor could he overlook the welcome gleaming in her eyes.

His cock bucked against its restraints, and sweat gathered at the base of his neck. He shot a glance toward the tree trunk where Bingham had propped himself, only to find the space empty. Either the old tar had faded into the trees to give them more privacy, or he felt his mistress was in capable hands and went back to the house. Either way, they were alone.

Sweat trickled down his spine.

Guy closed the distance between them, making no move to touch her. Beautiful green eyes rimmed in piercing blue skimmed his face and paused on his lips. There, they lingered for an unbearable moment, heating his already simmering blood.

Had she ever been intimate with a man that didn't require the pursuit of information? Did her body know what it meant to be truly loved? Another more insidious question surfaced, one dredged up from the primitive depths of his soul. Had she ever experienced a full and shuddering release?

He bent forward until their warm breaths mingled and was gratified when she held her ground. "If you're going to run away, now would be the time."

"Is that a threat?" she whispered, her words pelting softly against his cheek.

His nose nuzzled against hers, drinking in her salty feminine scent. "A friendly warning." If she retreated, he would be damn disappointed. He hadn't wanted to give her an excuse to withdraw, but his conscience wouldn't allow him to take advantage of her vulnerable state.

Her breath hitched, and he was certain she would step back, breaking the sensual haze enveloping them. His own breathing suspended, waiting for her recoil. But she remained in place, her chest rising in quick succession. Guy pressed on, skimming his lips across hers.

Once.

Twice.

Three times.

She tipped her head back—an invitation no mortal man could refuse, not even one who was burdened with altruistic purpose. He nipped at her lips, coaxing them to accept a deeper kiss. When they finally parted, his tongue slipped inside the moist, warm center they guarded with such concentrated care.

❧

The area between Cora's legs pulsed and clenched and pricked with each stroke of Guy's wicked tongue. A long-buried groan roared its way up her throat and into his mouth where he matched it with one of his own. Her fingers stabbed through his hair, holding him in place while she ravaged his lips with her desperation. She wanted to consume his very essence. She wanted to take all he would give before realization of whom he kissed struck.

Even now, he could be battling with his conscience— *she's too injured; she's my best friend's sister; she's slept with the enemy*. A pang of regret and fear seared her chest.

She deepened the kiss and fumbled with the leather strip holding his gorgeous hair. When she felt the thong give, she plunged her hands into the thick curtain of dark strands and flattened her body against his.

If she could overwhelm his senses, maybe he would push away the unpleasant questions until his carnal needs were fulfilled. Which, in turn, would satisfy hers. She deepened the kiss, determined to conquer the weakness in her mind that made her shy away from a man's touch.

After a moment, she drew back far enough to see his uncivilized appearance and to show him with her eyes how much she needed this. His full lips glistened from their passionate kiss, and his nostrils flared with each inhalation. His eyes, always dark and unreadable, glowed black as night.

He cupped her face in his large hands. "I've waited so long," he murmured. His confession confused her, but he didn't give her long to consider his words. "So beautiful. So much more than I deserve." His mouth covered hers, and a wild desperation overtook them both. This melding of lips was deeper, more consuming. More everything.

This he could not mask behind everyday courtesies like escorting her to dinner, handing her a flower, or helping her down the stairs. This was raw and intimate. This must be passion.

Her hands shook with unfettered need as they descended over his powerful arms, trembling arms that were locked in place at his side.

She frowned. When had he stopped holding her face?

After days of enduring his furtive touches and aching closeness, Cora was confused by his inaction, until she realized he waited for her invitation.

Warmth pierced her heart.

"Hold me." She spoke the beseeching words against his lips while her fingers coaxed his hands open.

"I don't want to frighten you, Cora. *This* goes beyond reassuring touches."

Her mind began its familiar descent into hell. She brushed her fingers over his cheek. *Conquer your fear.* "I understand."

"Do you, Cora?" he asked tenderly. "Your mind is already turning to a dark place. I can see it in your beautiful, troubled eyes. What if our desire takes us beyond the point of my control? Will you still crave my touch then?"

The barrier she had erected to mentally survive his lovemaking crumbled in the wake of his warning. She was so focused on obtaining her own pleasure that she hadn't stopped to think about the emotional torture she was inflicting on Guy. How could she be so consumed with her own wants and not notice the awful effect all this had on him?

Shame coated her thoughts, blurring her vision.

When his hands cupped her jaw this time, they were shaking. "Cora, sweet. Do not fret."

"How could I be so stupid?" she asked on a choked whisper.

He kissed her with exquisite care. "You're many things, Cora deBeau, but stupid does not make the list."

She stepped closer and placed both palms against his chest. His heart pounded in time with hers. "Idiot?"

He settled his hands on her waist. "No."

"Clodhead?"

His lips twitched, and he pulled her into his arms. "Uh-uh."

"Dimwit? Fuddlebrain?"

"Not even close."

"Foolish?"

He hesitated a moment too long, which struck a humorous chord with her. "Guess I should have stopped at fuddlebrain."

His hand stroked up the length of her back. "Now that we've established I'm a brutish ass and you're a foolish woman, I want to share something with you."

Excitement flared inside her veins. She snuggled closer. "Oh?"

"What I'm about to show you will change everything between us."

Cora's anxiety returned for reasons unrelated to her imprisonment. "I'm ready." And she was.

"Turn around, sweetheart."

Trepidation and a sweet taste of anticipation clutched her heart. "Why?"

"Trust me."

Even as she swiveled around, she realized presenting her back to him forced her into a vulnerable position, indicating a great deal of faith and a willingness to relinquish control. While she waited with trembling expectancy for the first touch of his hands, she also realized control was the last thing she wanted to retain at that moment.

He stepped up behind her and clasped her shoulders; the heat from his exertions penetrated the fine material of her silk tunic, sending chill bumps racing along the surface of her skin. He must have felt her resulting shiver, for his next words whispered across her cheek.

"Trust me."

She swallowed. "I do."

"Hmm." His warm hands brushed down her arms until his fingers could interlace over hers. Then he urged her open palms toward her *pai jamah*-covered thigh, coaxing her hands to glide against the smooth material, creating a delicious, forbidden friction. Her womb clenched against the sensation, searching, needing, grasping for something unfamiliar to her.

The scorching heat of his open-mouth kiss against the side of her neck sent a jolt of pure lust through her. She pressed her upper body against his chest, angling her head away to give him unimpeded access.

He accepted her offering, covering every inch of her bare flesh with moist, luscious kisses. His attack on her senses did not stop there. Oh, no.

If this were a skirmish, she would label his next move after the age-old war tactic of divide and conquer. With his hands still covering hers, he slid their entwined fingers beneath her tunic, caressing her stomach and skimming the underside of her left breast. The exotic feel of her own hand riding the planes of her body, studying every contour, made the area between her legs weep with excitement. She felt her nipples harden into tight nubs, flaunting their readiness.

Their clasped right hands broke off and burrowed inside the warm depths of her breeches, paralyzing her thoughts and locking her muscles. She focused on the downward descent of their hands with acute enthrallment.

She sucked in a sharp breath. "Guy?"

"Have I lost your trust so quickly, Cora?" he asked in a husky, teasing voice.

Turning her head slightly to the left, she sought the heat of his words. "N-no. I just… I don't—" she drew in a calming breath. "You startled me, is all."

The side of his nose lay against her temple, and his mouth brushed against her flushed cheeks as he spoke. "I'm going to do much more than startle you, my sweet."

Putting action to words, he guided her hand to the juncture between her legs. Cora braced herself against the security of his broad shoulders. She waited for the first illicit touch with the keenest anticipation. The tips of their joined middle fingers stopped short of the sensitive bud guarding her entrance. Then he moved his attention to their joined left hands, curling her fingers around her breast and positioning her thumb at the base of her nipple. Close enough to feel stimulating heat. Far enough away to feel bereft.

Divide and conquer.

She knew not where to focus her attention. Both hands teetered on the precipice of an abyss. One leap to the wrong side could either descend her into the licking flames of hell or raise her to the dazzling rays of heaven.

Even though she couldn't be sure which awaited her over the threshold, she wanted it, needed it. *Prayed* for it. Why did he hesitate? Why did he torture her with the longings of her own body? "Guy," she said in a breathless murmur.

"Ready?" His voice held a rough edge; his sharp breaths cooled her heated cheeks.

"Get on with it," she said through gritted teeth. She arched her back, forcing her breast against her palm, ignoring the pinch to her side. Then she rotated her spine, trying to capture a more satisfying contact with her aching nipple.

"Patience," he whispered on a low chuckle.

With a precision that nearly buckled her knees, he gently squeezed her nipple at the same time he plunged their long middle fingers into her slick, wet folds. Her back bowed higher and her bottom bucked against the hard ridge of his member. Their fingers pressed deeper into her center, as if anchoring her in place while a storm seethed all around them. Before long, he took over, kneading her breast and exploring her aching depths. She reached over her head and laced her fingers beneath the fall of his long hair, mooring herself in a web of sensual ecstasy.

Guy's manipulations and her new position created a maelstrom of oversensitive nerves and tingling expectation.

And then a new feeling emerged, one still too distant to grasp, one she knew instinctively would be like no other she had ever experienced. It pulsed closer, a bright light blinding her to the outside world. It throbbed with heat, flushing her body.

She grew wetter, hotter, more unrestrained.

Though her gaze flicked from tree branch to tree branch to azure painted sky, all her concentration was trained on the kneading action of his masterful finger. *Dear God*.

"Kiss me," he breathed, part command, part plea.

Eagerly, she turned to him. His mouth covered hers, and his tongue swept inside, scorching her already battered senses. The pulsing heat grew closer until Guy shifted his attention to her hard little nub. One flick was all it took to release the building inferno that propelled her to the heavens.

An ungovernable cry ripped from her throat, breaking their kiss. Pleasurable needles pricked along her spine and gathered in battering clusters between her legs. Guy's hand covered her mound until the throbbing deep in her center subsided.

Uncomprehending of what just happened, Cora stood frozen for several heartbeats. And then, her arms suddenly weighed ten stone, and they dropped to her side. Limp and useless.

Guy lifted his head from the crook of her neck, his hard breaths striking her flesh in pleasurable beats. He kissed his way up to her temple while easing his hands from beneath her clothes. The gentle lapping of the lake's water against the shore brought her to gradual awareness. Her languid body did not wish to move from the warm

shelter of his arms, and Guy seemed content to hold her
for as long as she would allow.

This time when she glanced around the secluded
glade, everything glowed brighter, more colorful, almost
cheerful. Perhaps she was projecting her own altered state
on her surroundings. To think she had left the house a
few hours ago, sick of the routine she had established to
avoid Guy's impossible charm, only to wind up dangling
languid and satiated in the comfort of his arms. His kisses
had shattered all the power behind the excuses she had
devised and ineffectually hidden behind.

"I hope you're not thinking," he said against her ear.

She turned in his arms. "And label myself an idiot again?"

He chuckled, burrowing his nose into the curve of
her neck.

"Thank you," she said suddenly.

"You are most welcome," he said. "But what exactly
are you thanking me for?"

Heat swept up her neck and into her cheeks. "I have
never… I mean that's never happened—"

"I think I understand," he said, interrupting her clumsy
attempt at an explanation. "And you are welcome. *Very*,
very welcome." He kissed the sensitive area behind her
earlobe before straightening, a rogue's grin on his face.

His intense gaze made her feel unsure. "What?"

"I cannot recall ever enjoying a Tai Chi session more."

She swatted his arm. "I should hope not. We were
children, and there are rules against such things."

When he laughed at her quip, his hardness came
into contact with her stomach. Her eyes widened.
"Guy, you didn't—" She glanced down between them.
"You're still—"

Bending forward, he kissed her. A gentle, featherlight
pressing of the lips. "So sweet." His dark gaze dropped
to her mouth. "Next time."

Next time. Longing sparked at the apex of her legs where Guy's fingers had soothed her sensual ache.

He grasped her hand and led her to a large, fallen tree. Atop the lichen-crusted trunk sat her red leather slippers. "Do you wear these so you can find them in the woods?"

She sat next to them, slanting him a cross look. "Noooo. I wear them because they make me happy." *As you do.* At that moment, she wished she had worn a pretty dress rather than her *pai jamahs*.

He knelt beside her and patted his knee, a request for her foot.

"I'm not so fragile, Guy. I can manage my own shoes."

"I know. Now give me your foot."

Reminiscent of his demand in the library, she knew he wouldn't budge until she complied. "Stubborn man." She extended her leg and couldn't help but smile when he dusted dirt and debris from her bare soles like a father would a recalcitrant child.

"We make a good pair."

Did they? She had always felt a connection to him. Something deeper than a mere friendship, something that had unfolded petal by fragile petal over the years.

A realization made all the more acute when her young girl's admiration had transformed into a woman's awakening. Her discernment of his masculine charms had gradually surfaced. She had noticed small things, like the magnificent length of his ebony eyelashes, the adorable dimple in his right cheek, and the fine hairs that peppered the backs of his hands.

She had felt awkward and guilty, especially once her focus shifted to admiring the breadth of his shoulders, the musculature of his thighs, and the beauty of his angular face. This was Guy, for goodness sake—practically her brother. Her thoughts had seemed immoral, wrong somehow, or at least that's how she had felt at the time.

Her preoccupation with her friend grew to a degree that had kept her insides in a quivering knot any time he drew near, and her normally easy quips would lodge in her throat with just one of his teasing winks.

When she began imagining all her days spent in his company and her lifelong quest to avenge her parents' murders began to fade, she started avoiding his company and eventually set off for France. She had hoped distance and the distraction of her mission would rid her of the unbearable longing he had stirred in her young heart.

She had hoped in vain.

During the intervening years, Cora had been able to shield her thoughts of him for long periods of time. Then she would catch a glimpse of an ebony-haired man or a whiff of spicy sandalwood that would spark her recollection, and she would wonder where he was at that moment, wonder if he missed her, thought of her, *yearned* for her.

When Cora had first spotted him in Valère's dungeon, she knew then—even through the pain and fear—that her feelings for Guy were more than a silly girl's infatuation. And she also realized those years in France had erased any chance of having a life with him.

She stared down at his bent head. Sunlight sheened off his black hair, creating an illusion of moonlight dancing over dark waters. Long waves cradled his massive shoulders while he guided her foot into an awaiting red slipper. Without thought, she combed her fingers through his thick strands, taming their wild disarray, and wishing—no, *longing*—for the courage to bury her nose amidst all that luxury.

He stilled, as if fearing any movement would make her stop. He worried for naught. She loved feeling the silky texture of his midnight locks against her skin. Had dreamt of running her fingers through their length for days. *Years*.

He sat back on his heels and met her gaze, his internal struggle obvious. He, no doubt, wanted to give her some time to absorb the intimacy they had shared, but the demands of his body were at war with his strong mind. A situation she knew all too well.

In a near whisper, she said, "Turn around, if you please."

His gaze sharpened, fired hot like a glowing cauldron. But he said nothing, simply maneuvered his body around until he faced the opposite direction, spine erect, senses alert.

She glanced down at the leather thong still wrapped around her middle finger. Its worn appearance was a testament to the many hours spent taming his gorgeous mane. She clamped the tie between her teeth while her hands smoothed over his hair.

"'Tis beautiful."

He tilted his head back, his eyes closed. "Nonsense. Men don't have beautiful hair."

Leaning forward, she swept the tail she had created over her face, inhaling the faint scent of sandalwood mixed with the fresh country air. "You do."

"Cora," he warned.

She laughed, enjoying the peaceful moment but not wanting to push him further. He couldn't be… comfortable.

Disturbed by the power he had over her senses, she made quick work of securing his hair.

When she finished, she patted his shoulders. "All done."

He murmured something that sounded like "Not even close, sweetheart" before rising to his feet and extending his arm.

"Pardon?" she asked.

He smiled, a secret curling of the mouth that caused Cora's heart to thrash against her chest. But all he said was, "Come. Let's go home and see what culinary masterpiece Cook has in store for us."

Her stomach growled at the mention of food, drowning out the cacophony inside her chest. She pressed her hand against her middle. "Seems my body is in agreement."

He lifted her chin and brushed the pad of his thumb over her bottom lip. "It appears I'm not the only one who enjoyed our Tai Chi session."

Fifteen

CORA TUMBLED INTO THE KITCHEN, WIPING TEARS OF laughter from her eyes. A few steps inside and her humor ground to a halt. The abrupt action forced Guy to grab her shoulders to keep from colliding into her. "What the——?"

Across the room, three solemn faces met their arrival.

At first, she worried that Bingham had shared her indiscretion with the others. However, once she searched their expressions, it wasn't disappointment she saw there but grief. Terrible grief.

Dread flooded her body. "What is it?"

Dinks and Bingham looked toward Jack, who stared at his scuffed boots. Her frowning maid gave the reluctant footman a poke in the ribs, receiving a swift glare in return.

"Tell her, boy," Bingham demanded. "Tell her what you found out in town. You're making it worse with your silence."

The footman swallowed hard several times, but no words emerged.

Cora stepped in front of him and held out her hand. "Be at ease, Jack." His haggard features surprised her. Deep lines etched between his eyebrows, and his shining bloodshot eyes darted about the room. "Tell me what's upset you."

He stared at her outstretched hand as if he were

afraid to accept her offer of encouragement. Finally, he relented, clasping her fingers in a bone-crushing embrace.

Still he said nothing.

"Jack?"

Cora watched his chest rise on a deep breath before his furious emerald gaze snagged hers. "That bastard toad-eater nabbed your brother."

"Toad-eater?" His statement, so unexpected, confused her. "Valère?" One word, two syllables—that's all it took to shatter Cora's brief reprieve.

He nodded.

"You're sure the Frenchman has Lord Danforth?" Guy asked.

The footman nodded, and the full impact of his words finally registered somewhere in the back of Cora's mind. Beyond the swirling black void of her consciousness, the realization that her brother was now in the hands of her enemy blocked all logical thought and eclipsed her vision. "No." Her mind swam with torturous possibilities, each one more abhorrent than the last. "No. You must be mistaken, Jack. You *must*."

Guy's firm hands settled on her shoulders; his agile thumbs attempted to gentle the aching knots of fear that had gathered between her muscles like a thousand festering wounds. "You're sure, Jack?"

"Yes, m'lord," Jack said with a slight quaver in his voice. "One of his lordship's regular messengers arrived in town soon after I did. Since we've exchanged information for our employers before, I figured I'd save him a trip to the house."

Cora looked to Dinks. The older woman's eyes shimmered in the early afternoon light. More than anyone there, Dinks understood how Jack's news sealed Cora's fate.

No longer able to bear the sympathy fracturing the

maid's face or the ephemeral strength she drew from Guy's reassuring hold, Cora forced herself to release Jack's hand and step away. "I want to hear everything Somerton's messenger said to you, Jack—word for word."

"Not much else to tell," the footman said. "Other than his lordship's ordering Lord Helsford back to London."

It was then she felt the first shift, from fear for her brother to terror for Guy. "Just Lord Helsford?"

"Yes."

"Not likely."

Guy's warning look affected her not at all. He knew nothing of her if he thought she would wait patiently in the country while he and Somerton plotted to save her brother.

"Taking Danforth is merely a ploy to draw you from hiding," Guy said.

"Of course it is," she shot back, although she wouldn't be surprised if Valère already hovered beyond these walls. "But I will not sit here and do nothing while Ethan..." Her words dwindled, and her eyes lost focus. She couldn't stand to think of the despair her brother would endure at Valère's hands. She would not—could not—allow him to be subjected to the Frenchman's awful vengeance.

"He will suffer, Guy," she said in a ragged voice. "Most horribly. Could be even now."

"Yes." He took a step toward her. "Ethan's my friend as well as your brother. I understand your need to rush to his aid, but I will not trade your safety for his. Your fate would be far worse than your brother's should Valère succeed in capturing you again. You outwitted him, Cora." His voice carried a hint of pride before it hardened. "Do not think he will be as circumspect in his methods the next time."

A violent shiver racked her body, and she wrapped her arms around her midsection to stem its assault. She would never survive that type of living death again. Never.

Toward the end, Valère had begun to suspect she was something more than a ballroom spy. She saw it in his assessing gaze and heard it in his probing tone. By now, Valère had likely pieced all the missing links together, and he must comprehend the trophy he let slip from his grasp.

And if Valère's superiors also figured out Raven's identity? They would surely reassess his loyalty to Napoleon. To be outmaneuvered by a woman—*une anglaise*—would reveal a dangerous sign of weakness, a disruption of loyalty. Napoleon's supporters hated the Raven and would not turn a blind eye on Valère's mistake. If they learned he had held the Raven and subsequently lost the notorious spy, they would most assuredly sever his ambitious path to the new emperor's side.

As thorough as ever, Somerton had made arrangements to fetch her great-aunt, Lady Kavanagh, at the same time he sent Guy to rescue her. She trembled to think of what the madman might have done to the dear old lady in his rage. Thank goodness her great-aunt was now tucked away in the Highlands of Scotland, far away from the evil pounding its way across England.

Cora glanced up, into the eyes of her little family. Without a doubt, she knew her servants would follow her, even if she ordered them to stay. Their indomitable loyalty would see them by her side, no matter the danger to themselves.

She faced the unbearable decision of choosing between her beloved brother and her faithful, loving friends. The cruelty of the situation caused her anger to flare to life, and she vowed to cut the reins of Valère's control over her, even if it meant her death.

"Jack," she said in her no-nonsense voice, "word for word."

Jack stabbed his fingers through his rumpled hair. "The man said Lord Danforth had gone off to kill the frog-eater, and now he's missing. That Lord Helsford needs to decipher a message received by his lordship, that…" His voice trailed off, his gaze downcast.

"And what, Jack?" Cora demanded, already knowing the answer.

Sweat gathered at his temples. Meeting her gaze, he cleared his throat. "That you are to stay here until further notice."

"Damn Somerton." Guy began to pace the small confines of the kitchen. "What the hell was the man thinking?"

"Did he explain how you were to enforce this edict?" Cora asked.

"Yes." Jack glanced at his two compatriots for help.

"Well?"

"To my knowledge, she's never killed a messenger before, boy," Bingham grumbled. "Spit it out."

"By whatever means possible." Jack's words rushed forth, barely intelligible. "His words, Miss Cora, not mine."

"Do not fret, Jack," Cora soothed. "I'm well aware of the lengths to which my former guardian will go to get his way."

"Miss Cora," Dinks said into the silence. "Lord Somerton is only trying to protect you. He knows this place is well guarded. The road is no place for you right now."

Cora knew this to be true. From the moment she crossed his threshold, Somerton had done what he could to protect her, even from herself. "Anything else, Jack?"

Beads of sweat dotted the young man's upper lip; his gaze dropped to the floor again while his hands twisted his hat. Cora wondered at his uncharacteristic nervousness.

"Jack?"

"Just that—" He cut off, his discomfort obviously rising to new heights. He fished something from his pocket. "He sent you a personal note."

She stared the ivory-colored dispatch, her heart constricting. She should refuse to read it and leave for London. No doubt the missive's contents would not be to her liking. Even as the thought whispered through her mind, she broke the seal and turned away.

> *Dearest Cora,*
>
> *You know by now of your brother's fate and of my request for you to remain safely behind. For the moment, I need Helsford at my side. You will be well guarded until we come for you—a sennight, no longer. Do me the favor of this one small request, so that I might have both my charges safely returned to me.*
>
> *Yours, Somerton*

Cora carefully read the letter a second time before handing it to Guy. A vast sense of helplessness washed over her, causing her shoulders to droop from sheer weight. Should she tell him it was likely a forgery? Never had Somerton signed his name to a missive. For three years, she had relied on his style of writing alone to identify him. The way his *R*'s broke away from the rest of the word and how the tail of his *Y*'s slashed down in a straight line.

The forgery was good. Extraordinarily good. But Somerton knew better than to leave a physical trail behind. Any path leading to the chief of the Nexus was a direct line to his agents. He wouldn't risk it—unless he was no longer concerned about the enemy intercepting his correspondence. Cora considered the possibility for a moment. The notion had merit, but Somerton was a cautious man, and some habits were difficult to break.

She also had the issue of Ethan's captivity to consider. Did that part of the letter reveal a truth, or was the whole thing an elaborate lie? If her brother was free, his whereabouts could be easily verified. Valère would anticipate this, and that knowledge led Cora to believe her brother's life now rested in the hands of a madman.

The thought threatened to overwhelm her with terror, but she found the strength to push it aside. She had to find a solution that would keep everyone safe. A task that seemed insurmountable from where she stood. Perhaps if she allowed Valère's ruse to play out, he would let slip Ethan's location. He was, at heart, a braggart, one who enjoyed waving his superiority over those beneath him.

Her strategy—and she used the term loosely—could work, but it was risky. Valère could kill her on sight, or he could take her to a location other than where he imprisoned Ethan. If she were blessed with good fortune, Valère would show her his new "trophy." However, she hadn't quite worked out what she would do after that revelation.

Every strategy carried its own extraordinary hazards. Determining which path to take placed an unholy pressure on her chest. One thing that niggled in the back of her mind had to do with Somerton. How had the missive's author known of the earl's involvement? Or of Guy's special talent? How much more did the author—Valère—know of the Nexus? The question sent a chill down her spine.

Yet a sliver of doubt lingered. Jack knew all of Somerton's messengers on sight. If the footman had any reservation regarding the messenger, he would not have sent the man on his way. More likely, he would have bashed the man's head and apologized later for any inconvenience.

If the dispatch was indeed from Somerton and he had made an uncharacteristic faux pas, Guy must go. Ignoring the missive would put Ethan's life in danger. However, if this was a clever form of redirection by Valère, then he was attempting to separate her from Guy, not the other way around. Which meant Guy would be safer away from her.

Her jaw ached from the force of her clenched teeth. One wrong decision could very well ensure the death of a loved one. But which one? Guy? Ethan? Her little family? She wanted to throw her hands over her face and hide from this responsibility. She didn't want it. Didn't want to be wrong, nor did she want to be right.

Oh, dear God. It was all too much. Never had she faced such an intolerable crossroad. Her path had always been clear. She'd had to weave around obstacles, for sure, but her direction had remained unaltered. And her decisions had never affected anyone so close to her.

Cora knew then, with devastating certainty, that she wasn't strong enough to choose.

Something brushed against the back of her leg, and she angled around to see Scrapper circling for another rub. Delighted by the distraction, she scooped the kitten up and buried the side of her face against his rumbling, soft body.

At once, she felt at ease, almost as if she had a direct conduit to the kitten's innocent strength.

Guy crushed the note. "I can't leave you here alone."

Cora saw his internal struggle carved on every plane of his handsome face. She understood his emotional torture, his doubts, his confusion. But she couldn't calm his anguished soul. Her demons of judgment were ripping at her own heart again.

A soft paw rested against her right cheek, startling her. When she turned her full attention back to the kitten, his other paw came up to frame her face. They stood there, green gazes meeting only inches apart. With uncanny stillness, the kitten stared at her with seemingly ancient, sympathetic eyes. Trapped inside their unblinking depths, she imagined generations of sacrifice, tragedy, and wisdom.

One of his paws moved like a caress down her cheek, and Cora's throat closed around the comfort she took from such an innocent gesture. *Sweet girl, there is nothing you cannot conquer. Trust in yourself, as I trust in you.* Her mother's voice swirled around her, clear and melodic. The whole situation reeked of familiarity, a moment in time she had longed for more than a dozen years.

Cora closed her eyes, convinced her mind had finally snapped, especially when her back straightened and a new resolve lifted her chin.

"You must," she said, coming to a decision. "Somerton wouldn't call you away unless it was vitally important. You must think of Ethan now. I beg you." Scrapper melted into the crook of her neck, and her chest constricted with unaccountable pride. Next stop... Bedlam.

Guy waved the wadded missive between them. "We're not even sure this is from Somerton. This might be an attempt by Valère to get to you."

"What if it's not?" she countered. "What if Somerton truly needs you? Are you willing to put Ethan's life at risk?"

Guy's burning gaze clashed with hers. "You have no idea what you're asking of me."

"Rest assured, I do. But, unlike Ethan, I'm not alone." She infused impatience into her tone, grabbing the note from him. "I've more than enough guards watching over me to keep Valère at bay. I can't even use the water closet without one of them lurking nearby."

Guy turned to Jack. "Are you sure you spoke to Somerton's messenger?"

Jack swallowed. "Yes, m'lord. As I mentioned, I've worked with the chap before."

"She'll be fine, my lord," Dinks interjected, elbowing Bingham.

"Right." Bingham squared his bent shoulders, looking slightly uncomfortable but no less determined.

Dinks continued, "You go read his lordship's message, my lord, and save that hothead. We'll see to things here."

He eyed her servants but didn't yield. It was then that Cora realized he wouldn't, or perhaps he couldn't, leave.

He was choosing her over his best friend.

An ache so keen pierced her heart that one might mistake it for a dagger. His unspoken acknowledgement was one of the most beautiful moments of her life.

And the darkest, for she couldn't allow him to stay.

Forgive me.

She called forth the Raven.

"Go, Guy." She made sure her tone had the perfect amount of indifference. "I don't need you here."

For as long as she lived, Cora would never forget the flash of hurt that crossed his face before it blanked. Her fingers wrapped around her thumb, squeezing.

His gaze flicked to her side, and Cora hid her hand behind her back. She held her breath, hoping she hadn't given herself away, hoping she hadn't hurt him for no reason.

Then he turned to her servants. "Do not let your mistress out of your sight. Not even for a second. Understood?"

"Yes," they said in unison.

To Cora, he said, "I need to know you'll stay put."

Releasing a slow breath, she smoothed her fingers over the wrinkled missive's words. The paper crackled in the silence like a crystal chandelier smashing against a marble floor.

"Where would I go?" She sent him an unconcerned

look, handing the missive back to him. "Do not dally, my lord."

With a heavy heart, she pivoted and began her slow retreat back to the lake, to the only sanctuary she had known since returning to England. To the place that had just become another prison.

Sixteen

"WHAT THE DEVIL ARE YOU DOING HERE?" SOMERTON demanded near midnight.

Guy froze in the act of removing his dust-covered overcoat. The warning voice he had heard since leaving Cora at Herrington Park turned into a full-fledged roar at his mentor's question.

"You didn't send for me?"

Somerton's features hardened. "No, I did not. Please tell me Cora is with you."

Guy shook his head, a flash of heat swept over him. His chest felt weighted down by fifteen stone, and nausea boiled low in his stomach. He should have listened to his instincts; he should have stayed by Cora's side. *Goddammit.*

Somerton closed his eyes, and his lips pressed into a grim line. "Come with me."

Pulling his coat back on, Guy made for the front door. "No. If you didn't send for me, that can mean only one thing, and I don't have a moment to waste."

"Helsford," Somerton said in a commanding voice. "You can spare me five minutes to explain your presence in town, especially given the fact I expressly ordered you to stay in the country with Cora." To his butler, he said, "Rucker, see that a fresh horse is brought around for Lord Helsford."

"Consider it done, my lord."

"Tell me what's happened," Somerton barked the moment the study door closed.

Guy pulled out the crumpled missive. "I received this from one of your messengers."

"I sent no one to you." Somerton scanned the note. "What does this mean by Danforth's 'fate'?"

"According to Jack, Valère has him."

His mentor's hard gaze returned to the missive. "Describe the messenger."

Guy spread his legs and clasped his hands behind his back. "I didn't speak with him. Cora's footman intercepted the man in town."

"Jack gave you this?"

"Yes, sir. He said he recognized the man." He should have verified the source before racing off to London, but he had no reason to distrust Jack's word, nor had Cora shown any signs of questioning her servant or the note's authenticity. Otherwise, he would never have left.

"He was either mistaken, or he lied." Somerton's face grew taut. "Find out which."

"Are we finished?" Guy had to get back to Herrington Park. To Cora. The need rose inside him like a volcano about to erupt. It sucked the air from his lungs and lodged fiery bile in the back of his throat.

"Not quite." Somerton's steady gaze locked with his.

"What is it?"

"I haven't heard from Danforth since before you left," his mentor revealed. "We have to consider that part of the dispatch possibly correct."

"It would not be unlike Danforth to go it alone." *Damned hothead.* The epithet Dinks had used proved quite accurate. More times than not, the viscount allowed his actions to be directed by emotion rather than logic. "Have you had any success in tracking down Valère's whereabouts or movements?"

"No specific sighting of Valère." Somerton paced behind his massive oak framed desk. "Given our current situation, one can only assume Valère is closer at hand than any of us realized."

"How the hell did he find my country estate?"

"I don't know," Somerton said. "I'll visit the Undersuperintendent of Aliens today to see if there are any new developments on the possible leak within the Foreign Office. Hopefully, Latymer has made some progress on that case while I'm occupied with this one."

"You think the two are linked?" He knew the answer before finishing the sentence. Valère would be a fool not to secure information from his informant while on foreign ground.

Guy held up his hand to forestall Somerton's affirmation. "Never mind. Of course they're linked." He prepared to leave. "Please send word as soon as you hear something."

"Helsford."

Guy steeled himself before turning back. "I've told you everything I know. I must get back *now*."

Somerton eyed him. "You know she's no longer there, don't you?"

He suspected as much, but he had to assess the situation with his own eyes. "Yes." The single word tore from his aching throat.

"Where are you going, then?" Somerton asked. "It would be best to wait here until my men pick up Valère's trail, or until the bastard sends word of where we can find Danforth and Cora."

"Her servants—"

"Are likely dead."

Guy closed his eyes. Dear God.

Suffocating emotions boiled inside him, making it

difficult to breathe. If by the grace of God Cora survived this, she would never forgive him the loss of her servants. They were as much family to her as Danforth.

He rubbed his aching chest. "I have to do something. I can't sit here twiddling my thumbs while waiting for news that will be, at best, intolerable."

"You won't be idle. There are other leads to check on, correspondence to review."

Guy strode to the fireplace. He braced both hands on the mantel and watched the flames flicker with eyes that burned hot as coals. "Give me what you have, and I'll be off."

Somerton opened a drawer and pulled out several letters. "These dispatches came in this morning. One is believed to be from Valère, but the cipher is too complex for my skills. Rather opportune, wouldn't you say?"

Guy accepted the packet; acid churned in his stomach.

"It's not your fault," Somerton said into the silence.

"The hell it's not." Guy stared at one of the few men whose opinion of him mattered. He had failed to protect Cora, and she may very well pay with her life for his incompetence. "Don't you understand? *I knew*. I knew something wasn't right about the situation when I left."

"Even so, you may not have been able to protect her," Somerton said. "Valère is determined to have her. If anyone is to blame, it is I who made the mistake of misjudging his resourcefulness on English soil."

"I have to go. I have to see for myself how things stand."

"Do what you must," Somerton relented. "Send word if you find something of importance in the letters. I will continue my search for Valère from here. When I speak to Latymer about the leak, I'll apprise him on this case, too. Not surprisingly, he was rather outraged by what happened to Cora and has authorized additional resources."

From Guy's perspective, Lord Latymer was the closest thing Somerton had to a friend. The two had gone to Cambridge together, and both began by assisting the Foreign Office right out of university. According to Somerton, Latymer had his eye on the Foreign Secretary position and, as the current Undersuperintendent of Aliens, he could very well attain his goal one day, whereas Somerton was content to oversee the affairs at the Alien Office—and more specifically, the Nexus—as its chief. Although Somerton now reported to Latymer, the two still worked in concert with each other.

Guy searched Somerton's eyes for a sign of the disappointment he must surely be feeling. He had not only let Cora down, but his mentor, too. Even though he didn't agree with all of Somerton's tactics, he still admired and respected the man. Would Somerton ever trust him again?

And more importantly, would Cora?

Seventeen

THE BEDCHAMBER DOOR EASED OPEN, AND TWO figures slid inside Cora's darkened room. She pressed farther into the shadows, her heartbeat nearly shattering the silence. Her muscles wound into taut readiness, waiting for the right moment. She had anticipated this visit since reading Somerton's so-called missive this morning. Being right about the forgery didn't make her feel proud, only regret for having sent Guy away. He might never forgive her for this breach of trust.

One of the men stayed near the door while the other crept across the room on silent feet. The masculine shadow drifted past the window, and a sliver of moon-light reflected off six inches of Spanish steel.

She flicked a glance at the man standing by the door, who followed his partner's progress. The man's anticipation was a palpable presence in the room, as was his tension. Dismissing him for the moment, she returned her attention back to her more immediate threat, now standing by the bed, his black-gloved hand reaching for the edge of the counterpane—

Cora pushed off the wall and slashed the fireplace poker through the air with all her might, connecting with the intruder's skull. A sickening crack resounded through the room before the man fell with an audible thud to the floor.

She whirled around to face the silhouette standing by the door. "Looking for me?" she asked.

Valère stepped into the moonlight. "I hope you have not killed poor Marcel, *ma chère*. I am running out of trained assassins."

Cora's blood pumped heavily within her veins. Her first sight of the man responsible for her torture severed her concentration for a brief second. She was transported back to her dank, cold cell, to the rats and rancid water, to the agony and humiliation. She recalled the fear and the moments of hopelessness. She remembered the hatred. For this man and all he represented.

Then Valère smiled. A beautiful smile, a charming smile. A malevolent smile that snapped her back to reality with the force of a slamming door.

Glancing at the bed, he gave the misshapen lump beneath the covers a derisive look before prowling toward her, a demon of death in an angel's façade. Cora widened her stance, battling her instincts to flee.

"You seem very thoughtful this evening, Cora, or do you prefer *Raven*?"

She wasn't fooled by his affable tone. He had hated the Raven as much as any of Napoleon's supporters. Discovering her secret identity must have sent him into a violent rage, especially if his superiors also learned of whom he had allowed to slip from his grasp.

She wondered what Guy thought about her alter ego. Would he embrace her as the Raven or try to destroy the connection? He had said little the day he'd revealed his awareness. Simply looked upon her with his unsettling gaze.

"Where are my servants?"

His smile broadened. "Quite indisposed, I'm afraid."

Fear sliced through her chest. Had he killed her

friends? Or incapacitated them? Unwilling to share her concerns about the missive, she had nonetheless warned them all to be at their most vigilant. An unnecessary warning, for they had already spoken to the guards and made arrangements for shorter intervals between watches in order to better stay alert.

He angled his body a little to the right, trying to force her into a vulnerable position. Years ago, she had been taught by—and trained with—the very best to deflect such obvious maneuverings. If Guy couldn't back her into a corner, a sniveling Frenchman wouldn't succeed.

"Whatever could be stirring inside that beautiful head of yours, *ma chère*? I suppose you may be wondering if I killed your servants. Is that it? Do you wonder how long your maid held out before she submitted to her first scream of agony? Perhaps you question whether your old coachman died from inhaling too much smoke, or if the flames consuming the barn got to him first?"

Her insides quavered at the images he wove. She prayed Valère had showed them mercy by locking them up somewhere. Someplace where they wouldn't do anything stupid—like try to save her.

Unfortunately for Valère, his experiment to discover the elusive chink in her indifference failed. She cast her mind to the sun-drenched grove near the lake where she and Guy had practiced their Tai Chi. His fluid movements had impressed and stirred her, reawakened lost memories and budding dreams. The memory helped her body relax, but her awareness remained centered on the madman at her feet.

"Quite the little ice queen, aren't you? Perhaps news of your brother would thaw that frigid façade of yours."

Cora knew as soon as she saw Valère's smile turn triumphant that she had slipped. Using her servants' welfare to force her hand was something he had attempted, although unsuccessfully, in the past. So she knew to prepare herself for his idle threats, but his casual reference to Ethan was most unexpected. Valère's intrusion confirmed the dispatch was a forgery. She had no reason to believe the missive's contents contained a grain of truth, so she had given the letter no further thought. She hoped the bastard was toying with her mind again, because the alternative was unthinkable. *Oh, Ethan.*

"Ahh, I knew there had to be something that would melt England's perfect little spy."

Cora allowed him to see her true feelings then. She allowed him to see, not her fear, but her absolute loathing. She allowed him to see *her* for the first time.

Her revelation wiped the smile off his face.

He drew a thin-bladed dagger from the depths of his sleeve, signaling flight was no longer an option. She switched the poker to her left hand and slipped her fingers beneath the white sash wrapped around her tunic.

"Put your weapon down, Valère."

"I think not."

Cora didn't bother to ask twice. She pulled back her arm and fired off one of her concealed knives. Moonlight caught the flash of steel as it sliced through the air, through the exact place Valère's throat had been moments ago. The thud of her knife embedding itself into the opposite wall barely registered past her disbelief. How could he have moved so quickly to avoid her blade? Or anticipate her target in the dark?

The Frenchman straightened from his awkward angle. Fury transformed his face into something far too feral to comprehend. His breaths pounded through the air, and she was certain he would rush her. But he surprised her yet again by sliding his dagger back up his sleeve.

"That bit of insolence won't go unpunished, *ma*

chère." His quietly stated promise frightened her more than any physical attack. "Renaud!"

Cora heard scuffling in the corridor. The sound grew louder until two struggling silhouettes appeared in the doorway. One masculine, one feminine.

"Perhaps we might shed some light on our new arrivals." Valère cocked his head to the side and waited.

Blood pounded in Cora's ears. Without a doubt she knew the feminine silhouette belonged to Dinks. She longed to see her friend's face to assure herself the maid was well. But she dared not let down her guard, not even to light a candle.

"Do you not wish to see how your beloved maid fares?" Valère taunted.

"What do you want?" Cora's confidence cracked. One wrong move and they would both surely die.

"An apology would be a good start."

She crossed her arms over her midsection and rubbed her fingers along the sash until she felt the comforting hardness of steel. "I'm sorry."

"Ah, but I didn't *feel* it, *mon ange*." He thumped his chest with his fist. "I want to experience the depth of your regret along with you, so that we might be one again."

As within his dungeon, what Valère said he wanted was nothing more than a precursor to debasement. He loved giving his captives hope and then laughing uproariously as he snatched it from their grasp. The Frenchman was cruel and unpredictable, which made him a very dangerous man.

"I'm not so trusting any longer, sir."

"Stubborn, stubborn, spy." He chuckled, as if pleased by her response. "You are very much like your father, did you know?" he asked. "Brilliant, cunning, and unwisely courageous. You have proved yourself more courageous than he, I think. But you are foolish to challenge me."

Cora's gaze sharpened. *Did he just say…?*

Valère's bark of laughter rent the air. "Poor orphaned Cora. Still haunted by your bastard father's and beautiful mother's deaths after so many years?"

"Murders," Cora corrected through stiff lips.

"Had your father followed instructions, he would still be alive and able to betray his country again and again."

Her heart constricted. "That's a lie." Was he toying with her again? She couldn't see his face clearly enough to judge. She hoped so. The alternative would be unbearable.

"If you wish to think so, who am I to disillusion you?"

Impotent rage fired through her veins. Her father was not a traitor. He loved England. He had instilled the same devotion in his children's hearts from the cradle. She would not allow this man to taint her childhood memory of her loving sire.

Another thought struck her. "You knew who I was?" Surely he hadn't known all along.

His gaze turned cool. "No, my little betrayer. I trust no one, especially *une belle anglaise*. After I found out who your parents were, I had my men follow you. You're quite adept at losing a trail, but I prevailed in the end."

She swallowed hard. "How long?"

His head canted to the side, a knowing smile on his lips. "*Ma chère?*"

Cora's gaze darted to where Dinks stood, struggling in earnest now. She dropped her voice. "Did you know who I was before…?"

"Before?"

She clenched her jaw so hard her teeth hurt from the pressure. "Before you slept with me, you bastard."

His bark of laughter was like knitting needles stabbing in her ears.

After an endless period of time, that was probably closer to five seconds, Valère rubbed his watery eyes and said, "You'll never know how much *I* regret not knowing the truth from the beginning, *ma petite*. Hours of endless amusement now lost to me." He shook his head remorsefully. "I came by the knowledge too late in our association. You might well recall that I have a most formidable temper."

Cora concentrated on calming her racing heart. She had always understood the cost of joining the Nexus. The work required its agents to reach beyond the bounds of proper society. For a woman of her standing, that meant being a spinster forever. No husband would accept such a stained reputation, and no children would survive such ridicule.

But now, she chafed against society's dual standard. A man in her position would be lauded a hero. Toasts would be raised in his honor. Women would flock to his bed. A man's duty to his country would not prevent him from having a family.

She had Guy to thank for this well of feminine need. If he hadn't awakened her heart and body, she would still be blissfully free of such futile yearnings.

The amusement lighting Valère's face faded. "I'm curious, *ma belle*. How far would you have gone for your precious island? Or was it your traitorous parents for whom you whored yourself?"

"Bastard."

He tsked. "I expected something far more creative from such a clever spy."

"I've had enough of your games, Valère," Cora said. "It's time for you and your men to leave."

"Is it?" He folded his arms in a thoughtful pose, tapping one slender finger against his bottom lip. "Renaud, I think your friend is trussed too tight for such a warm evening. Relieve her."

"*Avec plaisir, monsieur.*" The large masculine silhouette

pulled a small knife from his belt and lifted it toward the ties to Dinks's nightdress.

"Wait!" Cora dropped her clenched hands to her side.

"What is it, Cora? Would you prefer to offer a farewell kiss rather than see to your maid's comfort?"

If she got them out of this, it would be a fecking miracle, as Jack would say. Given Valère's speed, she had one opportunity to bring down both men and not kill Dinks in the process. One throw, two targets, and one flailing maid. She eyed the distance between Valère and Renaud and calculated approximately twelve feet. Sweat gathered between her breasts. A fecking miracle, indeed.

"Don't do it, Miss Cora!" Dinks said, wrenching her mouth free. "I'm an old woman." She dodged Renaud's massive hand. "You pay that rat bastard no mind."

"Quiet, *old woman*." A new tension entered Valère's voice. "Renaud, did I bring the wrong man?"

"No, *monsieur*."

A loud, eerie growl reverberated through the room. Everyone froze. The sound grew in intensity. Stark, furious, not of this world. With the room so dimly lit, the beast's exact location was difficult to isolate, but it seemed to zigzag across the room.

Valère twisted around, trying to locate the source, and Renaud backed up several steps until the light in the corridor illuminated his terrified face. "*Banshee*," he murmured.

Cora took advantage of the distraction. "Dinks, down!" The maid slumped to the floor like a bag of forgotten potatoes, her way eased by Renaud's sweaty, slackened grip. Cora threw the first knife and then the second, not stopping to see if the first found its mark. She heard the distinctive thud and the accompanying gurgle.

"Ahh!" Valère crumpled to his knees, cradling his wounded hand against his chest. Agony distorted his handsome features into a grotesque tangle of flesh.

She glanced back at Dinks, who was kicking the dead Frenchman off her. "Go free Bingham and Jack. Hurry!"

After ripping the long velvet draperies back to allow for more moonlight, she swiveled around to see Valère staggering to his feet. She picked up the fireplace poker she had dropped sometime during the foray and pointed it at him. "Back to your knees and leave my blade where it landed." The cacophony terminated so abruptly that the silence felt more terrifying than the howls and screams and barks of command.

Even injured, Valère was a dangerous man, especially with that knife up his sleeve. She had learned a long time ago to remain ever vigilant around him and never to reveal her trepidation. If she failed in either area, she was as good as dead.

"Orders, *mon ange*?" He sat back on his heels, wrapping his black cravat around his injury. "You are quite bold when you believe yourself to have the upper hand."

Everything about him repulsed her. In the beginning of their association, her young heart had held a mild infatuation for this French charmer, even knowing he was her enemy. For the first time ever, she had felt desirable and womanly and had gloried in her effect on the elusive Frenchman. Her warmer emotions proved transient once she had gathered more intelligence about him, and his true nature reared its conniving, murderous head.

"I'm not the one who was floundering on the floor like a stuck pig," she pointed out. "Now try not to be so enamored of your own voice and be quiet."

"Think you can make me?"

She waved the poker toward the corridor. "Look there to your man. He won't be speaking any time soon."

His lip curled into a smirk. "All this false courage. I hope you are not waiting for that sniveling Irishman to come to your rescue."

A ribbon of unease coursed down Cora's spine. "What are you talking about?"

"How is the boy's dear sister… Grace, is it? Yes. Such a beautiful name, Grace."

She lifted the poker and took a threatening step forward. "You didn't." Thunder cracked in the distance, rolling across the sky like a boulder tumbling down a three-hundred-foot cliff. Cora's heart felt much like the boulder, battered and plunging to its death.

A cunning gleam entered his sharp gaze. "Didn't what, *ma petite*?"

Cora frantically searched her mind for the common thread weaving amidst Valère's madness. This sort of thing was Guy's specialty, and she mourned his absence for more reasons than one. Not only would he have unraveled this mystery before her by now, but she would also have his indomitable strength to lean on. She wouldn't be alone.

But she was alone, and she had no one to blame but herself.

Think, Cora. The missive. Grace. Jack's unusual anxiety over delivering the message when his normal response would have been to attack the injustice with furious declarations of retribution. Her brow gathered in concentration, and then her eyes rounded in horror. "You kidnapped Jack's sister." Valère's duplicity came to her clear and certain. "Did you threaten to kill her if he didn't deliver the dispatch?" Her voice rose higher. "Dear God, Valère. Does your ambition know no bounds?"

Cora fought the ache of Jack's betrayal. Faced with the choice of saving his little sister or compromising his mistress's safety, the footman had stood in an untenable situation and likely had only minutes to make a decision. Although Jack was quite adept at getting out of trouble, he would have been no match for Valère's keen mind.

The mental torture Jack suffered must have been tremendous. Unable to seek counsel from the people he trusted most, and weighed down by a shattering helplessness, he made a decision that would surely cause him unbearable guilt for years to come. Even though she understood his impossible position, his choice had carved away a precious piece of their friendship that they might never recover.

"What is one little girl's life against an Empire, *ma belle*? Surely the Raven understands that the welfare of one insignificant child is nothing compared to the survival of a nation."

An incomprehensible evil stood before her, wearing a mocking, self-righteous smile. If she wasn't so consumed with fury, she would have lost what little dinner she had eaten that evening. "How ever did I miss the monster clawing beneath that beautiful, shallow shell?" Her ineptitude sickened her further. She knew of his passion for Napoleon, but never had she realized his love of the emperor was in truth a perverse obsession.

Somerton had entrusted her with the simple task of observance and report. How had she missed such menace, such disregard for innocence?

"Where is she?" Cora tightened her grip around the poker and raised the tip toward the ceiling.

"Why do you concern yourself with peasants?" Valère asked. "There are plenty more scurrying about this puny country to take her place."

She moved to within five feet of his kneeling form. "I won't ask you again."

"No." His eyes crinkled at the corners, and his lips curled into a smile that chilled the blood in her veins. "No, I don't suppose you will."

The blow forced Cora's head to jerk back. She stared at the bedchamber's ceiling, not actually seeing the fine lines zigzagging through the plaster, but more waiting for the terrible pain to reveal itself.

And then it did.

Her eyes rolled back in her head at the same time her knees buckled. The iron poker fell to the carpet with a dull, heavy thud. Or was it her skull sinking into the coarse fibers?

Cora's mind refused to sort it out. The room grew muffled, reminding her of the time pond water had burrowed deep in her ears. The only sound that registered was the sluggish beat of her pulse. Her body melted into the floor as if releasing a deep sigh. As if surrendering to a long, hard-fought battle.

A mere second before darkness engulfed her body, she was almost certain someone tickled her nose with the feathery end of a quill.

Eighteen

GUY'S WINDED HORSE TRUDGED DOWN THE NARROW, mud-thick lane leading toward the Golden Duck Inn in Witney. After Guy survived one of the longest nights of his life, he welcomed the sight of the small post town. During the long ride from London, he had spent hours torturing himself with various outcomes to Valère's carefully calculated visit to Herrington Park.

When he could take those images no longer, he began devising flawless methods of execution for Valère. With uncanny accuracy, he had visualized each placement of his blade and every entry point of his bullet. But the moment his finger moved to depress the trigger, his blood would ice, and his finger would freeze.

In the depths of his mind, a silent war raged. *Pull it! No! I'm not ready... must make sure... Just pull the damn trigger! Not yet! Give me a second.* On and on it went.

Guy squeezed his eyes shut for a moment. Even now, hours later, his throat grew thick with remorse. Somehow he had to overcome this paralyzing doubt. He must be sound of mind for the time when Cora needed him most.

He shifted in his saddle, chafing against his sodden clothes and the chill that had crept deep into his bones. As if his fear and guilt over Cora's disappearance wasn't enough, the good Lord challenged him further by blasting him with an unremitting rainstorm for the last two hours. His poor horse fared little better, with his rain-slicked coat and quivering withers.

His stomach chose that moment to remind him of his duty. He could not remember the last time he'd had a meal, possibly the morning he had abandoned Cora in the country and forced her to face her conniving enemy alone.

Sounds of life seeped into his consciousness. When he lifted his head, the muscles in his neck and back screamed in protest. He transferred the reins to his other hand and then stretched his arm out to the side, nearly groaning his pleasure aloud. He attempted the same with his stiff fingers, but his hand felt like that of an eighty-year-old man's. After a time, his fingers loosened, but he began to dread the moment he had to depend upon his leaden legs to carry his weight.

Dawn sprayed bright colors of purple, red, and golden yellow across the eastern horizon, heralding the beginnings of a clear summer day. As he approached the outskirts of town, he could see the residents of Witney already scurrying about—sweeping storefronts, loading wagons, and seeing to their animals.

He guided his hired horse toward the Golden Duck Inn, where he would hire a fresh mount and pay a handsome coin for the innkeeper's warmest loaf of bread. A young ostler, wearing breeches far too big for his narrow hips, ran up to Guy. "G'morning, sir." His small hand closed around the reins, while the other held onto his waistband. "Will you be staying at the Duck, sir?"

Guy dismounted and held onto the saddle until he was certain his legs were solid. He turned to the boy, tossing him a shilling. "No, lad. Have your stable's best horse saddled and ready to go in ten minutes, and you'll receive another one of those."

The boy's eyes rounded at the small fortune. "Thank you!"

Guy patted the horse's neck. "Take good care of him. He's had a difficult journey."

"Yes, sir." The boy tugged on the reins, coaxing the exhausted horse forward.

Pivoting toward the Golden Duck, Guy scanned the courtyard, cataloging every merchant and servant in sight. Everyone appeared to be about his normal business. No one seemed unduly interested in his presence.

He didn't immediately hear the approaching carriage. It could have been the clatter of wooden wheels, the jangle of a harness, or perhaps it was simply a bond that stretched across time and space that finally alerted him. Whatever the case, something inexplicable drew his attention to the lumbering carriage making its way toward the inn.

He glanced over his shoulder and followed the carriage's slow progress. The spent horses glistened with sweat, and their labored huffs reached his ears, even from this distance. The two occupants seated in the driver's box were slumped forward, their shoulders bent.

The conveyance drew closer, and the coachman glanced up. Recognition sent the fine hairs on Guy's nape standing tall, and his body pulsed with newfound hope. He sprinted across the cobblestone courtyard with his heart slamming against his rib cage, his gaze fixed on the passenger compartment. "Bingham! Jack!" He yelled from twenty feet away. "Where is she?"

"We're all fine, m'lord," Bingham answered around swollen, split lips. He nodded toward the passenger compartment. "Nicked in the nob a bit, but otherwise fine."

A vise clamped around Guy's chest, squeezing tighter and tighter, until he skidded to a halt in front of the carriage's window. Not knowing what he would find behind the shade, he tried to keep the panic from his voice. "Cora." He would give her two seconds, and two seconds only to show herself.

Then the shade lifted, and Cora's pale, bruised face appeared in the window. Her eyes shimmered with tears.

Guy wrenched open the door.

❧

Cora had maintained her composure up to the moment she heard Guy's voice. Her little family had needed her strength, and she had needed the illusion of control. But the sight of Guy standing outside the coach, concern carved into every tired groove of his handsome face, brought all the volatile emotions she had suppressed to the surface.

She crumpled. Huge, gulping sobs burst forth, causing her bruised ribs to throb and her aching head to splinter.

The door flew open, and she tumbled into Guy's arms. *Safe. We're safe. Oh, dear God, we're safe now.*

Immeasurable relief drugged her limbs, and she sagged against his solid body. All the anxiety and doubt she had lived with since rushing from Herrington Park had loosened its steely grip from around her chest.

"Cora, sweetheart." He wiped the tears from her face and pressed gentle, urgent kisses on her lips, cheeks, eyes, and forehead, caring nothing for the avid stares of passersby. "I was coming back... Somerton didn't send..." Then he hugged her to him. Not so hard as to crush her but firm enough to reassure. After a moment, he set her from him, inspecting her body. "Your injuries?"

"We're fine." She leaned into his hold, not wanting to be parted from his warmth. "I'm fine."

"Thanks to our ferocious little friend," Dinks said,

alighting after Cora. Her bottom lip was swollen and blood-encrusted. In her arms, she carried the damned ankle-biter like priceless cargo. The kitten gazed back at Guy with a wide, unblinking stare.

Cora nodded. "It's true. Scrapper provided an unearthly howl that distracted Valère's man, allowing me enough time to release two of my weapons."

Dinks smiled proudly. "That's right, my lord. Miss Cora killed the one holding me and maimed his master. If it weren't for that Marcel fellow, Miss Cora would be fit as a fiddle."

"What else?" he demanded.

A sense of desperation took hold of Cora, and she tightened her arms around Guy.

"Not much left to tell, my lord." Dinks scratched between the kitten's ears. "Injured as they were, the two Frenchies scurried out of there when they heard help storming up the stairs." She cast an admiring look toward Bingham, who still sat in the driver's box. When the coachman kept his gaze fixed forward, the maid scowled.

Valère's outraged commands to "kill the vermin" helped pull Cora from a concussion-induced fog. She would never forget waking to see Scrapper's tail whipping around angrily in front of her face while holding off Marcel's feeble attempts to bat him away. Those few precious minutes were enough time for Dinks to rush downstairs and free Bingham, Jack, and one of Guy's guards.

"I'm so sorry, sweetheart," Guy whispered against her hair. "I should have listened to my instincts."

The starkness, the aching quality to his voice made her blurt out, "No, I'm the one who should apologize. I should never have sent you away, but I wasn't certain about the missive—"

He stilled. "What are you saying, Cora?"

She felt more than saw Dinks's retreat. Realizing her error, a flash of cold heat swept through Cora's body.

Guy pressed, "You knew the letter wasn't from Somerton, didn't you?"

She couldn't answer him, couldn't get the awful words past the thickness in her throat.

"Didn't you?" His harsh rebuke matched his burning dark eyes.

"Guy, I couldn't be sure. Somerton doesn't normally sign his dispatches, but, since there was little chance his letter could fall into enemy hands, I had to consider he would not take such a precaution."

"Did it ever occur to you to discuss the matter with me before sending me off like a goddamned idiot?"

"No, Guy! It wasn't like that—"

He held up his hand, cutting off her explanation. "It was exactly like that." He closed his eyes briefly, pain-fully. When he opened them a few seconds later, his taut features were dull, passionless. Hurt. "I trusted your judgment on the matter." He released her, backing away. "But you didn't believe I could protect you."

She reached for him, wanting to bring back the man who had tenderly kissed her bruised face. "Please don't be angry, Guy."

His arms rose in a do-not-touch-me gesture, and a glint of something not quite human entered his gaze. "I have cracked men's necks with my bare hands. Broken bones and severed tendons. I have done unspeakable things in the name of England. Had you let me in on the ruse, I could have killed your Frenchman, and this nightmare would be over."

She now recalled their conversation in her bedchamber, where Guy had likened himself to a cold-blooded killer. His comment had given her little pause then, believing his masculine pride directed such boastful words, rather than any direct proficiency.

Her gaze swept down his body, taking in solid shoulders that needed no padding and upper arms far too thick to encircle with even two hands. Could it be true? In an effort to protect Guy and save her brother, had she missed an opportunity to destroy Valère?

Where would a cryptographer come across such unique skills? And why?

"You're right. I should have shared my concerns with you. But I didn't want—" *to lose another loved one.* First her parents, and then she was faced with losing her brother. Few experienced such unbearable losses, and even fewer understood the steps one would take to prevent others from being added to the list. "I told you in London that I didn't want you involved in this."

After a long, considering silence, he said, "I remember."

His low response spoke both of determination and hurt, and Cora's heart wrenched for her part in encouraging either emotion to surface.

"You should know Somerton has not heard from your brother since before we left for the country. So that part of Valère's subterfuge might be true."

Cora nodded. "Valère all but admitted he held Ethan."

He scrutinized the bruises on her face caused by her fall the night before. She fought the urge to hide her new injuries, even though she was aware he had seen her looking worse.

"Dinks," he called.

"Yes, sir?"

"Please see your mistress inside. I shall follow in a moment to make arrangements."

"Will do, my lord."

He strode to the driver's box and said a few quiet words to the men up top. Then Jack jumped down and

Bingham shifted over, gruffly handing the reins to Guy. With an expert flick of his wrists, he set the horses in motion and headed toward the stables.

The relieved joy Cora felt upon seeing Guy again vanished in a cloud of choking dust.

"Come, Miss Cora," Dinks coaxed. "Let's get you inside."

Numb and unsteady, she led their bedraggled group to the inn. A stern-faced Guy arrived a few minutes later, and he arranged rooms for everyone, including a hot bath and meal, holding firm against her servants' protests. As her three weary friends were led away, Cora sent Guy an uneasy glance. She wanted to make things right, soothe the hurt she had caused, but didn't know where to start. Her pulse quickened when he stopped before her.

"This issue of your lack of faith in me is not settled." He waved his hand toward the stairs. "Shall we?"

"It's not that—" Cora halted after only a few steps when her world began to tilt.

Guy steadied her. "What's wrong?"

She gently probed the painful lump on the back of her head. "Dinks warned I might have sustained a concussion when Valère's new henchman struck me. She wouldn't even allow me to sleep on the ride here."

"Smart woman," Guy murmured. "Prepare yourself."

She swallowed. "F-for what?"

"I'm about to carry you up to your bedchamber. You will no doubt protest, however. If you do, I shall object even more loudly, making a spectacle of us both."

She eyed him warily, unsure what to make of his mood. "I will endeavor not to make a scene, my lord."

"A wise decision." He gave her a moment to absorb his pronouncement, indicating it was up to her to decide how quietly they would make the journey.

A thousand tiny bees swarmed Cora's heart. Although

his words lacked warmth, her poor decision had not altered his determination to care for her. She reached up and traced the dark circles burrowed beneath his eyes. "How long has it been since you last slept?"

He ignored her question. "Ready?"

She drew in a deep breath and suppressed the small twinge of disquiet. With an expansive sweep of her hand, she said, "Carry away, my lord."

His left brow rose at her capitulation, but he did not delay. He lifted her into his arms and ascended the stairs after one of the inn's maids.

She ignored the tight clamp of his embrace and the cold sweat that coated her palms. At the end of the corridor, he entered a small yet well-appointed chamber. While the maid bent to light a fire, Cora took in the room with one thorough sweep of her gaze. Near the window sat a stained writing table and a chair that looked better suited to the rubbish rather than a guest room. A wash bowl filled one corner, and, to the right of the door stood a bed wide enough for two, with not-quite-matching night tables flanking each side.

The maid dusted off her hands. "Will you be needing anything else, sir?"

Guy strode toward the bed. "No, that will be all."

"Very well," she said with a curtsy. "The boys should be here soon with your bath."

Guy set Cora down on the edge of the bed, then knelt to remove her slippers. After dropping both shoes to the floor, he remained in place, his head bent. Silent. Contemplative. Tense.

"Why did you let me leave?" His question emerged harsh, bitter, and choked with suppressed rage. He lifted his head. "Why?"

Cora's heart beat too quickly. The answer he sought was stuck deep inside her throat, unwilling to surface for fear of further wounding him. But, as she gazed into his stormy dark eyes, she knew he deserved the truth, even if her confession exposed too much.

"I couldn't—" A knock sounded at the door, cutting her off.

Guy's gaze never wavered. He leaned forward, bracing his large hands on either side of her hips, trapping her in place. "Go on."

She sucked back a sharp rebuke. He wanted an answer to his question, but he also tested her resolve. He knew what inner turmoil such an aggressive position would cause her, and yet he still pushed her to resist the temptation to break free.

Her body and mind engaged in a soundless battle, and she fought to find the courage she once wore like an armored mantle. A quiver began in her stomach and then moved down to her legs. If she tried to speak now, the same tremor would garble her words.

When she stayed quiet, he pushed off the bed and stood. "Enter."

The owner's burly sons carried in a hip tub and retrieved several steaming buckets of water for her bath.

The taller boy asked, "Will you be needing anything else, m'lord?"

"Have you taken care of the others?"

"More water is heating as we speak, sir."

Guy flipped a coin to each of them. "That will be all for now."

As the two shuffled out, Guy strode to the fireplace and stared into the low flickering flames. With his demanding gaze no longer centered on her, Cora felt a measure of her control return. "I only suspected things weren't as they should be."

"And you said nothing?" The somber quality of his words made her throat ache with guilt.

"It was nothing tangible, Guy. I pieced together small nuances that seemed out of place."

He peered at her over his shoulder. "Somerton's signature?"

"Yes."

A muscle in his cheek jumped. "What else?"

She paused, reluctant to put into words actions that nearly broke her heart.

"Cora?"

"Jack," she said at last.

"What about him?"

"From the moment we stepped into the kitchen, I could sense his turmoil. At first, I thought his uncharacteristic behavior had to do with the news about my brother and his reluctance to deliver such news. But Valère made sure I knew of Jack's betrayal."

"Why would Jack take up with Valère? The footman's devoted to you."

A lump caught in her throat. "Valère took Jack's little sister to ensure he would convincingly deliver the note. He still has her, in fact."

Guy stabbed his fingers through his hair, locking them at the back of his head. "Good God. Why have I never heard of her before?"

"I don't know. She was rather shy as a young girl, avoided most people, especially imposing men. For the past six months, Grace's been staying at Miss Conrad's School for Girls near Bath. How Valère found her, I don't know."

Guy dropped his arms to his sides. "You should have shared your suspicions with me, Cora."

"What if I was wrong? Jack's odd behavior could easily have been explained away. What if Somerton needed you, and you stayed to protect me? What would have happened to my brother?"

He ripped the leather thong from his hair, freeing

his velvety black mane and obscuring his sharp features. Cora's breath hitched. His road-weary appearance transformed into wild sophistication. He resembled an untamed creature of the forest thrust into the civilized world. He exhibited an air of danger, and Cora wanted nothing more at that moment than to spear her fingers through his hair and draw him down for a thought-obliterating kiss.

"But you weren't wrong, were you? And you allowed—no, encouraged me to set off for London like a damned fool."

All thoughts of kisses disappeared. "If I hadn't, you'd be dead right now—just like your guards."

Explosive silence preceded his animal-like growl.

"Are you saying you were protecting *me*?" He marched toward her, and Cora jumped up from the bed. "Do you have any idea of the hell you put me through by remaining silent? No, of course you don't. You were too busy fighting for your bloody life and apparently protecting mine."

"I did what I was trained to do—protect and seek information. If it was a ruse by Valère, I thought he might take me to Ethan."

"And then what, Cora? If Valère had taken you to whatever pit of hell is currently holding Ethan, how could your going there alone have helped anyone?"

It wouldn't have—unless they followed her trail like last time. Given the circumstances, she hadn't had time to fully think through her stratagem. Only two things stood clear in her mind while staring down at Valère's note— help Ethan and get Guy to safety. That's all.

"Leave it to you to find the hole," she mumbled beneath her breath.

He must have heard her, for the fury left his face. However, the hurt lingered. It flowed deeply, as if she had cut out the core of his manhood and tossed it aside.

"Tell me the rest of it," he demanded. "After the hell you put me through, I deserve to know what that bastard did to you."

Deserve to know. Any remorse she might have been feeling suddenly leached away, leaving nothing but an exasperated Raven behind.

"What is this really about, Guy?"

"I haven't the faintest idea what you mean, my dear."

"Do not mistake me for one of your addlepated ladybirds, my lord."

He stepped forward. "What would you know of my ladybirds, Cora?"

She gritted her teeth against the pang of arousal his nearness caused. He looked fierce and volatile and so very dangerous to her heart. "Not a single thing, and I prefer to keep it that way."

He stared at her for the longest time before splaying his hand across his forehead to rub his temples. "I didn't heed my own damn instincts. My gut told me something was amiss, and still I left." He swung around to pace the small confines of the room. When he reached the far wall, he slammed his palm against it, the impact rattling the nearby window. "I should never have left you. I should have spoken to the messenger myself."

Comprehension dawned, and a morsel of sympathy pushed past her irritation. For the first time since arriving at the inn, the tension vibrating through her body eased.

"You trusted Jack, as I did, Guy." She hesitated. "And you trusted me. The fault does not lie with you." She flicked her hand in an unaffected gesture. "Besides a few scrapes and bruises, I'm fine. Do not castigate yourself any further."

He lifted his tormented gaze to hers, and Cora itched to pull him into her arms. But she had wounded him, and wounded him badly. Would he welcome her comforting touch? She didn't know, and she realized she was too much of a coward to find out. She clamped her hands behind her back.

"I thought…" He swallowed hard, his gaze burning brighter.

Cora stepped closer. "What, Guy?" Her heart clamored in her chest, and her hands tightened their hold.

"I thought he had killed you." Air bellowed through his nostrils.

She knew the agony such a thought carried. Had felt it when considering her alternatives with the forged missive. She had lost so much. The possibility of losing Guy, too, forced her to send him away. Away to safety.

For hours, he had believed her dead. She had never meant to put him through such pain. "Guy." One step, two steps, half-running, she threw herself into his arms. He didn't rebuff her, as she had feared. In fact, he seemed to need the contact as much as she. "I'm sorry, Guy. I don't know what else to say."

He cradled her face between his hands. "Say you'll never keep something like that from me again."

Tears clouded her eyes. "I'll always protect you, Guy. I won't promise otherwise."

"Damned stubborn fool." His mouth swept over hers in a timeless show of need and domination. She accepted his passion but exerted her own style of dominance. Little by little, she felt her mastery return. Her former self clawed its way back to the surface.

The pressure on her lips soon eased until their mouths were but a hairsbreadth apart, their foreheads resting against each other. "Promise me"—his lips skimmed hers with each syllable—"promise that you'll bring your suspicions to me the next time. We'll work through the problem together."

She kissed him. "You have my word."

Pulling her into his arms, he said, "There's hope for you yet, then."

She reared back, glaring at him. "Label me stubborn if you like, Guy Trevelyan, but my perseverance has saved lives."

The slight crinkling at the corners of his eyes faded. "For which England is eternally grateful. I, however, am selfish and do not want you placing yourself in danger any longer."

Mollified, she said, "Then it is good I bashed Valère when I did."

"What do you mean?" he asked on a half groan, half growl.

"I was waiting for Valère when he came for me." Even now, several hours later, her body still quivered with the aftershocks of her trepidation.

Deep lines bracketed his mouth. "*You* attacked *him*?"

Cora straightened her spine. She tried—Lord knew she tried—but she couldn't repress the smugness that entered her voice. "Yes."

His lips thinned. "Cora—"

"If I hadn't let my guard down for a mere second, he would now be languishing in your cellar at Herrington Park." Cora's gaze settled on the room's single window. Ominous black clouds loomed in the distance. "Instead, he's free to terrorize me and those I love again. He wants to break me, Guy, not kill me. And now that he has my brother and Jack's sister, he's the one in control of the game."

"Game?" he said. "Do you think this is a game? By God, we're talking about your life here."

"No, Guy, I don't think it's a game, but Valère does," she stated with as much calm as she could muster. "He will toy with me to the point of insanity; then he will kill everyone I hold dear."

"No, he will not."

His hand cradled her jaw, and his thumb fanned over her cheek. The intriguing scent of sweat, horse, and Guy sent tingles to her nose and trembles through her middle. He kissed her forehead. "I will never let you out of my sight again. Not until Valère's dead." He pressed his lips to her temple. "Maybe not even then."

The backs of Cora's eyes burned. She had no doubt he meant every word, and although it felt good to share the burden of Valère, Cora knew she would eventually chafe under such close scrutiny. But for now, Guy made her feel safe and womanly and loved. Things she hadn't known in a very long time.

As she lifted her head, Cora fixed a silly, wobbly smile on her face and relaxed a bit when Guy's tense features did the same. His gaze dipped to the jagged line on her cheek.

Cora's smile dimmed. She slanted the damaged side of her face away from him.

He cleared his throat. "Here, let's get you in the tub while the water's still warm."

If he thought her face was hideous—"I can manage on my own."

"I know you can. Lift your skirt, if you please."

Her jaw firmed. "I do not, please. I endured enough maltreatment while in France."

He pinned her with his gaze. "Are you comparing me to Valère, Cora?"

His quiet question tore at her conscience. "No, of course not."

"I'm glad to hear it." He pried her thumb from between her fingers and then held her hands a little away from her body. "I need to see the extent of your injuries, Cora. I'll do my best to preserve your modesty."

Her stomach churned at the mere thought of disrobing in front of Guy. She wouldn't be able to hide the evidence of Valère's violence. As much as she tried, she couldn't block the image of herself standing before Valère in a sheer chemise, his murderous fingers skimming down her breast...

Stop it!

Guy wasn't Valère, and Valère wasn't here. The Frenchman wanted to scare her, and he had succeeded. If Valère also believed he could dictate her every move, thought, and emotion, he was doomed for disappointment.

"Very well, my lord." She traipsed over to the bed and sat. Catching Guy's eye, she slid back into a reclining position. "Perhaps you would care to check the burns on my poor feet?" She twirled one foot in front of him, girding herself against the sharpening of his gaze.

He caught her foot and kissed the inside of her ankle. "A good beginning."

He removed first one silk stocking and then the other, searching for new injuries while kneading the soles of her feet and her cramped calves.

"That feels divine." A low groan escaped from between her lips.

Much too soon, he grasped her upper arms and pulled her into an upright position.

Even though he knelt on the floor, she faced him at eye level, no longer able to hide her marred visage. He visually caressed every cut and bruise, and his deft fingers untangled her knotted hair and rubbed her scalp. The soothing motion forced her eyes to close.

He pressed a lingering kiss to the corner of her mouth. "Come."

She allowed him to pull her boneless body to the fireplace where, with methodical care, he removed the rest of her clothing. When he reached for the hem of her chemise, she stayed his hands, still unable to reveal the hideous marks dotting her body.

"Thank you, Guy." She forced her arms to splay wide when all she wanted to do was use them as a shield. "As you can see, I'm intact."

He considered her for a long moment, as if he would demand a full accounting, before bending forward to whisper in her ear, "Never fear, sweet Cora. All the marks in the world will never outshine your beauty. But all that perfection isn't your brightest star." He kissed the corner of her mouth. "It's your inner strength and uncompromising love for your family and friends that holds a man captivated. And that shall last a lifetime."

Cora's stomach twisted into a spidery knot. His words left her shaken and tense, heightening her senses until her skin felt abraded along every line of her soft chemise.

"I'll be in the corridor while you finish your ablutions. I'm leaving the door ajar." His clipped tone left no room for discussion. "Do not take too long. I would enjoy a warm bath myself."

Cora's fevered mind almost missed his meaning. "What do you mean by 'enjoy a warm bath myself'? Speak to the innkeeper. He'll have a tub sent to your room."

"He did." He pointed in her direction. "It's right there."

Her eyes widened. "Absolutely not."

Ruthless determination transformed his handsome face into one of uncompromising lines. "I'll not debate this with you, Cora. I warned you that I'm not letting you out of my sight until Valère's dead."

At the door, he turned back. His soft look of encouragement surprised her. "Do hurry, my dear. My bathwater is getting cold." He left, closing the door just enough to afford her some privacy, and open enough to hear everything that went on inside.

Cora stood by the steaming tub, fuming over his commanding attitude. Did he think she was incapable of taking care of herself? Who did he believe looked after her while she was in France? Her great-aunt? Hardly. She was a dear lady but quite unable to keep up with Cora.

She jumped when Guy stuck his head around the door. "I suggest you make use of that bathwater with all due haste, my dear. I'm giving you precisely fifteen minutes, and then I'm coming in."

She stalked toward him, slowly, seductively. Carefully keeping her eyes hidden behind lowered lids. Guy's midnight gaze traveled the length of her, interest lighting his eyes. Cora knew the effect her body had on men, had used it many times over the years, but the intensity of his regard caused an involuntary shiver to track down her spine. When she stood close enough to feel his heightened breath waft across her face, she raised her hand as if to rest it on the door's edge. Instead, she smacked her palm against the heavy oak panel, forcing the door to ricochet off his forehead.

"Ow!" He rubbed his injured brow. "Why did you do that?"

"That is but a sampling of what I'll do if you don't cease ordering me about like an underling."

"I wasn't ordering you around. I simply wanted to make use of the warm bathwater."

"Then try asking me to hurry instead of barking orders at me. I'm closing the door."

"No—"

She slammed the door shut and, when she heard a growl on the other side, she allowed a small smile to lift the corners of her mouth.

"Fifteen minutes, Cora," came the muffled warning.

Feeling better, she yanked off her chemise and scampered back to the tub. She slowly sank into the water's heavenly, balmy depths. A few minutes later, her head lolled to the side, and with heavy lids, she stared at the chamber door. If she were honest with herself, it felt good to know that Guy was outside her room, that he worried about her. It had been so long since someone had.

She sighed and began rinsing the dirt from her exhausted body. Because he had been so thoughtful toward her servants, she would finish five minutes early.

At least she would have, had she not fallen asleep.

Nineteen

GUY'S IRRITATION OVER CORA'S TARDINESS MELTED away upon seeing her fast asleep in a tub full of water. Her race across country had taken its toll on her still-healing body and, of course, her recent confrontation with Valère hadn't helped matters any. When her carriage had rumbled into the inn's courtyard, his knees had nearly buckled under the weight of his relief. Seeing her sprite-like face appear in the window was the most glorious sight he had ever beheld.

While waiting for Cora to finish her ablutions, Guy took the opportunity to write a short message to Somerton to let him know she was safe. The information would be welcome news, even to a man whose ability to conceal his emotions was unrivaled. With Cora's safety secured, Somerton would be able to devote his full attention again to locating Valère.

Guy's thoughts veered toward the packet Somerton had given him in London. He had taken a moment to review the correspondence inside. From his preliminary assessment, he guessed the message was altered with a homophonic cipher, one of the most complex to breach. To create a homophonic cipher, the cryptographer generally assigned two digits, but sometimes more, to every letter in a word, creating an endless number of combinations to untangle.

His discovery was not good. No wonder Somerton handed the packet over to him. Few had the skill to break such a cipher. And Guy couldn't be certain he was one of the few.

As he approached the tub, his gaze lit upon Cora's nakedness, and sharp pangs of need shot through his body. She was so damn beautiful. Always had been, but her youthful innocence had shielded her against his admiring gaze. Not anymore.

When he stood at the edge of her watery haven, his eyes narrowed, cutting through the soapy surface. A macabre patchwork of fading bruises covered her torso, and one side of her face seemed to be darkening before his eyes. Guilt clawed at his stomach, scraping his soul raw.

Indicators of brutality were nothing new to Guy. In the last year, he had come upon the aftermath of violence often enough to build up a numbness against its sudden appearance.

Guy knelt at Cora's side, easing her awake with the gentle glide of his finger along her moist cheek and over the faint bruises encircling her slender neck. A small oval cameo depicting a delicate feminine profile lay nestled in the hollow between her breasts; the ivory-colored relief rose above a deep orange background.

He leaned closer, tracing the fine craftsmanship with the tip of his finger. A Phrygian cap sat atop the woman's wavy hair. His gaze searched Cora's sleeping features, wondering why she would be wearing France's national symbol of liberty.

She inhaled deeply, deflecting his attention back to her breasts. They broke the surface of the now-tepid water, almost as if they beckoned his touch. Pendant forgotten, he admired the way she awakened with languid sensuality. Her eyes fluttered open, widened, and Guy's insides twisted with pure, animalistic desire.

Without warning, her hand cut through the air and connected with his throat, a spray of soapy water following the burst of action. An explosion of excruciating pain sent him reeling to the floor, clutching his neck. He struggled for breath, vaguely aware of water splashing nearby and the rapid patter of feet. He wheezed his next breath.

Cora dropped to her knees beside him. "I'm so sorry! I didn't realize who you were at first." She patted his cheek. "Guy—can you speak?"

He turned his head away, rolling to his side. Not only could he not speak, he could not breathe.

She touched his shoulder and peered down at him. "Tilt your head back a bit so your neck's extended."

He tried, but the muscles in his throat had constricted, allowing for little movement. He shook his head.

"I know it hurts." She rubbed her fingers slowly down the length of his throat, easing the tightness. "Try again."

He raised his chin and was finally able to draw in some much-needed air.

When his labored breaths eased, she asked, "Better?"

"Yes," he rasped. He eased into a seated position and took a moment to get his more volatile emotions under control. Being laid low by a jab to the throat from an individual half his size was not something any man accepted with grace. When he thought he could finally look at her without murder swirling in his eyes, he lifted his gaze to find her sitting back on her heels, a distraught expression contorting her face. "I'm well, Cora."

"Only because I pulled back at the last second."

Pulled back? Jesus. If what she said was true, he was damned lucky. Had she followed through, he would be on the floor, clutching his crushed windpipe and slowly suffocating rather than sitting up and struggling with his damaged pride.

He rotated his neck around, stretching the tension from his rigid muscles. "I'm glad you did. I rather like being alive at the moment."

Rather than the smile he anticipated, her lower lip trembled, yet the rest of her face remained unchanged. The backs of his eyes burned. She was so bloody strong.

"Cora." He grasped her bare shoulder. "Never fault your instincts for keeping you alive. You knew not whether I was friend or foe. I should have made my presence known, but you looked so peaceful. I couldn't bear waking you." The fresh scent of clean woman drifted over him. He smoothed his thumb over a bead of water slipping down her shoulder.

Another droplet trailed over her collarbone, picking up speed as it dashed down her creamy, smooth breast until it met the barrier of her bath towel.

When she noticed the direction of his gaze, she fumbled with the top of the linen to make sure all was secure. She averted the injured side of her face. "Are you sure your throat is not damaged?"

Every time she sensed his interest, she hid her imperfections. He rested his weight on one hand while the other coaxed her face around. She glanced at him and then looked away.

"Yes, my throat is fine," he answered. "Why do you hide from me?"

A muscle ticked in her jaw. "Is it not obvious?"

"Cora, your injuries do not offend me. Valère offends me, however, and he should remain far out of my sight. I told you, it is your inner light—your courage and loyal nature—that draws a man's attention." He brushed his thumb over the curve of her flushed cheek. "My attention," he admitted softly.

Her eyes widened a little before they narrowed into a reproachful glare. "In order to see the light, a man must first weave his way through a tangle of gnarled branches and thorn-coated underbrush. How many men do you know who are willing to scuff their polished Hessians or rip their superfine coats?"

One. Guy clamped his teeth around the retort, knowing she was not ready to hear such a confession, understanding she would not believe him, anyway.

When he remained silent, she made to stand. As she made to stand, she clutched her arm to her side, and her brows scrunched together.

"Cora." He stood, grabbed a second towel and draped it over her wet hair, and then lifted her into his arms. Her body went rigid. "Easy."

"Guy, please put me down."

"As you wish." He sat in an old cushioned chair near the fireplace and settled her onto his lap.

She sent him a quelling look, pushing against his chest. "This isn't what I meant."

He grabbed one of her resisting hands and kissed her palm. "Let me see." He kept his voice low, soothing.

Some of the rigidity left her body, but she clutched the towel tighter to her chest and shook her head.

"Cora, if you don't open that towel, I will, and I won't try to protect your modesty this time."

Once again, her icy blue-green eyes shot daggers through his skull. When he stared back with the same determination, she closed her eyes for a bracing moment and then peeled back the linen, revealing the lower portion of her torso.

It was Guy's turn to close his eyes. The sight of her bruised body, free of the soap-clouded water, sent a violent shudder of retribution through his body.

Smooth alabaster skin blended into swirls of green, yellow, and purple where old and new injuries collided. He pulled the towel away from her left hip and leg, being careful not to reveal her most feminine center.

She had beautifully contoured legs. Legs that at any other time would conjure visions of him wrapped inside their erotic embrace. But now, all he could see was the long gash on her thigh that started on the outside of her hip and angled all the way down to the inside of her knee. An older wound, given its stage of healing. A wound that would undoubtedly leave a scar.

With trembling hands, she rearranged the linen and exposed an identical mark on her right leg. She pressed her thighs together to reveal a large, perfect V.

The fucking Frenchman had branded her. Had, in fact, marked his territory like a damn wolf in mating season.

"Jesus, Cora." A lump the size of a billiard ball lodged in his throat. The image of a much-younger Cora frolicking in the pond that separated their two properties flashed through his mind. The world-weary woman in his arms posed a stark contrast to the innocent girl's vitality.

Her tentative touch on his jaw brought him back to the present.

Tears spiked her eyelashes. "Do not mourn for me, Guy. The messages he leaves on my body are of little consequence."

"They are not—"

Her fingers moved to his lips, silencing him. "They are. I knew the moment I stepped foot on French soil that I was forsaking my destiny as a viscount's daughter. I knew no man of honor would ever accept the woman I had to become."

"Cora." He rested his forehead against hers and cupped her uninjured cheek. "You should never have been involved with a man like Valère."

"It was my decision to make."

"You were little more than a child."

She smiled wistfully. "I was twenty when I left for

France, Guy. Some ladies are well into motherhood at that age."

He ground his teeth together, unable to argue the point.

"Do not fret for me. I've underestimated my foe twice. There won't be a third time." She sealed the promise with a hesitant kiss to his cheek.

Guy's muscles contracted at her gentle touch. Her halting show of affection was one of the most compelling sensations he had ever experienced. He wanted to turn his head and pull her into a full, devouring kiss. One that would sate his growing desire and banish his overwhelming guilt. And show her he was not like any other man.

When she drew back, her tremulous gaze revealed a glimpse of the innocence she had lost while in France. "Be at ease, dear Guy."

In the face of all she had endured, she still sought to take care of others. He bent and kissed her, not the devouring kiss he desired, but a melding of lips to remind her of what they had shared in the glade at Herrington Park. She returned the pressure, almost desperately at first before settling in and following his lead. They lingered in this dreamlike state for several minutes, giving and taking, learning and reacting.

Soon, she sighed and melted into his embrace. The backs of her fingers caressed his injured throat before she placed delicate, apologetic kisses along the area where she had struck him. She pulled back and met his gaze.

He lost himself in that moment. The chamber disappeared; the world beyond vanished. All he could see was Cora. The only sensation he felt was the soft warmth of her body. He sank deeper into her inviting gaze, searching for the secret thought glinting in her unforgettable eyes.

The shift from friends to lovers was not heralded by a dazzling array of fireworks, nor was the change signified by the chiming of a thousand bells. No. For them, the transformation came in the form of her teary, joyful smile.

"I am at ease only while at your side." His confession emerged low, almost incomprehensible.

Her small hand smoothed over his hair as if she were taming a wild beast. She pressed her face into the side of his neck and whispered, "Then stay with me tonight."

A tidal wave of lust and possession drenched his already aroused body. He wanted to toss her onto the bed and strip away every filthy memory Valère had forced upon her and replace them with cherishing caresses and love-filled strokes. He wanted to offer her tender words of encouragement and to reassure her of his devotion and support. He wanted to obliterate every layer of darkness from her life. Instead, his aching body allowed him only a single-syllable response. "Yes."

She seemed content with his reply, for she nestled against him and gave herself over to the slumber she had forsaken the night before.

Guy closed his eyes and concentrated on her even breaths, resting his chin on top of her damp curls while he wrestled with the building pressure in his chest. Her courage and grace humbled him. Even at a young age, she had known her own mind. Seemed to have the course of her life set and followed it without fail.

Unlike him.

He had floundered for several years, not knowing his place or what he wanted. From the deBeau siblings, he had learned about family and friendship. From Somerton, he had learned about honor and duty—to his relatives and his estates and the people who worked them. But something vital had been missing from his life. It wasn't until he returned to England, after spending some time abroad searching for his elusive happiness, that he realized what he needed.

His epiphany presented itself in the form of a mature Cora dressed in an alluring red gown and traipsing around a masked ball. The moment she removed her black silk mask, he knew what he wanted. A home. A family. Cora.

And then she left. For three long years.

A soft snore brought him back to the present. To the woman in his arms, who had given herself over to him for safekeeping.

A treasure beyond compare.

Twenty

SEVERAL HOURS LATER, CORA WOKE TO A MILD ACHE IN her side. She blinked away the fog of sleep and was surprised to realize that she had slept away most of the day. How long had it been since she'd had such a restful sleep?

Now that she was awake, the pressure on her side grew more noticeable. She peered down at the source of her discomfort and found a large, sinewy male arm wrapped around her middle. She twisted around to locate its owner, her pulse pounding in her ears. When she found Guy sound asleep beside her, she released the alarmed breath she had been holding.

Tangled ebony waves framed his strong cheekbones, creating an untamed yet peaceful prospect. Until her gaze traveled below his chin.

The sheet rode low on his stomach, exhibiting a powerful combination of rippling muscles and hair-dusted skin. She followed the slow rise of his chest, noting with some dismay that her hammering heart did not match the even pace of his breathing.

When she averted her gaze, the small motion caused her nipples to rub against the cool sheet. Her eyes widened. *What on earth!*

Her gaze dropped to her bare arms and upper chest, to the sheet scarcely covering her chilled breasts, to the unclothed man at her back. A fresh wave of alarm surged through her, and she nearly bolted from the bed.

But the masculine planes of Guy's torso and his sheet-covered hip held her transfixed, immobile. The sight ignited a thrilling warmth deep inside that soon tempered her apprehension. Her gaze lingered on the sheet; her curiosity about what lay beneath eroded her good sense.

She inched her foot back until she found his leg. One tentative slide of her sole revealed she wasn't the only one naked beneath the covers. A low groan escaped from her throat, and she was transported to their time together at the lake. She relived the feel of his caress, the smell of his skin, the taste of his lips.

Although her initial anxiety had receded, her limbs continued to quiver. But for an entirely different reason, one that had to do with the inferno licking at her womb. Falling back to sleep with Guy's bare body mere inches away from hers would be utterly impossible. She could try slipping away but feared waking him. The worry and lack of sleep over the last few days had proven just as miserable for Guy as it had for her. He deserved a little uninterrupted relaxation before external forces called them to action again.

She lay there, counting his slumberous breaths and willing herself to relax. She made it to forty-one before throwing her hands up in defeat. There was absolutely no way to ignore something so... *tempting*.

Holding the sheet to her breasts, she slid out from beneath his arm and sat up, easing one leg over the edge of the bed. Guy's warm, far-too-close body stirred behind her. She froze, not daring to even blink. When no further movement came from behind, she chanced a quick peek over her shoulder.

Guy's bottomless gaze met hers. "Going somewhere?" His sleep-drugged voice slid down her spine like a trickle of warm water. It also shattered her last hope of slipping away undetected.

"Umm, yes. I seemed to have misplaced my clothes."

With a single finger, he caressed her exposed back. "So I see."

A violent shiver racked her body, and her breasts tingled with need. The darkened room, Guy's bare flesh and tousled hair, his musky scent—it all coalesced into a cocoon of intimacy and an unmistakable pulse of desire.

She scooted toward the edge of the bed. "I'm sorry to have disrupted your sleep."

"I'm not." He laid his hand on her elbow, halting her progress. The bed dipped, and then she felt the heat of his body against her back. "Stay." His seductive request whispered against the fine hairs blanketing her shoulder, causing a delicious shiver to track down her spine. "We have hours before dawn."

Cora closed her eyes. She could not be this close to Guy and remain unaffected. He tempted her, lured her into accepting his forbidden fruit.

"You know this is not a good idea, Guy." An entanglement with him could cost her dearly on many levels. Not only could she lose his friendship, she could fall in love with a man destined to wed an unblemished debutante to further the family name. So many reasons she should leave his bed. And yet she stayed.

"I know no such thing." He kissed the curve of her shoulder.

He leaned forward to kiss the corner of her mouth. "I'm willing to take the risk. Are you?"

Yes.

Cora was afraid she would risk a great deal for the simple pleasure of feeling his lips caress her skin. Touch by touch, thread by thread, he wove her into his sensual world, where nothing mattered but them. After their loving by the lake, she found herself yearning to experience the delectable release of passion again.

"Stay with me, Cora." His voice enthralled and tempted and tore at her resolve.

How could she deny him? *Them*. None of the reasons that seemed so important only minutes ago held any weight with her now. She felt herself dissolving into the cool bed linens, freeing her mind of Valère, and of perfect brides and lost brothers, loving the weight of his sleep-warmed body as it covered hers.

She felt decadent and beautiful, and her body writhed against the bottom sheet, enjoying the gentle abrasion on her sensitized skin and loving the press of his hard chest along hers.

Her restless legs came into contact with the fabric of his smalls. "You're not naked."

"No." His hand slid over her hip. "But you are." Then he kissed her. A possessive, thought-destroying mesh of lips that sank into the marrow of her bones.

She swept her arms around his torso and pulled him closer, luxuriating in the smooth strength of his back and trapping the evidence of his desire against her pelvis.

A shiver raced over the surface of her skin, and her nipples contracted into hard nubs. Desire, potent and heavy, pumped through her veins, leaving her gasping for air. The weight of her emotions was unfamiliar and frightening. And so addictive.

Misinterpreting her response, Guy lifted his head, concern and a hint of dread marking his handsome face. "Shall I stop?"

She lifted her right leg and hooked it over his waist, pushing her damp folds against his hard length. "Do I act as though I want you to stop?" She thrust her hips again.

A whisper of breath fanned her chest, and he answered her taunt with a driving thrust of his own. "I thought"—he swallowed hard—"I might have frightened you. And I was afraid it wouldn't matter. I want you so damn much, Cora. Too much, I fear."

She shook her head, weaving her fingers into his long, loose hair, kissing his unshaven jaw, his lips, his throat. "Never too much, Guy. Never too much."

He pressed a heart-stopping kiss between her breasts, and her eyes fluttered closed. With excruciating slowness, he turned his attention to the sensitive underside of each mound, kneading one while tasting the other. Then his tongue teased the rim of the aureole, and Cora's entire body bucked under the force of her need.

Guy laughed softly. "I like that spot, too, sweetheart."

A sound akin to a growl rumbled deep in her throat. "Cease your torment." She grasped his head and tried to force him to take her nipple into his mouth.

But he refused her demand.

His mouth hovered above her aching, rigid nipple, and no amount of prodding or pushing would entice him to take in her straining peak.

"Guuyyy," she groaned, arching her spine.

"Cora." He whispered her name over her fiery flesh, making chill bumps ripple across the surface. He thrust his member along her heated folds. "Do you *feel* me?"

She answered in kind with a roll of her hips. "Yes."

Still he held back.

She peered up at him, her voice thick with desire. "Do you wish for me to beg?"

He lifted his head enough for her to see the answer in his burning gaze.

"Please, Guy." She teased the seam of his lips with the tip of her tongue, showing him what she wanted. His breaths grew more labored, and his heartbeats pounded against her stomach. "Please take me into your mouth, my lord."

His control snapped.

He clamped the hot cavern of his mouth around her breast, flicking and drawing on the sensitive tip while one hand pushed down his smalls and guided his staff to the cleft of her moist center. He entered her with a slow and deliberate thoroughness that scoured her nerves raw. She wanted more of him, all of him. And she wanted it faster.

She arched her lower back and then pushed into him with all her strength, enveloping his entire length with her channel. They both groaned from the tantalizing friction her momentum created. Taking her cue, Guy began rocking against her with strong, sure thrusts, setting an anticipatory rhythm that made her grasp greedily for release.

Within seconds, something inside her exploded, and her body pulsed once again with exotic sensations. She held him closer, her mind fixed on the delicious vibrations thrumming in the vicinity of where their bodies connected. Suddenly, his muscles tensed, and she felt his seed pump into her, hot and forceful. Near her ear, she heard a low, unearthly growl rumble through his straining chest.

They lay frozen in a moment of charged silence before Guy released a slow exhale, his replete body sagging against hers. He languidly kissed her lips before resting his head in the curve of her neck. The pose was so comforting and warm and right.

Seconds later, he rose up on his elbows, looking down at her with sleepy contentment. "Are you well?"

Her body prickled with ethereal wonder. The momentary pleasure she had felt deep inside her womb transcended weeks of brutal torture. She wanted to experience that pleasure again.

And again.

She nodded. "You?"

His lips turned up into a wolfish, satisfied smile. "Quite."

She made lazy circles over his upper arms, searching for appropriate words.

"What is it, Cora?"

She allowed her gaze to roam over his dear features. She wanted to remember *everything* about this moment. Happiness strummed through her veins, her body, her heart.

How long would it be before she felt this way again? Two days? Two months? Never? A keen ache clutched her chest. She pressed a desperate kiss on his lips and tightened her internal muscles around his shaft still resting inside her.

Guy hissed a breath between his teeth and pushed his hips into her. Her back arched.

"Cora?"

"Hmm-mmm."

"As much as I'd like to make love to you all over again," he said through gritted teeth, pulling free, "I think it best if we wait a little while. Your body is still healing."

It was then Cora noticed the slight stinging sensation between her legs, and the area around her injured ribs ached from her exertions. "I suppose you are correct."

In the midst of trailing kisses along her bared shoulder, he chuckled at her disgruntled tone. "Never fear, my Insatiable One. I suspect 'a little while' will be here before you know it."

A lock of Guy's dark hair slid free and pooled onto her shoulder. The wispy, delicate strands were in such stark contrast to his broad masculine frame. She loved his hair. Loved lacing her fingers through the soft strands, as she did now, and loved the way his hair outlined the sharp planes of his cheeks when released from its constraining tie.

No matter how hard she concentrated on the sleek texture of Guy's hair, she could not hold back the layer of sadness that crept into her heart.

"Why so thoughtful, Cora?" he asked. "I expected you to collapse into a heap of satiated wonder after my lovemaking. Instead, you look like someone stole your favorite biscuit."

She tried to smile, she really did, but an insidious dark cloud of regret blotted out her euphoric mood.

He kissed her gently, coaxingly. "Tell me."

She sighed, knowing the time had come to face her lack of innocence. It could not be undone, nor would she apologize for its absence. But those conditions did not nullify the fact that she wished Guy had been the recipient of her gift, rather than Valère.

"I'm sorry I was not whole for you." Her words emerged on little more than a whisper, and she became quite entranced by a whisker on his jaw.

Guy tucked two fingers beneath her chin, bringing her gaze back to his. Slumberous midnight eyes spoke of understanding, even as a sad smile lifted one corner of his mouth.

"Did you not save the most intimate part for me? The part where your body accepted me as your mate?"

Was that why she had never found release with Valère? Because her body performed a duty rather than an act of love? She sent him a grateful, joyous smile. "Yes. I do believe you are right."

"I will not lie, Cora," Guy said. "The thought of you sharing another man's bed, especially Valère's, is like a cancer eating away at my heart."

Her smile dimmed. Her time in Valère's bed had been nothing compared to the time she had spent in Guy's arms.

Because Guy was correct. Her body's acceptance of him

felt like a gifting of her innocence. Not of the thin barrier coveted by men, but of something far more precious.

But what man of honor would want a woman who would give her virginity away for a morsel of information? The question splintered through her mind. No matter how justified her so-called noble reasons for gathering information in France, she could not change how society—she drew in a shuddering breath—or even Guy, would view her behavior.

"But," Guy said, giving her chin a little squeeze as if he had known she'd drifted off into her own thoughts, "know this, Cora deBeau. I shall be your last and only lover from this point forward, as you will be mine."

She stared at him, uncomprehending. "Pardon?"

His lips twitched. "What part of 'mine' did you not understand, sweetheart?"

The ache in her throat sharpened, and tears of profound joy blurred her vision. Could she be so lucky? Could a man of Guy's temperament accept such a breach in social behavior? The gentle look he sent her penetrated the depths of her long-held fears and filled her heart with a warmth that had been absent far too long.

She folded her lips between her teeth to stop their trembling.

Perhaps, just perhaps.

Twenty-One

GUY RAN DOWN THE STAIRS, STUFFING HIS SHIRTTAIL into his breeches as he went. When he woke to find Cora gone, disappointment pulled at his heart, quickly followed by a surge of white-hot panic and red-hot rage.

"Morning, m'lord," the innkeeper said with far more enthusiasm than a person should this early in the day. The man stood at the bottom of the stairs, his plump red face already slicked with sweat from his morning exertions. Although the innkeeper carried a few extra pounds, the retired pugilist's thick neck, massive upper arms, and disfigured ears were testaments to his many rounds in the boxing ring. "Are ye looking for your missus?"

Guy skidded to a halt on the last stair. *Missus?* Something warm slipped into his heart. "As a matter of fact, I am, Mr. Malone."

"You'll find her in the back parlor. She's sharing a cup of tea with her saucy maid." The innkeeper waved to the left of the stairs and then glanced down at Guy's bare feet with a wry smile.

She hadn't left him.

The tension drained from Guy's shoulders, and his breathing resumed its normal rhythm. When he had turned over this morning, expecting to nestle around a warm woman, his hand found nothing but cold sheet.

The realization that Cora had been gone from their bed for some time had sent a stab of dread through his gut. Why had she left the safety of their chamber without telling him of her intention? Had she needed something in the wee hours of the morning and hadn't wanted to disturb him? He sifted through the fog of his memories for an indication as to when she had left their bed. But his last conscious thought was of burying his nose in the crook of her neck, the fresh scent of her recent bath lulling him to sleep.

On top of the anxiety of not knowing her whereabouts sat a thick layer of old uncertainties. This morning's scenario brought back painful memories of his parents' abandonment while he had attended Eton. When it was time for the students to rejoin their parents at the end of each half, one of the schoolmasters, and sometimes the headmaster, would visit Guy and convey the unpleasant news of his parents' inability to return home in time for his term break.

The first year was a disappointment but not surprising. His parents had always followed their pleasures. They traveled the length of Britain, chasing one house party after another and, when they grew bored with local entertainments, they jumped on a ship and headed for more exotic amusements. Having a child, even his father's heir, had never slowed them down or caused them a moment's guilt.

If not for Ethan being within hearing distance of the master's announcement that first year, Guy might have gone mad stalking the corridors of his family's large estate. Instead, he had spent several holidays and summers with the fun-loving deBeaus—until the year before the great tragedy struck the close-knit family. During that long year, the earl's bouts of ill temper had steadily grown, as had the countess's affection for obscurity.

Shrugging off the dark memory, he trudged up the stairs to their chamber to finish dressing. Ten minutes later, when he entered the parlor, he still pondered the question of her disappearance. Spotting Dinks and a veiled Cora at the back of the room, Guy weaved past several of the inn's guests, taking note of each one. A young woman dressed in serviceable linen attended to two young children, who seemed intent on breaking free of her ironclad hold. Three disheveled young men sat in a darkened corner with their heads propped up on their hands.

Guy smiled, remembering many mornings when he and Ethan could barely hold their heads up after a long night of drinking and gambling. As he approached the ladies' table, he nodded to a gray-haired gentleman reading a paper in a booth at Cora's back.

He transferred his attention to Cora's veiled features. "Good morning, ladies."

"Morning, my lord," Dinks responded and stood to leave.

He held out a staying hand. "No need to scurry off. Please stay and break your fast with us."

"Thank you, my lord, but I've already had my fill." She patted her stomach with a contented smile and then glanced at Cora. "I need to check my chamber to make sure our Scrapper has left the place intact, and then I'll start preparations for our trip back to London."

Guy scanned the room again, caution compelling him to lean forward. "We're not going back to London, Dinks." He felt the slice of Cora's blue-green eyes.

Dinks dropped her voice. "Miss Cora?"

A full minute passed before her mistress spoke. "Please ask the innkeeper's daughter to pack a basket for our midday meal."

Understanding her mistress's unspoken request for privacy, Dinks nodded. "Might take me a bit of time. Got to stay clear of Seven Hands Malone and his annoying tendency to plump my bum." She scowled toward the door leading to the common area. "Them days for me are over. He tries that nonsense again, and I'll cut off those sausages he calls fingers and feed them to the stray dogs outside."

Guy leaned toward the maid and said, "If he touches you again, Dinks, you'll bring your grievance to me. Understood?" A peer could get away with bodily harm to another far more easily than a servant. Unfair, but in this instance, he relished an opportunity to defend Cora's steadfast maid.

Her full cheeks reddened. "Pardon, my lord. I shouldn't have spoken so. I know how to deal with the likes of the innkeeper."

"So do I. Promise me, Dinks."

She glanced down at Cora and then nodded. "Thank you, sir." The maid shuffled from foot to foot, seeming hesitant to leave.

"The basket," Cora reminded her.

"Right away. It's just that"—she cleared her throat—"until that Frenchie came and destroyed everything, I rather liked his lordship's pretty estate." She twisted her weathered hands together in an uncharacteristic show of nerves. "The place was cheery, like me mum's home." Her eyes narrowed in thought. "Well, like it was before she took to the gin." Straightening her spine, the maid's face scrunched up as if she were annoyed by her confession. "Never you mind me, Miss Cora. Nothing but the ramblings of an old woman. I'll be getting that basket now."

When Dinks turned to leave, she either winked at him or had something lodged in her eye. He held back a smile. Seems our Dinks missed her calling on the stage. Would her ruse work? Cora's success as a spy was due in large part to her ability to detect small nuances in an individual's speech, tiny details most people missed.

"Your estate is no longer safe, Guy," Cora said softly, interrupting his analysis of the maid's subterfuge. "No matter how pretty or comfy."

Ah, nice try, Dinks.

He settled in the maid's spot in time to receive a heaping plate of eggs, ham, bacon, and three slices of toasted bread brought in by a serving girl.

"There you go, m'lord," the girl said, sliding the plate in front of him. "Your missus didn't know what you'd be in the mood for this morning, so I brought you a little of everything."

Guy peered at the pile of food and wondered how any man could eat so much in one sitting. "This will do quite well. Thank you."

She dipped into a curtsy and scurried away.

He downed a slice of ham and a piece of bacon before addressing Cora's comment. "Correction. My estate is no longer a secret."

She lifted her veil, careful to leave one side hanging low enough to keep the curious at bay. "I fail to understand the distinction."

"The distinction," he said in the same quiet tone while slathering strawberry jam onto his toast, "is that Valère might be aware of our location, but he no longer has the advantage of surprise. I took the liberty of dispatching a message to Somerton to inform him of your safety and to request a half-dozen men posthaste."

"And you think he will be able to honor such a request? It would be rather difficult to amass that number of guards on such short notice."

"Somerton can be quite resourceful when provoked."

She rubbed her thumb along the edge of the table. "You may return to Herrington Park, Guy, but I must press on to London."

He stopped chewing. "Why is that?"

She stared back at him, her gaze defiant yet scored with resignation. *Valère*. He read her intention in the piercing depths of her eyes as clearly as if she had said the Frenchman's name aloud. Never one to sit around, she was obviously ready to take a more offensive position with her tormentor. Not that he blamed her, but they had to give Somerton's plan time to work, which suited Guy fine, because he wanted to keep her away from Valère.

"You're not going anywhere near that bastard again."

"Is that so?"

Dammit. He hadn't meant to be so blunt. It was exactly the wrong approach with his headstrong woman. He knew this, but that knowledge didn't prevent the words from flowing. "Yes."

Her nails brightened to red crescents with the force of her grip on the table. "He must be stopped."

"Rest assured, he will be."

"Somerton cannot find him on his own. Valère's too canny to leave any sort of trail." A dark curtain lowered over her features. "I know him, Guy. I know he hates crowds and loves the slick texture of oysters sliding down his throat. I know he can't survive without servants or in small places for extended periods of time." She squared her shoulders and hardened her gaze. "I know, despite his torture and hatred, he loves me."

The eggs attempted to make their way back up his throat. He swallowed hard and waited a second, not positive he had won the battle. When the burning sensation dwindled to a simmer, he said, "Don't be ridiculous. A man like that has no concept of love."

"You're wrong." Her tone was quiet, confident. "His version might be a damaged and ugly form of the emotion, but he feels it, all the same."

Guy was experiencing an ugly emotion of his own.

Jealousy roared through him like a lion bursting across the plains of Africa to ward off an approaching nomadic male interested in assuming control of his cherished pride.

Like the lion, Guy would crush Valère's throat before ever allowing him near his mate again, and the notion of Cora seeking her gaoler's company conjured equally violent thoughts.

"I can't… permit it, Cora."

"You can't stop it, Guy."

Her calm assurance stood out in stark contrast to the volatile emotions roiling inside him. She seemed to accept this dangerous path as her fate, uncompromising in her belief, unwilling to fight. *Fight?* Guy shook his head. Where the hell did that come from?

Cora had done nothing but fight since the moment she had lost her parents. He knew this, but knowing it did nothing to diffuse his anger. What did he want from her? What was it that he expected her to fight for?

For them.

The words flashed through his mind clear and vibrant and warm. He wanted more from her than a few trusting kisses and a handful of exquisite nights. He wanted her, all of her, but something kept her at arm's length, something besides her quest to stop Valère.

He wished he knew what was going on in that intelligent yet sometimes impetuous mind of hers. Was she trying to protect herself from a perceived future hurt? Or was she protecting him? And if so, from what?

The only thing he truly knew in that moment was if he allowed her to search for Valère, he would lose her.

The loud crackle of paper broke through the silence. Guy glanced behind Cora's shoulder to find the old man battling his newspaper into submission and mumbling something about dim-witted hunters. The disturbance was enough to lessen the tension between them.

She reached across the table and grasped his hand. "I don't want to argue. I simply want to finish my mission. We still don't know who has been leaking information out of the Foreign Office."

He stroked her fingers with his thumb. "And you think Valère's going to just present you with the man's name?"

"Don't be absurd. If I can find Valère, there's a chance Somerton can persuade the information from him."

"And perhaps avail you of a bit of justice, or do you have revenge on your mind?"

She released his hand and sat back. "Do you have any idea of what it's like to be ten years old and unable to avenge your parents' murders?"

"Even if you were older, no one knew the killer's identity."

"I knew enough."

"What do you mean?"

Her lips thinned, and her gaze clouded in remembrance. A few seconds later, awareness flickered, and he saw the half-truth she would deliver before the words ever seeped between her lips. Disappointment slashed his chest.

"A bauble, an accent, a murder scene. Enough information to send me to France, and when Somerton suspected Valère of being responsible for the missing British ships, my life's purpose narrowed down to one man."

An image of Cora soaking in the tub, with an ivory and orange pendant resting between her breasts, flashed through his mind and sent a deep ache to his groin. He briefly wondered if the symbol denoting France's freedom accounted for her "bauble," but something else she said distracted him from that fascinating puzzle.

"I thought you were assigned to Valère to discover the double agent."

"I was."

"Which came first, Cora?" He heard the harshness in his own voice, felt the throbbing at his temple.

Wariness entered her gaze. "Why does the order matter?"

He scanned the room, settling on every inhabitant, every dish, every piece of furniture, in an attempt to give his sickening sense of dread time to abate. It didn't help. His skin flushed with heat, and the bacon beneath his nose turned his stomach.

Ships. The answer to his question was as clear to him as the small freckle in the hollow beneath her ear. The message he had deciphered brought Valère to Somerton's attention and, therefore, Cora's.

Dammit. Dammit. *Dammit.*

He dropped his cutlery in his plate. "Somerton should not have told you about Valère's culpability." He lifted his gaze to hers, hardly able to maintain eye contact. In a thick, soft voice he said, "You were always too curious for your own damn good."

"Somerton acted appropriately." Her tone was stiff, defensive. "I was the lead agent for the region. Keeping intelligence of that magnitude a secret could have gotten me killed."

"Telling you nearly got you killed."

She studied him for a long, careful moment. "But it didn't. Thanks to you."

He closed his eyes. Gratitude was the last thing he deserved. He should tell her about the dispatch. Now was the perfect time. He could never hope to win her full affection with this kind of deception between them.

His eyelids were heavy, oddly sluggish when he lifted them. "Cora, I—" He swallowed back the thick knot clogging his throat. The confession was there, right on the tip of his tongue. *If not for me, you would never have spent time in Valère's dungeon.* She would be upset, at first. Maybe even hate him. But he could win her over, as he always had. She knew him well enough to understand that he would never intentionally hurt her. *Say it, Helsford!* "Cora, I-I almost left you." *Bloody coward*.

"Pardon?"

"In the dungeon. I came close to leaving you behind." Every word he said was the truth, but nothing more than a skirt to hide behind. He had missed his opportunity, the ideal time to remove this hidden barrier. Now he must prepare himself for the ultimate sacrifice of losing her. Forever. "We were there to retrieve a female spy, the Raven. Spread out as you were on that bloody table, with shorn hair, filthy limbs, and a swollen face, I thought you were a boy."

"Yet you still saved me."

He leaned forward, humiliation packing his voice with an uncalled-for roughness. "Stop making me sound like a goddamned hero. I'm the furthest thing from it."

"Perhaps in your mind." She reached up to pull the filmy veil down, but before she did, Guy caught the shimmer of tears in her beautiful eyes. "In my heart, you shall always be my savior."

Before he could say a word, a new voice intruded. "There now, Miss Cora." Dinks padded to their table. "The innkeeper's daughter packed a right big basket for our trip back to——?"

"Herrington Park," Cora finished.

Guy's heart lurched at her capitulation. Despite all the warning bells sounding in his head, he asked, "You're sure?"

She gathered her gloves and reticule, and then stood. "Yes."

He made to join her, but she placed a restraining hand on his shoulder. Her fingers felt confident and calm. Not at all like the mass of earthquakes ricocheting through his body.

"One more thing." She bent forward so only he could hear. "Did you tell the innkeeper that I was your wife?"

"No." He hated that damned veil, wished he could see her expression.

"Then why are the Malones referring to me as your 'missus'?"

"Might have something to do with my carrying you through the inn and sleeping in your room." God, he would kill to go back to that moment.

She nodded and straightened. "Yes, of course, that would make sense."

"Does it bother you?" Guy cursed his idiocy. Why ask a question whose answer might carve a section from his heart?

Her silence drew the first cut.

"Does it?" he pressed.

"I don't know how to answer such a question," she said in a low tone. "I have not contemplated marriage to any man."

He slid his hand over and curled his fingers around hers. They were cold now, trembling. "Do you find the idea distasteful, Cora?"

"No."

"Then why haven't you ever considered it?" He rubbed warmth back into her fingers. "I thought all females dreamed about being swept off their feet by a handsome prince and living happily ever after."

By the tilt of her head, she appeared to be staring at their entwined fingers. She said nothing for several seconds.

"No, Guy." She gently disengaged her hand. "Not all girls have the luxury of believing they will have a happily ever after. I'll meet you at the carriage in ten minutes."

He reached for her. "Cora—"

She swept out of the room, leaving him with his

barely touched plate of breakfast and a gut full of regret. Dinks sent him an unreadable look before following her mistress, an enormous basket laden with food hanging from her capable arm.

Guy shoved the plate away, wondering, if she ever *had* dreamed of a happily ever after, whom she would have picked for her handsome prince.

His heart skipped a beat when he imagined himself in the role. He might not be princely material, not after the grief he had caused her, but he could make sure she got her happy ending. She deserved so much more—*like the truth, you idiot*—but he would begin by removing Valère from her life.

I'll meet you at the carriage in ten minutes. An eternity.

To take his mind off the slow tick of time, Guy pulled a folded piece of paper from his coat pocket and smoothed it against the table. The cipher was never far from his thoughts. Such was the case any time he began a new assignment. Number and letter combinations constantly flowed through his mind until repetitions became apparent and patterns surfaced.

For certain, the message was short, decisive, and likely deadly, as indicated by the two blocks of numbers. Two words. One command.

78325026   2722153134012223

As with any cipher, he searched for the most common letter arrangements like *th*, *ing*, *er*, and a few others. When they reached the house, he would have to start graphing different possibilities. The code was far too complicated to unravel with mental willpower alone.

The crackle of paper struck the air. Guy looked up to see the older gentleman folding the daily news in half before tossing it on the table.

Turning, the gentleman caught Guy's eye and rasped, "Good morning."

Guy kept his greeting short, not interested in conversation. "Sir." He slid the missive back in his coat pocket.

With considerable effort, the gentleman levered himself from the bench. "The way these old bones are creaking, I daresay it's going to rain today," the stranger said. "Do you have far to travel?"

"A fair day's ride, sir."

"You and your lady wife take special care, then. One can never tell what perils await us when traveling nowadays, especially with those daft, careless hunters running about."

Guy's gaze narrowed. Something about the man's tone struck a discordant note with him. "Thank you for the warning, sir."

He studied the old man's features, but he saw nothing out of the ordinary except a bad haircut and the frailty of a man beyond his prime. He released an irritated breath. He was now seeing threats where none existed. "We shall stay extra vigilant."

The gentleman tipped his hat and shuffled out of the common room and labored down the two steps leading to the inn's courtyard. His manservant assisted him into the waiting carriage and shut the door behind them after he settled a blanket across his master's legs.

"Monsieur, did you learn their direction?" the gentleman's manservant asked.

The old man's stooped shoulders gradually rose to their full, broad width, his droopy eyes turned to steel cold awareness, and his slackened lips lifted into a feral smile.

"*Oui.*" Valère kept his eye on the inn's front entrance. "They are headed back to his country estate."

"The other will not follow."

"No."

What Marcel lacked in birthright, he made up for with his keen mind. The manservant's talent for detecting artifice made him an indispensable interrogator, and his ability to anticipate his master's next step saved Valère a great deal of time and inconvenience.

"Lord Helsford's decision displeases me. However, if our positions were reversed, it is exactly what I would do."

Marcel readjusted his low-brimmed hat. "Monsieur, shall we follow them or travel on to our final destination?"

"A moment."

Cora finally emerged from the inn, carrying a burgundy and gold portmanteau. Fury and desire wiped away his admiration of her lover's strategic acumen.

When he had overheard her discussing marriage with the earl, he'd had to restrain himself from turning around and plunging a knife into the witch's black heart. She was lucky he had sensed discord between them. Otherwise, he would have shot Helsford between the eyes and spirited her away. If not for the ensuing manhunt, the rash action would have perhaps enabled him to reach his goal more expeditiously but with far less stealth. Or enjoyment.

When Cora stepped into her carriage, Valère signaled his readiness to move on. He waited until Witney was a speck on the horizon before tearing off the itchy gray wig and accepting a damp cloth from Marcel to remove the actors' face paint he had used to age himself. He gloried in the fact that he had sat within striking distance of Cora, close enough to catch the faint whiff of her floral scent, and she had remained oblivious to his presence.

A surge of power pulsed through his body, replacing the fury. He liked holding her fate in his hands, knowing she lived by his beneficence alone. God was not the only one who had control over life and death. His chest expanded upon envisioning his emperor's pride once he learned of Valère's success. Napoleon's generosity would know no bounds, and Valère's ruthless ambitions would finally be realized.

He reached for the jasmine-scented handkerchief resting in his pocket, wanting to share this pivotal moment with Cora, but his manservant's presence stopped him. "I believe the driver requires your assistance."

Marcel peered at the passing landscape. "Of course, monsieur."

Valère watched his obedient manservant open the door and gracefully maneuver to the top of the moving carriage, shutting the door behind him. When Valère was alone, he pulled the ruffled handkerchief from his coat pocket and laid it unopened on his thigh.

A faint buzz of anticipation started low in his stomach. He looked forward to their next meeting, could imagine it already. Having Cora under his control again released feelings of ungovernable desire. Only she knew how to tame the raging beast within. The one that screamed for domination; the one that lashed out if a woman failed to feed his secret need. Nothing gave him greater release than being on the receiving end of a confident woman's riding crop.

He flinched and then shuddered with ecstasy, as if feeling the first slap of leather.

The sable curl beneath his finger felt like the finest silk from the Orient. He couldn't wait for her hair to regain its full glory, so he could see it draped around her flushed face and straining breasts. The scar on her temple and the brand on her thighs would take their love play to extraordinarily new heights.

Once he had completed his charge, he would see exactly how high they could fly.

Twenty-Two

A FEW DAYS LATER, SLEEPY CONTENTMENT ENFOLDED Cora as she lazed against one of Herrington Park's enormous trees. The rhythmic creak of its branches in the breeze lulled her into a deep well of blissful oblivion.

Finally.

Ever since she had fallen asleep in Guy's arms at the inn, sleep had come more easily. She was still plagued with nightmares but could generally get several hours' rest despite them.

She scratched between Scrapper's shoulders, prompting him to wiggle around and hang from her arm like an Amazonian sloth—only sloths did not use their long nails as tiny weapons of destruction. Cora clenched her teeth and disengaged her arm from the kitten's painful hold. The tiny dents left in her skin were a small price to pay for escaping Guy's persistent attentions.

"He watches me constantly, Scrap." The kitten cocked his head as if comprehending her words. "Everywhere I turn, his eyes follow me."

After their harsh words at the inn, she had avoided him whenever possible. The possibility of discussing her marital prospects—or lack of—was not a topic she wished to broach with him again.

She could blame only herself for arousing his curiosity.

If she had stopped to think for a moment, it would have been obvious to her why the innkeeper and his daughter thought they were married. Their reference to her as his "missus" had caught her off guard. The title had felt foreign, yet its use had awakened a long-abandoned dream, catching her unawares.

Not even after their mind-shattering lovemaking at the Golden Duck and his insistence that she would never attend another man's bed but his, had marriage entered her mind. She would not dare allow her thoughts to travel that far. The most she had hoped for was Guy's love and affection—in whatever form he could share it. His name was far too much to hope for, but that did not stop her female need to now test it on her tongue.

"Lady Helsford. Countess Helsford. Cora Trevelyan." She enjoyed the lyrical quality of the syllables twining together to form each grouping. If she'd had a quill and paper handy, she might have resorted to a more visual form of disillusionment.

After they had made love at the inn, she had forced herself to leave their bed. She had needed time to think and could not do that with the drugging effects of his sandalwood scent and musky, sleep-warmed skin taunting her to stay.

The few hours of contemplation away from him had helped her to see past the immediate needs of her body. As much as she adored him, she realized how their love-making had unbearably complicated their situation. She could not be his mistress and share him with a wife. Even the thought of such an arrangement caused her stomach to churn. And if Guy took it into his gentlemanly head to ask for her hand in marriage, she would refuse him. She must, because being the object of his social ruin would place an intolerable strain on her, and it would eventually be the death of their marriage.

She tickled beneath the kitten's chin, and he promptly sank his razor-sharp teeth into her fingertip. "The *ton* would eat him alive," she said, tugging her finger away. "They have a knack for sniffing out the sordid areas of one's past. If they ever learned of my activities in France, Guy would most assuredly suffer for it, as would any of our children." And they would find out. It wasn't as if she had gadded about Paris under an assumed name. Her exploits would soon follow her to London. She had no doubt. "I won't let him suffer for my decisions. He deserves so much better than a life of mockery."

Since they had arrived at Herrington Park, Guy's eyes and tone of voice had remained seductively warm, but his body withdrew into cool formality. He kept himself near but at a discreet distance, touching her only when necessary. While he physically pulled away from her, she was more drawn to him than ever, like a sweet pea vine reaching for the support of its trellis.

She knew her behavior at the inn's breakfast table confused him, but she simply couldn't bring herself to care. Her damaged body and worry for her brother had sapped all her strength. She didn't have the fortitude to explain the obvious to him. He would eventually figure out why marriage was dead to her. Her fingers pressed against both of her eyelids to rub the sting away.

"God, I hate this," she swore beneath her breath. Hated this feeling of helplessness. Of hopelessness. She had always been strong, even before she had sailed to France. This *yearning* to lean on Guy battled viciously with her drive for self-reliance.

She buried her face in Scrapper's soft fur. On one level, Guy's protectiveness drove her to fits of temper, and on another level—one where she kept her deepest desires hidden—he exhilarated her. That's why she had requested a few hours to herself each morning after returning to the country. She needed to reestablish her independence, and she couldn't do that with Guy constantly underfoot.

Scrapper's little body vibrated with happiness, making her smile. She lifted her head, and her gaze drifted around the sun-dappled glade. She hadn't wanted to return to Herrington Park. She would rather be in London, helping Somerton find Ethan, instead of in the country doing nothing but strolling and sleeping and thinking. Always thinking. But she was glad to return to the tranquility of this hidden paradise. It was the perfect spot to perform her Tai Chi each morning.

She glimpsed her servants' bobbing heads in the distance. While keeping a keen eye on her, they collected greens and berries for their luncheon salad. Bingham's low grumblings and Dinks's snappish retorts carried across the distance of the small lake. A wave of nostalgia gripped her insides, causing her nose and eyes to sting.

She would never have survived France without them. Never. Their unflagging loyalty, strength, and friendship had kept her motivated and focused on her one true goal: finding the man who murdered her parents.

Horrific scenes from that fateful night flashed before her eyes. Scenes that over a decade later had the ability to slice open her chest, exposing her terror, her mortification, her shame. She curled her fingers into Scrapper's soft fur.

"Mrrreow."

The kitten's cry of distress forced her to ease her grip. "Sorry, Scrap." She rubbed along his tiny back, hoping to soothe any hurt she had caused, but tension still thrummed through his quivering body.

Then his claws pierced the linen covering her left breast, hooking into her tender flesh. She sucked in a breath and tried to disengage his hold. "Scrapper, what's wrong—?"

"Mrrreow!" He hissed and made to bolt. She caught him by the scruff of his neck and pressed him against her body.

"What's the matter?" She cradled his small head and noticed his big green eyes were almost entirely black... and they were focused on something beyond her shoulder.

Like the kitten's stinging claws, dread curled around her heart, squeezing away the last of her contentment.

"Your kitten doesn't appear to like me, *mon coeur.*"

Cora's pulse stuttered to a halt. She reached for her skirt pocket, but Valère's gun barrel rammed into the pit of her arm, stopping her cold. A killing shot, one that would rip her life's blood out of her body in a matter of minutes.

"If you scream, my men will cut down your servants before you can catch your next breath," Valère said. "Keep your hands wrapped around that gray vermin where I can see them, and leave them there. Understood?"

She glanced at Dinks and Bingham, finding no discernible threat near them. The fact that she had missed Valère's approach forced her to keep her mouth shut and her senses open.

She nodded.

"Good. Now rest your head against the tree and close your eyes."

No. A cold sweat coated Cora's palms.

"Are you testing me, Cora?"

The same helplessness she had experienced in his dungeon pervaded her body now. Her strong-willed defiance had bought her time while imprisoned, where she was alone, but that tactic would not work in this instance.

She peered at her friends, knowing they would

observe only what Valère wanted them to see—their mistress resting beneath a large tree.

Valère had discovered her weakness for her servants and was now using them to his advantage. Another failure on her part. Something else to regret.

"Bastard."

"On occasion. Now do as I say."

Cora eased her head back. No matter how hard she tried to see Valère out of the corner of her eye, she couldn't. The strange condition of conversing with a bodiless voice heightened her unease. There was no way to judge his mood or his next action. No way to defend herself.

Guy's image flitted through her mind. He would blame himself for what was to come, believing he shouldn't have left her in the care of others. He wouldn't understand that he couldn't be with her every minute of every day, no matter how hard he tried.

Her enemy would always find that one moment, that fragment of a second that would distract her protector, pulling him away.

Valère jabbed her with the muzzle of his gun. "Do not test me, *ma chère*."

Releasing an unsteady breath, she closed her eyes and waited for the blow.

Instead, he slid the gun barrel along the side of her breast. "Good girl." His breath fanned over her neck as he spoke. "Speaking of obedience, why do you keep that mewling footman around? The boy betrayed you."

"You kidnapped his sister," Cora said. "He had few options."

"He could have told you the truth. Does he not love you as he loves his sister?"

Disappointment pierced her heart, tightening the walls of her chest. She knew he baited her, but the wound was still fresh, and her affection for Jack spanned many years. "And risk losing the only family he has left? You are a cold-blooded bastard, Valère."

The barrel dug into her ribs, and Cora gritted her teeth, wishing she hadn't forsaken her stays since coming to the country. "What do you want? Why not kill me and be done with it?"

He laughed low. "I will. However, right now, I must keep you alive for my emperor. Once he has no further use of you and I have sated my own desires, I will make a gift of you to Marcel. What do you think of my plan?"

"Sounds like you're still relying on your servants to do your dirty work."

Cora braced herself for another vicious thrust, but he replaced his gun with something sharp. Sharp enough to slice through the fabric of her dress and pierce the tender skin of her lower back. She recoiled, but the motion was halted by four sets of barbed feline claws embedding themselves in her upper arm. She bit her lip against the pain while she eased Scrapper's claws from her skin.

"Sit back," he demanded. "You think to amuse yourself at my expense, *ma chère?*"

Calming her wild breaths, she resumed her position against the tree.

"Because of you, my superiors now question my loyalty to the emperor. *Mine.*" He punctuated the word with the point of the knife. "One of his most loyal of subjects. My appointment as *Maréchal de France* is all but gone, thanks to you."

"Marshal of France?" Cora snorted. "Where is your army, Valère? Only the finest military men are appointed to such a prestigious position."

"My army surrounds you." The blade burrowed deeper into her back, slicing through flesh. "Can you not feel their presence?" She gritted her teeth and arched her spine.

She wouldn't scream, wouldn't cry out. If she did, Dinks and Bingham were as good as dead. Much to her disgrace, she couldn't stop her breaths from bellowing through her nostrils in her bid to remain quiet. Where were Somerton's men?

"I will collect my apology," he continued in a lethal voice, "while you are taking me into your body."

A violent tremor shook her core. "Never."

"You think not?" Valère's sudden burst of movement and the feel of his fingers wrapping around her neck triggered years of disciplined training.

She swept around and threw the only weapon she had readily at hand—right into his arrogant face.

Scrapper's claws sank into Valère's flesh, piercing his cheeks and throat. "Ahhh!" He grabbed the kitten by the neck and made to yank him away, but Scrapper refused to release the Frenchman and grasped for a better hold, connecting with Valère's right eye.

"*Fils de pute!*" Valère pried the kitten's front paws off and flung him away with a vicious twist of his wrist.

Cora fumbled for the knife in her skirt pocket, staring at the spot where Scrapper's little gray body disappeared inside a cluster of leaves and spindly branches. One lone yellow leaf dangled above the dark opening. She couldn't see a single gray hair.

In the distance, she heard a feminine scream and a baritone yell, and then nothing. *Dinks. Bingham.* Oh, God.

Valère swiped his coat sleeve over the lines of blood trickling down his face; his right eye squeezed shut. "English whore." He scanned the ground around them. "I'm going to rip the skin from your bones and feed it to my men."

Ignoring his threat, she crouched into a battle stance,

her knife extended. To her astonishment, Valère appeared to have lost his weapons during his scuffle with Scrapper.

Blood pumped more richly through her veins, for her odds of surviving this encounter improved tenfold, a hundredfold if she counted his half-blind status.

At least that was the case until she heard the swoosh of low-hanging branches and the pounding of feet off to her left, reminding her that Valère wasn't the only threat lurking in the woods. Cocking her head slightly to the side, she bided her time.

"Lose something, Valère?" Scrapper had not only gouged holes in the Frenchman's eye, he had shredded the man's face in several places. Cora fought the impulse to touch the scar near her temple.

Thank you, Scrap.

Another disturbance behind her, closer now. She couldn't tell how many were approaching, but the sickening smile stretching across Valère's mouth didn't bode well.

Five.

Four.

"Not for long," he said.

Sweat trickled down the center of her back, joining the growing patch of blood. A wave of light-headedness struck her, and she drew in a deep breath to conquer its effect.

Three.

Two.

The whir of air nearby propelled her into action. She spun, slashing her blade against the back of the man's knee and followed through with a jab to his temple with the heel of her hand. He fell to the ground, roaring in agony.

She barely had time to take a breath before she heard another hum of air. This time, she didn't react fast enough. The club struck against her lower back and glanced off her contused scalp. The pain was incredible, and her sight narrowed to tiny pinpricks of light. She fell to her knees, dazed and barely able to catch her breath. She blinked, trying to regain her senses. Bile roiled in her stomach and threatened to rise into her throat.

Marcel walked around her as if he were a gladiator in the great Coliseum, sizing up his foe for the killing blow.

Where was Valère? She needed to scan the area, but her muscles refused to cooperate.

"Knock her out." Valère said from behind her. "We must be away."

"With pleasure, monsieur." When Marcel drew back his arm, Cora willed her shoulder to tuck and her body to roll. But neither followed her command. Her body seemed disconnected from her head, swaying in the breeze like a bedsheet draped across a line. All she could do was stare as Marcel's fist slammed down toward her temple.

Then a shot rang out, and the henchman collapsed beside her on one knee before his fist connected. He held his shoulder, panting from the pain of the bullet's impact. His eyes bore into hers with such malice that she felt their evil across the short distance separating them.

"Stop the earl," Valère said to someone she couldn't see. "You two, help my man and the other."

"Are we not bringing her, monsieur?"

"Not this time."

Marcel was lifted away by his compatriots, and they disappeared from view.

Cora found the equilibrium to turn and look behind her. Valère stood at the edge of the woods. The sight of him sickened her. There were so many things she wanted to say to him, rage at him. He had not only abused her body, but he also tortured her soul. At that moment, however, her fear for Guy and her servants and the awful image of Scrapper's tiny body flying through the air plagued her mind far more than words of retribution.

"Very nice, little spy." He stared at her almost calmly in the face of the chaos around them. "Perhaps your lover won't be around to save you next time."

Still disoriented, she swiveled back to locate Guy, but could see nothing beyond the green foliage. When she tried to stand, her knees buckled like a newborn calf's.

"I fear Marcel hit you too hard," Valère mused. "Before I leave, *mon coeur*, I wonder if you would be so kind as to answer something for me."

Cora slid her hand into her skirt pocket.

"Is your brother as terrified of rats as you?"

His not-so-gentle reminder of Ethan's circumstance was more than her fractured mind could handle. She released an agonized wail that sent birds rushing from treetops. "*What have you done with him, you bastard?*"

A cacophony of sound crashed through the brush not far away. "Cora!" Guy called.

Valère's gaze flicked behind her then back. "I will keep him safe for you, Raven. Come to me when I call." He stepped into the woods.

"No, take me now," she demanded, stumbling to her feet.

"Too late, little spy." A burst of wind carried his laughing reply to her ears.

His threat to Ethan still rang in her ears. "You're not going anywhere." Her hand tightened on the knife, and she moved forward, intending to protect her brother from this monster.

"No!" She tripped, and her knife went flying from her grasp.

"Cora," Guy said again, pulling her upright and shielding her with his body.

Cora strained against his hold, at once relieved and

irritated to be in Guy's arms. "I'm fine. Let me go." She stared into the woods, terror crushing her heart. *Ethan. Dear God, what have I done?*

"In a moment." Guy rubbed soothing circles on her back. "Where are the damned guards?"

Disheveled and panting, Bingham broke through the underbrush. Blood smeared one side of his face. "Bastards are gone, m'lord." He ducked his head. "Pardon, Miss Cora."

"Dammit," Guy fumed. "How is this happening?"

"Somerton suspects the French got to someone in the Foreign Office."

"Indeed." His hold around her tightened. "Still doesn't explain how four guards disappear in the middle of skirmish. How the hell could they *all* turn tail?"

"I must check on Bingham." Cora pushed out of Guy's arms. She yearned to take off after Valère, but one look at Guy's face told her he was ready for such an attempt.

She spread her hands out to the side to check her balance before approaching the coachman. "Let me see." She turned his grizzled head from side to side, ensuring he sustained nothing more than the slash to his skull. "Looks like you'll live. Dinks?" she asked around a lump of guilt. She pulled a handkerchief from her sleeve and pressed it to the open wound on his head.

"She's fine." He wiped blood from the corner of his eye. "Take more than a clubbing to hold that harridan down. She set off to find Jack and the other guards." A note of admiration edged his gruff words.

Knowing her friends were safe sent a wave of relief rushing into her limbs. She coiled her fingers into a taut fist to stop their trembling.

"You're going to need a few stitches, Bingham. I'll see if Dinks is up for the task."

He stiffened. "I'll not let that woman within a league of my wound."

"She has a much better hand for needlework than I, old friend."

"No need to worry about marring this mug, Miss Cora. It didn't start out pretty, so there ain't no sense in worrying about it ending pretty."

Cora squeezed her coachman's brawny hand, her mind shifting to Scrapper. She hadn't liked the lifeless quality to his body when he tumbled through the air.

"Let's get you inside," Guy said. "I don't like having you out in the open like this. Valère or one of his men might double back."

She understood Guy's concern, but she also knew Valère was long gone. *Come to me when I call.* The bastard knew what the wait would do to her. He knew his taunting words about rats would slam her back into a hell of his making.

"He's gone," she said simply. "I must find S-scrap." Her throat closed around the kitten's name. The thought that he might be dead—by her hand—was tearing at her chest.

On feet heavy with dread, she strode toward the cluster of bushes that held Scrapper, with Guy at her side. She focused on the lone yellow leaf dangling from an otherwise bare limb. As she watched, the dying leaf broke free and drifted to the ground, joining the fallen remains of its brethren.

The air inside her lungs strained for release, and her heart pounded at a jarring rate. The truly alarming realization was the utter absence of warmth in her body, inside and out. Her limbs felt frozen and brittle, ready to shatter at the slightest provocation.

"Cora, allow me," Guy urged.

"No." She could manage no more, for this was her burden to bear.

As she knelt near the dark hollow, blocked by briars and spindly branches, images of Scrapper attacking Guy's boots, swiping the quill, and cradling her face with his tiny paws pelted her mind. Like all those close to her, Scrapper was a valiant warrior. Brave, fierce, and protective. And in a few short days, she had grown to love the little ankle-biter, as she did all her warriors. *Please, dear Lord, don't take him, too.*

The ache in her throat grew so sharp she couldn't breathe. By the time she peeled back the branches to see within, all thought, all feeling, had withered away with the sure knowledge that she had killed her kitten.

Fighting a wave of dizziness, she bent low to peer into the gloomy interior of the underbrush and saw the kitten's big green eyes staring back.

Tears clogged her throat, and her vision blurred. "Hello, Scrap." She peered up at Guy, overwhelmed with relief. "He's alive. I didn't kill him."

"Of course you didn't." Guy kissed her forehead. "Now move aside, sweetheart, so I can pull him free."

She shifted to the side, and Guy reached in. And froze.

He sat back on his heels, not looking at her, and Cora felt her joy splinter. Then Guy settled his empathetic gaze on her briefly before bellowing, "Bingham."

"Yes, sir."

"Take your mistress to the house."

The coachman grasped Cora's arm. "Come with me, Miss Cora."

She shrugged him off. "What's wrong?" she asked. "Why aren't you pulling him out of that hole?"

Guy's voice was harsh. "Go with Bingham, Cora. I'll see to Scrapper."

"No! He's alive. I saw him staring at me." She tried to shove Guy away, but it was like pushing against the side of a mountain. "Move."

"He's gone, Cora. There's no need to subject yourself to the sight."

"You're wrong." Panic seized her body, and she dug the pendant from her bodice and clutched it in her fist. She needed to see Scrapper, needed to show Guy the kitten was simply injured. Not dead. Not like her mama and papa.

Guy glanced behind her. "Get. Her. Out of here."

Strong hands grasped her shoulders and lifted her into a standing position. "No, Bingham. Let me go. I must see him." Somehow she broke free of the coachman's iron clasp, and she threw her body into Guy's, catching him by surprise.

"Cora, no!"

Her hands burrowed into the darkness until her fingers wrapped around the kitten's reassuringly warm body. She pulled him onto her lap and smiled when Scrapper's gaze locked with hers. "You see?" She glanced at Guy, certain he would share in her elation, but his face was blank, emotionless.

The kitten moved, drawing away her attention. Cora stared in horror as his head cocked back at an unnatural angle, and his sightless eyes stared into the distance. Sightless. Not staring, but sightless.

For the second time in the span of a quarter hour, Cora lost her mind. "No. No. Noooo!" She closed her eyes and clamped her hands over her ears to block the voices and images screeching through her skull. The madness moved from her head and channeled its way into her chest, squeezing with all its might. "Not Scrapper, too."

A yawning white tunnel formed in her mind's eye, bright and swirling, beckoning her inside. Blood drained from her face, and her fingers turned to ice. The tunnel started to close, swirled tighter until her eyes strained to see it. She swayed, feeling the blackness closing in on her. "Oh, Scrap. I'm so sorry. So, so sorry for failing you, too."

Someone removed the small body from her lap as she rocked back and forth in her grief. Then warm arms pulled her into a solid chest, bringing her back from the edge of darkness. Distantly, she recognized Guy's unique scent. He lifted her onto his lap and resumed the gentle rocking. "Cora." His voice cracked. "You did not cause this, sweetheart."

"I used him as a weapon, Guy. If not me, who? Who else would do such a disgusting thing?"

He shook her. Hard.

"Valère killed Scrapper. No one else. Certainly not you."

"You don't understand," she cried.

He clamped his hands around her jaw and shoved his face to within inches of hers. "I understand more than you know. When we're fighting for our lives, we act on instinct. Would you do anything different, Cora? If you could turn back time to the second Valère attacked you, would you act in any other way?"

"Yes," she said.

"Really?" Guy prodded. "How would you change your reaction to the threat? In that moment, when your mind recognized the danger and your training took control, how would you deflect Valère's assault?"

She could hear the panic in her sharp, staccato breaths. Desperately, she searched for an alternative reaction, something that would save both her and the kitten. She went through scheme after scheme, discarding each one. "My mind is too muddled to think right now. There must be—"

"No there mustn't." His voice was calmer, reassuring. "Your training guided you down the correct path. If you hadn't followed, we would be mourning your death rather than the kitten's."

She released a slow, defeated breath. Now that the

first rush of emotions had withered to a trickle, her head reminded her of the knock it had taken. Again. Rubbing her temples, she said, "May we go inside?"

"Of course."

When she made to rise, Guy's arms tightened and he rose with her in one smooth movement. She didn't know if he was right or wrong about what she had done. All she could think about was closing her eyes and not opening them again for at least a sennight.

"Little mite," Dinks said, rushing up to them. Her hair stuck out at various angles and contained bits of leaves and twigs. "Are you injured?"

"No, Dinks." She snuggled deeper into Guy's arms. "Did you hear about Scrap?"

Matching tears welled in the older woman's eyes. "Yes. Just spoke to the old goat. We'll give him a proper burial, we will."

"Thank you."

"Did the wee rascal get in a good swipe?"

A tear spilled over Cora's cheek when she smiled. "More than a swipe, Dinks."

Delight shined in the maid's eyes. "That's my boy. How much more?"

"Skewered his right eye."

Dinks squealed, and Cora glanced up to see Guy's smile. Although the terrible guilt remained, warmth flooded her chest.

Guy started toward the house. "Put on some hot water, will you, Dinks?"

"Right away, sir."

"Dinks?" Cora called over Guy's shoulder.

"Yes, Miss Cora."

"Bingham's head needs stitching. Will you see to it?"

A short pause. "I'll tend the old goat, don't you worry none."

"And Dinks?"

"I promise not to poke him too hard."

Cora shared a look with Guy. "That's not what I wanted, but please do." She swallowed. "Don't bury Scrapper without me."

"Are you sure, little mite?"

"Never more so."

Guy kissed the top of her head. "Rest first, sweetheart."

Cora didn't think she would ever rest again. Her mind sped through recent events with an almost inhuman speed. However, somewhere between the front lawn and the grand staircase, her body began to relax and her thoughts slowed. With Guy's arms supporting her and his scent surrounding her, she began to drift into slumber before her head ever touched the bed.

Twenty-Three

WHEN HE HEARD A TENTATIVE KNOCK ON HIS bedchamber door, Guy paused in the act of removing his stockings. Having just extracted his timepiece from the pocket of his discarded waistcoat, he knew it was a few minutes before eleven. To have a visitor at such a late hour generally meant the deliverance of unpleasant news or the appearance of a delectable evening companion. Since Cora was presently fighting a horrible megrim in her room, Guy steeled himself for the disagreeable news.

Glancing down at his untucked shirt, bare feet, and loose hair, he briefly considered throwing on his silk banyan but discarded the notion. He wasn't feeling particularly civilized at the moment and, besides, it was much too warm to wear the voluminous dressing gown. He braced his left hand on the door frame and opened the door wide. "Yes?"

Cora stood on the other side, looking lost and heartbreakingly frail in her wispy cream nightdress and with her sleep-rumpled hair. His heart dipped into his stomach. "What's wrong, sweetheart?"

"Am I disturbing you?" She took in his dishabille with a mixture of chagrin and avid interest. "Please tell me if I am… I don't wish to bother you, but I—"

He grasped her hand and drew her inside. "Nonsense. How is your head?"

Guy's chest expanded at her slow response. From the way her gaze stayed affixed below his chin, he did not think she minded his current state of dishabille. When awareness softened her features, he was suddenly glad he did not take the time to draw on his banyan.

Closing the door, he led her to one of the two high-backed chairs curling around the low-burning fire. Instead of sitting anxiously on the edge, she sank into the depths of the soft cushions and folded her legs to the side. She looked so young and vulnerable in that moment. He liked the fact that she felt so at ease with him. It was hard to believe this was the same woman who had spent three years bedeviling the French with her wit, beauty, and keen observational skills. Her ability to adapt to her ever-changing circumstance was nothing short of remarkable.

She brushed her fingers over her forehead and along her temple. "Down to a dull ache. Thank you for asking."

"Dinks showed me how to make her megrim concoction," he said. "Shall I mix you another dose?" As always, the maid's special brews contained a healthy measure of brandy.

She shook her head. "I'm tired of sleeping and do not wish to have a fuzzy head any longer."

The subdued quality of her voice unnerved him. He knew how to deal with her anger, her fear, and even her stubbornness. But the hint of defeat he heard slipping between syllables was a sentiment he knew not how to manage.

An uncomfortable feeling of helplessness kept him silent and watchful. He studied her like a naturalist studies the mating rituals of a puffin. But she gave no sign or provided any clue as to how he could help her cope with her most recent setback. He realized then that it had always been thus with Cora. At an early age, she had experienced the staggering loss of her parents, and later, the loss of a young lady's come-out ball. But she had not allowed those events to destroy her, although her parents' murders had come close.

The scene of Cora digging a small grave for Scrapper seared through his mind. Although the somber ceremony had occurred several hours ago, the knot in his gut seemed as tight as ever. Other than accepting a shovel from Bingham, Cora had refused all other offers of help. So her servants and he had stood quietly by while she labored over the hole, sweating and growing weaker by the moment. They had all breathed a collective sigh of relief when the last shovel of dirt was carefully spread on top of the small grave.

Guy did not know what had possessed him to reach down and remove his boot tassels. When he had handed them to Cora to place on the grave, she had given him a grateful, watery smile before securing them with a small stone at the head of the mound. He still felt foolish about the gesture, especially after recalling Bingham's wide-eyed stare. But Cora seemed to take comfort from the pathetic little headstone, which, in turn, brought him contentment.

He kept his voice gentle. "Did you have a particular purpose for coming to see me?"

She leaned her head back against the chair. "Not really. I just needed not to be alone anymore."

Guy's muscles lost some of their tension. "So you came to see me." Perhaps redirecting her thoughts into more comfortable territory—at least for him—would remove the sadness from her blue-green eyes. "Why not Dinks?"

"She loved Scrapper as much as I." Her lips twitched the slightest bit. "One hopes she is similarly engaged."

Guy raised a brow. "With whom?"

"Is it not obvious?"

"Apparently not," he mused, not really liking the images circulating around his mind. There were some areas one simply did not tread. "Bingham seems the only prospect, but it can't be him."

"And why is that?" Her mouth definitely quirked then.

"Come now," he said, all amusement gone. "You can't be serious. The two can barely tolerate breathing the same air. I've never even heard of half the names Dinks flings at Bingham's head."

"Guy, you astonish me." She tugged her rose-colored shawl more securely around her shoulders. "I would have thought a worldly man such as yourself would recognize love play."

Love play? "Evidently, I'm not that worldly."

The low chuckle she emitted strummed across his heart like a well-tuned harp. Affable silence followed while they shared a conspiratorial smile, a silent communication they had conferred on one another many times over the years while dealing with Ethan's high-strung antics. However, this time, their amusement faded into pulsing awareness.

"Do you ever wonder what our lives would be like had we not joined the Nexus?" Cora asked softly.

Guy reclined back in his chair, matching Cora's restful pose, though his body was anything but relaxed. A peculiar feeling of anticipation reverberated beneath his skin, heightening all of his senses. The Nexus was the conduit for her life's ambition. The secret unit had given her the means to locate the man who had murdered her parents. For nearly a decade, she had trained for this one purpose. Somerton, and his band of anonymous spies, represented the last hope of a grieving girl's desire for justice.

For her to now question that choice was staggering.

And it also reminded him of a situation he very much wished to forget, but he knew he could not until Cora understood the full story behind her captivity. The thought soured his stomach. Her pensive mood did not seem conducive to such confessions, though. At least that is what he told himself. He would find the right moment. Soon.

Returning to her question, he settled on a rather blurry version of the truth. "No, not really." His involvement in the Nexus had been a natural transition from pupil to active status. Once he became an agent, he had enjoyed the rush of unraveling the enemy's secrets and the intense gratification of thwarting Napoleon's various dreams of conquest. He had felt necessary to the cause, vital even. Yet something had kept him from fully relishing the moment. The same something that had plagued him for most of his life—the absence of a family. Staying with the deBeaus over the years had periodically filled the void. But the craving to come home to the joyous smiles of a wife he loved and children he adored lingered in his heart like the faint memory of a beloved pet.

So the answer to her query of what his life would be like without the Nexus was carved into the very marrow of his dreams. And once Valère was no longer a threat, Guy had every intention of pursuing his long-deferred wish.

For him, the real question had always been with whom he would share his life after the Nexus. His gaze dropped to her plump lower lip, and he felt an immediate punch of desire. It was not until the masked ball that the answer had come to him in a vision of shimmering red and catlike blue-green eyes.

"Do you regret your decision to join the Nexus?" he asked, intensely curious about her answer.

She considered him for a long moment, as if she were on the verge of sharing a great confidence but undecided about how it would be received. When her expression shuttered, Guy experienced a stabbing disappointment.

But his disappointment turned to surprise when she said,

"Since my imprisonment, I have given thought to many things I have done and many decisions I have made."

"Any you care to share?"

Shaking her head, she said, "No. You might feel compelled to discuss such things with Somerton. I do not wish to disconcert him, for I am committed to my present course."

Irritation sharpened his tone. "Did I betray you to the chief when I learned of your fear of guns?"

Her gaze jerked to his. "I don't believe so."

His eyes narrowed. "No, I did not. One word from me, and he would have removed you. The Nexus cannot have an agent who is afraid to defend herself with whatever means are available. Instead, I worked with you until the gun you dreaded so much became an extension of your arm."

She flinched at the reminder. "Yes, of course. I did not mean to offend you with my caution. Your bond with Somerton and my brother is strong. I simply did not want to put you in an awkward position."

"So you thought I would choose Somerton over you."

She frowned. "As you should, Guy. Protecting the Nexus's interests is far more important than the silly reflections of one woman."

"I don't consider your dreams as silly, Cora." He waved his hand around the chamber. "You deserve something better than this"—he stumbled for the appropriate word—"this constant intrigue."

Her eyes crinkled at the corners in a self-deprecating manner. "Do I." Not a question. It was a simple, noncommittal response. She continued, "The success of the Nexus depends upon the unwavering dedication of its members, Guy, and that includes me."

He leaned forward and rested his elbows on his knees. "Forget the Nexus. I'm interested in hearing about those 'silly reflections' you mentioned." Guy clasped his hands together to keep from rolling them into fists. A thundering expectation took up residence inside his chest. All of his senses were focused on her next revelation. Would her vision of a Nexus-free future equal his? He swallowed back a sudden lump of thick dread. Would he have a place in her future at all?

She gave him a cross look. "I do not regret my decision of becoming an agent. The role has filled my life in immeasurable ways." A hiss sounded from the crackling fire, drawing her thoughtful gaze. "However, I do confess to longing for a bit of boredom. I would love to wake up in the morning with nothing worse to worry about than the day's menu and what frippery I'm going to wear."

The first pang of unease tapped Guy's stomach. "Why don't you? Resign from your position, I mean. Somerton would not fault such a decision."

She turned and searched his face. His words had emerged harsher, more insistent than he had intended, but the stoic quality of her voice had struck a nerve.

"While Valère is still wreaking havoc, I have no intention of setting aside the Nexus, especially not until I find the murderer and see to Ethan's and Grace's safe return. Even then, my notion of what is normal will be vastly different from other ladies of the *ton*."

The pang twisted into a knot. "In what way?" he heard himself ask, already knowing the answer.

"In all the ways that matter, Guy."

He shot to his feet and strode to the window. Outside, the waxing moon glinted off a thousand leaves in a nearby elm tree, bestowing upon them a silvery sheen. Her quietly stated words could not have been clearer. She still believed that her past and the scars on her body would be an obstruction to any man's desire. Little fool.

"Cora, I don't know how to make you understand—"

"I was not completely honest with you earlier," she said.

He glanced over his shoulder, arching a brow. "Indeed? I take it you wish to change the subject."

She didn't look away, but he noticed the flush darkening her cheeks, even in the low firelight.

A gust of wind slammed against the windowpane, testing the glass's strength. The moonlit leaves no longer hung lazily from their arboreal perches; they now clung with tenacity. With so much force working against them, it was inevitable for a few to lose their grip and fall soundlessly to the ground.

Guy closed his eyes and drew in an exhausted breath. He didn't want to let go of the subject of her suitability. He wanted her to fight for her place in society, despite the *ton*'s wagging tongues and contemptuous looks. He wanted her to fight for a place at his side like those leaves fought to retain their spot within the arms of the enormous elm tree.

He opened his eyes once more, realizing she had gone through too much and forecasted her future for too long to see anything but a singular existence. It was up to him to show her how perfectly she would fit in his future. *Their* future.

"You win this round, Cora-bell," He used the old endearment with a familiar threat of retribution. "But *I* have no intention of setting this subject aside."

"Do not try to use your old bullying tactics with me, Guy Trevelyan. I'm not Ethan's runt anymore."

Indeed not, he thought. Circling back toward the fireplace, he allowed his gaze to skim over her body, taking profound pleasure when she burrowed her exposed toes in the crease between the chair's arm and seat cushion. "Why do you persist in this need to challenge my manhood?"

"I'm doing no such thing."

He grasped the back of his shirt and pulled it over his head.

Her eyes rounded. "What are you doing?"

"Reminding you of what you are up against should you be entertaining thoughts of victory in a scuffle between us." He tossed his shirt onto his abandoned chair.

"I have no desire to scuffle with you, Guy," she said to his chest.

He flexed his pectorals.

The look of startled wonder on her face made him want to do it again for good measure, but he resisted the urge. Unfortunately, his cock was not so circumspect.

Her attention dipped lower for a fraction of a second. "Nor do I desire to be ordered about."

Stepping forward, he unfastened the top button on his waistband. "You mentioned something about dishonesty, I believe."

"W-what?"

Another button popped free. "When you were trying to distract me from telling you how much my body burns for yours, you suggested some deceit on your part."

"Not deceit exactly." She unfolded her long legs and slid her feet to the ground, her pretty shawl slithering off her shoulders. "More like withholding unnecessary information, or so it seemed at the time."

His fingers moved to one of the three horizontal buttons securing the narrow fall of his breeches. "And now?"

She swallowed, riveted on his progress. "Crucially important."

He stopped a foot away. "Perhaps we should discuss it, then."

"Yes." Cora lost the thread of their conversation. Everything but the opening to Guy's breeches faded into the background. The left side of his fall drooped toward the center, giving her a glimpse of... nothing.

She stared at the center button with something akin to hatred until his fingers blocked her view.

"What is it you're withholding from me, Cora?" His voice, low and dangerous, slid down her spine with tingling warmth.

"Are you going to free that button, my lord," she breathed, catching his eye, "or toy with it all evening?"

His hand fell to his side, making her heart lurch and her mouth go dry.

He moved closer, his pulsing erection within her reach. "Perhaps you could do better."

The compulsion to do just that was strong. Incredibly strong. She dug her nails into the seat cushion, where she hung on with a strange mixture of trepidation and passion.

"No?" He made to close his open fall. "Ah, I see you are more interested in discussing your misdeed."

"Wait." She placed her hand over his to halt his action. Her heart hammered against her chest like a relentless battering ram. Each thump seemed to shake her whole body, as if to say "Wake up!" Her fingers tightened their hold. "Wait."

Frozen with indecision, she sat immobile for long seconds, staring at their hands. For a brief spell, her thoughts had centered around a basic driving need to feel the scorching heat of Guy's staff in her hands. *She* wanted to toy with it. She wanted to grasp his length, feel the glide of his hardness beneath her palm, and glory in his response to her touch.

She wanted to know him in the most intimate way. Her mouth watered with the inexplicable desire to close her lips over the soft head of his erection and to run her tongue along the pearling slit.

In that moment, she had not thought of danger or failure or what was best for others. She had thought only of herself and, God forgive her, it felt good.

Guy eased his hand from beneath hers and switched their positions, placing gentle pressure on top of her hand while at the same time flexing his hips. "What are you withholding from me, Cora?" he asked again in a low, guttural voice.

She molded her fingers around his length. Guy's harsh breaths above her increased her own excitement, but a nagging voice inside her head warned her of how such intimacies complicated matters between them. How they made her yearn for a life he could not deliver. With the vengeance of a jilted bride, the voice persisted until it dampened her desire.

His finger smoothed over the middle button. "Change your mind, Cora?"

Heat spread into her loins, fiery and wet. She stared at the beguiling button. Sweat gathered beneath her arms and beaded at her temples. She was melting in a pool of lust, and the only thing stopping her was a damned button. Was it a gateway to heaven? Or hell?

The buckskin-covered fastening sprang free easier than she would have believed, what with the material below being stretched so tight. As the front fall gave way, inches of pure masculinity was revealed. Before her eyes, he elongated and throbbed. His stomach muscles clenched into deep valleys and hard ridges. Emboldened, she released the final barrier.

The narrow front fall dropped from sight, leaving behind an indecent amount of flesh and curly black hair. An anticipatory silence beat through the chamber. It was as if all life suspended in those seconds of admiration. "Guy, may I?" Her gazed remained locked on that part of him that would bring her so much pleasure.

"If you don't," he said with gritted teeth, "I might have to finish it myself."

A very feminine gratification stirred between her

legs, prickling her insides and infusing determination into her veins.

His thumb caressed one corner of her mouth, which unbeknownst to her had turned up into a knowing smile. "Why am I all of a sudden afraid?" he asked.

She cradled the base of his staff in the palm of one hand, as one would hold a pistol, while her other hand enveloped the girth of his erection. Using the pad of her thumb, she applied enough pressure against the smooth skin of his erection to create an exquisite friction beneath. Then she began to move her hand, slowly, methodically, sensuously. His hips picked up the pace.

She chanced a glance up at Guy and found his impassioned gaze fastened on her face. His long black hair was loose, flowing around his chiseled jaw. He looked like a mythical Greek god—powerful, handsome, and more than a bit dangerous to human females. She saw him swallow hard and then close his eyes. He looked to be caught in a terrible struggle for control.

His big hands clasped her head. For stability or encouragement, she didn't know. Didn't care. She knew what she wanted. Had known it from the moment she tapped on his door, escaping memories and vicious nightmares that would not allow her rest. She needed him in the most selfish of ways, and she couldn't bring herself to feel shame. That would come later.

Right now, her passions guided her. They lured her down a forbidden path that not even Valère, at his most insistent, could force her down. No one was compelling her in that moment, only her own curiosity and unshakable need.

Her mouth closed around Guy's satiny tip, and her tongue removed the salty moisture weeping from the small slit. Pleasure drenched her body as she tasted him and explored his length. When she hit on a particularly special spot, Guy would let her know with a low groan or a tighter grip. His response fueled her desire to please him, because somewhere along the way her focus shifted to satisfying his cravings rather than hers.

And that's when everything exploded out of control.

"Cora... sweetheart," he panted, his fingers grasping her head more strongly, "remove your mouth. I'm about to spend."

She ignored his plea. Instead, she tightened her hold and slid her hand almost to the apex, and with her mouth, she drew from him what he tried to deny her.

"Bloody—" His head tipped back, and he cried out her name while his body bucked with release.

Soon, Cora eased away, her muscles trembling. She bent her head and used the back of her forefinger to wipe away the moisture. Although her body still vibrated with unspent desire, she felt an unbearable shyness overcome her.

Guy did not give her long to dwell on the matter. He dropped his breeches and scooped her up into his arms and then carried her to his massive, curtained bed. She slipped her arms around his neck and felt the dampness coating his skin. When he released her legs, she turned into his embrace and stretched her body along his to reach the hollow of his neck, his throat, his ear.

He found her greedy lips and delivered a bone-melting, all-consuming kiss. Her mind blanked, and she was engulfed in sweet darkness. Tonight, his unique musky scent was stronger, more pronounced, allowing only a trace of sandalwood to break through.

"Quid pro quo," he said with a devilish slant to his lips that made her burn with excitement. Bending, he seized the hem of her nightdress and drew it up her body until her arms slid free.

At the inn, she had flinched at the thought of him

seeing the ugly marks left behind from her captivity. But he had inspected each injury with a keen eye and had never once recoiled in disgust. Fury, yes. Disgust, no.

The backs of his fingers smoothed down her arm and then up again. They skimmed over her collarbone before curving toward the outer rim of her breast. There, he lingered, caressing every available inch until she thought she would scream.

"Cora." The word whispered across her eyelashes. "Do you *feel* this?"

She nodded, unable to speak. *I feel, I taste, I want…* He finally took pity on her and cupped both of her breasts, plumping them high to meet his warm tongue.

Her back arched into his mouth, and she hugged his head to her bosom, rubbing her cheek against the silky skeins of his hair. She inhaled deeply of his distinctive fragrance and suppressed a shudder when he drew her nipple farther into his mouth. An unholy thrill pulsed through her, leaving her feeling raw with excitement. She pressed into him, wanting to meld their bodies into one, so that maybe the ache deep in her womb would be appeased.

His arms clamped around her bottom, raising her up for a more complete taste. Once he had his fill, he laid her over the soft counterpane.

She swept her arms above her head and elevated one knee in invitation. The position made her feel decadent and luxurious, beautiful and desirable. He stood at the side of the bed, devouring her with his black eyes. His chest expanded with each harsh breath, and his shaft, flaccid a few minutes ago, arced toward his navel again.

"Raise your other knee," he said in a voice saturated with desire.

Cora hesitated. Until that moment, she had experienced

no anxiety over the wicked things they had done to one another. But now, he wanted her open to him. Open to his inspection and laid bare to his sensual exploration. She did not know if she could give so freely of herself and then walk away later with her heart intact.

His hand skimmed the underside of her uplifted leg, making her inner folds clench when his fingers came to within mere inches of her most intimate parts. Moisture flooded her entrance, preparing for him. She shoved away her apprehension and did as he requested. She would deal with the consequences of her decision later. Much later.

The massive bed was high enough for him to bend at the waist and be able to stretch his body comfortably below hers. He hooked his arms around her hips and placed hungry, slow kisses along her inner thighs. Her legs began to quake, a tremor that became more violent with each attempt she strove for calm.

"Shhh, my sweet." He crawled up her length to cover her lips, gentling her with his alluring kisses while his big hands kneaded her quivering muscles. "Shhh." He coaxed her legs around his hips.

Before long, her stimulated senses overpowered the barriers of her mind. She became aware of the intimate press of their stomachs and the whisper of air separating their chests. If she arched her spine just so, the hard peaks of her breasts would tangle in the wavy dark hairs covering his chest. The resulting teasing tickle curled her toes.

"All better?" he murmured against her throat.

"Yes. Thank you."

"Cora, never fear our passion," he said in a thick, reassuring voice. "It is pure and true"—he brushed his lips against the tip of her breast—"and beautiful. In my arms and in my eyes, you shall never be anything but utterly perfect and entirely safe." He caught her gaze. "Do you believe me?"

Liquid warmth spread into every pore of her body. She felt the truth of his words clamp lovingly around her heart, and the last of her doubts sifted away. Although she was far from perfect, years of friendship had enabled Guy to look beyond her faults, where others would only stare in horror. When this was all over and she had to hand him over to a proper wife, she would have to leave. Not just the city, but also the country. Even a chance meeting with the happy couple would devastate her, making the time she had spent in Valère's dungeon seem like a holiday.

She threw off the maudlin thought and lifted her hand to cradle his cheek. "I understand very well, sir." She sealed their accord with a kiss. However, she could not help but feel Guy's question held a much more profound meaning than her muddled mind could comprehend.

Moving her right leg higher against his back, she nearly burst out of her skin when her slick center came in contact with his scorching length. She tested the delicious friction by rolling her pelvis, and this time Guy hissed a curse.

"I'm trying to be gentle here, woman," he bit out.

She loved watching the myriad of emotions track across his features. In the midst of his fraying self-control hovered vulnerability, a trait not often seen in Guy or any of the other men in her life. But she also saw him struggle with the same unquenchable need that compelled her to investigate the deep expanse of his lower back. The farther down her fingers journeyed, the more force she exerted. "I have no further need of your light touch, Guy. In fact"—she laid her palms against his broad shoulders and pushed her hips upward—"I would prefer you resume your previous examination."

An unholy grin split the hard planes of his face. Something feral entered his eyes as he slowly backed away on all fours, never releasing her gaze.

With great deliberation and male satisfaction, he lowered his mouth to her throbbing center and licked her. There was no other word for it. His tongue started at the base and slid between her plump folds until he reached a place that made her hips shoot into the air. "Oh, dear Lord." She stared at the dark canopy above with astonished eyes.

Then she felt him tuck a pillow beneath her bottom and spread her wide for another round of carnal bliss. While easing two fingers inside her, he grazed her sensitive peak with his teeth before soothing it with his lips. He alternated between the two forces for several tormenting seconds and, at pivotal moments, replaced his fingers with his tongue.

She speared her fingers into his long hair, holding his mouth in that one spot. She did not trust him to release her from the inferno consuming her from the inside out. At least, not without further suffering on her part. Any more stimulation than what she was presently enduring would surely stop her heart.

Then it did. For one brief, glorious minute, time suspended, and she lost all sense of place. It was, perhaps, the most freeing moment of her life.

And Guy, dear generous Guy, was there to unlock it for her.

Twenty-Four

GUY ROUSED HIS SATED BODY ENOUGH TO GLANCE AT the unmoving woman beside him. Cora lay partially on her side with her palm tucked beneath her cheek in an adorable fashion and her left leg angled invitingly toward him. A perfect resting spot for his hand.

He stroked her thigh, feeling the thin scar of Valère's brand. The euphoric sensation drugging his muscles vanished. How could a man brutalize a woman in such a way? He closed his eyes and took a deliberately calming breath. He would not allow thoughts of the Frenchman take this small piece of happiness away from them. There would be time enough to ponder the man's insanity later.

Instead, while he contemplated their evening together, he concentrated on her delicate scent drifting in the air around him and the soft flesh beneath his thumb. She had taken him into her mouth. The vivid image burned through his mind with the speed of a runaway horse. Even now, hours later, his cock readied itself for another invasion. *Greedy bastard*.

One would think a gentleman of his experience would be satisfied by Cora's gratifying and selfless offering, but no. Not him. Once he had come down from his release, all he wanted to do was burrow his face between her sweet legs and give her the same glimpse of heaven.

The genuine way in which she had responded to his touch had nearly crushed his self-control. Her trembling legs, rapid breaths, and coaxing hands had contained an air of innocence about them that had driven him a little mad. And when she exploded around his tongue, he nearly spent himself on his aunt's embroidered counterpane.

Almost out of his mind with lust, he had been unable to deny her hesitant request to relieve his "burden" once again. His second release was even more powerful than the first. Barely able to lift his leaden arm, Guy had settled her against his chest and waited until he heard her even breathing before closing his eyes and giving into the demands of his replete body.

Now, delicate fingers glided over his hand where it rested on her thigh, bringing him back to the reassuring presence of Cora in his bed.

"What's the matter?" she asked quietly.

He became aware of the desperate grip he had on her leg and eased his hold. "Sorry, sweetheart." He turned on his side and kissed her forehead. "Did I hurt you?"

"Not at all. Is something weighing on your mind?"

She traced the edge of his jaw with a reverence that made his throat ache. After so many years of watching her single-minded and oftentimes masculine approach to her training, he liked seeing this facet of her.

He tapped the end of her nose. "Only you."

"Are you implying I am a burden, my lord?" Her voice carried a teasing note, but even in the dim light, he could detect a slight frozen quality to her features.

"Never a burden, Cora," he said. "If you must know, I was enjoying a rather vivid recollection of our... what did you call it? Ah, yes. Our *love play*."

Her eyes widened, and then she sent him a conspiratorial smile. "Were you?"

"I see you do not believe me. Would you care to feel the evidence of my excellent memory?"

She sat up, fluffing the pillow behind her and holding the sheet securely above her breasts. "I don't recall you being so very wicked in our youth."

Guy followed suit but did not bother to adjust the sheet when it pooled around his hips. "Do you not? I seem to recall you commenting on my mischief not but a few days ago." For the first time, he noticed the pretty oval pendant dangling from her neck. It was the same one she wore in the bathing tub at the inn. The same one that celebrated France's revolution.

"Indeed, I did. In your case, mischievousness equates to annoying. Like an insect. Wickedness is an entirely different matter."

He laid his hand over his chest. "You likened me to a gnat?"

The smile she sent him was several degrees warmer than wicked. "Aye. One I wanted to swat many times."

Guy threw back his head and laughed. This was the side of Cora he had missed. Since escaping the French, she had regained a modicum of her humor back, but her easy quips had been much slower in coming. "Impudent wench. Come here. I am getting a crick in my neck."

He grasped her beneath the arms and helped her straddle him. The moment she settled across his lap, her searing cleft enveloped his shaft. Guy's buttocks clenched in reaction, the small motion driving him farther into her heat. He sucked in a sharp breath. "Blast it, Cora."

She braced her hands on his shoulders. "My s-sentiments exactly," she panted. "Is this your idea of revenge?"

He clutched her hips in a steadying hold, being careful of the wound on her lower back. "Hardly. I merely wanted a better view." The backs of his fingers smoothed down her flat stomach. "Which I now have."

Awareness gleamed in her heavy-lidded gaze, and she followed his teasing caress over her stomach, ribs, and breasts. Then her attention turned to him. She raked her fingertips through the short hairs covering his chest, seemingly fascinated by their springy quality. "Yes, I see what you mean." She straightened from her bent position, giving him a better aspect of her beautiful body and—he swallowed when her sleek center skimmed along his cock—a captivating measure on her intimate thoughts.

To distract himself from the building inferno between his legs, he touched his finger to the pendant arranged against her alabaster skin like a priceless gem in a jeweler's display case. "That's an unusual cameo. Do you always wear it?"

She looked down and traced her fingers over a feminine profile. "Much of the time."

"A family heirloom, perhaps?" He didn't think so, but the proprietary way in which she stroked the cameo drew forth a very male desire to know how she came by the piece.

"Yes and no." Her words were low, hesitant.

Something like dread rippled through his stomach. "Which one, my dear? It can't be both."

"It has not been in my family's possession long." Her hand resumed its tortuous study of his chest. "My mother left it for me before she died. I keep it as a remembrance."

He reflected on her words, noting her response left much to the imagination. She obviously wanted him to believe the pendant held sentimental value, and it might. However, the cryptographer in him reasoned there was much more to the story.

"I see." A hundred questions circled around his mind, but he tossed them away one by one, deeming them all a bit too pointed. He wanted to ask who had given the necklace to her mother, and when. Why keep a trinket depicting France's break with the *Ancien Régime* as a remembrance of her mother? Especially when Lady Danforth's wedding ring or her great-grandmother's pearls would perhaps be more appropriate.

"Is there anything you fear, Guy?"

At her softly spoken question, he glanced up and found her lips parted and worry lines carved into her forehead.

The tips of her fingers grazed the line where smooth skin met a thatch of dark hair encircling his groin. *Yes*, he thought, trapping her hand beneath his.

With painful clarity, he recalled the scene in the woods, the awful moment when he saw Valère's man-servant rounding on Cora, hatred distorting his features. He recalled the moment he realized he would not reach her in time.

When he had stopped long enough to brace his feet apart and aim his pistol at the center of Marcel's back, his hand jerked at the last second, sending his killing shot wide of its mark.

Guy gritted his teeth against the memory. What use was a protector—an assassin—who was unable to kill? He could not allow his conscience to forever hold his actions hostage. He had every intention of killing Valère, and this newfound weakness would not—must not—stand in his way.

During his ruminations, Cora's wandering fingers wiggled out from beneath his restraining grip to tunnel into the dark patch of hair between his legs.

His head fell back against the cushioned bed frame, and his bollocks tautened. For a self-indulgent moment, he considered allowing her the freedom of discovery. But, like his current inability to slay his enemy, Guy feared the effect of Cora's touch on his resolve. Far too easily, he could turn his back on the world outside and spend the rest of his life wrapped in the firm clasp of Cora's loving hands. And her loyal heart.

His eyes popped open at her first tentative caress on his fully extended shaft. He grasped her wrist. "Cora."

"You did not answer my question, my lord."

He had to cut through his passion-fogged mind for her original query. Ah, yes. Did he fear anything? "Of course. What man does not?" Releasing her, he cupped the back of her neck and pulled her down for a kiss. "What is troubling you, Cora? Why did you really come to me tonight?"

She resumed her place at his side, making Guy regret his probing questions.

"The dark."

She spoke not to him but to her lap.

"What of the dark, sweetheart?"

The muscles in her throat pulsed before she said, "It frightens me." Her statement, so plainly spoken, boomed through the shadow-laden room.

On one hand, his chest swelled with male satisfaction that she would seek him out to hold back the witching hour. But his unruly heart wanted her motive to be far more personal.

He seized her hand beneath the sheet. "I don't recall you, or better yet, Ethan, mentioning this particular trepidation."

"No." Her eyes took on a haunted look, and she drew the counterpane up to her chin.

Bleak understanding crashed into Guy. *The dungeon.* The underground labyrinth of fathomless darkness. "Bloody hell." He slid his arm around her shoulders and dragged her into his embrace. "Cora—"

"The horrible images," she said in a rush of words, "they won't allow me a moment's respite. I have tried to ignore them, Guy. I truly have, but they persist." She hid her face against his chest. "My skin feels like it is crawling with insects, and I hear the patter of a thousand tiny malevolent feet stalking toward me. And now... now I can add Scrapper's death to the macabre scene." Air billowed between her lips as if she had run the length of the estate's vast parkland. "There are times when I am certain I'm losing my mind. But that night at the inn, when I slept in your arms, the nightmares never came."

Guy's heart shattered at the aching quality of her voice. Helpless rage stung his eyes and clogged his throat. "I will keep you safe through all the nights of your life, Cora."

She lifted her sweet, ravaged face up to his. "I know."

There was nothing for it but to kiss her again. The volatile emotions battering his insides would not allow for a simple reassuring press of the lips. No, this kiss was designed to banish one's demons.

When she responded with equal fervor, Guy moved between her legs and entered her. Her passage was slick, allowing him to set an urgent tempo that brought them both to a splintering release within minutes. He kissed her softly, gently, before easing away.

She exhaled a contented sigh, pulled him down next to her, and snuggled into the shelter of his arms. After adjusting the covers around them, Guy tightened his hold, giving her the peace of mind she sought from him. "Sleep, Cora. Tomorrow, we shall return to London, where I can provide better protection. Does that suit you?"

She nodded, toying with her necklace.

Guy regretted his decision to tell her now rather than waiting until the morning. Although she remained pliant, he sensed a new restlessness thrumming through her small frame. Then her next words confirmed his suspicion.

"I won't allow Valère to take another loved one, Guy."

He smoothed his hand down her bare arm. "We will find Ethan, I swear it."

Both their vows hung heavily in the darkened chamber. Both held unspoken promises by the speaker.

It was some time later before either of them fell asleep.

Twenty-Five

THE SUN FELL BELOW THE HORIZON AS GUY STARED AT the cloaked figure. "Are you sure it was Danforth?" He ignored the sounds of London's underworld coming to life, but the smell of human waste and rotten food scattered over the alleyway's cobblestones could not be so easily dismissed. The acrid odor burned through his nose and landed in the back of his mouth, leaving a bitter, gripping taste behind. The constant drip from the roof's eave thundered over the pounding of his heart.

"Several witnesses reported seeing a man of Lord Danforth's description being thrown into a carriage several nights ago," his informant said in a raspy, indistinguishable whisper.

The last snag of hope that Danforth, covertly disguised and inaccessible, was searching for Valère tore free. The intelligence his informant had passed on over the years had proven eerily accurate. And Guy had no reason to believe this time was any different.

His heart lurched with the knowledge. Cora would have to be told that Valère's taunts about her brother were true. He wondered if she, like he, had held onto a fragment of hope.

"I have a veritable army with their ear to the ground, my lord." The cloaked figure stood in the shadow of a nearby building. After meeting briefly two days ago to outline Danforth's situation, the Specter had prearranged today's tête-à-tête. "They have been instructed to bring all possible leads to my attention, no matter how small. Never fear, I will find the overeager lord."

What Guy knew of his mysterious informant could be ticked off on one hand. They had collaborated on a number of cases over the last two years without incident. Guy sought information, and the shadowed figure asked for nothing in return, except anonymity and the occasional inquiry into Somerton's health.

At first, Guy had been suspicious of the informant's interest in Somerton. After all, the cloaked figure had first come to his notice during a rather harrowing back-alley discussion, where Guy had been held at gunpoint while his informant conveyed the details of a large shipment of ammunitions scheduled to disembark from an English port to make its merry way to a French shore.

But the cloaked figure never went beyond inquiring about Somerton's health. Guy soon realized the informant was not seeking answers but rather hinting at what was already known. Quite clever and decidedly dangerous.

After the success of their first *discussion*, he learned the figure was known as Specter. From that moment on, any time he needed help, he would scribble "Specter" on a note and leave it at one of a dozen locations throughout the city. In a matter of hours, the two of them would be conversing in a darkened alcove similar to the one they currently occupied.

Honoring the Specter's need for secrecy had posed no moral dilemmas for Guy. The informant's web of contacts had proved to be an invaluable resource in their war against the rabid Corsican.

"You will contact me if more details arise?" Guy asked.

"Yes, my lord." The dark silhouette shifted, taking

Guy's measure. "For the Raven, it would be my honor to dispatch the Frenchman once Lord Danforth has been recovered."

A razor-sharp pang of jealousy punched Guy in the chest. Why would the informant be "honored" to kill a man for the Raven? Were they acquainted with each other? Had Specter also worked with Cora? Or was their relationship something more personal? Myriad questions continued to plague him until the quiet rasp of "my lord?" penetrated the territorial fog enveloping his mind.

Eyeing the black depths of his informant's hood, Guy said in an even voice, "That won't be necessary. We have a few questions for Valère first."

The hood dipped, and the cloaked figure stepped farther into the shadows of the building. "As you wish, my lord. I will be in touch."

When Specter melted into the darkness, Guy turned and headed for Somerton's town house. He strode down the narrow alley, dodging piles of rancid offal dotting the cobblestones and watching the occupants of each abyss-like nook along the buildings' outer walls.

The Frenchman's ability to breach each of Guy's safeguards had forced him to swallow his pride and return Cora to London. With Cora once again under Somerton's roof, Guy could no longer see her on a whim. As her self-proclaimed bodyguard, he could see her during the day but not the night. Did she sleep all through the evening, or was she still plagued by images of the past?

They had to bring this mission to a conclusion soon, for all their sakes, but mostly for Cora's. Which led him to the packet of missives Somerton had given him to decipher. With a stroke of luck, he had finally managed to break two critical letters in one of the newer messages:

T32E26   272215E34T2223

He would likely have more letters within the next few days. Excitement rumbled through him. With a disturbing certainty, he sensed the power behind the two distinct words. Why else would the French use one of the most difficult ciphers? Not for any ordinary communication between agents. No, something told Guy this message would affect England—and possibly the Nexus—in a monumental, irreversible way.

He had come to another revelation, of sorts, regarding Cora's view on marriage. What appeared to be aversion at the Golden Duck turned out to be a rather faulty belief that her actions in France made her an unworthy candidate for a happy marriage. Although he had every intention of setting her straight on the matter, the confirmation of her innermost desire was welcome news. She yearned for a normal existence—just as he did—which meant she wanted a family. A home, friends, children, a *husband*.

The fact that she had admitted her fear of the dark and sought the safety of his arms was a significant turning point. One he would always cherish. There would no doubt be other barriers standing in the way of making her whole once again. But he would meet each one head-on and tear it down for her.

For now, he must focus on the challenge ahead. As he drew closer to Somerton's town house, he rehearsed how he would reveal the latest details about her brother. He feared the knowledge would send her mind spiraling back to the past. The past she still refused to discuss.

❧

The large clock in Somerton's entry hall struck nine times, signaling the lateness of the hour. Cora leaned against the wall, her gaze focused on the library door. For nearly an hour, she had prowled the dimly lit corridor, waiting for Guy to finish his conversation with

Somerton. She could hear their low murmurings but nothing so distinct as to warn her of what was to come, and the waiting was starting to grate on her patience.

Her intuition shrieked that this meeting did not bode well for her brother. Not for the first time, a ripple of unbidden panic ricocheted through her. Valère had picked his tool for vengeance with exquisite care. She could no more fault Jack's instincts to protect his sister than she could turn her back on Ethan's plight. When the talons of terror grip your heart, you will do anything you are told to save a loved one.

She blinked to dispel the menacing images clouding her mind. She must not let the past take control. Closing her eyes, she inhaled deeply several times. By the time the library door finally opened, Cora felt much the way she had in France when she was faced with a difficult case—controlled, determined, ruthless. *Raven.*

Guy emerged, and Cora noted his troubled expression before he could mask it. She pushed away from the wall and waved in the general direction of the drawing room. "Shall we?"

Surprise flickered across his feature before resignation set in. "Indeed," he said, waving her ahead. They managed about six paces before he noticed her attire. "What the hell are you wearing?" he asked with a trace of annoyance and admiration.

"We have already been through this, my lord. You have seen me in breeches before."

His eyes narrowed. "Must you cavort about in them in front of *everyone*?"

"I'm hardly cavorting, Guy. And the servants have seen me in far worse costumes." She shook her head and sat cross-legged at the end of the ivory-colored divan, hugging a silk pillow against her chest.

"Would you care for something to drink?" she asked.

"No, thank you." He strode to the window, choosing the view outside rather than facing her.

"I assume you have news of Ethan."

"I'm afraid so."

"It is cruel to keep me in such suspense, Guy," she said when he lapsed back into silence.

His shoulders sagged a fraction before he turned from the window to join her on the divan. "A reliable source confirmed footpads carted off a man matching your brother's description several nights ago."

She nodded, having already prepared herself for such news. "What did you and Somerton discuss in the way of a rescue?"

He hesitated, as if he were puzzled by her reaction, or perhaps he was debating whether or not to share his information.

She targeted on the latter. "Stop trying to protect me."

He sent her an even look. "Never."

If he wasn't keeping information about Ethan from her, his vow would have made her womanly heart sting. But he was withholding details, which made his pledge rather annoying. "Tell me what you have planned, or I will discuss this with Somerton instead."

"Can you not leave this to us?"

A thunderbolt slammed into her gut. "No, Guy, I can't. We're talking about saving my brother. Do you really think I will sit around and do nothing but wait?"

He leveled an uncompromising stare on her.

"I can be of use. There is no need for your coddling."

"I'm not interested in coddling you, but I will do what I must to keep you safe. Valère has proven himself to be more dangerous and cunning than any of us expected."

"All the more reason for us to work together."

"I can't," Guy ground out. He knew he risked killing the fragile trust they had built in the country. But the combination of Somerton's guards abandoning their post and the discovery of one of their top agent's naked, mutilated body yesterday morning indicated the elusive double agent Somerton sought held a much higher position in the Foreign Office than they originally imagined. Which meant no one was safe. "The line between foe and friend has blurred significantly while we were away."

The air around them grew thick with her quiet rage.

"Let me make one thing perfectly clear, my lord." She unfurled her legs and rose from her seat. "I will do whatever it takes to free my brother and won't hesitate to remove any obstacle standing in my way."

"And I will do *whatever it takes* to stop you." He reached for her at the same time he rose to block her path.

A flash of outrage burst forth and, in the next moment, he found himself cartwheeling through the air, and the next, staring at the ceiling. He blinked several times, surprised by his rapid change in circumstance. He attempted an indrawn breath. However, his air-deprived lungs were of no help. It was not lost on him that he had been in a similar position not long ago. His wheezing effort to breathe echoed through the room.

Cora hovered over him, as if waiting for his lungs to expand with air again. When they did, a veil of indifference coated her words.

"I will free my brother and Grace—with or without your assistance. I hope you choose the former." She turned away.

He twisted around into a crouching position. A toxic mix of anger, humiliation, and respect churned in his gut. He had underestimated her for the last time.

In a whirlwind of motion, he extended his leg and caught the back of her ankles. She emitted a short, high-pitched shriek while her arms fought for purchase. She found none, except the hardness of his chest and the viselike anchor of his arms. She slammed into him, hurling them both to the floor. Their breaths sawed through the air, and Guy had to fight his desire to roll her over and claim a victory kiss. "Still challenging my manhood, Cora? I obviously did not make my threat plain enough last time."

"Release me at once," she demanded, struggling.

He lifted his head from the floor until his face was even with hers. As he spoke, his lips skimmed her flushed cheek. "Do not attempt such a maneuver on me again unless we are in a bedchamber and quite naked. As you have come to discover, I do not mind having a feisty woman in my bed."

Her eyes narrowed on him. A tremor heaved through her body, flushing her cheeks.

Guy could no longer resist such temptation. His lips explored the silky texture of her neck, and he gentled her with long, thorough caresses down her back. When her tense muscles loosened and she sagged against him, his chest swelled in pleasure.

"Leave off with the battle skills, Cora," he said in a soft voice. "Next time, I vow you won't get off so easily."

When he opened his arms, she scurried away, but not before digging one of her bony elbows into his ribs.

"Your threats do not scare me, Guy Trevelyan." She stared down at him, her body heaving with feigned indignation. He saw the truth of her words written across her adorable, mutinous features.

He suppressed an aching smile. Cora-bell was back.

Her lips firmed as if understanding his thoughts, and she let loose a soft snort and marched away.

The door closed behind her with a thud, and Guy's head sagged to the floor. She grew stronger every day, and he was glad of it. But her comment about freeing her brother was not an idle threat. Her ultimatum was clear—work with her or choke on her dust.

There was no way he would take the chance of her crossing paths with Valère again. The mere thought made his stomach churn with acid.

He longed for the days of old when the lord could lock his woman in her solar and set a few guards outside her door, or order the castle hag to brew up a sleeping concoction. He enjoyed the images for perhaps a bit too long before he cast them aside and sought a more civilized approach.

When none came to mind but the one Cora had offered, a wave of foreboding slithered down his spine. He would have to join forces with her.

She had survived three years in relative seclusion, fighting the French on their soil. Intelligence, beauty, and a noble cause had carried her through mission after successful mission. However, allowing her to face Valère again scraped his nerves raw. The Frenchman's plan had been foiled one too many times now. That made him even more dangerous than normal. And, if Guy were honest with himself, he didn't want her coming face-to-face with her ex-lover. He knew better than to believe that she would succumb to the man's wiles, but the thought of the bastard's knowing gaze on her made him want to rip out the Frenchman's eyes.

He rubbed his hands over his face, realizing what he must do and not liking it one whit. At least this way he could keep an eye on her and continue to assault her senses.

Guy sighed. How did she manage to turn the tide of control to her advantage with every encounter?

Pushing himself into a sitting position, he shook his head and relived her graceful exit. How did one glide in a pair of breeches? He recalled how her silken *pai jamahs* had molded over her rounded bottom and swished around her long legs. She had managed the feat somehow, and damned if his body didn't stir just thinking about it.

Twenty-Six

CORA CLOSED THE DRAWING ROOM DOOR WITH A trembling hand and an explosive anger that threatened to break free of her iron grip. She stared at the oak panel for several seconds, certain her fury would burn a hole in the thick wood.

Damn the man! How could he turn a battle of wills into sexual longing? She briefly considered storming back inside and giving the idiot earl a swift kick in the ribs for making her want him while she was mad at him. Barely recovered from their last wondrous night in the country, she did not need him to remind her of how quickly their bantering could turn into hours of intoxicating pleasure.

Oh, such pleasure, she thought and then scowled upon remembering she was supposed to be angry with him.

Instead of damaging his ribs, she headed for the grand staircase and scrambled up two flights of stairs until she reached her bedchamber. She darted inside to grab a couple items from the trunk at the foot of her bed before proceeding up another flight of stairs. After a few more strides, she stood before the attic door.

Fond remembrance surrounded her, quelling her anger to a low simmer. She turned the knob and eased her way in, and then waited for her eyes to adjust to the gloom of the enormous room filled with decades of memories.

At the far end, moonlight streamed through an oval window, providing a small amount of illumination. She weaved her way through a mountain of trunks and various types of furniture until she found Winnie. Nostalgia clenched the deep recesses of her throat when she lifted the Holland cover to find her old friend.

She smoothed her hand over the velvety fabric of the faded red chair and braced herself for the wave of remembrances to hit. The chair had belonged to her father, who had refused her mother's constant urgings to dispose of it. When Somerton came to collect her and Ethan all those years ago, he'd had to pry her from the depths of Winnie's bosom. A few days later, her brother had brought her to the attic and presented her with this quiet alcove of her own, compliments of their guardian.

Not everyone would appreciate such a gift, but for Cora, it was perfect.

She slipped around to the front and eased into her old friend's embrace. "Hello, Winnie." Why she gave a chair a name, she could no longer recall. It was one of those pieces of memory that had faded with time.

She made a table with her lap and placed in the center the small lacquered box she had plucked from her room. Made of sturdy, fine-grained walnut from the Orient, the beautiful box was decorated with an ivory overlay that depicted a Siberian tiger hunt scene. With reverence, her fingers skimmed across the familiar pattern, an image that made her feel alternately happy and sad. The artist had spent a great deal of time on the hunt scene. The level of detail carved into the ivory still amazed her, even after a decade of admiration.

If not for Dinks, she would have lost her most treasured gift. At the first sign of trouble in France, her thoughtful maid had packed this box and her mother's necklace, knowing Cora would mourn their loss if left behind. A kindness Cora would never be able to repay, but it was always thus with her friend. Dinks had always given selflessly of herself for Cora's benefit. Like following her mistress to a country full of war-hungry men, whose avaricious eyes were constantly cast toward England.

Unhooking the brass clasp on the box, Cora raised the lid to find three equally beautiful throwing knives. A stinging sensation pierced the backs of her eyes when she recalled the day Ethan had bestowed them on her at the tender age of eight.

Her family had visited the Bartholomew Fair in London that year. Their day had started out dreary, but by luncheon the sun had cut through the thick layer of gray clouds to illuminate the vendors' displayed goods to their best effect.

Otherwise, she might never have seen the flash of metal.

Without bothering to tell her parents or brother, she had dashed away from her family and made straight for the shiny object. Seeing her wide-eyed fascination, the vendor, garbed in bright, loose-fitted clothing, motioned her over for a better look at his wares. The knife set had held her enthralled until her brother had finally tracked her down and dragged her reluctantly away. After leaving the booth, she had nattered on for the rest of the day about the artist's craftsmanship. On her next birthday, much to her mother's dismay, Ethan had presented the precious gift to her.

Leaning back in the cushioned chair, she removed one of the knives. Moonlight sparkled off the silvery blade as she rotated it in a circle. The handle displayed an intricate carving of a wingless dragon with an enormous tongue, its slender scaled body twined intimately around the handle. The carved relief was menacing and, at the same time, utterly captivating.

Her fingertips wandered down the flat sides of the blade, stopping a few inches above the tip. She closed her eyes, allowing her inner eye to guide her. Drawing back her arm, she sent the knife flying across the room. It landed with a solid *thwack* on the opposite wall. The other two knives followed in rapid succession.

Cora strode over to the wall and was pleased to see all three knives protruded from the center of the crude target she and her brother had designed many years ago. Although Ethan was quite skilled at the sport, he had not spent the time needed to perfect his technique. Cora, on the other hand, had devoted hours to the craft.

Walking back to the chair, she retrieved the second item she had filched from her room. Strapping the specially made leather belt around her waist, she then secured the knives in their holders. The belt fit around her trim hips perfectly, and the knives were set at the precise angle she needed for smooth, efficient access. Just as she had designed it.

How she wished she'd had the ensemble when facing Valère at Herrington Park. She had not thought to bring them during their unexpected flight to the country. She had not had time to think of many things before being shoved out of Somerton's front door. But thankfully, she always carried a less ornate set in the lining of her reticule. An agent can never be too careful.

She moved to stand in front of the target again. From various distances, she repeated the exercise several times, adjusting her aim when a throw would go wide. During those shots, she could almost hear her brother's voice, teasing her, telling her that she was losing her edge, and then the boom of his laughter when she proved him wrong. Tears pricked behind her eyes.

She wouldn't allow Guy to closet her in this house. If he wouldn't share his information, then she would have to gather her own. One knife after the next hurled against the target, each one becoming more exact.

The calm focus she had been waiting for finally settled over her, and she began assembling her own plan. One that would free her brother and Grace, protect Somerton and her servants, and drive Guy away forever.

Twenty-Seven

SITTING ON A WHITE BENCH IN SOMERTON'S REAR garden, Cora curled a long blade of grass around her index finger while Dinks, who sat beside her, replaced the tattered forest green trim on a straw bonnet with a bright, cheery ribbon the color of marigolds.

Another dull, tedious beginning to a new day. After three such mornings, Cora worried she would not have the resilience needed to wait out Valère. She held back her deep sigh that begged to be heard and gave the vane of grass another whirl around her finger.

It was only a matter of time before Valère struck again. Unfortunately, she had no way of knowing when that moment would come. Her contacts had failed to supply her with anything of substance, and all her knowledge of the Frenchman's likes and dislikes had gained her nothing but wasted time. But she knew he would come. He had promised.

Come to me when I call.

Well, she was waiting for his bloody calling card. He had always had a penchant for theatrics. Why should her kidnapping be any different?

"If you jiggle this bench any faster, I'm sure to get a case of… What do the Frenchies call seasickness? *Mal de muke?*" Dinks grumbled as she secured one end of the yellow ribbon.

Cora stopped bouncing her knee. "*Mal de mer*."

"That's right. Pluck some more grass or rip apart one of those pretty flowers to calm your nerves," Dinks suggested. "Preferably the yellow ones."

Cora glanced down at Dinks's slow progress. "Why don't you have Maddie do that? She loves working with such fripperies, and I know how much you dislike taking care of my wardrobe."

"A lady's maid who doesn't look after her mistress's clothes?" Dinks replied in feigned affront. "I'll do no such thing."

"You are more companion than maid, Dinks. You always have been." Cora's gaze skimmed their surroundings. "Why you insist on acting the lady's maid, I do not know."

Dinks made a snorting sound. "As a maid, I can run about the house—*any* house—with nary a glance from its occupants. Not so as a companion. Besides, all they do is sit, talk, read, sleep, and walk. I like to stay busy. Can you imagine what would become of my hips if I did nothing but keep you company? Bah!"

Cora chuckled, unable to stop her gaze from slashing down to Dinks's ample hips. It hadn't always been so. Years ago, when Dinks first arrived at Somerton's, her tall, svelte figure moved with catlike precision and her voice purred with velvety undertones. As the years ticked by, her façade—the one she had dedicated years to hone—had melted away until the real Dinks felt safe to appear.

In a way Cora was only now beginning to understand. She had connected with this woman, had sensed a kinship in her that Cora had experienced with only one other individual in her life. A dark-haired, fire-beneath-his-feet boy. Both had made her smile, both had felt like home.

Dinks's reasoning for taking on the role of lady's maid penetrated her reveries. Sly girl.

While Cora roamed the ballrooms of Paris, listening for morsels of intelligence, Dinks had prowled below stairs of the homes they had visited. Cora had always marveled at the seedy gossip Dinks had collected on society's most influential and powerful members but never paused to consider the maid's methods. From the first days of their acquaintance, Dinks's knowledge was something Cora had relied on, even expected. Something that just *was*. And when they left England for France, the maid's *on-dits* never ceased.

Cora studied the older woman's face. Indeterminate years left their mark in a spray of lines around her brown eyes and deep brackets framing her full mouth. Never had Dinks bemoaned her circumstances or sought pity for her difficult past. She greeted each day like a courageous frigate determined to survive the endless battering waves of a midsummer storm. Did she never tire of the constant struggle? Did she never wish to share her burdens with the right man? "Your life could be one of leisure instead of toil. Don't you think you deserve a little rest, Dinks?"

The older woman's lips thinned. "Now is not the time to be reclining in my frilly bed and sipping on my hot chocolate, Miss Cora. Plenty of years to do that later."

Guilt pierced Cora's heart. Dinks and the others should never have been this involved in government affairs or been dragged into Cora's personal mission to find a killer. Gathering and sharing information was one thing, but participating in a war with the enemy was quite another. "I'm sorry, Dinks. This situation with Valère will soon be over."

She kept telling herself that, praying it would come true. If only one of their sources would come through with the Frenchman's location, pointing them in the right direction.

Valère's suspicious mind, dislike of people, and dependence on finer things likely had him holed up at a large estate not far from the city's borders, or possibly at a luxurious town house in an area like Grosvenor Square. A rustic cabin in the woods or a small flat over the bakery—with no access to servants, silk sheets, or expensive wine—would not do for the Frenchman's sophisticated tastes. No, he thrived on decadence, pampering, and an army of staff at his command.

Dinks straightened and cast Cora an unhappy look. "Now what nonsense do you have bashing around that too active mind of yours?"

"Too active?" Cora wanted to smile, but the muscles in her cheeks felt heavy and leaden.

"You're not feeling responsible for those two scapegraces and me again, are you?"

Cora's gaze shifted to the sliver of grass coiled around her finger. "Of course not. Why on earth would I feel responsible for those in my employ?"

"There now, someone's been sipping the vinegar this morning." Dinks smoothed the ribbon in place. "If we're going to get particular about the issue, those two mutton-heads and me receive our wages from Lord Somerton."

Cora refused to take the maid's bait. With her mood already gray, her musings had taken her to a dark place, one filled with melancholy, longing, and regret. She was not a particularly patient person, and Valère's silence was fraying the edges of her taut nerves. And no matter who paid their wages, Cora would always take care of her little family, as they had her.

Dinks sighed and stopped fussing with the bonnet. "I'm a woman grown, Miss Cora, quite capable of taking care of myself. You needn't place that kind of burden on your wee shoulders."

The image of Dinks fighting her captor's hold while

commanding Cora not to give in to Valère's petty need for vengeance flared bright in her mind. "Valère could have killed you."

"I've got nowhere else to be, little mite. Here, I have purpose." She nodded her head beyond the garden's walls, toward the city at large. "There, I have nothing."

Cora covered her friend's work-worn hand and blinked back the sting of tears. Kinship. And devotion. How she loved this sharp-tongued woman.

Dinks had inadvertently touched on a very real fear of Cora's. A fear she strove to ignore, even though she had felt the first nick of its deadly claws a few days ago. What would she do when Valère no longer terrorized her and she no longer hunted a killer? It's not as though she could go husband-hunting or produce a brood of children. Would she continue working for the government in some other capacity? Would she retire to the country, a spinster? She simply didn't know, and her inability to see into her future haunted her present.

Dinks sniffed. "Well now," she said, her words rough with emotion. "How much longer are we going to wait for that Frenchie to make an appearance?"

Cora cleared her own throat. "Another quarter hour, and we can begin Act II."

Since Guy and Somerton had made only a cursory attempt to take her into their confidence, she had devised her own strategy. Contrary to their wishes, she left the safety of Somerton's house every day, visiting old acquaintances, the museums, the theater, and even a ball or two. She became predictable, visible, and made herself appear vulnerable.

The bruises on her face had faded to the extent that cleverly applied powder covered the rest. The jagged scar running down her cheek drew less attention than her cropped hair. Although an oddity, many of the women loved the style and bemoaned their own cumbersome locks. Oddly enough, she noticed several men sending appreciative looks her way—Guy noticed, too.

As with everything, her forays back into society came with a price. A tall, too-handsome-to-ignore price. A Guy price.

Without invitation, he would appear on her doorstep, ready to provide escort. He had obviously wheedled her schedule out of Dinks. It would not have taken much convincing on his part, though. Dinks considered Guy's constant presence a boon, not a hindrance.

Never before had the maid gone against Cora's wishes. Cora found the other woman's covert actions endearing and irritating at the same time. The pesky devil inside of her brain tried to view Dinks's endorsement of Guy as a slow-moving fracture of her loyalty, of her shift to Guy's side. Of her first horrid step to leaving Cora.

No matter how much she wished an easier existence for Dinks, she didn't want to move through this life without her. The thought of losing her friend—her confidant, her anchor—was intolerable. In many ways, the maid had picked up the fallen maternal reins of Olivia deBeau and in her mother's absence, helped guide Cora down her unusual path.

Reflecting on their years together, Cora realized she had learned as much from Dinks as she had from Somerton. Her former guardian had taught her how to protect herself, how to peel off layers of intrigue to get to the juicy, sweet middle. How to hide her emotions.

Dinks had educated Cora on how to survive as a woman, how to use her wits, and how to laugh when faced with insurmountable adversity. Because Dinks knew a thing or two about adversity. She had lived with it her entire life. Had pulled herself out of the stews of London's East End, dusted herself off, and used her assets to learn about the world around her and build a better life. One of her own making.

Dinks was a survivor, and she had given Cora the tools to become one, too.

She sent her companion a sidelong glance. "I should warn you, Madame Matchmaker, that I am on to your underhanded tactics."

The older woman's eyebrows shot up. "Are you? What cunning thing have I gone and done now?"

"In a wily attempt to keep Guy and me in each other's pockets, you have turned traitor by sharing my schedule with him."

Dinks's lips twitched. "You're lucky to have such a handsome, capable man offering you his protection. Besides, you needed an escort, and his lordship was happy to oblige. Seemed perfectly straightforward to me."

"He obliged because he wants to keep me under his thumb."

A wicked smile rent across the maid's face. "Not a bad problem to have, as long as the thumb is pressed in the right spot."

"Dinks!" Cora couldn't keep the pink from sliding into her cheeks. Her inner muscles clenched at the mere thought of having Guy's strong, warm hands on her *anywhere*, but most especially on the sensitive spot that throbbed with anticipation with little more than a hint of his approach.

She didn't want a few marvelous moments with him; she wanted them all. Every aggravating, breathtaking, joyous, grief-stricken moment of his life, and the realization terrified her.

In truth, the part of her that was female to the core didn't mind his being by her side. His supporting hand at her back allowed her to walk into any room with her head held high and a secretive smile on her lips.

But the harder, more determined, more ruthless part of her knew his constant attendance placed them all in danger.

His nearness muddled her mind and made her careless. She foolishly imagined a gentler, less world-weary version of herself in a future drenched with images of Guy.

So instead of skimming ballrooms for any sign of her enemy, she stole glances at Guy from the corner of her eye. Instead of checking behind every tree and shrub for Valère as they dashed along Rotten Row in Guy's curricle, she gazed with envy at fresh-faced debutantes smiling shyly up at their chosen beaux. Instead of slicing through crowds to lose her brooding escort, she slowed her step so she could feel his subtle strength at her back.

Yes, Guy was a danger, on levels she had yet to comprehend.

She dropped the shredded blade of grass and bent to pluck a new one, inhaling the earthy green scent. Her daily routine began here, in Somerton's garden. She selected the location for its visibility and also to give her a spot of solitude before the day's carefully planned theatricals began.

A breeze collected a profusion of scents as it glided over herbs, roses, and scores of perennials. Cora lifted her nose and filled her lungs, cleansing her mind in the process. She glanced around, as she did every morning. Everywhere she looked, her vision was assaulted by color. Dazzling shades of heartsease sprinkled the borders of the gravel walking path, and hardy spires of foxglove bugled and swayed in the distance, while a cluster of forget-me-nots wove their gentle petals between thorny, white rose blossoms.

Here, among all this beauty and peace, she waited for Valère to make his move, waited for him to follow through on his threat to come for her. The submissive role was punishing for one whose success stemmed from her ability to act decisively, without waiting. By keeping her in a constant state of anticipation, Valère controlled their high-stakes chess game.

She wished she could share her plan with Guy, yearned for the use of his clever mind and reassuring companionship. Although he was never far from her side, their views on her involvement in this mission had chiseled an enormous chasm between them. She held fast against her urge to look over her shoulder. Would she find him in his usual place—standing guard in one of the upper windows, scanning the garden's various outbuildings and entrances? Or would he be strolling the perimeter and checking the many walking paths?

"What if I desired a different escort? Did you consider that possibility?" Cora winced at the petulant note in her tone.

"No." Dinks cast a worried glance behind her back. "And neither did you."

Disquiet spiked through Cora's heart, and her muscles locked in a silent battle—turn, don't turn, turn, don't turn. "Is he behind us?"

"More than likely, but I don't see him."

Cora breathed a slow, steadying sigh of relief.

"Don't know why you don't just tup the man and be done with it," Dinks said.

Raising a brow, Cora angled her body around until she faced her friend. "Tup?" Dinks no doubt already knew she and Guy had already *tupped*. Her wily maid was likely talking about something far more serious than making love.

"Aye. Tup." The maid leaned forward as if she were revealing a state secret. "Need me to explain?" Her eyes glittered with mischief.

Cora's gaze narrowed in mock reproach. "No, I do not." It took everything she had not to laugh aloud. She enjoyed their playful battle of wills. Turning back to give the garden another inspection, she said, "You should take your own advice."

"Bah, he's a fine, handsome man, Miss Cora, but his lordship has eyes only for you."

"I wasn't talking about Guy—"

"Of course, if I were twenty years younger, I might try to steal him away."

The confident gleam in Dinks's eyes drew forth the laughter Cora had been suppressing since they had started this ridiculous conversation. When the convulsions in her stomach finally calmed to a soft rumble, Cora asked, "Why do you like him so much?"

Dinks picked up her needle and dug it into the delicate silk fabric. She sat silent through a half-dozen stitches, as if weighing her answer. "His lordship is a right honorable man. He's handsome. Smart. Brave. Handsome. Kind to animals and common folk. Handsome—"

"Diiinks." Her warning emerged as a low growl.

"And because he loves you."

Cora's heart paused midbeat, and her breath caught in the back of her throat, sharp and uncertain. The breeze calmed, and the birds grew silent. The pungent smell of crushed grass disappeared, and the bitter taste of fear drenched her tongue.

Not looking Dinks's way, she swallowed down a painful knot. "Yes, he has always been a good friend."

"I'm not talking about friend love, missy, and you know it."

"No, I don't know it," Cora retorted.

"Then we need to find you some spectacles."

She could feel Dinks studying her, but she refused to look the older woman's way.

"Never took you for a cloud gazer."

That did it. Cora lifted her brow. "A what?"

"A cloud gazer doesn't allow herself to see the sun lurking just beyond the billowing gray clouds. It's a dismal way to live, it is."

Speech eluded Cora. Aristotle had nothing on Dinks. The woman was a constant source of amazement and amusement. "Why, Dinks, you've turned philosopher on me." She had also hit on a difficult truth, one Cora tried hard to ignore.

If she stopped to see the sun's power, a desperate hope would blossom. A hope she had cleaved from her heart four years ago when she had gazed upon Guy with the innocent yearnings of a young girl, but had followed the calling of a vengeful daughter.

"His lordship might be able to overlook your antics in France, but a man like that has certain needs and obligations. He won't wait forever."

"Let us for the moment ignore the fact that present circumstances have heightened our awareness of our own mortality and, given such, Guy and I might now look upon each other with greater favor—"

"Bah!" Dinks said.

Cora shot her maid a quelling look. "Forget that we are two young people caught up in a dangerous game of intrigue. Forget that we enjoy the familiarity of a decade-long friendship. When this is all over, what then? What would you have me do?"

"Besides tupping the man?"

Cora closed her eyes and prayed for an infusion of more patience.

"Marry him, of course."

She sent Dinks a sidelong glance. "You would have me destroy him?"

"Ain't no destroying a man like that," Dinks said.

"If you're worried about how society will react to your union, you're upsetting yourself for nothing."

"And how do you think society will treat the children of a seductress?"

In a quiet, admonishing tone, Dinks said, "Do you have no faith in your man, at all?"

Your man. The possessive quality of Dinks's reference to Guy felt both thrilling and right. But she did not lack faith in Guy; she lacked faith in society's benevolence to those who do not fit in the *ton*'s mold.

"Perhaps it would be best to turn our minds back to the Frenchman who has a rather murderous dislike of me."

Dinks shook her head and murmured something beneath her breath that sounded decidedly like "coward." Cora chose to ignore the maid's ill humor and peered around the empty garden with disappointment. She did not know how Valère would summon her and briefly worried she would miss his sign. In the next instant, she shook her head in disgust. He was as likely to bash her on the head and drag her off as he was to show up on her doorstep and offer her his arm for escort.

Either way, Valère was not one to go unnoticed. He thrived on attention, whether good or bad. For her, it seemed to be mostly bad.

She sighed. A head bashing it was, then.

Twenty-Eight

CORA NEEDED A BREAK FROM THE SUFFOCATING CONFINES of the Rothams' ballroom. Lords and ladies, bedecked in their finest silks, satins, and jewels, packed the edges of the dance floor so efficiently that one would think royalty graced the room. If she could get only a bit of relief from the heat of a hundred fragrant bodies. But every time she flicked open her mother-of-pearl fan, she would whack some poor, unfortunate soul's body part, transforming the pretty bit of silk into an effective weapon. More than one guest had sent her a look of retribution since her arrival.

One bit of pulsing heat she did not mind, though, was the Earl of Helsford's hand resting on the curve of her lower back. She loved the possessive message his simple touch conveyed to curious onlookers. And she appreciated the air of calm his attention suffused into her jangled nerves. What she did not care for was how he commanded her admiring gaze time and again.

Guy had paid particular attention to his appearance this evening, she noted with some suspicion. He was always impeccably dressed. However, on most occasions he seemed "thrown together," as if he had more important things on his mind. But tonight, his starched muslin cravat was tied in folds more intricate than his normal *Cravate à la Maratte*, and his silver-patterned waistcoat gave his somber black assemble an aura of majestic sophistication.

The most astonishing transformation, the one that arrested her breathing with every glance at his profile, was the revelation of his perfectly sculpted features. With his midnight hair pulled into a tight, sleek queue and fastened with a new leather thong, she could feel the full masculine effect of his chiseled cheeks and strong, angular jaw. He looked both seductively elegant and dangerously handsome.

The object of her considerable attention bent near her ear and said, "I need to discuss something with you."

His solemn tone gave her pause. She peered over her shoulder to discern what the "something" might be, but she could see only resigned determination. A strange, unwanted churning developed in the pit of her stomach. Lowering her voice, she said, "Is it Ethan?"

Someone jostled against her, and Guy steadied her with one hand while nudging the gentleman away. "Take care, sir. There is a lady behind you."

"What's this?" the gentleman exclaimed, clearly oblivious of his infraction. "Pardon my clumsiness—" His apology stopped abruptly when his gaze fell on Cora. One thorough scan of her scarred face and chopped hair was all it took for his countenance to change from contrite to disdainful. "Lady, you say?" The gentleman's gaze shifted to Guy. "A rather broad use of such a refined epithet, Helsford."

The cream-and-buff-colored ballroom floor rumbled beneath the thin soles of Cora's lavender dancing slippers. With each shudder, another piece of swirled marble broke off until nothing remained but the scarce bit of flooring beneath her feet. And she knew it was only a matter of time before her tottering perch buckled under the pressure into the yawning abyss. If not for Guy's hold on her arm, she might have fallen into a full, desperate swoon to delay the inevitable banishment.

Word of her flirtations in Paris had finally reached England's shores—and the ears of the *ton*'s most discriminating peer. Cora had heard more than one hushed conversation about the fastidious marquess and his propensity toward delivering scathing comments. According to the gossip, any young lady who dared to make a misstep, either in fashion or behavior, received a harsh correction from the peer, which set off a tide of narrowed gazes and pitiless rebukes from his followers.

Briefly, Cora wondered who had betrayed her. So far she had not crossed paths with any of her Parisian acquaintances, but her abrupt departure from the Continent likely engendered a letter or two to relations in England. Then again, it could have nothing to do with her time in France. Perhaps the marquess was simply offended by her marred face and unfashionable coiffure. Although she barely took notice of either feature any longer, no amount of rice powder would completely disguise the faint line bisecting her cheek.

With long-practiced ruthlessness, she vanquished such musings from her thoughts. Neither concern mattered, for this was the moment she had dreaded since rejoining society; the moment the *ton* would hike up their hypocritical noses in the air at Cora and then turn their scathing sights on Guy.

"Chittendale," Guy said in a deceptively calm tone. "I suggest you point your barbarous tongue elsewhere."

The marquess paused in the act of sipping his claret. "Do you indeed?"

Those guests closest to their circle did not even try to mask their avid stares. One by one, they shifted their attention from the twirling dancers to the tableau before her. She yanked on Guy's sleeve. "My lord, I am in need of refreshment."

In answer, he drew her hand through the crook of his elbow, bringing her body close to his and curving his hand possessively over hers. Then, in a bold move that would later bring tears to her eyes when she would think on it, he bent and placed a gentle kiss on her cheek. Her scarred cheek. "A moment, sweetheart."

When Guy lifted his black gaze to Chittendale, the marquess wore the same startled expression as Cora. "I do, sir," Guy said. "In fact, I insist."

Although the two men were of a similar height, and the marquess outranked her escort, Guy's years with the Nexus had hardened him in imperceptible ways. One sensed more than saw the threat lurking behind Guy's handsome features. He carried himself with the confidence of a man who had survived a great many trials in his life.

And the idiot had just declared himself in a ballroom full of London's most influential men and women. A rabble of anxious butterflies flittered inside her stomach. She waited for the marquess and his followers to turn as one, presenting their backs in the sharpest cut society would have seen since a drunken Lady Bridgeview stumbled into the Duke of Devonshire's ball some ten years ago, looking for her wayward husband and his newly pregnant mistress.

As the stares grew uncomfortably intense, Cora fought the conflicting desire to kiss Guy senseless for his heart-warming proclamation and to kick his shin as hard as her slippered foot would allow for placing himself between her and the vultures.

"I see." The marquess handed his glass to a friend before facing Cora.

She braced herself for another snide remark, her fingers tightened around Guy's arm. His body remained deathly still, hard to the touch. She took little comfort from the soothing circles his thumb traced over the back of her hand.

"It seems I have a case of mistaken identity, dear lady." The marquess bowed low before her. "I hope my comment did not offend you—" He peered at Guy for an introduction.

"Miss deBeau," Guy offered.

"DeBeau." The marquess stiffened. He seemed to be rolling her name around his mouth as if he were identifying the subtle flavors of a fine wine. "Somerton's ward?"

Guy nodded. "Formerly. And Danforth's sister."

Lord Chittendale's thin faced blanched. "I have indeed made a mistake. Please accept my most sincere apology, Miss deBeau."

Stunned, Cora said nothing for a full two seconds while her mind tried to understand what had happened. No matter which way she looked at the scene, she arrived at the same conclusion. One of the *ton*'s most notable peers just begged her forgiveness, effectively wrapping her in his mantle of approval. How could this be?

Guy squeezed her fingers in a silent command, rousing her from a fog of confusion. She curtsied. "No harm done, my lord."

As the marquess straightened, something caught his attention beyond her shoulder. In an aside to one of his companions, he said, "Tell me young Fitzgerald did not wear his Hessians." The same disdainful, wrinkling-of-the-nose sneer he graced on her moments ago was now redirected on poor Fitzgerald, who clearly did not realize pumps were the more fashionable choice. The marquess inclined his head toward Cora. "Please give my kind regards to Lord Somerton." He swallowed what looked like a rather large piece of humble pie before lifting his chin in a haughty angle. "And your brother."

Then he wove his way toward Fitzgerald, his courtiers in tow.

In a state of stupefaction, Cora watched the thicket of guests fill in behind the marquess. The whole incident could not have taken more than a few minutes, but she felt as though she teetered on the edge of disaster for an eternity. "What just happened?"

He guided her out of the ballroom to a less-crowded portion of Rotham mansion. "A rather judicious attempt at self-preservation."

"But his rank—"

"Is nothing compared to Somerton's power or your brother's temper," Guy said gently, weaving them around the last cluster of laughing guests. "Nor is he willing to test my heretofore silence about his peccadillo."

"What sort of peccadillo?" Cora asked.

"The kind that can get a man hanged, if made public."

Cora's mouth dropped open. "No."

"Yes," Guy said in an even tone. "The marquess's tastes run on the eclectic side, if you know what I mean."

During her years in France, she had come across men and women who preferred the delights of their own gender. In most cases, the men tended toward a more delicate frame, and their voices carried a higher pitch. Neither was the case with Lord Chittendale.

"He did not strike me as such," she said.

"No," Guy agreed, entering a long gallery of Rotham ancestors. "I know only because I happened upon an *interlude* when we were both at Oxford."

The emphasis he placed on the word interlude sent a wave of heat up her neck. To be caught in such a vulnerable state, at university of all places, must have been terrifying for the young nobleman. If the marquess was not so mean-spirited, she might have experienced a twinge of sympathy for him. But he was, and she didn't.

"Were you friends at the time?"

"Not particularly," Guy said. "Chittendale has changed little over the intervening years."

"You never spoke of the assignation?"

"Why would I? His actions hurt no one." His gaze took on a faraway look. "Besides, I know what it is like to be shunned. It is not a state I should wish on anyone. Not even Chittendale."

He referred to his parents and their propensity to leave him behind or forget about him altogether. Cora's heart sank at the implicit meaning behind his words. Had he stood up for her merely because he could not bear for her to be cast aside by society? "So your threat to reveal his secret was nothing more than a ruse. Well played, my lord."

"No, Cora. It was not a ruse," he said. "If the marquess had continued down such a foolish path, I would have broken more than my silence."

Gratitude warmed her heart. Up and down, up and down. If her emotions did not find an even keel soon, she really might become a candidate for Bedlam.

Turning a corner, Cora could see a few ladies milling around a room at the far end of the corridor. She guessed they had come across the ladies' withdrawing rooms, which were normally as crowded as the high-ceilinged ballroom.

Guy drew them to a stop near a console table decorated with an assortment of hothouse flowers and a triple-tiered candelabra. A few feet away, the corridor ended in a charming alcove, complete with a scarlet cushioned seat.

Guy escorted her toward the cushioned seat, which rested on a raised dais. Once she was settled, he positioned himself in a manner to block curious stares from passersby. "Better?"

His look of concern helped Cora shrug off any

lingering unpleasantness caused by her encounter with Lord Chittendale. Her perch put her at eye level with his chin, which meant his chest was within easy reaching distance. Unable to meet his gaze due to the nasty little needles pricking the backs of her eyes, she began fiddling with one of his gleaming coat buttons. "Yes, thanks to you."

He said nothing, so she moved on to another silver button. "I did nothing but stand there like a buffoon."

"Not true. You made a very diverting comment about refreshments."

She put a bit of pout in her tone. "It is not at all humorous."

Guy tipped her chin up with a crooked finger. "Were you trying to protect me again, Cora?"

Remembering the row they'd had last time the topic came up, she wasn't about to answer truthfully. "No, I was merely thirsty."

His lips twitched. "I should have called him out, or better yet, laid him low on Lady Rotham's ballroom floor."

"But you did call him out, didn't you? Not in so many words, of course, but your message was as clear as his disdain."

"It seemed a good time to make my feelings known on the matter."

She came close to asking about those feelings. She actually opened her mouth to draw in a breath for the first syllables... and promptly choked them back. "You took a horrible chance, my lord," she said a little unsteadily. "What of the next person? The one who does not have a secret to hide or have a fear of my family? How will you silence them all?"

A wicked smile caught at the corner of his mouth. "The same way we silence any of our enemies, my love," he whispered, kissing the underside of her jaw. "I shall make them disappear." Although his words were teasing, they held a quality of truth in them that sent a shiver down her spine.

"Guy, I do not think you are taking this seriously. Attaching yourself to me could ruin any chance you have of making a good marriage."

"You think so?"

"Of course." She punctuated her opinion with a tug on his button, and it popped free. Right into her hand. "Oh!"

Guy plucked the silver from her palm and dropped it into his coat pocket. "Spare my buttons, if you please."

She stared at the frayed threads that used to anchor his polished button, feeling desolate and incredibly inadequate.

"Cora, believe me when I say that being linked with you will have absolutely no ill effect on my finding a wife." He paused, sliding the backs of his fingers down her bare arm. "Quite the contrary, I should think."

Probably because all the eligible young ladies wished to protect him from her villainous clutches. Jealousy slithered its way through her body.

Cora no longer cared to pursue their discussion. The thought of Guy with another woman did nasty things to her disposition. In a desperate attempt to change the subject, she recalled Guy's comment about needing to speak with her. *Ethan.*

She pulled at his coat, dislodging his fingers. "What was it you wanted to speak with me about? Did you learn something about Ethan?"

"No. What I have to say has nothing to do with your brother." He uncurled from his loose-limbed stance. "When you are ready to leave, we will take a circuitous route back to Somerton's town house. The closed carriage will afford some privacy." His grim countenance and reserved tone put her on guard.

She rubbed her temples, questioning her ability to

keep up with the constant tangle of events. Did she have the fortitude to fight this new threat, whatever it may be? Lord, she hoped so. Glancing toward the withdrawing rooms, Cora said, "Give me a moment, and I will be ready to leave."

Guy followed her gaze and then examined the area. Satisfied with what he saw, he helped her down and turned toward the withdrawing rooms.

Cora's heels dug into the carpet. "I can manage this on my own."

Her attempt to stop his forward momentum failed. "I have no doubt."

"Do not even think of following me into the ladies' retiring room."

He sent her a sideways glance. "Such a vulgar mind you have, Cora deBeau."

Cora heard a rustle of fabric to her left at the same time Guy's attention shifted behind them.

"Good evening, Lord Helsford," a woman called out.

Guy slowed their progress until a woman in an eye-boggling combination of pomona green and pale pink sailed passed and then planted herself in their path. Bowing, he said, "Lady Meacham, what a pleasant surprise."

"I'm sure it is, my boy. Introduce me to your lady."

"My lady, this is Miss Cora deBeau. Miss deBeau, Lady Meacham was my aunt's closest friend."

Cora curtsied. "Then I like her already."

Lady Meacham raised her penciled eyebrows at Cora's bold declaration. "You knew Phoebe, young lady?"

"Indeed, I did," Cora said. "My friendship with Lord Helsford spans many years."

The older woman's eyes narrowed on Guy. "And you are just now escorting this pretty lady around town?"

Guy inclined his head. "As much as it pains me to admit such a fault…"

"Phoebe would be none too pleased with your taking so long to come up to scratch," Lady Meacham declared.

Uncomfortable with the woman's assumptions, Cora said, "Um, my lady, I must beg your pardon, but I was on my way to the retiring room—"

Lady Meacham waved her off. "Go, go. I will stay here and keep the earl company." Her lips thinned into a disapproving line as she gazed upon Guy. "Need to make sure he does not waste any more time."

Cora nearly groaned on Guy's behalf as she made her escape. A few feet from the ladies' room, she peered back at Guy to see how he fared. Instead of resignation and an air of hurry-up-or-you-will-regret-it, she found his amused gaze on her, his head tilted at an angle that would indicate keen interest in his companion's conversation. Cora frowned, unsure what to make of the scene and even more confused when Guy winked at her. Winked. As if this were all a great lark.

A man of his ilk—wealth, looks, title, and land— should understand the havoc one determined matron could mete out on an eligible bachelor. If she insinuated the wrong thing to the right person, he could be betrothed before the night was over. After the Chittendale debacle, he likely already was.

Shaking her head, Cora ignored the twinge of pleasure the thought provoked and hurried into the small room, incredibly grateful when she found the ladies, who were milling around, gone. She dropped onto a stool to rub away the dull ache at her temples.

Guy was a complication. He made her want things. Impossible things. Things that ceased to be within her reach the moment she learned how to pleasure a man, without taking any in return.

The oval looking glass propped on the dressing table beckoned her closer. The red, crescent-moon-shaped scar wrapped around her eye like an eagle's talon closing in for the kill. She could still picture Valère's gold-clad fist coming toward her, crashing into the side of her face, the warm trickle of blood seeping into her hair. She averted her gaze, unwilling to walk down the path of self-pity again.

Instead, she submerged her handkerchief in a nearby basin and blotted away the sheen of perspiration around her neck and in between her breasts. The cool water against her heated skin felt heavenly and helped restore her spirits. Somewhat.

She glanced at her reflection to ensure her coiffure was still in place, and then set off to join her self-appointed bodyguard. There was nothing for it. She could not wait until this mission was over to end this flirtation between them—or whatever this maddening desire to be with him every minute of every day was. Once Guy finished delivering his dreaded message, she would tell him no more kisses or caresses or mingled body heat or—anything.

She knew her thoughts were cowardly, but she couldn't take the chance, not after having lost so much already. As things were, she would already suffer for the decisions she had made. Gathering her nerve, she pulled in a shaky breath before rejoining Guy and Lady Meacham.

A massive hand clamped over her mouth a second before she reached the door handle. She elbowed him in the gut and met with a wall of granite, the impact jarring her shoulder. Her assailant locked a crushing arm around her waist, forcing the air from her lungs as he lifted her off the ground. It all happened so quickly she had no opportunity to scream.

The brute half-carried her, half-dragged her back into the retiring room, shoving open a door she had barely registered earlier, which led into an adjoining bedchamber. When they passed the bed, she reached out and grabbed one of the tall posts, but he yanked her body so hard her arms felt like they were ripped from their sockets.

He opened another door leading out into an empty corridor. Seeing her opportunity for rescue slipping away, she tried incapacitating him one more time with a kick to his instep and a head butt to the nose.

"Damme," he said under his breath, his hold loosening.

Cora surged forward with all her strength. It wasn't enough.

The beefy hand covering the lower half of her face kept her head anchored to his chest, and her body slammed back into his bulk.

Then his other hand arced in front of her, she could barely see over his thick fingers, but she felt the blinding sharp pain searing through her shoulder. She stopped struggling.

"That's a good girl," the brute crooned next to her ear. "If you start squirming again, I'll be tempted to use me shiv to carve up the other side of your pretty face." He yanked the knife from her shoulder.

Black spots appeared before her eyes. The agonizing pain in her shoulder concerned her far less than her present lack of air. Her lungs burned with the effort to draw in a single breath. A cavernous black void seeped around the edges of her vision, and she slowly sagged against him.

"I thought ye might see it my way, missy." Spittle sprayed the side of her face. He sniffed her neck and ran his tongue along its exposed length. "You're much nicer than the wagtails down at the corner. Maybe when the guv'nor's done with you, I'll have me a better taste."

Not until her eyes rolled back in her head did he loosen his grip. Cora sucked in big gulps of air, filling her lungs and bringing back her senses.

Without the clumsiness one would expect from a man his size, he replaced his hand with a sweat-soaked rag, securing it with a long strip of cloth tied at the back of her head. Tears pricked her eyes when her hair caught in the too-tight knot.

"Remember what I said about your squirming." With that pronouncement, he hefted her up onto his shoulder and set off down the narrow corridor. Her arms hung limply down his back, and an occasional bead of blood dripped from her middle finger and splattered on the carpet behind them.

After the first rush of terror faded, Cora saw this for the opportunity it was. She had finally managed to flush Valère from his hiding place. She would have preferred doing so without being kidnapped, and definitely without being stabbed, but she gave the sacrifices no further thought.

She did, however, consider Guy. He would be furious once he found her missing. She wondered how long it would take him to realize she had been kidnapped and was not merely evading the scheming machinations of Lady Meacham. She imagined his terrible fear, his helplessness in the face of her disappearance. She imagined him searching for her in vain.

Her resignation turned to anger on Guy's behalf. She reared up and put the full force of her body weight behind her downward momentum. Her elbow plowed into her captor's lower back, eliciting a grunt of pain and a severe pinch on the back of her thigh. Cora winced but didn't regret her show of ire. The action helped take the edge off her volatile emotions. She had to focus, to develop a plan before entering Valère's hidden lair.

The brute's thick fingers dug into the tender flesh of her leg, and Cora clamped her jaw shut, which probably saved her several broken teeth. Because in the next instant, the beast propelled her into the air and then let her crash down on his solid shoulder. The force of her own weight *whooshed* the air from her body, and the cracking sound of her still-healing ribs was the last thing she heard before darkness claimed her. The death grip she'd had on her dampened handkerchief loosened.

Twenty-Nine

FIVE MINUTES. GUY DROPPED HIS WATCH BACK INTO HIS pocket and glanced in the direction of the retiring room again. It felt more like an eternity since Cora skipped away from Lady Meacham's none-too-subtle hints about matrimony.

The horrified look on Cora's face had been the highlight of this evening's affair. Now that he understood she was not put off by the prospect of marrying him, her escape had amused more than affronted him. She was so damned set on making sure his reputation remained untarnished, so society's mamas would not set their sights on some other poor fool with a title.

If not for her inclination to tumble him through the air every time she was caught by surprise, he would have informed her that the *ton* already knew he was off the market. Until tonight, he had managed to stifle advancing mamas and acerbic voices without Cora being the wiser. He was rather surprised Chittendale had not received the message, being a connoisseur of gossip and all. But Guy realized he had not seen the marquess at any of the other functions they had attended, so perhaps he had only just returned to town.

He would have preferred to have spared Cora the scene, but she could no longer be in doubt of his commitment, even if she continued to fall back on old habits.

Speaking of which, where the hell was she?

"Did you get that, my lord?" Lady Meacham's commanding tone cut through his musings.

If not for his growing apprehension for Cora, he would have fenced words with this woman who reminded him so much of his aunt Phoebe. The two were sharp-witted and motherly, both elements he had come to adore. But instead of engaging him in droll repartee, the older woman's words had blurred into an incoherent murmur.

"Excuse me, my lady, but I must ask a favor of you," Guy said, keeping the retiring room door in his sights. There was no way Cora could have left the room without his notice. Absolutely no way.

A spark of interest flashed across Lady Meacham's rounded face. "Certainly. I would be happy to assist in any way."

"Would you be so kind as to check on my companion?" He nodded toward the room. "She should have emerged by now, but she complained of a headache earlier, and I—"

Lady Meacham's affable countenance turned cross. "You think she fainted or some other cock-brained notion? Women swoon to be caught by eligible young bucks, not to bounce their head off the hardwood floor." She pivoted for the retiring room. "Probably just her monthly flux."

She stopped abruptly and settled a disapproving eye on Guy. "You are not going to pucker up over the term 'flux,' are you?"

Guy raised a brow, somehow keeping his lips in a stern line. "Of course not. Use it all the time."

The lady humphed and set off to check on Cora. Guy strolled to within a few feet of the door, each second ticking in his head like the Abbey Bells ringing at a funeral. Even with Lady Meacham's incessant chatter, Guy had not taken his attention away from this chamber.

The door opened, and Guy's breath caught—and released on a disappointed hiss—when the third lady who had entered and exited since Cora sought the shelter of the retiring room, emerged. The lady's eyes widened at seeing Guy lurking so close to the women's sanctuary. He nodded, and the young miss scurried away before he could ask her about Cora.

When the door opened the second time and Lady Meacham's confused visage appeared, Guy knew something had gone wrong. Very wrong.

"She's not there, my lord."

Panic sucked the breath from his lungs. "She must be."

Her lips thinned. "The room is quite empty, my dear boy."

Guy wasted no more time. He sprinted the short distance separating him from Cora. She had to be in there. The alternative was too terrible even to consider.

"Lord Helsford! You mustn't enter."

Ignoring Lady Meacham's admonishment, he breached the hallowed walls of the ladies' retiring room. Yanking open the door, he nearly ripped it from its hinges. "Cora!"

A quick glance around the small room confirmed Lady Meacham's assertion. A cold, tingling sweat covered his body. He shoved open a privacy curtain separating a chamber pot from the main room. Nothing.

He turned back to the small room and caught the lingering scent of jasmine. Closing his eyes, he pushed back the dread. *Think, Helsford!* When he opened them again, his gaze landed on another door adjacent to the chamber's entrance. His throat tightened.

In two quick strides, he was through the portal and inside a bedchamber decorated in lavender and green and all manner of lace. Light filtering through a door left ajar on the far side of the room drew his attention. When he found the door led into an empty corridor, his heart plummeted. He knew in an instant she had been kidnapped, for Cora would never play so maniacal a trick on him.

Had Valère or one of his men spied on the women's comings and goings all night until his quarry arrived? There was no other explanation. Ever a brilliant strategist, Valère could not have been so lucky to have chanced upon Cora pacing the lavender and green room while she plotted ways to free him of Lady Meacham's marriage-scheming clutches.

Sick bastard.

A white object lying on the carpet caught his gaze. He rushed down the corridor. When he bent to pick it up, he realized it was a handkerchief. Correction: a *wet* handkerchief.

Guy's upper lip curled in disgust and he made to flick the offending object away, when the scent of jasmine reached his nose. His pulse leapt. He inspected the silken square more closely and noticed Cora's initials embroidered on one corner.

He made to stand, when something else caught his attention a few feet away. He rubbed his white-gloved fingers over the carpet, his heart thundered in his ears, and crystals shattered behind his eyes. He stared down in horror at the crimson stain.

No! Not again. Goddammit, not again.

Thirty

"WHAT IS THE MEANING OF THIS?" VALÈRE DEMANDED, stalking toward the giant he had hired to fetch Cora. The ruffian, dressed in ill-fitting servant's clothing filched from the Rothams' laundry, looked out of place in his informant's opulent foyer. The Foreign Office official had been rather displeased when Valère had requested the use of his country estate. The man seemed to be growing an inconvenient conscience at this stage of the game.

But Valère knew how to control such troublesome states of mind. Everyone, including traitors, had a weakness, and he already had his informant's well in hand.

"What do you mean?" the behemoth responded in confusion. "I got your woman just like you asked."

Cora's limp body slid off his massive shoulder, and she staggered like a newborn foal taking its first step. A dark, wet stain snaked down her left shoulder, ending in a narrow rivulet on her middle finger.

"She's been injured." Valère reached out to steady her.

"Aye, well, she tried to run away. So's I had to give her a little taste of me shiv."

"You stabbed her?" Valère drew Cora to his side and cupped her jaw, lifting her pale face up for inspection. The black centers of her eyes swallowed the beautiful blue-green rims, and her lips had turned an unbecoming blue from loss of blood. "I did not give you leave to hurt her. Your job was to bring her to me. That is all."

"If I didn't give her something else to think about, she would've screamed for help. And her gentleman friend was right around the corner."

Her eyes fluttered shut right before her legs gave way. Valère lifted her into his arms and headed for the staircase.

Marcel, who had been hovering behind the giant, stepped forward to take Cora. "Monsieur?"

Valère caught his manservant's eyes. "I have no further need of Mr. Porter. See that he is adequately compensated."

"My pleasure, monsieur."

"Thank you, guv'nor." The behemoth beamed. "Any time you need ole Billy, you know where to find me. Don't you worry about that little prick in your lady's shoulder. It'll heal in no time."

"Come with me, Mr. Porter," Marcel said. The manservant's hand stole inside the sleeve of his jacket. "I have your payment ready in the other room."

When Valère heard a heavy thud echo through the entryway, some of the furious tension left his body. Once he reached the top stair, he looked back to see Marcel emerge from the drawing room. Nodding, his manservant slid the knife back into the protective casing hidden beneath his sleeve. Valère gave the dead man no further thought. He tightened his hold around Cora and continued on to his borrowed bedchamber.

He draped her unconscious body over the expensive silk counterpane, not caring about the scarlet liquid seeping between its threads. Flicking open a small pocket-knife, he cut away her ruined ball gown.

And swore.

The opening was as long as the pad of his thumb, and blood oozed from the deep wound. The stupid bastard did not even try to stop the bleeding. It was no wonder she could not support her own weight, not after being jostled around in a carriage for the past three hours. She had lost a great deal more blood than he had originally thought.

Impotent fury poured through Valère. Cora's delicate beauty, even scarred and pale as death, called to him, and he could not countenance anyone marring her perfection—unless he deemed it necessary.

"Excuse me, my lord." The housekeeper nudged the door open with her elbow. "Your manservant said you'd need these." She set the tray containing bandages, warm water, brandy, and various other items on a nearby table. "Is there anything I can do? Oh, my!" she exclaimed upon seeing Cora's damaged shoulder.

He adjusted the black patch over his right eye, chafing at the restriction. He hoped to God the cat was dead, because if he ever saw the vermin again, he would rip its claws out one by one and stuff them down its rabid mouth.

He turned to the woman responsible for his blind eye, calculating how best to make her pay. "Help me remove her gown."

The housekeeper scurried to the other side of the bed and gently pulled the flimsy material down Cora's body as Valère lifted her. He turned her onto her side in order to cut the bindings holding her corset in place.

"Is she shot, my lord?"

"Stabbed," he said. "Find something for her to sleep in."

"Yes, my lord."

Valère sliced open Cora's chemise from neck to hem and opened the left side to wipe away the drying blood. The warm, wet towel removed the traces of her encounter with the footpad. The trail led to her exposed breast. Its perfection drew forth an unwanted craving.

He should be repulsed by the betraying bitch's body,

not drawn to it. With each swallow of desire, the clicking in his ears magnified.

An image of his informant's special room came to mind, and his cock pushed against his breeches. Valère's gaze slid to the hidden panel to the right of the bed, remembering the baron's instruction on how to access the chamber. A series of three intricate maneuvers, and the wall opened without a sound.

A large bed sat in the middle of the room, adorned in red silk and black lace. Pulleys and ropes, straps and tethers, manacles and blindfolds, and other devices Valère could not name dotted the room.

They were all there for a man's amusement, affixed to every conceivable surface of the bed, walls, and floor. Valère shifted his gaze back to Cora, to her bared breast. His heart raced with visions of him sprawled naked on the silken bed, of his wrists and ankles secured at the four corners, of Cora standing over him in a transparent negligee, a cat o' nines slithering through her capable fingers.

His hand slid over her breast, and his cock tested the fabric of his restraint. He closed his eyes, curling his fingers into her soft flesh...

"Here we are, my lord," the housekeeper said, striding to the bedside.

She stopped, frozen by the tableau before her.

Valère, nearly insensible with his need to take Cora into the side chamber, stared at the plain-faced servant. All he had to do was throw the English *salope* out and drag Cora into the side chamber, where he could relive some of their most memorable moments.

"My lord?" the housekeeper ventured.

And then, when he'd had his fill and his plan was fully executed, he would command her to take out her own eye before he killed her.

"Sir?" the housekeeper tried again, her voice shaking.

He blinked and pulled in a deep breath, forcing calm into his quivering muscles. Within seconds, his icy reserve returned. There would be time enough later to make use of the red room.

"Apply pressure on the wound for ten minutes," he ordered the housekeeper, wiping the sweat from his upper lip. "Then stitch her up."

Fear flashed across her plain face. "I've only ever worked with cloth, my lord."

He shrugged. "Here is your opportunity to expand your skills. I will be back in thirty minutes to inspect your handiwork."

Thirty-One

GUY WROTE ONE WORD ON A SHEET OF PAPER, STASHED it under the loose brick, and set off at a breakneck pace for Somerton's town house. The twenty minutes it took to reach his destination seemed like an eternity, much as it had when they had brought Cora across the Channel.

While waving him inside, Somerton's butler peered over Guy's shoulder. "Did Miss Cora remain at the ball, my lord?"

A heated flush suffused Guy's face despite his best efforts to remain impassive. "Rucker, where is Lord Somerton?"

"In the library, my lord."

Guy continued on to the library while divesting himself of his hat and gloves. "I'm expecting a message. Please deliver it right away."

Rucker nodded. "Certainly, my lord."

Guy rapped on the door twice before entering. Somerton sat behind his desk, piles of reports stacked before him. At Guy's entrance, the older man rose to his feet with a smile of welcome, which quickly faded when Guy moved to the center of the room and clasped his hands tightly behind his back. "We've got a problem, sir."

Somerton braced his hands on the polished surface of his desk, his head bent low in an unusual show of emotion. "Tell me."

Guy did. Every detail, leaving nothing out. He would not try to cover up his own culpability in this debacle. Desolation churned in his gut. His fear for Cora, his anger at his own incompetence, and his need for vengeance were vying for supremacy, breaking his legendary control in the process.

Halfway through Guy's accounting, Somerton moved to stand in front of the window. Who could blame him? He would not be able to stand the sight of the man who had succeeded in losing his charge—not once, but twice—either. Because of him, Cora must face Valère again. Guy balled his hand behind his back. With any luck, Specter would respond to his note posthaste. Although he did not hold out much hope, he nevertheless prayed the informant had some information—any information—on Valère's whereabouts.

"A hundred pardons, sir, for failing you both," Guy finished.

Somerton pivoted and pinned him with the superior stare he had used many times on Guy as a boy. "Let us hope she can be located before Valère does her serious harm."

Guy nodded, a thousand vicious images filling his mind. Another thought intruded, one that had surfaced on his walk back to Somerton's. "It is possible she was using herself as bait."

Somerton's head snapped up. His intelligent eyes glared at him while his calculating mind worked through the evidence.

Guy said, "Cora was never one for society, though she was adept at playing the part. After we returned to London, she threw herself with remarkable fervor into making the rounds. Now that I think on it more, she seemed to follow the same pattern every day—an unusual trait for a seasoned agent."

"She was luring Valère from his cave," Somerton said with a blend of admiration and seething anger.

"Why would she place herself in a position to be tortured again?"

"For the same reason you or I would."

Guy stared at the dark blemishes on Somerton's desk. "To protect her loved ones. *My God.*"

"Indeed."

"If I had discerned her scheme earlier, I would have put an end to it," Guy said. "In the beginning, I was delighted that she was recapturing a measure of her former life. Not until this evening did I start putting all of the pieces together."

"Her cunning is commendable," Somerton said, "but I would have preferred some notice. I could have set a few men on her."

With a sick heart, Guy stared at his mentor. "There was no need for her to be at risk. Our men were closing in on Valère's position."

Somerton sent him a repressive look, a silent reminder of who was in charge. "We tried hiding her. We tried protecting her. Both to no avail, I might add," Somerton said with cold logic. "I agree with her tactics but not her method. If she had confided in us, we would now be in possession of Valère's location. Because she chose to keep her own counsel, we will be bloody lucky to find either deBeau now."

Cold-blooded bastard. Even though Somerton's words had a ring of truth to them, the sacrificial lamb he spoke of with such dispassion was the man's ward, the closest he would ever come to having a daughter.

Guy choked back his disappointment and fear. "What now? We have no idea where he's taken her."

Somerton resumed his seat behind his desk. "Have a seat while we figure out our best course of action."

Guy hesitated, not wanting to sit. The need to act burned strongly in his blood.

"Helsford. Sit."

A knock heralded the butler's entry. "Excuse me, my lord, but Lord Helsford asked that I deliver this message straight away when it came."

Guy accepted the crumpled scrap of paper. "Thank you, Rucker."

"My pleasure." The butler bowed and then backed out of the room.

Guy scanned the short missive. "It's from my informant. We are to meet in one hour."

"Good. That will give us time—"

"Pardon me, my lord," Rucker said, a harassed expression on his face.

"What is it?" Somerton asked, distracted.

"Miss Cora's servants would like to have a word with you."

"Not now, Rucker," Somerton said. "I'll speak with them in the morning."

"I'm sorry, your lordship, but this can't wait 'til morning," Dinks declared, elbowing the butler aside.

"What's the meaning of this, Dinks?" Somerton asked, coming to his feet.

Bingham, towing a reluctant Jack, followed Dinks into the library. They squared off in front of them. "We have news of Miss Cora."

Guy met Somerton's look of confusion.

Bingham nudged Jack forward. The young man looked as though he was headed for the gallows. Wrinkled clothing and disheveled hair capped the dark circles ringing his bloodshot eyes. Sunken hollows etched the bristled planes of his cheeks, and his tall frame looked to be caving into itself.

"Tell 'em, boy," Bingham snapped.

Jack stared at the rug in front of him, strangling his hat between his hands. He swallowed several times in an attempt to speak, but no words emerged.

"Is there something you wish to tell us, Jack," Somerton asked in a coaxing tone.

"Y-yes, sir."

"Go on, then. If you have information about Miss Cora, I should like to hear it."

Again, Jack hesitated.

The smack Dinks delivered to the footman's head echoed across the room. "Stop yer shilly-shallying around, Jackson O'Reilly," Dinks said, fury causing her to slip into her childhood accents. "Stand tall and tell his lordship what you know, or I swear I'll beat it from you meself."

"And I'll hold ye down," Bingham added.

Jack stepped away from his two friends, obviously aware their threats weren't idle. His spine straightened, and his emerald eyes settled on Somerton.

"Jack, you have exactly ten seconds to tell us what you know, or there will be three of us extracting the information out of you." Guy felt a stab of pity for the footman, even though he meant every word. The devil-may-care man had vanished, and in his place stood a guilt-ridden, frightened boy.

"I know where Miss Cora's headed."

"Explain yourself, Jack," Somerton interjected in a measured voice.

"You see… his lordship… my sister… do what he said… she'd die…"

"Jack!" Dinks and Bingham yelled at the same time.

"Calm yourself, boy. Start from the beginning," Bingham instructed in a gently firm voice. "Leave *nothing* out."

After a deep breath, the young man closed his eyes and began his heartrending tale, one that left those present feeling a mixture of sympathy, betrayal, and a desire to commit murder.

"Not long after we arrived at Herrington Park, Lord Valère's man, Marcel, approached me," Jack began, focused on a distant memory. "He said they had my sister, Grace, and, if I didn't do what they said, I'd never see her again."

Guy had already heard the story from Cora, but he could not help asking, "And you believed him? Without any proof?"

Jack scowled. "I'm not an idiot, m'lord. Miss Cora would have my hide if I believed such a thing without knowing the truth of it firsthand."

Guy's eyes narrowed at the footman's tone. "Go on."

"Well, as I was saying," Jack continued, his voice growing stronger, "I didn't believe him at first. I told the frog-eater I wanted proof."

"Did he give it to you, Jack?" Somerton asked.

"Yes," he snarled. "The bastard held a lantern outside the carriage window—"

Dinks wrapped a plump arm around him while he struggled to finish the story. Her silent support seemed to be what he needed to continue. He hugged her briefly, and she stepped away as he continued.

"Someone smashed Grace's face against the carriage window. She's only eleven years old, m'lord, and didn't understand what was happening. She b-begged me to help her as she squirmed and cried for release."

"What did Valère demand of you in exchange for your sister's safe return?" Somerton asked.

"His man handed me a folded note with instructions on how to deliver it. They wanted to separate Lord Helsford from Miss Cora."

"Did Valère free your sister, Jack?" Somerton asked.

"No."

The footman's face crumpled with the knowledge he had failed both his sister and mistress. Guy knew a moment of kinship with the young man, as he, too, had failed Cora.

"Do you have anything else to add, Jack?" Somerton queried.

"Yes, m'lord. Marcel came to me again."

A charged silence ignited inside the room.

Guy stepped forward, hands curling into ready weapons. "Jack, did you play a role in what happened this evening?" An undercurrent of menace shifted along the edge of his voice.

"No, m'lord, I swear it. Marcel wanted me to give him Miss Cora's schedule, but I refused. He was not happy about it and swore Grace was lost to me forever—" A catch in his throat choked off the words. He fought to compose himself and, after a moment, his glittering eyes flashed in triumph. "I followed him."

Somerton stepped around his desk and leaned against its massive front. "Did he lead you back to Valère?"

A spark of pride lit Jack's features. "That he did, m'lord."

"Can you find the place again?" Guy demanded.

"Without a doubt."

Somerton looked to Bingham. "I need three horses readied."

"Right away, m'lord."

"Make it five horses." Dinks crossed her arms over her bosom with a look that dared Somerton to gainsay her.

"What are you about, Dinks?" Somerton asked.

"We'll not be left behind, Bingham and me. Miss Cora needs us."

Somerton's lips thinned. "You can trust us to deal with this situation."

"Yes, I have no doubt you will. However, with our help, the little mite will be home that much sooner."

"How?"

"Just stating a fact, my lord. There are places servants can go and people we can speak to that fine lords, such as yourself, cannot."

"We will be riding hard and fast."

A knowing smile spread across Dinks's face. "I'd have it no other way, my lord."

Her double entendre was not lost on the group of men. It eased the tension permeating the room by a degree and seemed to infuse a new determination among those present.

"Very well," Somerton said. "You can follow behind in the carriage. We may need a conveyance to carry Cora and the others home, anyway."

Guy looked to Somerton. "I must make my rendezvous. My informant might have uncovered information we can use during the rescue." He looked to Jack. "What direction will you be heading?"

"Due west, m'lord."

"I'll meet you all at The King's Arms, then."

"I should apprise Lord Latymer on our progress," Somerton said. "While I am at the Alien Office, I will recruit additional men to bring along. Let us regroup at The King's Arms in one hour."

As Guy cantered away, Somerton's words echoed through his mind. *We may need a conveyance to carry Cora and the others home.* The words conjured up the searing image of Cora lying motionless on the filthy table in France. He could not dispel it. Never would he allow her to go through that again.

God help him, he could not go through it again, either.

Thirty-Two

CORA BUCKED INTO WAKEFULNESS WITH THE FIRST puncture of the needle. The metallic smell of blood coiled its way into her consciousness, and two female voices murmured inches above her. Light flickered nearby, but it was too bright for a mere candle. An oil lamp? Possibly. However, given the plush quality of the bed beneath her, she was not in a barren cell but a well-appointed bedchamber. Therefore, the illumination was likely coming from one of those lovely Argand lamps now found in every aristocratic home in London.

All this she registered before cracking her heavy eyelids open. Once she did, she was treated to the slow, steady draw of a needle near her face, followed by a sharp tug on her throbbing shoulder when the woman pulled the thread tight.

So her plan to flush Valère from hiding had finally worked. All had gone well, except the part where she, rather than Valère, got stabbed and was carried away. That little chink in her scheme complicated the situation more than she wanted to admit.

"Who are you?" The question emerged rusty, barely audible.

The older woman jumped, pricking Cora's shoulder. "Sorry, miss. I'm the housekeeper, Mrs. Pettigrew, and this is Lydie, one of the upstairs maids."

"W-water."

"Lydie, fetch a glass, girl. Be quick about it."

Such an ordinary action as drinking proved to be an awkward, arduous task. Cora slumped back on the bed, flushed and perspiring from her exertions. So reminiscent of a few weeks ago.

"Miss, I have a few more stitches to set," Mrs. Pettigrew informed her, uncertainty lacing her voice.

"Proceed, Mrs. Pettigrew. My shoulder is numb now—I won't be able to feel it," Cora lied. Her shoulder muscles tensed in anticipation of the needle's next entry. She turned her face into the pillow at the first bite of the needle piercing her raw, angry flesh.

Three stitches later, the housekeeper finished, and the three of them labored to wriggle Cora into a nightdress before tucking her under the covers. After the servants left, she closed her eyes, succumbing to exhaustion, only to open them again minutes later when she heard the heavy tread of someone stepping into the chamber.

Valère.

His confident stride brought him to the side of her bed. Cora's eyes opened wider as he approached. She learned her lesson well the last time they were in a bedchamber together. She would never lose sight of him again. Then she noticed the black patch over his eye and fought to keep the smile off her face. *Thanks, Scrap.*

Valère's fingers closed around the neckline of her gown, ruining her euphoria. Quick as a whip, she clasped his wrist in a grip less iron-like than she would have preferred.

Steel gray eyes slammed into hers. "Release me."

Cora's hold tightened at his low command. It was obvious he could break her grasp with a quick flexing of his wrist, but he didn't. His lack of action confused her.

"I don't think you heard me, *mon ange.* Release. Me."

Bracing herself for the worst, she eased away her fingers and watched the blood rush into the slender white lines encircling his wrist.

The edge of her gown slid down her shoulder, uncovering one pale breast. With teeth clamped together, she stared at his chest. She didn't flinch or show any outward sign of the fury, of the terror churning beneath the surface. His hand rested on the mattress above her head while he trailed a finger around the sensitive rim of her wound. She clutched the bedsheet and contracted her shoulder muscles to lessen the raw tingling sensation his touch created.

His finger continued its descent.

She called upon the skills she had honed as the Raven to help her through what was to come. "Stop."

"Why?"

She made to sit up, but his finger didn't move, and it dug into her chest. Excruciating pain slashed through her shoulder, causing her breath to catch. She dropped back onto the bed, perspiration coating her brow.

"Now, look at what you made me do."

"Bastard," she wheezed.

"Ah, has that old rumor surfaced again?" Ignoring the painful twitches racking her body, he walked over to the wall next to the bed.

She heard a series of noises, and then a whoosh of incense-misted air wafted into the chamber. Valère threw back her covers, lifted her into his arms, and carried her into a hidden room. With something akin to reverence, he propped her up against a profusion of black and red satin pillows of various shapes and sizes. Cora drew her gown over her nudity, feeling more vulnerable in this room than the last.

While Valère went to light several candles, her gaze took in the forbidden decadence layering every nook and cranny. The room was large, perhaps twice the size of the adjoining bedchamber. Across the way, a wide plank of wood was suspended several feet in the air by two thick ropes anchored at the ceiling. The whole ensemble looked like a child's swing but far more provocative. The braided ropes were wrapped in black silk for the first seven feet or so, and a long train of red silk was attached to the underside of the plank rather than covering the rough grains of the seat.

Everywhere she looked, carnal toys abounded. Cora recalled enough about their time together to know that she had just become the most useful toy of all. Bile, hot and thick, surged into her throat. "I am going to be sick," she said, pressing the back of her hand to her mouth.

Valère jerked around. "Do not. Or you will regret it."

She closed her eyes against the awful room and swallowed back her dread. *Concentrate on getting through the next hour. Do not think about your revulsion or how you are about to betray Guy. Just get through the next h-hour.* Even in her mind, the word shuddered through her body. Good God, an hour with this murderer would surely sink her into the abyss of madness.

When she opened her eyes again, it was to find Valère standing by the bed with his coat gone and his cravat hanging limply from his neck. He eyed her as if she were a loathsome insect leaving feces behind on his newly laundered handkerchief. "Are you quite done?"

Perhaps he would fall asleep after—afterwards, and she could try to locate Ethan. She held onto the hope, even though Valère had never fallen asleep in her presence. Smart man. "Yes, my lord." She plastered what she trusted was a welcoming smile on her face. "My apologies. I fear the loss of blood has weakened my stomach."

His harsh features softened, and he unfastened the two buttons at the top of his shirt as he sat on the edge of the bed, facing her. The rapt set to his features conveyed a determination that would not be swayed by a weak stomach, injured shoulders, or change of heart. "Then we must be careful not to shake the bed too much, *mon coeur*."

He braced one hand next to her thigh, leaning into her. His breath fanned across her sweat-dampened face while his fingers peeled back the flimsy protection of her gown. Every instinct begged her to strike out and end this torture. But Cora's logical mind kept her pinned to the bed, allowing the nightmare to continue. She needed a few days to heal. There was no way she could fight off Valère, locate Ethan and Grace, sneak out of the house, and make her way back to London in her current condition.

She didn't even know where she was.

As was her custom when faced with a terrible prospect, her mind turned to Guy for solace. She focused on his dark, penetrating eyes, his silky, long hair, and the husky timbre of his voice. She imagined his arms lifting her from this strange bed and whisking her to Herrington Park, where they could begin anew.

But her reckless bid for revenge had likely destroyed any chance she'd had for true happiness. She ignored the fact that she had made up her mind at the Rotham ball to end their romantic relationship. Her treacherous heart would not release him so easily.

Valère's cold hand closed around her breast, and she heard a low rumble of appreciation. She had miscalculated in the worst possible way. Not only would she suffer the consequences of her single-mindedness, but so would Guy. Their deepening bond and her disappearance would ensure he would sustain an unforgivable torment, wondering where she had been taken, envisioning what Valère was doing to her. Unforgivable.

A knock on the outer chamber door interrupted his cruel torment.

"Monsieur?" Marcel called, opening the door.

"In a moment," Valère snarled. When the door closed, he resumed his punishing manipulation of her breast while his hooded gaze skimmed her features. He bent and drew her earlobe into his mouth; his thumb flicked over her nipple.

Unable to remain passive, she jerked her head to the side to dislodge him. Undeterred, he clamped down on the soft flesh of her ear with his teeth. Tears welled in her eyes.

"My lord?" a muffled voice said through the thick chamber door.

Valère released an unsteady breath. "You have been given a bit of a reprieve, my beautiful betrayer." He sat up and gave her nipple one last vicious squeeze.

Cora bit back a painful gasp.

Valère chuckled. "Perhaps your stomach will be stronger upon my return." He rose from the bed, straightening his clothes, and repositioned his erection with the slow glide of his fingers, staring at her all the while. "Soon," he said with a dangerous undercurrent before joining Marcel in the corridor.

Cora pulled the nightdress over her nakedness again. She counted to fifty before allowing the steady stream of tears to slide down her cheeks. Her ragged breaths rent the air while her forearm pressed against her abused breast. A sense of desolation overwhelmed her. She could not bear to go through such degradation again. While she was in his dungeon, Valère used torture as a means of drawing knowledge from her about the Nexus. Now he meant to inflict a different kind of torture upon her. One that preyed on her emotional fears, one that time rarely healed.

Thirty-Three

"GOOD EVENING, MY LORD."

Guy twisted around at the raspy greeting. Specter stood in the misty shadows of a large oak tree. Their rendezvous did not take place in a rotting back alley, as was their norm, but in an old cemetery adjacent to Bunhill Row.

"I do not have time for pleasantries," Guy said. "Do you have any information on Lord Danforth?"

"I do." The informant paused. No doubt to remind Guy who was helping whom. "An associate of mine is caring for him at present. The Frenchman's footpads were not kind."

"Danforth's with your people?" Relief pooled in Guy's stomach. Cora's brother was alive. He could not wait to tell her.

"Yes, my lord."

"Why have you not informed me before now?"

Specter's stance widened. "Because I did not know before now."

Guy backed off. The benevolent phantom had never given him any reason to distrust his word. "My apologies. His injuries are severe?"

"Not life-threatening, though he will be in a great deal of discomfort for a while."

Danforth's tolerance for pain was legendary, so Guy let the comment pass. "Thank you for helping him. His sister will be most pleased. Any word on Valère's whereabouts?"

The skeptic in him did not want to follow Jack blindly into what could be another trap—no matter how convincing the footman's tale.

Specter's hood dipped down. "The Frenchman's taken up residence at a country estate just outside of the city."

"Who owns the estate?"

"A name I think you'll recognize."

Guy locked his jaw in impatience. "Which is?"

"Lord Latymer."

Stunned, Guy said nothing. His hands curled into fists, and his jaw clenched tight. Of all the possibilities at the Foreign Office, never once had they considered Latymer as the traitor. The undersuperintendent was the only man Somerton had ever called friend. *Jesus*, what a muddle. Valère's occupation of the undersuperintendent's home did not bode well—on many levels, not just this mission.

"Are you sure it is Latymer's estate?"

"Without a doubt."

Latymer's involvement would explain a lot. Valère always seemed to be one step ahead of them and able to penetrate their defenses. Whatever information Somerton had shared with Latymer no doubt went straight into the Frenchman's ear.

Latymer must have alerted Valère to Cora's real purpose in France, too. Even though Somerton considered Latymer his friend, Guy suspected the traitor had not learned about Cora's secret identity from Somerton. The chief of England's Secret Service did not share that kind of information with anyone. Even his family. The bastard probably intercepted missives between

Somerton and Cora, and then forwarded them on to
Valère for money or power or whatever the hell bound
the two.

Indecision sliced through Guy. Cora's life could be
measured in minutes now, and Somerton could stroll
unawares into an equally lethal situation when he went
to update his superior.

"Problem, my lord?" the raspy voice mused.

"Somerton is on his way to see Latymer now."

"Ah, I see your dilemma."

The dark shadow shifted; waves of menace vibrated
off his informant. There was something different about
Specter tonight. The informant's tone conveyed a
powerful, barely contained derision—one quite different
from its usual amused indifference.

"Do you have something on your mind?" Guy asked.

"As a matter of fact, I do," the cloaked figure said.
"Minutes before your summons arrived, I received
word that the Raven is under the Frenchman's control
once again."

Guy's nostrils flared at the unnecessary reminder.
"You are well informed."

"It's my job to be so," Specter returned. "You have
benefited quite well from that fact over the years."

Guy bit down on the inside of his cheek, unable to
deny the truth of his informant's words.

"Wasn't she under your protection, my lord?"

Silence skidded off the stone walls surrounding them.

"Yes," Guy clipped out.

Another lengthy stillness ensued. Guy allowed the
hooded informant to see the humiliation and anger
burning in his soul. "What does your chief think about
the Raven's disappearance?"

Guy frowned. "What do you mean?"

"What I asked, of course," Specter said. "Does

Somerton mourn her disappearance, or is he indifferent to the problem?"

What was it about Somerton that snagged this shadowed figure's curiosity? Guy recalled the streak of pain that crossed Somerton's face upon hearing of Cora's kidnapping. "He is quite upset, I should think. Why do you ask?"

"Go to Raven," came the quiet order. "I will see to your distressed leader."

Guy nodded and turned to leave. He should have felt relief that Specter took the issue of Cora's disappearance no further than a simple inquiry. But relief was only a small part of what fired through his veins. A very small part. The bulk of his emotion equated to ungovernable rage. Rage against Valère, rage against Jack and himself, and he even felt rage against the mysterious informant at his back.

"My lord?"

Guy halted, squared his shoulders, and waited for the delayed tongue-lashing. "Yes?"

"Be careful. The estate is well guarded."

Guy glanced back. "I assumed no less. If you have nothing further to offer…"

He did not wait for an answer, simply allowed the growing fog to envelop him. For the first time in their clandestine relationship, it was Guy who disappeared into the shadows.

Guy reached The King's Arms at the appointed time, after first stopping at his town house to change out of his formal clothes and to grab a small arsenal of weapons. He located Somerton's carriage outside the inn's stables and startled Cora's servants awake when he opened the door. They scrambled out, apologizing as they went. He held up a hand. "No need to apologize. It has been a long evening."

"How long do you expect Lord Somerton to be, my lord?" Dinks asked, covering a yawn.

Guy thought on the Specter's revelations about Lord Latymer. He had to consider it would be some time before Somerton and reinforcements arrived. Time that Cora did not have.

"I will give him another hour to join us. If he is not here by then, we will continue on to Latymer's without him. In the meantime, let us all get a few minutes' rest."

"Latymer, my lord?" Dinks asked, a quizzical look on her face.

"That's right," Guy said. "You recognize the under-superintendent's name?"

"Undersuperintendent?" Dinks shook her head. "No, sir. At least I don't think so. Are you speaking of Maurice Pencavell?"

Something stirred low in Guy's gut. "No, his younger brother Pierce. Maurice died under mysterious circumstances a few months ago, and the middle son took the title."

"Yes," Dinks mused. "Just as I thought."

"Dinks, what do you have yammering inside that brilliant head of yours?"

She sent Bingham a brief glance, which made the coachman's face scrunch up and turn a ghastly shade of purple.

"I'll be off for a bit of sleep if you don't need me, m'lord." Bingham didn't wait for an answer. He stalked off toward the stable, his shoulders hunched.

Jack looked at the maid. "I'll see to him, Dinkie."

Dinks nodded before giving herself a hard shake. "Many years ago, I spent a few weeks inside that estate, entertaining the former baron." She squared her shoulders. "I'm not proud of those days, my lord. But they kept me off the streets. Some would suggest one stew is no different from the other, and to those kettle-brains, I say go spend the night on a urine-stained stoop in the middle of winter and see if you feel the same in the morning."

"I am no kettle-brain, Dinks." He lifted her rough hand to his lips. "Now I understand why Cora loves you so."

Tears welled in the maid's eyes. "We'll get her, my lord."

"I have no doubt," he said, handing her a handkerchief and wrapping an arm around her sturdy shoulders. "Especially with you by my side."

She batted at his chest. "Oh, now, go on with you, my lord. I'll send Jack up with a change of clothes for you and your shaving soap."

"Shall I have a maid prepare a chamber for you?" he asked, already knowing her answer.

"No, thank you, my lord." She waved her hand in the vicinity of the carriage and the stable beyond. "I have a few things to take care of down here."

"As you wish." Guy took a few steps toward the inn and then glanced back over his shoulder. Dinks stood there, staring at the stable, looking uncharacteristically lost. "Dinks?"

She started. "Yes, sir?"

"Bingham is no kettle-brain, either."

He knew the moment his words registered, for Dinks drew herself up and lifted her chin to a determined angle.

Guy nodded to the maid and turned back to the inn. He almost felt sorry for the coachman.

The following morning, Guy and Cora's servants strolled into the hunting box on the backside of Latymer's vast estate. Dinks had recalled seeing the structure and its accompanying outbuildings when she had been here as a guest of the former Lord Latymer. Since hunting season was still a few months away, the odds of discovery this far away from the main house were negligible.

Before leaving The King's Arms, Guy sent a messenger back to Somerton, with a coded note detailing their location. Guy tried not to think about why Somerton had not met them as planned. He could only hope Specter had been able to warn the old warhorse in time.

He swiped through a thin layer of cobwebs at the entrance to the small saloon and dropped his valise on a sheet-covered sofa, ushering up a cloud of dust. "We've some time before evening yet," he said to his newly appointed agents. "Let's make this place a little bit more habitable." Knocking down the cobwebs and airing out the sheets would give them something to focus on besides their worry.

"Yes, sir," Cora's servants said in unison, scurrying in opposite directions.

Being this close to Cora, his body hummed with anticipation. The next few hours of waiting would be the longest of his life. He had no way of knowing what would be awaiting him once he entered the house, or in what condition he would find Cora. She had sustained some type of injury at the Rothams', and he feared Valère would leave it untended.

He pulled his mind away from such unsettling thoughts and used the afternoon to concentrate on Cora's rescue.

When the sun fell below the tree line, Dinks and Bingham borrowed a pony cart from the barn and set off for the village to see what information they could collect on the new tenants at Latymer House, while Guy and Jack headed in the opposite direction on horseback.

They arrived at the edge of Latymer's parkland and secured their horses out of sight before making their way closer to the house on foot. "Jack, I will head east and angle my way north. You take the west side. Can you do that?"

"Yes, m'lord." The footman's earnest face revealed he was more than ready to do his part in retrieving his mistress.

"Count the number of men standing guard and note where they are located. Keep a lookout for signs of Miss Cora and your sister. Meet back here in half an hour."

"Yes, sir."

Guy knelt in the bracken and followed Jack's progress before beginning his own circuit. The young man wanted desperately to make up for his previous error in judgment, and Guy took a huge risk in allowing Jack to help gather intelligence. But, given their lack of manpower, he had few options.

Guy cut through the trees, stopping periodically to listen and count guards. After reaching the northeast corner of the house, he knelt again and waited for any sign of life inside the building.

"Cora, where are you?" he whispered. She was still alive. He felt it in his bones. If she were dead, he would sense it in the hollowness of his heart. He had to find her, had to tell her—

His attention was drawn to the second floor. To the dark outline of a woman's silhouette pacing slowly, almost painfully, before a curtained window. His pulse leaped in recognition.

Cora.

He stepped forward, intent on going to her, until a second, more masculine silhouette stepped behind her. The man's head bent toward the curve of her neck, setting up a roaring in Guy's ears that deafened him to the night calls of insects chattering all around him.

Valère.

He stared at the entwined figures; a flush of fury crept up his neck. His insides twisted with conflict. Being held in a bedchamber was far more hospitable than a damp cell, but what awaited her in that bedchamber could be even more destructive.

His unblinking gaze burned from focusing on the

couple for so long. From the way Cora carried herself, the injury she had sustained was to her upper body. And the goddamned French parasite was taking advantage of her weakened state. Guy's hand stole beneath his coat, and his fingers curled around the butt of a pistol. He prayed her injuries would keep Valère at bay long enough for him to get inside and rescue her.

"M'lord?"

Guy spun on his heel and aimed dead center at the man's chest. Blood thundered behind his eyes. The loathsome image from the window continued to dance before him, blurring reality. He cocked the pistol's hammer.

"M'lord! It's Jack."

The footman's harsh whisper penetrated the bloodlust whirring through Guy's mind. He squeezed his eyes shut and then reopened them. Jack's anxious features finally materialized and sharpened. Guy lowered his weapon.

"Forgive me, Jack," he said in a strained voice. "I could not make you out in the dim light."

The footman swallowed hard and swiped his forehead. "Any sign of Miss Cora or my sister?"

Guy glanced over his shoulder toward the house, toward the now-empty second-floor window. "I caught a glimpse of Miss Cora in one of the chambers on the second floor, three windows from the right."

Jack followed his gaze, silently counting to himself. "What do we do now?"

Guy stood. "We'll reassemble back at the hunting box."

As they trudged through the forest, Guy glanced back at the vacant window one last time. Leaving her behind was one of the hardest things he had ever done. He had counted a half-dozen men on his side of the house, and Jack likely counted an equal number on the west side. They needed a plan to remove the guards. Waiting for

Somerton and reinforcements was now out of the question. "Hold on, Cora," he whispered.

Two hours later, Dinks and Bingham returned from the village.

"The folks in the village are real tight-lipped about the goings-on at the Big House, as they call it," Dinks said.

"That garden fellow didn't seem none too quiet to me," Bingham grumbled.

A flush covered Dinks's face. "He did have a bit to say, but none of it had to do with Miss Cora."

"Then why'd you waste so much time on him?"

"Isn't that why we went there?" Dinks asked in exasperation. "To charm information from his lordship's servants and neighbors? The gardener might not know anything at the moment, but he'll keep his eyes and ears open now."

Bingham plopped his hat back on his head. "I'll be out in the barn if you need me, m'lord," he said, glaring at Dinks on his way out.

"He's been in a foul mood ever since we arrived," Dinks said in frustration.

"Can you not see why, Dinkie?" Jack asked with a crooked grin.

"I haven't the faintest idea what's going on in that old codger's head." She moved about the room, straightening this and that. "It's neither here nor there, anyway. What do we do now, my lord?"

"We must get rid of the guards."

"How many are we talking about, m'lord?"

"Valère has at least a score of men stationed around the house." Guy tried to control his own impatience.

"How about we take them out one by one, sir?" Jack said.

"It might come to that, Jack." Guy rubbed his tired eyes. "However, I'm hoping for something a bit more efficient and with far better odds of survival."

"Come, my lord," Dinks coaxed. "You're running

low and need to rest. We've established there's nothing more to be done tonight but worry."

"You're right, as always, Dinks."

"Do you plan on waiting until Lord Somerton arrives, m'lord?" Jack asked.

"I'll give him until tomorrow evening."

"Then what?"

"Then I'll take my chances."

Thirty-Four

MOONLIGHT SPILLED THROUGH THE BALCONY DOOR, casting a silver beacon of light onto the bedchamber floor a few feet from where Cora sat propped against the wall. But it was the ticking of the clock on the bedside table that held her rapt attention.

She had run out of time.

When the maid brought her dinner tray, she had cheerily told Cora that his lordship would be leaving first thing in the morning.

Cora's head fell back against the wall, and she stared at the ceiling. Other than a few taunting visits, Valère had not forced his attentions on her. That would all change tonight. How would he exact his revenge? Rape? Torture? Murder? All three? A sliver of ice ran down her spine. As if any of those options were amenable.

Good God. She wondered if the thin thread holding her sanity intact would survive the horrifying events Valère planned for her. He had begun his sensual torment last night, touching and kissing, leading her to believe her cooperation was the only thing that would keep her brother breathing. Her fingers worried the makeshift sling supporting her wounded left shoulder as images of the previous evening flashed before her eyes.

She had agonized over the possibility of Ethan being

alive and under the same roof. Valère would not think twice about using her dead brother to further his goals. In the end, she endured Valère's revolting touches, because she could not bear being the cause of another's death. Poor Scrapper. The kitten had used his last heartbeat to give her a chance to survive.

She had survived and would continue to do so by pretending it was Guy's lips pressed against her neck, not Valère's.

The Frenchman excelled at prolonging her anxiety. He knew she would focus on little else but his return. His enjoyment would end soon, for all would be resolved this evening. At least, for her.

Why had she thought she could defeat Valère alone? Why had she not confided her plans to Guy? Had she really thought she could outwit Valère?

Cora closed her eyes. Since her parents' murders, she had followed her own path for so long, certain of her course. She knew no other way.

She rolled her head to the side and shifted her gaze to the sheer curtain swaying in the evening summer breeze. Where was Guy? Did he search for her? Of course, he did. Guy was her friend. *Friend*. The word tore at her soul. Considering what her most recent decision was putting him through, such might not be the case any longer.

Her exhausted mind envisioned Guy hovering beyond the fluttering curtain, his broad shoulders adjusting to the narrow width of the open balcony door. With a veritable army patrolling the grounds, Valère knew door locks were unnecessary.

Guy's hazy image solidified when he stepped farther into the room. His handsome profile, so familiar and dear, caused the backs of her eyes to sting. She had missed him—every provoking inch. A sob welled deep in her throat.

He turned at the sound, spotted her shivering in the corner, and breathed her name into the evening breeze.

"Cora, love," he whispered, holding out his hand, coaxing her from the shadows. "I'm going to take you home now."

"You came."

"Did you think I would not?"

"I-I… how did you find me?"

"I will explain later," he said, urgency cutting his words short, "but first we must get you to safety."

"Yes. P-please."

"Please what, *mon ange*?"

"*Mon ange*?" she asked in confusion.

"Dreaming about your lover?" Valère's languid voice cut through the fog of sleep. She glanced around and found him sitting on the edge of her bed, not six feet away.

She scrambled to her feet, jarring her injury. Pain exploded in her shoulder. She gritted her teeth and worked to keep her body from swaying. Her gaze swept the room, looking for Guy. Was it just an apparition? *No!* God would not be so cruel.

"I d-don't know what you mean."

"You seem to have developed an unbecoming stutter, *ma chère*," he said in a casual tone. Too casual.

She stared at him, shaken by the vividness of her dream.

"What? The Raven has nothing to say? You did not seem to be at a loss for words a few minutes ago."

"Perhaps I dreamed of you."

His silky half smile disappeared. Valère's lean body unfolded, and he stood, menace humming around him like a swarm of bees. He tilted his head in a predatory manner, studying her. Silence stretched.

Cora reached for the wall behind her, seeking its solid strength in a miserable attempt to steady her nerves and stay upright.

"What did you dream?"

The next several hours yawned before her. She could see the revolving cycle of his revenge as clearly as if she had already lived it. In a way, she had. He would toy with her mind, touch her body, and feed her fear. But this time his attentions would be condensed to a twelve-hour period, not a fortnight.

She rolled her shoulders to relieve the tension. If she had weathered two weeks in his company, a half day—no matter how magnified—was barely worth her concern. She swallowed hard.

A false sense of courage fortified her spine, and she pushed away from the wall. Away from her haven of darkness, she realized with some surprise.

Every wile she had learned from Somerton's former mistress, and a few she had picked up on her own, led her down the familiar path of securing this man's attention, of using his own need as a means of control.

The rose-colored silk nightdress pressed against the outline of her body, leaving nothing to the onlooker's imagination. She inched closer, her gaze drifting over his lean body, ensuring he felt the scorching trail of her interest.

Forgive me, Guy. "I dreamed..." Cora allowed her words to float in the air between them. Her fingertips feathered up the length of his arm, along his shoulder, and hovered over his lips. She caressed the air above, the heat radiating from her fingertips her only contact.

"What?" he rasped, reaching for her waist.

"Ah, ah, my lord, you must keep your hands to yourself."

Valère lowered his arms, clenching his hands into ready weapons. "I do not like to be trifled with."

"What a pity," she purred. Her free hand tugged his coat off one shoulder and then the other, allowing it to fall about his elbows. "Because that is exactly what I intend to do."

Thirty-Five

WHEN SOMERTON FAILED TO SHOW THE FOLLOWING evening, Guy knew he could wait no longer. To leave Cora under Valère's thumb another day was unthinkable. He would have to follow through with his plan and pray Somerton arrived soon with reinforcements.

However, the wait had given him several quiet hours to work on the cipher. He was so damned close.

T 32 E 26   27 22 15 E R T 22 23

His heart thundered with the taste of triumph close at hand. Just a few more days. Maybe even hours.

"Lord Helsford!" Dinks burst through the front door of the hunting box, Bingham and Jack following behind at a more sedate pace.

"What is it? Have you heard something?"

"Yes," she gasped. "I know how to get you into the house with none the wiser." Dinks pressed a calming hand against her ample chest.

Tugging on her arm, Guy settled her into a nearby chair. "Have a seat so you can catch your breath."

"Oh, thank you, my lord."

"Better?"

"Yes."

"Go on."

"I know where they're storing their ale casks." Dinks

beamed at him, her hands prayer-like against her bosom, as though all their worries had been resolved.

"I see," Guy lied.

"Henry let it slip that his lordship's servants sneak down for an extra pint or two more than their daily ration."

Guy struggled to make a beneficial connection. "And Henry would be?"

"The garden fellow," Bingham spat.

Dinks's sunbeam smile turned to a scowl at Bingham's tone.

"Why did he tell you this information, Dinks?"

"The daft man would have told her anything as long as she kept jiggling her wares under his nose." Bingham crossed his burly arms over his chest. Bushy eyebrows dusted with a hint of gray turned down into a severe vee, giving him a sinister appearance.

"Why, you four-legged loving, shite-scooping mongrel." Dinks rose from her chair. "I did what I had to do to help Miss Cora. And, for your information, I'd have done a lot worse than baring a bit of my melons to loosen a lonely man's tongue. I owe Miss Cora my life, and you owe her for your own miserable existence, too."

The two stared at each other, neither backing down an inch. Guy wondered if the two realized they were in the midst of a courtship. A volatile one, but a courtship, nonetheless. Did they even realize that's what this was all about? He glanced at Jack. The footman wore the same roguish I-know-something-you-don't-know look that had lit his features the previous evening.

"Dinks," Guy said with growing impatience, "please continue."

"As I was saying"—she threw one last dagger look at Bingham before resuming her seat—"*Henry* also overheard his lordship ordering preparations for their departure."

"Departure?"

"Yes. Back to France."

Guy turned away to stare into the low, hissing fire. "Any mention of the prisoners?"

"No, my lord."

Desperation bloomed. He could feel its tentacles crawling along the edges of his thoughts. He had one chance to save Cora and the others. The likelihood that Valère would take Cora and Jack's sister to France was slim. Very slim. They would be a complication he could ill afford at this stage in the game.

"I can poison the ale," Dinks said.

"What?" Guy swung around. His gaze slashed between the three servants; each sported a devilish grin of satisfaction.

"Well, not exactly poison, but they might wish for the Almighty to take them away."

"How so?"

"Horehound, my lord."

"Horehound?"

"Oh, yes. It's good for cleaning out the system, if you know what I mean."

He felt the first stirrings of a smile. "I'm beginning to."

Dinks's grin turned evil. "If I can gather enough horehound leaves, I can create a purging brew to slip into the casks." She clasped her hands in glee. "It will have them guards sitting in the shiter for the rest of the evening."

The trio held their collective breaths while Guy sifted through this new scheme. His slow smile of agreement had them all grinning from ear to ear and elbowing each other in the ribs.

He swooped Dinks into a celebratory whirl. "Well done, my wily Dinks."

She shrieked her delight before exclaiming, "Put me down, you mad man, you'll break your back acting like such a fool."

He settled the maid back on her feet and, with a loud smacking noise, kissed her on the cheek.

Guy rubbed his hands together. "Now, let us get down to business, shall we?"

Later that night, Guy hunkered down to observe the stillness surrounding the grounds of Latymer's house. Not a guard in sight.

His lips curled into a triumphant smile. Their plan had worked. They had sent Dinks to charm the gardener—much to Bingham's consternation—into showing her where the casks were stored. A suggestion for an evening nip had given her an opportunity to empty her home-made concoction into the barrels.

Cora's little group of misfits was more resourceful than an elite band of spies. She would be so proud of them. He relished the moment when he could tell her how the trio had helped save her life again. And he could not wait to tell her how much he—

An owl shrieked low overhead, and Guy ducked. The bird's massive wings gracefully maneuvered the maze of limbs and branches.

The distraction refocused Guy on the mission ahead, on getting inside the house undetected. He had no way of knowing how many guards, unaffected by Dinks's potion, were inside. The maid had given him a rough sketch of the mansion's floor plan, along with a whispered warning of a secret room off the master's bedchamber. There, she feared, was where that Frenchie kept their little mite.

The thought of Cora bound in such a chamber made his blood run cold. Casting away the image, he moved to take a closer look and was stopped by a distinctive click near his ear.

"I think it best if you stay right where you are, my lord," a refined voice said.

A slender, well-dressed man edged into his line of sight. The gun he pointed at Guy's head never wavered.

"Toss your weapons to me," he ordered. "Slowly."

"I have no need for weapons, sir," Guy hedged, stalling for time.

"Indeed? Then you will not mind removing the gun tucked inside your waistband and the knife resting under your right hand."

Guy swore. How long had the guard been observing him?

"Do you know the gentleman you work for is an enemy to England?"

The guard laughed. "Your puny attempt to tweak my conscience is wasted, monsieur. Toss your weapons. Now."

Dread trickled down Guy's spine. The man shifted from flawless English to pure Parisian French. His garments were not of the quality worn by hired mercenaries but ones any London gentleman would be pleased to wear.

"Lord Helsford, I would prefer not to make a mess in Lord Latymer's woods, but I will."

Guy narrowed his eyes. "Are you the chap who enjoys beating women?"

"Depends upon the woman, my lord." Marcel raised the gun higher.

"What's the matter, Marcel?" Guy nodded toward the man's waist. "Equipment doesn't work well anymore?"

The Frenchman's finger curled around the trigger. "Ask your lady, English dog. She can provide great detail on how well my equipment operates."

Guy heard the crackle of leaves right before the first loud thud rent the air, followed swiftly by a second. Marcel's eyes rolled into the back of his head, and his now weaponless hand hung limply by his side. His legs buckled, and he teetered on his knees a moment before falling face forward into the bracken.

A wild-eyed Jack holding a large tree branch stood above the fallen man, his handsome face contorted into something wild and savage.

"Jack?"

"Yes, sir." He continued to stare at the Frenchman.

"You did well." Guy nodded toward the footman's hand still clutching the makeshift weapon. "You won't need that any longer."

Jack's gaze flicked to the branch and then to the prone man on the ground before tossing the weapon away. Without warning, he plunged his boot deep into the man's ribs. "That's for my sister, you fecker." He stomped his broken wrist. "And that's for Miss Cora."

Jack's labored breaths rent the air. Guy kept a wary eye on the footman when he bent to retrieve the unconscious man's gun.

"Jack." He waited for the footman to look up. "Do you still have your rope?"

"Yes, sir."

"Let us make sure he does not cause any more trouble."

While Jack secured Marcel's limbs, Guy tied a handkerchief around the Frenchman's mouth.

"Help me move him farther into the woods," Guy said.

They stowed Marcel in a shallow den beneath a large, fallen oak tree.

"Thank you." Guy squeezed the young man's bony shoulder and received a jerky nod in response.

"Bingham is covering the back of the house. I need you to take the front and keep an eye on the drive," Guy instructed. "God willing, Somerton is on his way to the hunting box, and Dinks can bring him here straightaway."

"But, m'lord—"

"No buts, Jack. Given the lack of guards, Dinks's concoction must have done its job. The handful of able servants inside will pose no problem."

Jack's scowl conveyed his displeasure at the order, but he moved to comply.

Guy surveyed the manor's stone edifice, making his way to a side entrance. The fewer of their people inside the house, the fewer they would mourn if all went wrong.

It was his second to last thought before something solid connected with the back of his head and pain splintered through his skull. His last thought, the one that plowed through his mind a second before his face smashed into the ground, was the realization that at least one other guard had dodged the effects of Dinks's concoction.

Thirty-Six

CORA FOUGHT TO HOLD BACK A SIGH OF RELIEF. THE pounding on the bedchamber door could not have come at a better time. Of course, Valère did not share her opinion.

"Do. Not. Move." He shrugged his coat back on and stomped across the room. He threw the door open, slamming it into the wall. "What is it?"

Mrs. Pettigrew stood in the doorway, wringing her apron between work-worn hands. Her eyes shifted about the room, landing on Cora near the bed.

"Speak up, you English cow!"

The housekeeper stammered out, "T-there's something wrong with your men, my lord."

"What do you mean?"

"I'm not sure. They all seem to have a putrid stomach."

"All of them?"

"Yes, my lord."

"Dammit." Valère stormed into the corridor, his French curses bouncing off the walls. "Lock the damn door. Marcel!"

The housekeeper stared at Valère's retreating back, lines bracketing her compressed lips. She turned to Cora. "How are you, miss?"

Cora peered out the balcony door. "I have been better, Mrs. Pettigrew." Something was definitely amiss. Not more than an hour ago, two dozen men milled around the grounds. And now, nothing but a curious stillness greeted her inspection. Switching her attention to the bedchamber door, she wondered if the guards stationed in the corridor were also affected by the mysterious outbreak.

"His lordship said you were set upon by highwaymen, and that's how you received your wound."

"Did he?" Cora responded in a neutral voice, not wanting to drag an innocent into their dance of death. She edged toward the bedchamber door.

"Yes." The housekeeper glanced down the corridor before stepping closer. She lowered her voice. "I found it odd that he brought back no luggage or lady's maid for you."

"Mrs. Pettigrew." Cora inched forward and instilled all the haughtiness she could muster into her next words. "I have no luggage because the distance I traveled was not so great and, women such as I do not need maids, only a man's hands."

The housekeeper's eyes widened and, just as quickly, focused on her with an unnerving regard.

"I, and a few others, are close at hand should you need us." Mrs. Pettigrew pulled the door shut.

"Mrs. Pettigrew!"

The housekeeper paused. "Yes, miss?"

"Are you aware of any other guests staying with his lordship? Perhaps a gentleman or a little girl?"

The housekeeper nodded. "His lordship's niece."

"Niece?"

"Grace is her name," the housekeeper said. "A sweet child with a mane of red hair and an endearing gap between her front teeth. When his lordship first brought her here, the little thing cried day and night. His lordship said she had recently lost her brother, her last remaining relative. Besides him, of course."

Although Cora had not seen Jack's sister in a while, the description seemed to match. "Can you take me to her room?"

"Woman," a man called from down the corridor, "stop your prattling and lock the door."

The housekeeper's friendly demeanor shifted to stoicism. "I'm afraid not, miss." Before closing the door, she met Cora's gaze. "Remember my offer."

Cora's throat clenched at the sound of Mrs. Pettigrew's key clicking in the lock. The housekeeper made no mention of Ethan. Was he even here? Had she allowed herself to endure the Frenchman's touch for nothing?

She shook her head. No, Grace was here. If Valère had not dangled Ethan in front of her, he would have used Jack's sister. Cora's decision would have been the same.

Devising a plan, Cora paced by the window and was once again struck by the absence of guards. Nervous excitement pulsed through her muscles.

Guy.

Bone-shattering fear and exhilaration filled her mind. He had found her. My God, he had come for her—*the idiot.*

If Valère managed to capture Guy, the unbearable days she had spent locked in his dungeon would seem like nothing more than a fanciful dream compared to what Guy would endure. The thought of her brother's torture was enough to eat at her sanity. If Valère succeeded in taking Guy, she would be lost. All would be lost.

In desperation, Cora ran to the door and pounded. "Guard!" When he did not answer, she pounded again. Still no answer.

She glanced around the room for a long, thin item she could use as a pick. Nothing. Valère had made certain to remove all potential threats. She did not even have a pin for her hair.

Turning back to the door, she struck the panel several times, yelling for the guard. Past rational thinking, she hiked up her nightdress and flattened her foot against the wall. She grabbed the knob with both hands and pulled as hard as she could. The door remained closed tight.

In a fury, she jerked on the handle over and over, growling her frustration at the locked door. The next thing she knew she was hurdling backward, landing half on her bottom, half on her back, her bare legs sprawled in an unladylike manner toward the corridor.

The corridor.

She scrambled to her feet, feeling a twinge in her back. Dumbfounded, she stared at the open door. Then she remembered the knob turning in her grasp during her frenzy to be free. The housekeeper had not locked the door, only rattled the key a bit for the guard's benefit. All she had to do was turn the damn handle.

She hastened from the chamber, almost colliding with the door in her haste. At the top of the stairs, she paused to listen for movement below.

When all appeared quiet, she inched her way down the stairs one at a time. Halfway down, she heard a pair of masculine voices streaming through a partially opened door to her right.

With careful steps, she continued her descent, keeping a wary eye out for a stray guard or the ever-present Marcel. An undercurrent of familiarity drifted at the edge of her conscience, almost as if she had lived this scene at another time and place.

Bracing a trembling hand against the door frame, Cora set her eye to the opening. Several candles illuminated a well-appointed study and, in its center, she found Valère towering over someone in a chair, with two guards flanking the French doors that opened onto the terrace.

Unable to see around Valère's back, she shifted her position to get a better look at the chair's occupant, but all she got was a perfect view of Valère's hand slashing through the air, connecting with flesh.

Every instinct told her Guy was sitting in that chair. The disturbance with the guards, Valère's flight from her bed, the housekeeper's assistance—it all pointed to an intruder. Another flesh-against-flesh impact sent her heart slamming against her rib cage. Blood rushed to her head, making her feel light-headed and slightly nauseous.

Squeezing her forehead, she took a couple of breaths, willing it back. She needed all of her mental faculties to be in proper working order, not be swooning like an overexcited debutante. Satisfied she would not fall flat on her face, she pushed the door open a little more with the tip of her finger.

"I'll ask you one more time." Valère's angry words carried to her hiding place. "How many more of your comrades are outside?"

"My bare hands are enough to see you dead," taunted a familiar voice. "What need do I have of others?"

Valère moved to the side, and Cora spotted Guy tied to a sturdy wooden chair, bloodied and breathless. The skin over his right eye was already swelling with fluid, and blood oozed from the deep slash in his full bottom lip. Cora clapped a hand over her mouth to silence a helpless scream.

"I would have given you a quick death had you answered my question the first time," Valère said in a voice most people used to discuss the weather. "However, you have forced me to make this a very ugly scene."

Valère turned to one of the guards. "Find Marcel."

"That wouldn't be chap I met in the woods, would it?" Guy spit out a ball of thick red phlegm.

Valère's body stiffened. "What have you done with him?"

"I threw the bastard in a hole."

A small, wobbly smile split across Cora's face. How she would love to see Marcel crammed in a dirty, insect-infested hole. If they all came out of this alive, she would insist Guy take her to the henchman's burrow. Such a fitting place for such a vile man.

Valère's feral gaze landed on the guard again. "Do not come back until you have found him."

"Yes, my lord." The guard rushed from the study.

"You will pay dearly if my servant's dead, Helsford."

Seeing Valère's furious intent, Cora pressed her hands against her ears and backed away from the door. Shielding herself from the violence did not stop her body's physical reaction to the goings-on inside the room.

She had been here before.

As old memories flooded into her mind, a flush of cold sweat coated her skin. Her body trembled against the onslaught of so many troubling images. From one moment to the next, she was ten years old again, terrified and alone.

Cora crept down the staircase, bending her ear toward the raised voices muffled behind her father's thick library door. Several times over the last fortnight, she had heard her father's rage pelt the four walls of what was once his quiet sanctuary. She paused in indecision, and then her father yelled something indecipherable.

Sighing, she turned to go back to her bedchamber. She wished her old papa would return, the loving and jovial man who had hugged her each morning and asked about her day every evening. This new papa, who had haunted their home for over a month, frightened her with his constant ranting and demand for solitude. His merry blue eyes had dulled to a lifeless gray, and he smelled of strong spirits more often than not.

A loud pop exploded through the lower level of the house,

followed by her father's wail. Cora's head whipped around at the sound of anguish in her father's voice.

She scurried down the stairs, her heart hammering against the wall of her chest. She reached for the door handle but stopped short when she heard an unfamiliar voice. Something told her to take caution rather than rush into the room. The decision to proceed slowly was distressing, for she knew her papa needed her. Edging closer, she peered into the room. Her father sat bound to a chair with tears streaming down his face. His tormented blue eyes were trained on the floor.

She followed the direction of his tearful gaze. At first, the azure slippers and silk-clad legs lying sprawled in an indelicate tangle on the floor did not register in her ten-year-old mind. Her gaze flicked to her father and then back down to the slippers. Understanding finally dawned. The loud pop, her father's cry, her mother's dainty feet.

Cora clamped her hand around her mouth to hold back a shriek of terror. She stumbled back a few feet from the door, keeping her father's face in view. Numb with grief and overwhelmed with the awful events, Cora could do nothing but stare at her father as if he held all the answers.

"You will share your wife's fate, Danforth," said a male voice with a French accent, "if you do not tell me what I wish to know."

Rustling from within penetrated the haze of anguish coating her heart. She rushed back to the door, hoping to glimpse the foreign stranger. But her view was limited to the half of the room containing her father and—she gulped for air—her mother's prone body.

Her father fought the bindings holding him. "I told you I know nothing about a deployment of troops!" he snarled.

"So you have said a hundred times, and yet, I have intelligence that tells me otherwise. Very well," the Frenchman said. "Since you cannot provide the information I need..."

Inches before her eyes, a black-gloved hand holding a gun

*materialized from the wall, its owner out of sight. The shiny
barrel pointed directly at her father's chest, and then an explosion pierced her eardrums.*

*A hand wrapped around her mouth, pulling her away from
the door. She glanced over her shoulder to see a twelve-year-old
Jack. His frightened gaze locked with hers. He urged her
away, pulling her hard when she refused. Unable to battle his
greater strength, she stumbled away. Hand in hand with Jack,
she escaped all the way up to the attic. To Winnie-the-Chair
and safety.*

Another demand for information brought Cora back
to the present. After fleeing the murderous scene, she and
Jack had huddled in Winnie's red depths for what seemed
like hours, waiting for the murderers to leave. Not until
the house grew eerily quiet had they been brave enough
to venture out of their hiding spot.

The jeweled pendant hanging about her neck burned
a reminder against her chest. She wrapped her fingers
around the cameo, drawing strength from its reassuring
presence. When they tiptoed into the library, they had
found several of her father's books and important papers
littering the floor. And the pendant.

She would never forget how the cameo lay forlornly
on the carpet not far from her mother's grasping, claw-
like fingers. Remorse for her parents' stolen moment
still sat heavily on her heart. Had the killers interrupted
a tender time between her mother and father? Had her
father given the beautiful cameo to her mother for a
secret celebration? Cora feared these answers would
remain forever unanswered.

Tears clogged Cora's throat. If only she had gone for
help rather than run for safety. There was a chance—a
small possibility—that her father had not died right
away. Instead of sniveling in a chair, she could have
gone downstairs and untied the servants, escaped to

a neighbor's house, screamed all the way down the
street... anything but hide.

She had deserted her parents all those years ago, and
that poor choice would haunt her always. Tonight, she
would not bury her face in plush red comfort. Tonight,
she would act. Instead of desertion, she would employ
coercion. She would do anything—everything—but hide.

Swiping the tears from her face, Cora stormed into the
adjacent room and hurried to the desk. She rummaged
through several drawers, taking precious minutes to find a
suitable weapon she could conceal in her sling. Then she
found it. After testing its mettle, she slid the slender object
into the tight space under her forearm for easy access.

When she rounded the desk, a second item caught her
attention. She picked up the round crystal paperweight,
testing its heaviness and her ability to grip it well. The
cold mass fit perfectly within the palm of her damp hand.
After a second's hesitation, she secured it inside her sling,
this time resting the piece on top of her forearm before
rushing from the salon.

Standing outside the drawing-room door, Cora drew
three deep breaths to help steady her nerves. She had one
chance. One chance to convince Valère that Guy meant
nothing to her. She must smother the truth into the
depths of her soul. Would Guy recognize her subterfuge
or be wounded by her perceived betrayal? She could not
warn him of her intent, and she may never get a chance
to explain, if things went awry.

So much was at stake—Guy, Ethan, Grace—they all
needed her to succeed. She could not fathom the loss of
any one of them. However, losing Guy would be like
erasing her future. Without Guy, nothing but a never-
ending wall of darkness towered before her.

*Focus on the goal and move forward without hesitation,
Cora. If you falter, even for a moment, all could be lost.* She

heard Somerton's voice as if he stood by her side, both of them staring at the formidable door separating her from Guy. She had called on his words of wisdom many times over the years. Not once had he failed her. Not once.

She checked to make sure her little arsenal was secured in the depths of her sling. Satisfied all was as it should be, she lifted her chin and pushed open the door.

Thirty-Seven

GUY'S MIND REELED FROM THE BLOWS VALÈRE DELIV-
ered. The Frenchman's relentless demand for information hammered against every sinew in Guy's already
weakened body.

It was his sheer unfortunate luck that the two guards,
who had ambushed him the moment he had emerged
from the forest, had been carved from the Rock of
Gibraltar, and neither evidently imbibed. Not even a sip.

Dammit, his head hurt. The back of his skull felt as if
it were cleaved in half, laid open for the world to see the
source of his stupidity. What the hell had they used on
him? The blows suddenly halted, and Guy's head sagged
to his chest, a prayer of thanks whispering between his
split lips.

Then he heard her voice.

"What is going on here?" Cora asked in a tone that
reeked of indolent boredom.

Guy's head snapped up, taking in her bandaged arm and
languid stride. She looked incredibly beautiful with her hair
curling softly around her face and her nightdress molding
the curves of her body with each step. The bandage
supporting her injured arm and the faint bruises smudging
her skin presented a delicate contrast. But her eyes, her
Raven eyes, conveyed a completely different message.

Determination. Hatred. *Sacrifice*.

His relief at seeing her alive was overshadowed by a gut-burning rage and a mind-numbing helplessness.

"Ah, the Raven emerges from her nest," Valère said with acid disdain. He rubbed his bloodied knuckles against the remaining guard's coat.

"You left my bed for this?" Cora asked.

Valère studied her. "Your lover came to fetch you home, *ma belle*."

Guy's gaze flicked between the two while applying pressure to his restraints. They did not stretch so much as a hairsbreadth. Damned efficient guards.

"Really?" she said. "I made it quite clear to him that our liaison was over. If not for Somerton's insistence that I have a bodyguard"—she sent Valère a cross look—"I would have been quit of the wretch days ago. It takes some men longer than others to understand such things."

"You wish me to believe you do not welcome his interference?"

The skepticism in Valère's voice set Guy's teeth on edge. From the way his cold gaze regarded Cora, he did not completely believe her lack of interest. The Frenchman was obviously suspicious and seemed to be waiting for her to make a misstep.

Cora moved to stand behind Guy, draping her arm over his shoulder in a negligent and highly sensual fashion. He stiffened, not knowing where she was going with this new tactic. With her defiant gaze on Valère, she stroked Guy's swollen jaw so dispassionately one could almost label the intimate action a mockery.

"Lord Helsford is a childhood friend and a man I slept with for a few unremarkable nights—nothing more." She rubbed the backs of her fingers down his throat, and Guy clenched his teeth against her impersonal touch. Her caress made his blood run hot and cold in equal parts.

"Please tell me that it is not jealousy sparkling in your eyes, monsieur." She shifted around until she appeared on his left. "I find such sentiments tedious." She smoothed her hand down his front, all the way until she covered his crotch. "Don't you?"

The impact of the hard, slender object sliding against his spine turned his tense muscles to impenetrable granite. His fingers latched onto the object as it made its slow descent into his palm. After a few exploratory twists and turns of the item, a flush of excitement gripped his chest when he realized Cora had slipped him a knife.

The Raven had come through for them again. Guy took a moment to assess the weapon. Latymer's cutler did an excellent job curving the haft to fit a man's hand. Approximately four inches in length, the smooth handle connected to a much shorter blade. Likely one of Latymer's penknives, used for mending quill nibs.

Guy glanced up at Valère, certain the man would be furious over Cora's bold display. Instead, the Frenchman watched her hand with a burning intensity that made Guy's stomach knot with revulsion. If he were not so terrified for her safety, he would be in awe of her cunning ploy.

With a jarring abruptness, Cora straightened and sauntered to where Valère leaned against the back of a sofa. She draped herself around the Frenchman, her fingers smoothing across his blood-splattered shirt. "Perhaps we could convince him to join us upstairs. You may keep him bound, if you like."

Predatory interest gleamed in Valère's dark eyes. "You think to control the both of us, *ma petite*?"

The corners of Cora's mouth turned up into a confident smile filled with knowing secrets. Her hand hooked around the Frenchman's neck, and she answered his challenge with an ardent kiss to the bastard's lips. With his role now reversed with Valère's, Guy followed her beguiling movements much as the Frenchman had moments ago, but with none of Valère's lust.

Guy turned away, resentment and a maddening fury choking the air from his lungs. He could not watch her debase herself to save his miserable hide. If he had not gotten himself captured, she would have been spared this humiliation. Twisting the penknife around, he made his first ineffectual slice to his bindings.

"So very convincing," Valère said. "Perhaps I should take you right here in front of your *childhood friend*."

The husky menace in Valère's voice brought Guy's gaze back to the entwined couple, and his stomach cringed with dread.

Valère clasped Cora's throat in a viselike grip with one hand and ran his index finger, sticky with Guy's blood, over the pale surface of her cheek. Cora did not so much as flinch. She merely regarded the Frenchman with an air of patience, almost as if she had expected his response.

Guy tried to increase his efforts, but the guard had done his job well. The tight restraints allowed for little maneuvering.

"Tempting, *mon loup*." She peeled Valère's fingers from around her throat. "But I am well enough now to see to your... needs. Why waste your host's special room upstairs?"

The Frenchman considered her for a long moment, his aroused breaths reaching Guy's ears.

"Alas," Valère said. "I must disappoint you. The place I have in mind is far superior to Latymer's red room." He seized her upper arm and headed for the door.

Cora's confident expression cracked, and her gaze

slashed to his. That one brief glance was all it took for
him to see her fear. Not for herself, but for him.

To the guard, Valère said, "I'll be back in ten minutes.
Do not let the prisoner out of your sight."

"Yes, my lord." The guard uncoiled his massive arms.

With every desperate stroke of the small blade, Guy
ripped through flesh. The blood from his wrist trickled
into the hand holding the penknife, making it difficult
to retain his grasp. He tested his bindings again and felt
the tension give. His pulse leapt, not only because of his
progress but because he had run out of time.

"Valère, you bastard," Guy yelled. "Where are you
taking her?" He could not let them leave the room.

The Frenchman turned his gaze, so filled with hate
and malevolence, on him. "She will be in good hands,
monsieur. You should be more concerned about your
own fate."

"Goddamn it! Do not touch her." Guy came to his
feet—chair and all. Sweat and blood seeped into the
corner of his eye, and the damn bindings tightened with
the weight of the chair pulling on them.

Valère smirked at Guy's rash act. "Make sure Lord
Helsford is secure before my return. Break his ankles, if
you must."

The guard grabbed Guy's arm, intending to follow
his master's orders. Guy shrugged him off, his gaze never
leaving Cora's retreating back.

"Hold on, Cora," he demanded.

She turned, sending him a tremulous smile, and then
she mouthed the three most beautiful words in the
English language.

Valère jerked her forward, the door slamming behind
them.

Silence flooded the room.

I love you. He had not imagined the words. Her

beautiful mouth had formed the words with perfect clarity. She loved him. A tide of helpless wonder crashed into his stomach while he stared at the wooden barrier separating him from Cora.

This was not the time for him to act like a besotted idiot, nor was it the time for him to rejoice in the knowledge that his efforts to draw forth his old friend had netted results far greater. And much more precious.

He blinked hard to clear the bloody sweat from his swelling eye and began tearing at his bindings in earnest.

Pain shot through his midsection when the guard's beefy fist connected with his stomach. Guy staggered, and the chair bounced into the backs of his knees, buckling them. He fell to the ground in a heap at the guard's feet, his arms pinned beneath the chair.

"Now look at what you've done." The guard drew a two-foot-long wooden club from his leather belt. Made of what looked to be solid English oak, the weapon could kill a man with a single crushing blow to the throat.

Guy swallowed and then lifted his hips up to take the pressure off his hands. And that's when he realized he no longer held Cora's knife.

Thirty-Eight

CORA FOCUSED ON PUTTING ONE FOOT IN FRONT OF THE other. Leaving Guy bound to the chair was an unbearable decision, but she knew he had a better chance of freeing himself with Valère absent. Dear Lord, she hoped the penknife was strong enough to cut through his bindings.

Hold on, Cora. Guy's agonized expression and wrenching plea haunted her as she trudged toward her destiny. It had taken every last ounce of courage she possessed to face Guy and to reveal her true feelings when he must surely hate her after witnessing such a disgusting spectacle.

Even she was repulsed by her own behavior.

Valère stopped in the middle of the entrance hall, and he clamped his hands around her face with brutal force. "Stop thinking about him." He devoured her lips in a raw attempt to force her compliance, until the metallic taste of blood reached her tongue. He finished the kiss by sucking her bottom lip between his teeth, and then bit down hard until a fresh wave of warm liquid spread into her mouth. She was unable to contain her gasp of pain.

"If you continue thinking of the Englishman while in my possession, I will kill him." He caught a droplet of scarlet liquid on his thumb before it beaded off the edge of her bottom lip. "I should think that knowledge would provide proper motivation, no?" His sneering lips encircled his blood-slicked thumb.

"As always, monsieur, your logic is sound."

Her satiric response was not lost on him. "Your mockery will be short-lived."

Instead of continuing up the grand staircase as she had suspected, he pulled her deeper into the lower level of the house. They passed the formal dining room, with its elaborate mural-covered ceiling and large, richly decorated table, before traipsing down a long, dank corridor and a set of narrow stairs. They emerged into a large kitchen stocked with hanging herbs and pots of various sizes. Propped against an immense wooden table stood another hale guard, although this one looked as if he could benefit from a hearty meal or two.

The table drew Cora's gaze, and a flush of heated dread scoured her body. A fortnight of memories crowded her mind, many spent shackled to a similar structure in Valère's dungeon. Without conscious thought, she began backing away.

Valère glanced at her, a scowl on his face as he finished whispering unintelligible instructions to the guard. She could hear nothing beyond the furious pounding in her ears. Before darting out of her line of sight, the guard grabbed a nearby lantern and retrieved a burlap sack stored beneath the table. She backed up another step, and Valère's hold tightened. He followed the direction of her gaze and chuckled low.

"No, *ma petite*." He nudged her toward a low-framed door. "I have much more sumptuous accommodations planned for you." He swung open the door to reveal another set of narrow stairs, only these emptied into absolute darkness.

No! Cora dug her heels into the floor, knowing

exactly where those steps led. Cold sweat saturated her body, and her limbs began to tremble.

Valère glanced down at her; a knowing look danced across his rat-bastard face. "Why do you hesitate?"

She tugged on her arm. "I'm not going down there."

His fingers bit into her flesh. "You make it sound as if you have a choice, *ma petite*."

Cora wrenched free of Valère's grasp and jammed the heel of her hand into the black patch covering his damaged eye. He roared, and she bolted for the stairs leading up to the first floor, her feet slapping a desperate tattoo across the wood planks. Her only sane thought—*Guy*!

She made it as far as the dining room before powerful, claw-like fingers snagged her by the hair, stopping her flight in an instant. She cried out and then pressed her lips together, unwilling to show him any more weakness.

Valère yanked her back, her body plowing into his solid chest. She used the momentum to jab her elbow into his ribs and slam her foot into the inside of his knee.

Air burst from his lungs. "*Salope!*" he hissed, grabbing a handful of hair. Her eyes pricked with tears.

"Do not do that again." His harsh breaths beat against her ear. The arm he clamped around her waist felt more like a steel rod against her injured ribs than a human limb.

Slowly, inexorably, he tilted her head back until she could see nothing but Valère's harsh face and a single trail of blood escaping from beneath his black eye patch. She experienced a moment of pride until she tried to swallow and could not. The severe angle of her neck held her completely at his mercy. Cora tried to tamp down the panic bubbling deep inside, and failed.

"You don't want to miss the best part, *mon ange*." He nipped her neck hard enough to make her flinch. "Do you not wish to see your friends?"

She tried to look at his expression, to check his

sincerity, but she could no longer see his face. Was he speaking of Ethan and Grace? Or had he imprisoned Dinks and the others, too?

Oh, God. Nausea roiled deep in her stomach.

"What have you done, Valère?"

One side of his mouth curled into a cruel smile. "Come with me, and you will find out."

She shook her head, fear consuming her mind.

He regarded her for a moment. "Because you are my favorite pet, I shall be generous and tell you this. If you refuse to follow me below, I will reenact on your friends some of the more interesting aspects of your previous stay in my dungeon." He glanced at the drawing-room door. "*All* of them."

Cora drew in a ragged breath and closed her eyes. The thought of walking into the cellar, into the darkness, and into all the evil that awaited her there, made her stomach heave.

How would she find the strength? For her friends and brother? For Guy? Their lives depended upon her cooperation with this monster, unless she killed him first. Could she set aside weeks of remembered torture and isolation to save them?

A shudder of terror turned her bones to jelly, and she sagged against Valère. God forgive her, she was not strong enough. She did not have the courage to face her greatest fear. Not even for those she loved.

"Go to hell, Valère."

Rage burned across his features, contorting his once-handsome face into a thing of ugliness and evil.

"You shall regret your decision." He raised his hand.

Noise from down the hall caught their attention. The drawing-room door muffled what sounded like a drunken brawl. Then a loud pop resounded through the house, followed quickly by an awful silence.

Cora had heard that sound once before, many years ago, when an unknown gunman murdered her parents.

"No!" she cried at the same time Valère muttered a foul French curse.

She heaved against his iron grip, ignoring the excruciating pain of ripping hair and bending ribs. She had to help Guy. He would not have had enough time to cut his bindings.

"Let go of me, you bastard."

"You will forget him soon enough." Valère picked her up and carried her toward the cellar. "I vow it."

She kicked at his knees again and head-butted his nose.

"Ahhh," he growled, his grip loosening. But he regained his bearings and, after a hard shake that rattled her teeth, he threw her over his shoulder.

The paperweight shifted, and she made to catch it, giving up her ability to brace herself against the shock of his shoulder punching into her ribs. Unlike last time, she managed to stay conscious and save her weapon. But not without consequences.

Darkness dimmed her vision, and her head swirled until the pain of impact receded. When Cora's wits returned, she pounded his back with all her strength. "Let me go, let me go!"

In answer, he whipped around, the movement throwing her off-balance and into the kitchen's door frame. Her head cracked against the solid wood, and her vision dimmed once again. By the time she could regain her equilibrium, Valère was descending into the cellar.

She daren't put up a struggle now for fear of Valère's missing a step and breaking both their necks. She stared up at the door's rectangle of light while pitch black enfolded her, pulling her farther into its inky depths. She imagined Guy lying on the floor, with a gaping hole in his chest, his eyes staring sightlessly toward the door, toward her retreating back.

She shook her head. *No!* He was alive, and he needed her. Over the years, she had made a point to learn all she could about gunshot wounds and their care. But all her knowledge was for naught if she could not see the patient and assess the damage.

Valère reached the bottom of the staircase and rounded the corner, snuffing out the light, the window to her sanity.

Squeezing her eyes shut, she fought to hold on. She had to work through her fear, hold on until an opportunity of escape presented itself. She would not desert Guy as she had her parents. She. Would. Not.

"Guard," Valère called.

"Here, sir," With a lantern held aloft, the thin guard scurried out of a room.

"Is all in readiness?"

"Yes, sir."

Cora glanced around, looking for Dinks and the others. The mixture of rotting food and cold, damp air made her skin crawl. The absence of her friends sent terror ripping through her. "Where are my friends?"

"Patience," Valère said. "After your poor behavior, I should not allow you to see them. But I am feeling magnanimous at present and will honor my promise."

Taking the lantern from the guard, Valère made his way across the cellar, weaving around casks, bins, and sacks of God-knows-what, until he drew even with a walled cell. It looked to be an exact replica of the cell she had inhabited in France, except it lacked Boucher's blood-soaked table and lethal devices.

Cora, hanging from his shoulder, had to swallow hard to keep the bile down. As she had done with the giant who had kidnapped her from the Rothams' ball, Cora arched her back and put the full force of her weight behind her elbow.

Anticipating her move, Valère dropped his shoulder and released her legs. She tumbled to the hard-packed dirt floor. The force knocked the air from her lungs, and bright spots whirled before her eyes. She was starting to question her ability to survive. One more knock to the head, and it was certain to explode.

"I am through being a gentleman." He grabbed a handful of hair and dragged her backward into the cell.

She clawed at his hand, and her feet fought for purchase, trying to mitigate the excruciating pain driving into her scalp.

He flung her against the rough stone wall, her back smacked the surface with a dull thud, and she slid to the reeking floor like a ball of mud sliding down a fence post. She barely had time to get her bearings when his hand clamped around her throat and drew her battered body up, inch by slow inch. Her head scraped against the uneven surface until they stood eye to eye.

Her neck stretched tight, and her slippered toes ached from the weight of her body. Her hold on the heavy paperweight tightened. She must not drop it—no matter what. Given the grim condition of the cell, the paperweight would likely be her only salvation.

A glowing lantern hanging from a wrought-iron hook cast wavering light over Valère's face. His chiseled features were cold, his eyes hollow with vengeance.

"Do not be frightened, *ma petite*. Your friends will soon be here to keep you company." He released her. "In the meantime, turn around."

Cora's breath hitched at his quiet command. She had sworn to remain vigilant around him after her lack of focus at Herrington Park. Presenting her back to him was out of the question. In a pathetic attempt to shield herself with something—anything—she scanned the room once more and found it still devoid of furnishings. No bed, no cot, no mound of straw. Not even a bedpan.

His eyes narrowed when she did not immediately comply. "You think to challenge me? Shall I bring your pitiful friends in here and kill them one at a time? Perhaps the sight of your brother would provide more incentive?"

A well of grief opened up inside her. The French had stolen so much from her. Monsters like Valère, who believed they could determine another's destiny with a single word. Her hand inched toward her only weapon. She would not lose any more of her loved ones to the French, especially not this fiend.

The skinny guard stepped into the room. "Where would you like the sack, my lord?"

Cora's hand returned to her side.

"Anywhere." Valère's jaw clenched at the interruption. "Except by the door. Did you get the bucket?"

"Yes, sir."

"Place it near the sack, and get out."

Cora angled her head to see past Valère's broad shoulders, but he moved to block her view. With unexpected swiftness, he twirled her around and ripped open the back of her borrowed nightdress. She stared at the stone wall as the rose-colored silk sagged around her shoulders. If not for her sling, she would be standing in nothing but a thin shift, for she wore no corset.

The cool air penetrated the fine material, and her body began to quiver inside. That small movement pierced the fog of her shock, and her muscles coiled for action.

Sensing her intention, he forced her against the wall, pressing his forearm against her neck, the rough stone cutting into her cheek.

Cora gulped for air. There was none to be had.

"Do not test my patience. When I remove my

arm, you will get rid of that damn sling and drop your garment. Understood?"

Unable to speak, she nodded.

He stepped away, and Cora's reeling mind searched for a means of escape. She needed the Raven's keen wit, and she needed it now.

When the Raven refused to surface, Cora pulled in a shuddering breath and drew the sling from around her neck. She crouched low, stripping the garment from her shoulders and piling everything, including the paperweight, in a crumpled heap at her feet.

She turned to face her captor.

A deluge of vile-smelling liquid hit her in the chest, splashing her face and stinging her eyes. Her breath lodged in her throat. Cold, fat clumps ran down her body, coating her from head to toe. The filth dripped like fat raindrops from her fingertips.

She blinked several times to clear her vision. Valère stood across the room, a calculating expression on his face. He tossed the empty slop bucket into the corridor, where it splintered against a far wall.

And that was when she heard the squealing.

Her gaze shot to the large burlap sack lying at Valère's feet. The top was tied with a narrow rope. The sack writhed with the activity of several bulbous bodies.

Cora's heart nearly exploded with terror. She glanced down at her fetid, wet body, and then to the sack of squirming rats, and finally, to Valère's triumphant, evil mien.

He produced a knife; the blade sparkled in the lantern's light. "Your friends have arrived, *mon coeur.*"

Thirty-Nine

GUY CLENCHED AND UNCLENCHED HIS FINGERS TO restore feeling to his bound hands. After Valère hauled Cora from the room, the guard smirked at Guy's awkward position and left him to rot on the floor. But that did not stop the guard from taunting him about what "his master" was doing with "his lordship's woman."

While furtively searching for the penknife with his gaze, he noticed a forgotten letter on the floor beneath Latymer's desk. The sight reminded him of his unfinished cipher. He had run out of time, yet his instincts continued to assert the message was somehow vitally important. He had only a few more letters to go. Closing his eyes, he concentrated on what he had deciphered thus far.

T 32 E 26   27 O 15 E R T O 23

His mind ticked off each letter, one by one, over and over and over. Various combinations slid into place, and when they did not suit, Guy quickly banished them, making room for others.

T_EZ _O_ERTO_

And then, like a painter transferring a landscape onto canvas with a single stroke of his brush, the blanks filled in almost simultaneously.

TUEZ   SOMERTON

Sweet God, no.

Why the combination became so clear to him now, while he was fighting for his life and Cora's, he would never know. Perhaps he needed the swell of immediate danger to help his mind focus with a diamond-point accuracy.

In the end, it did not matter, for he had deciphered the message too late. Too damnably late.

"*Dites-moi, anglais.*" Furious with Guy's lack of response, the guard kicked at Guy's knee and missed. But his boot connected with the chair, and both Guy and the chair tilted onto their side.

The new position allowed him to search the floor for the missing penknife while keeping an eye on the circling guard. After what seemed like hours but was only a matter of seconds, his fingertip caught on cool metal.

With a terrified single-mindedness, he attacked his restraints, sawing through rope and sometimes flesh.

Becoming suspicious of his movements, the guard pulled a pistol from the depths of his coat. "What are you doing behind your back?"

Guy ignored the guard, feeling the rope growing weaker with each slice. So close. Just a little—the binding gave way, and Guy pushed off the floor in one smooth motion.

The guard's momentary disbelief gave way to ferocity. He lifted his weapon and aimed it at Guy's chest.

Time slowed.

With uncanny clarity, Guy watched the guard's finger curl around the trigger and squeeze.

Guy dove to the side; the whiz of the bullet sliced through the air near his ear. His shoulder slammed against the hard floor, jarring his body. The penknife flew from his hand.

Throwing the spent gun away, the guard jumped on

top of Guy like a feral cat pouncing on a field mouse.
They were well matched in size, but Guy's strength was
potent, sharper, and far more desperate.

With two well-connected jabs to the guard's
jaw, Guy reversed their positions. Incredible power
surged into his muscles, and Guy attacked the guard
like a man possessed. Even consumed by bloodlust, he made sure each blow served to incapacitate
his enemy.

His mission remained clear—save Cora.

With that in mind, he smacked both hands against
the guard's protruding ears, eliciting a roar of pain. The
guard crumpled, hitting the Aubusson rug hard and
holding his ears.

Guy scrambled to his feet and grabbed the nearest
weapon he could find. He smashed the gilded clock over
the guard's big head.

The guard sprawled across Latymer's expensive
carpet, unmoving. Guy used his shirtsleeve to swipe
away a stream of blood oozing from a scalp wound
before it reached his eye. Satisfied the priceless clock
had done its job, Guy retrieved Cora's knife and sprinted
from the drawing room. He turned the corner and
collided with Jack.

"What the hell are you doing in here?" Guy said in
a harsh whisper. "I ordered you to keep an eye out for
Somerton."

"Yes, m'lord," Jack bent over his knees to catch his
breath, pointing toward the entrance door. "Coming up
the drive."

No! "Keep him away from here," Guy demanded.

"Pardon, sir?"

"Get Lord Somerton to safety. Use any means necessary to get him off this estate. Is that understood?"

Jack nodded. "Yes, m'lord."

"Excellent, Jack. Hand me your pistol. Did Somerton bring any men?"

The footman handed over his weapon. "Yes, sir."

"Send someone to secure the guard in the drawing room."

Guy checked to make sure the pistol was loaded, and made for the staircase.

Dinks skidded to a halt in front of him. "My lord," she panted, "did you find our little mite?"

Brimming with impatience, Guy said, his words clipped, "No. I can't seem to get out of the damned entrance hall without bumping into someone." He turned to the footman, hardening his gaze. "Jack, go! Do not let Somerton in this house."

Jack rushed out the door, and Guy turned once again toward the staircase. Dinks huffed along by his side. He stopped. "No, Dinks."

"I can lead you to Latymer's bedchamber, my lord, a lot faster than you can find it on your own," Dinks insisted. "Spent enough time there that I could locate it with my eyes closed."

"That may be, Dinks. But I don't know what we are going to find up there, and I would as soon not to have to worry about Cora *and* you." At the bottom of the staircase, he paused. "Tell me, Dinks. Tell me where to find her."

The maid was not happy with being left behind, but he did not have time to reason with her. "Second floor," she relented, "turn to the left and follow the corridor until it ends. The master's suite is the last door on the right."

He kissed her cheek and then took the stairs two at a time.

When Guy was about fifteen feet from the master suite's bedchamber door, a woman in servant's garb exited the room. Given the number of keys jangling from her waist, he guessed this was Latymer's housekeeper.

She glanced at his bloody wrists with solemn eyes. "You won't find her up here, sir."

He stepped forward, his finger sliding over the trigger. This was Valère's household at the moment. Guy knew better than to blindly trust anyone here.

"If not here, where?" he asked, moving closer.

Her lips thinned. "The cellar."

Guy's heart sank into the pit of his stomach, recalling the awful image of Cora's frail body shackled to a bloody table in Valère's dungeon. Throwing caution to the wind, he stormed past her to see for himself that Cora was not within. In one wide sweep, his gaze took in the massive bed, the high windows, and the masculine accessories strewn about. To the right of the bed, he noticed a door standing ajar.

Conscious of time sifting away, he hurried to the door and pushed it wide. A blast of incense struck his nose a second before nausea engulfed his stomach. He took in the opulent room designed for all manner of sophisticated, and not-so-sophisticated pleasures, and felt his knees weaken.

"She has not been here since the first night, sir," the housekeeper said quietly.

"You are sure?" he asked, unable to wrench his astonished gaze away from the high-mounted swing.

"Yes, my lord," she said. "I moved her myself."

He whirled around to face the housekeeper. "The cellar?"

"Back the same way you came, my lord. Turn left at the bottom of the staircase. The cellar is off the kitchen."

He wasted no more time. Turning on his heel, he ran. When he stormed into the kitchen, he found Dinks standing next to the table, wielding a wrought-iron pan, with tears bubbling in her eyes. "I didn't know, my lord," she whispered. "I sent you up there… wasted time. I didn't realize—" Her words choked off.

He squeezed her shoulder. "You could not have known, Dinks."

Dinks swiped her nose and kicked at something on the floor. "Thanks to Lydie, I took care of this blighter. Come morning, he'll wish he drank the poisoned ale."

Guy noticed two things then—a little black-haired maid standing near a low-framed door and a pair of men's boots peeking out from beneath the worktable. He peered around the corner for a better look and found a rather thin man, unconscious, with his mouth agape.

"You'd better make haste, sir." The little maid quietly opened the small door and pointed down the dark stairs.

"You kill that rat-bastard, my lord," Dinks said in a cold voice. "You kill that Frenchie for what he's done to our little mite."

Dinks's chin trembled with suppressed rage and heart-wrenching grief. He recognized her turmoil, because he could feel his own emotions cracking under the burden. "You may count on it, Dinks."

Guy slipped into the cellar. After only a few cautious steps, he was instantly immersed in darkness so thick he could not see his own hands.

He paused a moment for his eyes to adjust. It took an interminable amount of time, but finally, shadows shifted into more pronounced lines.

Continuing his descent, he tested each stair before putting his full weight on it. The last thing he needed was a creaky board heralding his arrival.

Before long, he was able to see into the vast room. Much was cloaked in darkness, but a halo of light near the back drew his attention. With excruciating care, he moved toward the light, careful not to bump into anything while taking time to search behind every corner for a waiting guard.

About twenty feet from the chamber housing the flickering light, his boot caught on something. He sensed it falling and grabbed for it. His heart skidded to a halt when he missed, and then jolted to a start after his next attempt stopped the broom only a few inches from the floor. Pausing to catch his breath, he measured its sturdy weight and long length, and decided to hold on to it.

"Your friends have arrived, *mon coeur*," Valère said.

Guy's muscles locked, certain Valère had heard his approach, despite all his caution. The knowledge that Cora might be around the corner sent his pulse hammering through his veins. When this was over, he would spend the rest of his life surrounding her with safety and love.

"You do not look happy to see them," Valère taunted. "They sound quite anxious to make your acquaintance."

Guy frowned. The Frenchman's words made no sense.

He edged closer to the door, easing forward until he spotted Cora, her body flattened against a wall, wearing nothing but her chemise. Her eyes were wide, staring at something across the room. Something he could not see. Her pale skin glistened in the wavering light, and he realized she was soaked from head to toe.

A foul odor reached his nose. He glanced around the corridor and found a bucket a few feet away, splintered and leaking a watery substance. Then he heard the distinctive squeal of rats from inside the chamber. Understanding dawned. His gaze slid slowly to Cora, and a heavy dread sat in the pit of his stomach.

"Nothing to say, *mon ange*?" Valère asked, amusement tinting his voice.

"It's a shame," Cora said, standing a little taller.

"What is?" the Frenchman asked.

"All that keen intelligence being wasted on childish games."

Valère went silent. When he finally spoke, malice oozed from his lips.

"You think me childish, *ma petite*?"

Valère moved around the room as he spoke. Guy tensed, wishing he could see the blackguard. At the moment, he knew not what weapons the Frenchman possessed or whether another guard was inside.

All he had to measure the activity within the room was Cora's shifting expressions. And at that precise second, she projected keen distress.

His grip tightened around the broom handle, and his finger smoothed over the trigger of his gun.

"All this for a woman who betrayed you," she said. "If you do not call that childish, what do you call it?"

"*Pour l'Empereur.*"

Her brow furrowed, and Valère laughed. "You did not think I traveled to this miserable English island for you alone, did you?"

When her eyes widened, Valère's amusement increased. "How precious."

His circuit continued. "Although I had a personal interest in making you suffer and… partaking of a few of your talents, you were nothing more than a means to an end."

Guy's gaze sharpened on Cora, already knowing what Valère would say.

"I don't understand," she said, inching away. "If you did not come to England to kill me, why are you here?"

"To kill your hero, *bien sûr.*"

TUEZ SOMERTON

Kill Somerton.

"What?" she asked in a disbelieving whisper.

Valère's laughed boomed again. "The chief of

England's Secret Service is a far greater threat to the emperor's plans than a ballroom spy, do you not think? When I leave you here with your friends, I will go upstairs to finish your lover and then wait for Lord Somerton to come riding to your rescue. I expect that happy event any minute."

Guy closed his eyes. Everything fit together beautifully—Valère's constant taunts to Cora and his association to Latymer, Jack's recruitment, Danforth's disappearance, and finally, Cora's abduction—all carefully plotted to lure Somerton to this remote location.

From the look on Cora's face, she had pieced it all together, too.

"How will Lord Latymer explain Somerton's death?" she asked.

"Latymer's ready to swear that he invited Somerton and his family to his country estate and, while here, they attempted to stop a group of thieves from stealing the baron's priceless collection of oil paintings and perished in the process. For who would not give their life to protect a Raphael? Tragic, really."

"And highly implausible."

The Frenchman's lips thinned. "People die during robberies every day."

"Why the elaborate ruse, Valère?" Cora asked, anger lacing her words. "Why not just go to Somerton's town house and shoot him in his bed?"

"My instructions were to make it look like an accident," Valère said, his voice growing impatient. "An execution-style death would have raised too many questions."

"Yes, but your henchmen are going to murder two earls, a viscount, a child, and a woman? You don't think a casualty list of that magnitude won't raise a few eyebrows?"

"Of course it will," Valère said evenly. "But all evidence will point to an unfortunate tragedy, nothing more."

Guy's stomach churned at the way they had all been duped by this madman. *Somerton*. The chief could be upstairs, even now.

"Besides, had I completed my task in such a vulgar manner as you suggest, I would have been deprived of my little amusements." His chest expanded, and his features transformed into an expression of victory and complete insanity. "I will most assuredly receive a marshal appointment now."

Cora pressed farther into the stone wall, her gaze intent. "I am so pleased for you. I can think of few people more qualified to stand at Napoleon's side."

After what Somerton revealed about the slaughter in the West Indies, Guy could not agree more.

"Your tone displeases me, *ma petite*. Perhaps it is time to reacquaint you with your friends."

She shot a fearful glance toward Guy, or rather, the doorway leading to escape, gauging the distance.

In a move reminiscent of his rescue mission in France, Guy risked discovery and leaned forward until her startled gaze locked with his.

Forty

CORA'S BODY QUAKED WITH RELIEF WHEN GUY'S shadowed face came into view. He was alive. From what she could see, he appeared to be intact, too. No gaping bullet wounds, no plunging dagger holes, only a few more cuts and bruises. Afraid she would alert Valère to Guy's presence, she turned her gaze to the squirming bag.

The Frenchman knelt down beside the sack of crawling rodents and slid his knife beneath the knotted rope. The woven cloth sagged open, and a dozen brown angry rats grappled for freedom.

Another quick glance at Guy, and Cora knew what she had to do.

Taking three wide steps to the left, away from the door, she drew Valère's gaze back to her.

The Frenchman stood, watching her with a feral gleam of amusement while kicking away a rat that came too close.

"Where do you go, *mon coeur?*" He followed her progress around the room.

The rats' whiskered noses lifted in the air, tracking the foul scent covering her body. Cora's courage faded when, as one, they turned toward her.

Her skin itched and pricked as she recalled the scrape of their tiny claws on her bare flesh and the piercing pain of their sharp teeth. She allowed herself one cleansing shudder and then shored up her nerves and concentrated on her current task—keep Valère's attention on her.

The rats scuttled closer.

As she moved farther into the recesses of the dank cell, Cora raked her hands down her breasts, molding the soaked chemise to her chilled skin.

"The personal revenge you seek," Cora said to Valère, gratified to find his hard gaze on her hands. "It confuses me."

"Why is that?" Valère asked in a hoarse voice.

"You and I, we are spies. We deal in lies and deceptions."

She paused, flinging the excess slop off her fingers. It slapped against the walls.

Several rats broke off from the pack, scurrying toward her to investigate the new source of potential food.

"Your point, *ma chère*?"

Her hands skimmed over her hips. "It is rare to come across another agent who matches either of us in intelligence and cunning."

She sensed more than saw Guy slip into the room. With his back facing the door, Valère took no notice of the intrusion.

Valère's chest heaved, his breaths now audible in the small room. "I grow weary of your verbal games. Say what you mean. I have business upstairs, and your friends are hungry."

Using the same scraping motion, Cora smoothed her cupped fingers down her offal-caked arms. "I would have expected you to consider my flawless penetration of your company with a modicum of admiration and mutual respect. But instead of appreciation, you showed yourself to be petty and ridiculous. You acted like a spoiled child who had his sweets taken away."

"I will show you spoiled, you stupid English cow." He lunged for her.

Cora flung a stream of stinking filth into his face.

"Ah!" He stopped short, wiping the liquid from his good eye.

Guy swooped in, bringing a long cudgel—no, a broomstick—down on the back of Valère's head with enough force to snap it in half. The blow sent the Frenchman to his knees, and his knife skidded into a corner.

Cora ran toward her clothing piled on the floor.

Holding his head, Valère squinted up at Guy. "You!" He made to rise, but his knees buckled again. "English *cochon*!"

"Cow, swine, dog," Guy said. "The French really need to be more creative with their curses. So dull, wouldn't you agree, my dear?"

Cora stood, hiding the paperweight behind her back. "Indeed," she said, unable to come up with anything more clever.

Guy pulled a pistol from the back of his breeches and pointed the barrel at Valère's head. With a voice devoid of amusement, he said, "Your reign of brutality ends tonight, Valère."

Cora's heart pounded in anticipation, and nervous excitement hummed through her body. Years of searching, intrigue, and compromised morals narrowed down to this one moment in time. She wanted Valère to die, had envisioned it for weeks.

"Wait," she said. "I wish to see his face."

"Stay where you are, Cora," Guy said in a rough voice. "This is not a memory you want to keep."

Ignoring his command, she approached Guy's side and noticed a trickle of sweat gliding down his temple. "Of course, it is. I shall sleep better knowing the deed is done."

Guy swiped away a layer of sweat from his forehead. "You will know without having to see the damned thing."

Something about the quality of Guy's voice and the

intensity of his burning gaze alerted Cora to his inner struggle, but she could not discern the source.

"My, my," Valère said, sitting back on his heels. "The two of you make quite a pair."

"Shut up," Guy warned.

"That is a pretty trinket you have wrapped around your neck, *mon coeur*. Now where did you come by such an unusual cameo?"

Cora's hand went to the necklace. Her fingers found it glazed with the same filth covering her body. Without thought, she rubbed it away until the ivory relief of a female profile set against the orange background materialized.

"Ah, yes. There she is," Valère said with unexaggerated wonder. "*Marianne*. Our beloved *Déesse de la Liberté*. With such a treasure at my emperor's side, France will be invincible."

Guy snorted. "You dare use emperor and equality in the same breath, Valère?"

"Once the world embraces French ideals, my emperor's generosity will know no bounds."

"And if the world does not embrace Napoleon's oppression?"

Valère's smile was condescending. "Hardly oppression, my lord. But to answer your question, it is not a matter of if, but when."

Cora heard the men's discourse, but in the way one overhears a conversation in another room. Valère's notice of her mother's necklace disturbed a haze of thoughts and images buried in Cora's mind. But everything was jumbled, and nothing would align in any logical order.

Why would her father give her mother a symbol of France's freedom? Both her parents had familial connections to the country, but to present one's wife with such a revolutionary icon reeked of unpatriotic alliances. Valère's taunt surfaced again. "*Had your father followed instructions, he would still be alive and able to betray his country again and again."*

"Tell me, *mon coeur*," Valère said, interrupting her disturbing line of thought. "Where did you come by the cameo?"

Her hand tightened around the pendant.

"Cora," Guy said. "Do not engage this bastard in conversation. He is only trying to confuse you."

She did not have to be reminded of Valère's treacherous nature. But she sensed long-sought-after answers stood just outside her grasp. "My father gave it to my mother."

"Oh," Valère said. "When was this? Before or after his silence killed her?"

Cora stepped forward. "What?!" Bile clogged Cora's throat, and her mind began to spin out of control.

Guy grasped her arm and kicked at Valère. "I told you to shut up, you bloody bastard." Pulling her back to a safe distance, he admonished, "Don't go any closer."

"And why would I listen to an Englishman afraid of his own shadow?" Disdain dripped from Valère's voice. "Your father thought he could outmaneuver me, but in the end it was I who won our little game of—how is it you English say it? Ah, yes—cat and mouse."

Cat and mouse? Cora didn't have time to sift through Valère's verbal swordplay. Her attention was drawn to Guy's unsteady grip on the pistol. His hand shook so badly he would never have been able to hit Valère, not even at this close distance. Her gaze shot to Guy's face, and her heart stuttered at his transformation in so short a time. His healthy, sun-kissed skin was now devoid of color with the exception of the black hollows beneath his dark eyes. Eyes that bore into Valère as if they had just witnessed the terrible atrocities of hell.

Not understanding Valère's insults or Guy's reaction, she ventured a tentative, "Guy?"

He did not respond, simply blinked his eyes hard, as if he were trying to force away an image.

"What does Somerton think of his assassin now, *my lord*?"

Guy's grip on her arm turned bruising as he cocked the hammer. Fearful he would kill the Frenchman before she got her answers, she blurted out, "I found the cameo on the carpet near my mother's body."

"Of course." Valère's face lit with a sickening triumph. "Your mother must have torn it free of my fob chain during... her last moments. The cameo's loss did not come to my notice until I was safely ensconced in my carriage. I experienced a trying few days of worry and disappointment at being deprived of my favorite adornment. But you have protected it for me all of these years, *mon coeur. Merci.*"

A lifetime of memories crashed in on her.

Their family's frequent trips to the Continent, her father's rages, her parents' murders, the murderer's French accent, the cameo, her training, the British ships, Valère... Where before, she could not make sense of it all. Now, everything aligned in perfect symmetry.

All of this time she had held the key to the murderer's identity around her bloody neck. Why did she never mention the cameo to Somerton? Surely he would have understood the symbol's importance. Instead, she had kept Valère's trinket to herself, thinking she held a precious memory of her mother and father's last intimate moment together. What a complete, melodramatic fool she had been.

Fury unlike anything she had ever experienced before welled up inside of her. She ripped the necklace from her neck and threw it at Valère.

But he seemed to have anticipated such a response, for he used the distraction to his advantage. In a violent whirl of movement, the Frenchman grabbed a nearby rat and threw it at Guy's head. Guy ducked and fired his weapon, nicking Valère's right shoulder.

It was not enough to slow him down. He seized Cora by the waist and pinned her to his chest. From a concealed pocket, he drew forth another knife and pressed it against her throat.

It all happened so fast that Cora had no time to react.

"You English, with all of your high morals and petty emotions, make it too easy," Valère said.

Cora stood on her toes to keep the knife's sharp edge from slicing her skin. She peered at Guy and was taken aback by the savagery marring his handsome face.

"And you should have stayed on your knees." Guy's hand tightened around the spent gun. "Before I am through, you will be begging for a bullet."

"You exhibit a great deal of confidence for a man without a weapon."

The knife quivered against Cora's neck, scoring her skin and releasing a soft trickle of warm blood.

She considered Valère's shaking arm and realized the bullet wound must be worse than she had originally thought. Cora took comfort from the solid mass of the paperweight in her right hand, her fingers curled around its smooth surface. She would have one chance, and one chance only, to make her escape.

Guy said, "I do not need a weapon to kill a man who hides behind women's skirts."

Valère spat on the ground. "*Merde!* I do not hide—"

Cora arched her hand wide and bashed the paperweight into his temple, wincing when the crunch of bone reached her ears. The arm around her slackened, and in one smooth motion, she flipped Valère over her shoulder and onto his back.

A wildness overtook her. She had dropped the

paperweight so she could assault Valère with her bare hands. Hands that had been taught how to kill and to caress. Hands that had cradled her mother's head and Scrapper's lifeless body. Hands that had loved Guy.

She used them now, as she had been trained, plowing her fists into Valère's neck, his injured eye and arm, any area that would give her an advantage over her enemy. She had no plan of attack; her only focus was on eliminating the threat. As he had her parents.

And all the while she meted out her revenge on the man who had destroyed her life, she felt a piece of her soul—her humanity—flit away. Everything that separated her from monsters like Valère was vanishing beneath the pounding of her grief. She was becoming all Raven. Ruthless. Driven. Vengeful.

Strong hands wrenched her up and away, pushing her into the corridor outside the cell's doorway. Guy cupped her face, his thumbs wiping something wet off her cheeks. "Wait here, Cora-bell," he commanded. "Do you hear me? Wait here." The look on his face was wrought with a combination of fear, concern, fury, and determination.

She nodded, words lost to her. He needn't have worried. She could not have moved had her life depended upon it. Everything felt numb and leaden, from the fine hairs on her head to the tips of her toes. Nothing worked but the lock on her knees.

"My lord?" A harsh, feminine whisper penetrated the shadows to Cora's right.

"Take her upstairs, Dinks. Now."

"Yes, sir." Dinks wrapped an arm around Cora's shoulders, and Guy reentered the cell. "Come, Miss Cora."

Cora's feet remained rooted in place. Her maid understood her silent communication, for she settled in next to Cora, offering her familiar, unshakable support.

"I've got you, little mite." Dinks used her ever-present handkerchief that smelled refreshingly crisp and clean to wipe off Cora's face, neck, and arms while murmuring beneath her breath. Busy work, Cora realized distantly. Something Dinks had always done when anxious or upset.

Although Cora appreciated Dinks's efforts, it was not the maid's vague reassurances that held Cora's rapt attention, but rather the macabre tableau playing out in the adjacent chamber. No longer stunned by the blow from the paperweight, Valère made a valiant attempt to rouse himself, while Guy retrieved the Frenchman's discarded knife.

Guy stood over Valère, his chest rising high with each inhalation. He stashed the longer knife in the back of his breeches and then held up the penknife she had given him. "This is the weapon that will bring about your defeat, Valère. This, a woman, and a paperweight."

Valère laughed. "What do you plan to do with that puny knife, Helsford? Trim my nails?"

Remembering how devastated she felt only moments ago, when her brutality sifted away the essence of her humanity, she attempted to absolve Guy of what he no doubt felt was his duty. "Guy."

He did not lift his gaze from Valère's prone body, but by the slight tilt of his head, she sensed he was listening to her.

"You do not have to do this, love."

The tension eased from his shoulders, and she released a pent-up breath. She would have to content herself with the fact that Valère would rot in the dankest prison cell money could buy until it was his turn on the gibbet.

"I love you, Cora," Guy said quietly. In a swift and violent move, he drew his arm back and drove the small knife—

Cora squeezed her eyes shut, unable to watch Guy

plunge the knife into Valère's throat. Dinks's arms went taut, and Cora sensed more than saw the maid's retreat, as well.

After a few breathless seconds, Cora shifted her attention back to the chamber and found Guy checking Valère's neck for a pulse.

Smelling new blood, the rats squealed their delight, inching their way toward Valère.

"Is he d–dead?" she asked with a catch in her voice.

Guy got to his feet, kicking away rats as he made his way over to the hanging lantern. Once he returned to Valère's side, he held the lantern aloft and peered into each of the Frenchman's eyes. "Both dilated."

Dead. A profound weight lifted from her shoulders, a lightness of spirit amidst a macabre scene of evil. She glanced up at Dinks and found tears streaming down the older woman's face.

"It's over, little mite."

Cora lifted her lips into a bittersweet smile. "Yes. Yes, it is." She nodded in the direction of the cellar door. "Why don't you see what the others are about?"

"You're sure?"

Cora nodded.

Dinks chucked Cora on the chin. "Such a brave little mite. Don't be long."

"I won't." When Dinks disappeared in the shadows once again, Cora peered at Guy, wondering what was going through his mind as he stared down at Valère.

And then, he raised his dark gaze to Cora's. After what she had witnessed in the last quarter hour, she had expected to find sadness, regret, or some other form of torment lurking in the black depths of his eyes.

But she found something entirely different, something completely unexpected.

What she found was… redemption.

I love you, Cora. He had said the words aloud. Words they had danced around for so long. He had said them and then killed the man responsible for murdering so many of her loved ones. A deep ache closed in around her throat, shutting off her ability to breathe even as her heart beat with excitement.

He set the lantern down and then stepped around the dead body of their enemy. "Cora."

The next thing she knew, she was flying into him.

Strong arms encased her in a cocoon of sheer comfort and safety. She sensed his fear, his regret, his relief. And she felt his love in the tightness of his embrace.

"Are you well?" he asked against her forehead. "Are you injured?"

With the demon of Cora's nightmares vanquished, how could she not be well? "The housekeeper sewed up my newest wound." She pulled back her chemise to show him the bandage. "Just a prick. At this rate, I will have to draw up a map to find them all."

Her amusement dimmed as she looked over his body for telltale signs of serious injury. "And you, Guy? I heard a gunshot. I thought for certain the guard had killed you."

"Nothing a few bandages won't cure." He inspected her neck and then used his sleeve to dab at the cut made by Valère's knife.

Cora studied him for a long moment, recalling his physical reaction to Valère's jeering remarks. She reached up and used the pad of her thumb to swipe away a bead of sweat rolling down his cheek. "Earlier, when you were pointing the gun at Valère, you seemed… distressed."

Guy's body shuddered at the gentle press of her fingers against his overheated skin. A part of him hoped she had not noticed his flare of panic, and another part of him was profoundly happy she had.

Drawing in a deep, steadying breath, he said, "Earlier this year, Somerton received intelligence that a small coalition of French sympathizers had shifted from having harmless, clandestine meetings to stockpiling firearms and other weapons of destruction in an abandoned textile building in Soho."

She reached out and wrapped her fingers around his. "Drawing-room politics?"

"Indeed," he said. "But far more deadly in this instance. With Napoleon's forces gaining strength to the south and the ever-present danger of another Irish uprising, the government's resources were being stretched across the seas, the continent, *and* British soil. To add yet another worrisome threat in our capital city was simply too much. We did not have the necessary men to watch our back door."

Her fingers tightened. "I take it you were sent on a field assignment."

"Yes," he said. "The chief sent me and another agent to remove the leader of this growing faction. The mission was straightforward, and our intelligence was quite detailed. We had the leader's name, his description, and a rendezvous date and time."

She lifted their clasped hands and pressed a kiss against his knuckles.

He appreciated the calming gesture, because the nightmarish panic began to pulse through his mind once again. "A few minutes after the appointed rendezvous, we made our way into the dimly lit warehouse and found a man fitting the leader's description sorting through a crate of munitions."

He rubbed his hand over his damp upper lip, his throat suddenly dry. He wanted nothing more than to finish this bloody story quickly. A distant, hopeful part of him had believed talking about the mission would help put closure to the terrible incident.

But discussing it made it all too real, something he had tried to hide for several months.

A slender arm snaked around his middle, holding him close. He loved her so damn much in that moment.

"We emerged from our hiding spot and commanded the leader to stand down." He pressed his lips to the top of her head. "At the sound of my voice, the man whipped around, brandishing a pistol. I did not think twice, simply raised my own weapon and took the shot."

Cora kissed his chest, and Guy felt the delicate touch all the way to his toes.

"The story is more than a case of self-defense," she reasoned.

"You are correct." His heart beat hard and fast, gaining momentum with each revelation. "The echo of my shot had barely faded before a young boy, maybe nine years of age, came careening around the corner, yelling to his papa about a gunshot."

She squeezed him harder. "Guy, no."

"I see you comprehend the situation," he said in an unsteady voice. "Not only did I kill the young boy's father—virtually before his eyes—I killed the wrong man."

"What?" Her head jerked up, and she caught his gaze. "The man you shot wasn't the leader?"

He shook his head. "No, and to add further injury to an already tragic situation, the man was wielding an unloaded weapon from the crate."

"Guy," she said gently, clutching his nape. "You could not have known the weapon was not a threat. You were in an unfamiliar, darkened warehouse, hunting an enemy. Whether or not the pistol was loaded is immaterial. All your intelligence pointed to the man as the leader of the sympathizers."

He chucked her beneath the chin. "Still playing the part of my protector, Raven?"

"It appears someone must," she said. "How did you discover the man was not your intended target?"

"The boy was our first clue, of course." He absently rubbed her back. "After lighting a lamp, we noticed the man's clothing was not that of the merchant, or a shop-keeper, or even a gentleman, but rather that of someone making a living of working off the streets. We deduced he had either grown curious about the goings-on in the warehouse and started poking about, or he was a very unlucky thief."

"What of the boy?"

"He ran away." Guy rubbed his temples with shaking fingers. "We watched the warehouse for several more days, hoping the boy would return, but he never did. After a fruitless sennight of monitoring the building and making inquiries of the locals, we finally gave up." He dropped his hand to his side. "For all I know, I orphaned that boy the same as Valère orphaned you and Ethan."

A tear spilled over her cheek. "No, Guy. You must not compare the two. Your situation was a mistake, a terrible, horrible mistake that any agent would have made in your shoes."

He dropped his gaze to the floor. "Ah, but I am the agent who made the mistake."

She turned more fully toward him, cradling his jaw in the palm of her hands. "No wonder your body reacted so physically against shooting another. It is the stuff of nightmares."

"As well I know."

"What about the leader of the French sympathizers?" she asked. "Did you complete your original assignment?"

"No. The leader surfaced a few days later, but I couldn't—" He glanced away, clenching his teeth against a wave of humiliation. "I couldn't pull the damned trigger. My partner had to finish it."

She smoothed her thumbs over his cheeks. "Your partner. Would he be anyone with whom I'm acquainted?"

Guy knew she spoke of Ethan, but he could not confirm or deny her brother's part in the botched mission. As much as he loved her, he would not reveal the details of any missions that did not personally concern her. And he suspected she would do the same with him.

"Never mind," she said as if reading his mind. "I do not wish to know." She rose up on her tiptoes and kissed him with a gentle, thorough passion. She drew back far enough to say, "'Twas not your fault, Guy."

Some of the tension eased from his shoulders, and Guy flexed open his hands before settling them on Cora's hips. His kissed her nose. "I will try to remember your words."

The detestable sound of a dozen gnashing teeth echoed through the cell.

Cora stiffened in Guy's arms and glanced down at the encroaching rats. "I think it's time for us to leave."

"Agreed." He released her and then bent to scoop up the cameo necklace.

"No." She grabbed his arm. "Leave it. I don't need that any longer."

They both stared down at the delicate female profile. *Goddess of Liberty*. "Ironic, isn't?" she asked. "That France's symbol of freedom is being used to oppress entire nations?"

"The French are not unlike citizens of other countries," Guy said quietly. "Everyone needs a hero, someone they can trust to care for their needs and make them feel safe. Napoleon fulfills that role now, but his greed for power will one day be his downfall, and then the French will rally around their next savior."

Cora stared up into Guy's dark eyes. "You are right. Everyone does need a hero… and you are mine."

She saw his nostrils flare and his eyes well a moment before he swooped down to cover her mouth, kissing her until she was nearly senseless. Cora melted into him, forgetting about the rats. Then he drew back and said, "As you are mine."

Her vision blurred, and then it was her turn to kiss him.

"Come, sweetheart," he said against her lips. "Let us leave this place."

Cora nodded and allowed Guy to help her into her ruined dress. The back gaped open, and it was hopelessly wrinkled, but it kept her modesty intact. Pausing at the door, she scanned the dank cell, vowing it would be the last time she ever stepped foot inside one again.

"Ready?" Guy asked softly.

"Yes."

As they made their way through the death-filled cellar, Cora left her past behind, amidst the squeal of excited rats.

Forty-One

"HELLO, RUNT."

Climbing the last few stairs leading up from the cellar, Guy nearly bashed into Cora's back when she stopped abruptly at the sound of her brother's voice. Guy peered over her stiff shoulders and noticed Danforth and several others crowding into the kitchen. Including Somerton.

Closing the cellar door, he gave her a gentle nudge. That was all it took for her to break free of her disbelieving stupor. She screeched her excitement across the short distance and catapulted herself into Danforth's open arms.

The contact must have hurt like the devil. Danforth's chiseled features still carried deep shades of purple mixed with greens and yellows. Lord only knew what injuries lay beneath his rumpled coat. But her brother did not make a sound, merely enclosed his sobbing sister in his arms.

"Ethan," Cora said in a croaked whisper. "You're alive." She shrieked again, hugging him closer.

Guy smiled, understanding her relief. The two siblings had always been close, especially after they were orphaned and began training together.

As poignant as their reunion was, Guy's nerves felt abraded and raw. He wanted to be quit of this place. Logically, he knew Valère was dead, but instincts urged him to get Cora as far away from the Frenchman as possible.

He stepped forward to shake Somerton's hand. "All clear up here?"

Somerton nodded. "Valère?"

Guy caught Danforth's eye over Cora's head. "Dead."

Pulling in a deep breath, his mentor said, "Good." Then more to himself. "Good."

"Jack was supposed to keep you away," Guy said, knowing he sent the footman on a fool's errand.

"He tried." Somerton eyed him. "Care to tell me why?"

"I finally deciphered one of the letters you gave me."

"You were the target," Cora said with a catch in her voice. "Not me. It was you they wanted all along. I was merely the bait."

The chief's nostrils flared on a deep breath, and his gaze shuttered.

In the silence that followed, Danforth draped his coat over Cora's shoulders, and she smiled her appreciation before turning to Guy. Tears sparkled in her eyes, and a trembling smile graced her beautiful face. He noticed that she no longer bothered to hide her scar.

Although she looked upon him with fondness, Guy sensed something of a goodbye in her tearful smile. His heart clenched around a painful knot. She would not be free of him so easily.

She might have had a chance—a slim chance—to run had she not mouthed those three little words *and* called him "love." In her infuriating need to protect him, she had attempted to pardon him from avenging her honor.

Foolish, beautiful, stubborn woman.

By killing Valère, he had removed a vital piece of Napoleon's grand scheme, protected the woman he loved, and freed himself from a terrible mistake. Whatever decision she had made in that rat-infested cell below did not stand a chance against their age-old connection. He would break through whatever barrier she had erected. In the drawing room, she told him she loved him, and he would never let her forget it.

Jack squeezed passed Bingham, Dinks, and Somerton, toting a redheaded poppet beneath his arm. "Miss Cora?"

Cora glanced between the two, and her face lit with joy. "Grace?"

Jack nodded.

Cora strode forward and started to place her hand on the young girl's cheek, but thought better of it. "Excuse my abominable appearance, Grace. I had an altercation with some rubbish."

Instead of smiling, the girl rooted farther into the safety of her brother's embrace.

Cora tried again. "You've grown into a beautiful young woman while I was abroad."

Jack covered the girl's fingers twisting one of the buttons on his coat. "Gracie, you remember Miss Cora now, don't you?"

The girl shook her head.

"Jack, I am rather altered since last she saw me. It's no matter." To his sister, she said, "You're safe now, Grace. We shall not let anything happen to you. I vow it."

Jack squeezed his sister's shoulder. "Miss Cora always keeps her promises."

The girl sent Cora a timid smile.

Straightening to her full height, Cora sent Jack a questioning look. She did not want to upset the girl by making inquiries about her well-being.

Jack understood her silent communication and responded with a slight nod. Although relieved, she would send for a doctor to see to the girl.

"How did you find this place?" Cora asked Guy, changing the focus away from the girl.

He nodded toward Jack. "Your friend followed Valère's man then led us back here."

Pride shone in her eyes, and she kissed both the footman's cheeks. "Thank you, Jack."

A flush blanketed Jack's face. "Was the least I could do after all the trouble I caused." He lifted guilt-stricken eyes. "Can you ever forgive, Miss Cora?"

She sent the footman a warm smile. "It is already done. We shall speak of it no more."

"Thank you," he whispered.

"Perhaps we would all be more comfortable back at the hunting box," Guy suggested. "There is plenty of room, and nothing more to be done here, except call the local constable."

"A fine idea," Somerton agreed, ushering everyone from the kitchen. "I'll leave a few guards and return to deal with this later."

Danforth threw an arm over Cora's shoulder. "Come on, runt. Let's see if we can find you a hot bath. You smell like someone dropped a slop bucket on you."

Guy's jaw clenched, and he stepped forward to intervene. His friend had no idea of the horrors Cora faced below.

Cora punched her brother in the stomach.

"Ow!" he said, not feigning the pain.

Her eyes narrowed. "I'm well aware of how foul I smell, you dolt, as is everyone else. I do not need you to express the obvious."

Guy could not hold back his smile. He should have known the little spitfire would not need his help. She had managed her brother's speak-first-think-later attitude far longer than Guy had.

She sent Guy a sidelong glance, her cheeks rosy despite her chiding words.

"So does that mean you don't want a hot bath?" Danforth quipped.

Before she could whack him again, her brother bolted awkwardly from the room, leaving a devilish laugh in his wake.

"Ethan!" Cora yelled, fast on her brother's heels. Both of them hobbled more than ran.

Guy's smile grew wider, and he noted the others' expressions had lightened. The siblings' antics were reminiscent of when they were children. How they had all cherished those few years when grief no longer suffocated them and duty had yet to call.

He hoped their laughter was a sign that the healing process had already begun. When he recalled Cora's withdrawal, his good humor darkened.

But only for a moment. He had a barrier to breach. And this time, he would leave nothing behind for her to reconstruct.

Forty-Two

AFTER CORA'S BATH, DINKS WRAPPED A TIGHT LENGTH of linen around Cora's rib cage and bundled her arm in a new sling. She then applied a thick ointment to Guy's sliced wrists before covering them with a secure bandage.

Guy gently squeezed each wrist. "What did you put on my wounds? Stings like the devil."

Dinks smiled. "Means it's working, my lord."

At Somerton's request, Jack poured healthy levels of rum into glasses of various sizes for everyone. The small saloon's occupants diligently finished their drinks while watching Dinks move from one patient to the next.

"Please don't take this the wrong way, Danforth," Guy said. "But where the hell have you been?" Knowing Specter watched over the hothead for several days, he asked the question more for Cora than himself.

"Searching for Valère, of course," Danforth said, toying with a long stalk of grass he'd picked from the unkempt grounds surrounding the hunting box.

"Indeed." Somerton leveled a do-not-try-my-patience look on his former ward.

Danforth sighed. "After we returned from France, I started making inquiries at various ports about Valère's whereabouts—official and otherwise. A few days later, the Frenchman's men plucked me off the street, and I gained intimate knowledge of their carriage's boot. Quite uncomfortable, I might add." He paused for a moment, his brow knitted in a scowl as if reliving the ride.

"Do not dawdle, Ethan," Cora admonished. "Tell us what happened next."

Guy smiled. He had tried to get her to rest, but she had tucked a pillow against her injured side and insisted on staying.

"It is not a pretty tale, Sister." Danforth glowered at Cora.

"Spare me your melodrama, Brother. I have seen worse, I'm sure."

Danforth sobered at the reminder. "Seen and experienced worse, I have no doubt."

Cora's flush was all the confirmation they needed.

"Once we reached our destination near the docks," Danforth continued, "three Goliaths gave me a sound beating and left me for dead in an alleyway."

"Since you did not perish," Somerton said, "I assume you received an act of kindness from a dock worker."

"I'm not altogether sure," Danforth replied with a furrowed brow. "Someone pulled me from the alleyway and transported me to an abandoned building. I have only flashes of memory from those first few days of my recovery."

"You never saw who saved you?" Guy had a hard time visualizing his brawny friend incapacitated.

Danforth's lips thinned into a frustrated line, and he slapped the stalk of grass against his chair.

"Come now, Danforth, you had to have seen something," Guy pressed.

A crimson flush suffused Danforth's ears. "What I remember makes no sense." He looked around the room. "I remember a cloaked figure with gentle hands in the alley, then nothing. When I returned to awareness in the abandoned building, a pretty maid, rather than my savior, greeted me. And then she disappeared once I started asking questions about the cloaked figure. Damn me, but I would like to thank the chap."

A fierce scowl blanketed Cora's features. "They left you there to fend for yourself?"

"No." Danforth stared at the amber liquid he swirled in his glass. "I don't think I was ever left alone. I had adequate food and clean bandages at all times."

It did not surprise Guy that his informant had avoided Danforth, especially once Cora's brother began asking probing questions. Specter's motives for helping Guy over the years had never been clear, but the informant's demand for secrecy had been quite explicit.

Guy shrugged. He had stopped pondering the mystery of Specter some time ago. Danforth was returned to them safely. That was all that mattered.

Guy looked to Somerton. "I assume you learned of Lord Latymer's part in all of this."

"Indeed, I did," Somerton said. "A timely note alerted me to be careful of the man. Dealing with the intricacies and layers of Latymer's involvement forced me to stay in town longer than I had anticipated. I sent a note ahead, but my messenger's horse went lame. By the time he arrived at The King's Arms, you were already gone."

Somerton stared at his empty glass. "I trusted him. Information I had supplied to him became instruments of death. I was charged with protecting England, not be a source of its downfall—" The older man broke off, swallowing hard.

Guy suspected greed lay at the heart of Latymer's enterprise, its claws always a powerful persuader. He was gratified to learn Specter had succeeded in both endeavors, finding Danforth and alerting Somerton. The informant continued to be a powerful ally.

Cora reached across the short distance and laid her hand over Somerton's. "You could not have known."

Somerton's smile was self-deprecating. "Could I not?"

He patted her hand and rose from his seat to pour himself another drink. By the time he turned back to the room, all sign of emotion was gone. "The Foreign Office is still sorting through Latymer's web of deceit. Unfortunately, they will have to do it without the traitor's confession."

"Why?" Danforth asked.

"Because he escaped."

Silence shot through the room.

"When?" Cora asked.

Somerton sighed. "Not long after I left London. A messenger tracked me down on the road to Latymer's estate."

Five minutes ago, they had believed the case closed. Now everyone recognized that Latymer's disappearance left a gaping hole that would need to be sewn shut. Soon.

"Why did you not notify any of us that you planned to investigate on your own?" Cora prompted her brother in an obvious attempt to change the subject. And probably because she wanted to rattle his wits.

"There was not time," he said vaguely. "For the first sennight, I was following one false clue after another. Every time I thought I was close to a breakthrough, I met with another wall."

"Had you followed protocol," Somerton said in an even voice, "you could have saved yourself a beating and a great deal of wasted time."

"And your family a great deal of worry," Cora added.

Danforth tipped back the rest of his rum. "There is that. Sorry, runt."

"Helsford," Somerton said. "Why don't you take

Cora and Grace to the village inn for the evening? Danforth and I will deal with matters at the house." He turned to the coachman standing uncomfortably by the door. "Bingham, would you be so kind as to bring the carriage around?"

"Yes, m'lord," Bingham mumbled, obviously relieved to return to familiar tasks.

"Come, Miss Cora," Dinks said, helping Cora rise from her chair. "I brought along something a wee more appropriate than that borrowed wrapper you're wearing."

Cora turned to Somerton, "I have not had an opportunity to thank Mrs. Pettigrew for her help. She intervened at a most opportune moment, and I shall never forget her kindness."

Guy's muscles tensed at the implication buried in her words. He had wanted to beat Valère with his bare hands, to have felt the give of the man's flesh and bones beneath his knuckles. The bastard had died too quickly. He had wanted him to suffer in the same way Cora had suffered.

He tamped down his anger. "The housekeeper and the little maid helped me, as well. As did our fair Dinks."

The corners of Dinks's mouth turned down. "Not before I sent you a wild-goose chase, my lord." She averted her gaze from Cora's. "Wasted precious time on an old woman's memory."

Cora kissed her cheek, which brought forth a handkerchief.

Guy said, "Your memory was faultless, Dinks. Latymer's bedchamber was already going to be my first stop. Your instructions got me there much faster than my bungling about."

Dinks flapped her handkerchief at Guy. "Don't be wasting your charm on me, my lord. I've got my sights set elsewhere."

Somerton smiled. "Thank you, Dinks. As for Mrs. Pettigrew and—

"Lydie, my lord," Dinks said.

"And Lydie, I will convey our collective gratitude."

Cora stood to leave. "We'll return in a few minutes—"

"Ow!" Danforth yelled.

Guy turned to look at his friend. At first, he did not know what to make of Danforth's sprawled position. The viscount's arms were spread wide and his right leg was hiked high in the air. But it was his friend's look of horror that had Guy doubling over with laughter.

"My boot!" he exclaimed. "Get it off."

Cora rushed to her brother's side and gently pried the little white kitten from his expensive boot. From ten feet away, Guy could hear the scratch of leather beneath the kitten's claws.

"Ack! Be careful, will you?"

Cora ripped the grass stem from Danforth's hand. "If you thought you could do better, you should have."

"I'm not touching that stray," Danforth said. "Probably carries rabies or some other foul disease. How did it get in here, anyway?"

Dinks hurried forward. "We have the doors open, my lord, to air out the place. The kitten must have made its way up from the barn. What a curious and brave beastie."

Danforth stood, backing away. "Shouldn't the animal be afraid of humans?" He bent forward to inspect the damage to his Hessians while keeping one eye on the kitten.

"Ethan, it's just a kitten, for goodness sake."

"Blast," he said, finding the gouge marks in his boot. "The damned—"

"Ankle-biter," Guy offered.

"Right. The damned ankle-biter ruined my boot."

"Such a pretty little thing," Dinks said, ignoring

Danforth's outburst. "All that snowy white. Oh, and it has two gray boots."

Guy watched Cora turn the kitten around and peer into its face.

She glanced at Guy with a luminous smile. "Green eyes," she said in a shaky voice.

His heart clenched, knowing she was thinking of Scrapper. "And gray boots."

"Shall we keep him, Miss Cora?" Dinks asked eagerly.

"Hell no—" Danforth began.

"Yes," Cora said over her brother's protest.

Then, as if communicating its thanks, the kitten rested his gray-booted paws against Cora's cheeks. A startled expression flashed across her face, and to Guy's surprise, a tear rolled down her cheek.

Dinks pulled her ever-present handkerchief out of her skirt pocket and offered it to Cora. "Up with you, little mite. We must get you dressed."

Cora rose and made her way toward the door, with the kitten in her arms and Dinks by her side.

"Cora," Guy called.

She glanced over her shoulder, happy in a way he had not seen her in a very long time. "Yes?"

"What will you name your new friend?"

Her smile turned mischievous. "Fang. The name has a certain poignancy to it, don't you think?"

Guy sent her a knowing smile. "Indeed, I do."

She laughed, and the trio retreated to an upstairs bedchamber.

"What the hell was all of that about?" Danforth demanded.

Guy tossed back the rest of his rum. "A small jest between your sister and me."

Danforth's eyes narrowed. "Now, listen here, Helsford—"

"What happened in the cellar?" Somerton asked.

Guy's pleasant mood fled at the thought of retelling the events that led up to Valère's death. Although the bastard received the comeuppance he deserved, he did not know how Cora would cope with her part in the man's death.

In the end, he decided to let Cora tell the story, if she chose. "A well-placed paperweight and a razor-sharp penknife ushered the bastard along to his rightful place in hell. And none too soon, sir."

Somerton eyed him. "What do you mean?"

"As Cora mentioned, he was sent here to kill you, not her. She was merely a decoy to lure you to Latymer's estate, where he could make your death look like an accident."

Somerton rubbed his eyes, looking as if he had aged ten years. He dropped his hand and met Guy's gaze. "I will get the full details later. For now, I need to ask a final favor."

"Name it."

"I would like for you to take Cora away for a few weeks. There is a great deal to be done with this mess yet, and I would rather she not be around while this incident unfolds. She has been through enough."

"There is no need to bother Helsford with this anymore," Danforth said. "I will take care of my sister."

Guy eyed his friend, his teeth clenching. Had Danforth noticed their sidelong glances and shared smiles? Had her brother's protective instincts kicked in? Against *him*?

"It is no bother at all," Guy rejoined, returning Danforth's hard look with a more determined one.

"See here, Helsford," Danforth growled. "I don't like the way you have been looking at Cora tonight. If you lay one hand—"

"Calm yourself, Danforth," Somerton said. "Cora's reputation will not suffer under Helsford's care."

Somerton slanted Guy a commanding look, his message clear. *Don't disappoint me.*

A pang of chagrin thwacked Guy in the stomach. He hated to take advantage of his mentor's trust, but in this case, where Cora was concerned, he would use every opportunity to draw her closer. To awaken her body and deepen her trust.

To remind her of her words of love.

Warmth settled in his bones.

Cora chose that second to step back into the room, wearing a lovely blue dress.

Their gazes met. Cora's eyebrows flared high, and a flush of crimson blanketed her features. Guy tried to stem the tide of affection he felt for her, tried to shield her from its impact. But she had caught him at a vulnerable moment, and he could only yield to the rush of emotion.

"Cora," Somerton said, visibly bracing himself for an argument, "Helsford will escort you ladies to the inn for the evening, and then on to Herrington Park until we can bring order to this chaos."

Her considering gaze settled on Guy before she nodded to Somerton. "I've had enough intrigue for the moment." She clasped her hands together. "I would like to request your assistance."

"What would you have me do?" Somerton asked.

She raised her chin. "I want you to check for any possible connections Father might have had with Valère."

"Cora, you can't be serious," her brother said.

"I am. Valère said if Father had followed instructions he would still be alive. He also mentioned something about Father trying to outwit him." She glanced away for a moment, as if gathering her thoughts. "I know you don't understand, Ethan. But things changed after you left for Eton. Father always seemed on edge and angry, and Mama dealt with it by not dealing with it. Laudanum became her new companion during those months. Valère's taunts opened a door to memories I had long forgotten and have never understood." She leveled her pain-filled yet determined gaze on her former guardian. "I need to know if there is any truth to what Valère said."

She had not backed down from her brother's disbelief, and Guy knew this conversation had to be ripping her apart.

Somerton stepped forward and, in an unusual show of affection, kissed the crown of her head. "Leave it to me, Cora." He nudged her toward the door. "Now go with Helsford."

Her voice cracked. "T-thank you."

Guy loaded the women into the carriage and headed for the inn. As they rambled down the narrow road, his mind focused on the hours that lay ahead.

He would finally have an opportunity to explain his role in her imprisonment. A long overdue explanation, one he had fully intended to deliver after the Rothams' ball. He was not looking forward to the discussion, but he knew his confession was one of the keys to building a future together.

Would she understand why he acted as he did? It was the one answer he feared the most.

If the worst happened and she could not forgive him, he would respect her decision and leave her be when Somerton called them back to London. Somehow, he would summon the strength to walk away from the only woman he had ever loved. But until then, he was not letting her out of his sight.

Which meant they would be sleeping in the same bedchamber tonight.

Forty-Three

CORA'S EARS VIBRATED FROM THE CLAMOR GOING ON inside her head. The closer they got to their destination, the harder her heart pounded.

Guy's need reached across the carriage, searching for a small sign of acceptance, but Cora kept her gaze on Grace. She spoke in soft tones to Jack's sister to keep the girl's mind off her recent ordeal. At a glance, Jack's sister appeared unharmed, but Cora recognized the hollow tones in Grace's speech and the tightness around her eyes. She also knew some wounds were visible only from the inside.

Guy sighed and shifted in his seat, drawing her attention away from Grace. She peeked from beneath her lashes and noticed his clenched hand resting on his powerful thigh. The area between her legs tingled, and Cora pressed her legs together to prolong the effect. His body called to hers as a canvas calls to its master. Excitement, fear, and guilt all clambered for supremacy in her mind.

She wanted him. Cora closed her eyes as the truth filled her soul. They were both adults, with adult desires. Surely, when they were ready to end their liaison, they could walk away with no regrets. She recalled the twinge of hope she had felt after their wondrous time together at the Golden Duck. For one precious moment, she saw their future together, replete with children and happiness and love.

Guy had always held a special place in her life. From their earliest acquaintance, he had watched over her, guided her, cared for her. She could no longer remember a time that he didn't occupy a space in her memory.

When the time came to give him up, would she be able to hand him over into a wife's keeping? The question clawed at her insides like a hungry dog digging for a scrap of food. Frantic. Intent. Fruitless.

The temptation of spending several days, and nights, in Guy's arms was proving too enticing. Nowhere else did she feel complete and happy and hopeful. Nowhere else did she feel loved. Were a few days of unalloyed joy too much to ask? No, she decided.

Calm poured through her mind, quieting her concerns, and her normally confident nature returned. With a languid sweep of her lashes, she locked eyes with Guy. His features revealed a moment's confusion, and then an explosive expression of longing ripped away that paltry reaction. The carriage hummed and heated with undeniable, irresistible tension.

Guy stared at her mouth, his breathing heavy. On impulse, she slid her tongue along the edge of her lower lip. The planes of his face sharpened, and he released a low groan of need.

"Got a sour stomach, my lord?" Dinks asked.

Cora flinched, and Guy's lips firmed, both having forgotten the carriage's other occupants.

"Pardon?" His voice was low, husky.

"I asked if you had a sour stomach," Dinks repeated, smoothing a hand over Fang's purring body. "Thought I heard a bit of rumbling there."

With obvious reluctance, he turned his attention to

her maid. "Ah, no. I'm afraid you caught me trying to stifle a yawn."

Dinks smiled and sent Cora a sideways glance. "I see. No doubt we will all sleep like wee babes tonight."

"Indeed," Guy murmured.

Cora worked to hide a smile. Dinks knew men, and Guy's feeble attempt at deception did not fool her. If Cora's body wasn't vibrating with its need for release, she would have shared her friend's amusement over the situation. Instead of returning a secretive smile, Cora was forced to shut her mind to her body's demands and pray that this interminable ride would end. Soon.

The moon hovered high in the sky by time everyone was settled in for the night. Cora tipped her head back against the iron bed frame and watched Guy pace the chamber with an uneven gait like an anxious soon-to-be father. She frowned, making a mental note to check his leg for injuries—after she got him out of his clothes.

Once they reached the Grinning Buck Inn, their routine was quite reminiscent of the time they had stayed at the Golden Duck. The only difference was Grace occupied a cot in Dinks's room, and it was not Scrapper nestled warmly in a linen-filled trunk, but Fang.

The moment she and Guy turned toward their shared room, Cora sensed Guy's slow withdrawal. All the vivid promises they had made with their eyes in the carriage had disappeared beneath the weight of Guy's thoughts.

She made another attempt to get him to talk about whatever was bothering him. "Guy, won't you tell me what is weighing on your mind?"

"Yes," he said, tugging on his cravat. "In a minute."

Cora clasped her hands together on her lap and prayed for patience. One minute turned into five. Five turned to ten. The longer he delayed, the more her nerves frayed. Then she recalled Guy's comment at the Rothams' ball.

"*I need to discuss something with you.*" Lord Chittendale's rude interruption and Valère's uncouth henchman had prevented them from ever having their discussion.

"Is this the conversation you wanted to have after the Rothams' ball?"

He set his hands on his waist and stared at the tattered carpet, as if all the answers in the world were scribbled at his feet. In all the years that she had known him, she could not recollect ever seeing him so torn. "Yes."

She held out her hand. "Guy, come sit with me." When he stared at her outstretched hand, with a mixture of yearning and consternation, she said more softly, "Please."

His chest caved in on a long exhalation, and he muttered something low that sounded like, "In for a penny." He strode around to the side of the bed and brought her fingers up to his lips, kissing them with a heart-aching reverence. Easing onto the bed, he sat on the edge—half-facing her and half-facing one corner of the room.

"It is time I confess my role in your captivity," he said in one unbroken breath.

Cora's heart thumped once, hard against her rib cage. An eternity elapsed before the organ gathered enough strength to send the next beat crashing into the wall of her chest. "Which one?" she asked stupidly.

His lips thinned. "The first one, of course."

She heard the words he spoke but could make no logical sense of them. "Guy, that is not possible—"

He cast her a quelling look. "Allow me to finish, Impatient One, before I change my mind."

Not a chance, she thought. One cannot make a statement like that and think to leave the receiver hanging midexplanation. At least, not if said speaker wanted to wake up with all his appendages intact. "All this pausing for effect smacks of Ethan. Do get on with it, my lord."

Cora refrained from smiling her satisfaction when Guy's countenance no longer carried the evidence of his mental burdens. She was pleased to see the impressive look of irritation shining in his dark eyes.

"As I was saying," he said with precise enunciation. "Over the past year, I received an unusually high number of coded missives to decipher. Some of the messages were nothing more than poorly scribbled decoys designed to waste our time." His hold tightened around her fingers. "But others brought us closer and closer to the man responsible for the loss of a number of British ships."

A spark of memory flashed through her mind of Guy questioning her about what inciting incident had led to her association with Valère. He had wanted to know what came first—the investigation of the double spy or that of the British ships. At the time, she considered the answer to be of little significance. Both needed her attention. But in light of Guy's current confession, she feared the sequence of events might mean the difference between purgatory and salvation.

Good Lord. For the life of her, she could not recall her answer.

In a toneless murmur, he continued, "The contents of the last missive confirmed our suspicions."

"Let me guess," she said. "The coded trail led you to Valère."

His burning gaze met hers. "Yes."

"So you were the one who finally unraveled the cipher." She heard the note of wonder in her own voice. "A cipher three other agents were unable to break."

He studied her with a look of intense concentration, one she imagined he reserved only for his ciphers. "Do you not comprehend, Cora? Do you not understand how I contributed to your imprisonment?"

Emotion cracked his voice, and Cora's heart ached with the knowledge of how long he had kept this secret bottled up inside. "Guy." She edged forward until she could feel the hard puffs of his breaths against her cheek. "Oh, Guy." She smoothed her fingers over his jaw and cupped his chin with her hand. He turned his face into her palm, delivering a fervent kiss in its center. "Please tell me you have not placed the responsibility of my imprisonment upon your own shoulders."

He covered her hand with his. "Had I not deciphered that final message, Somerton would never have brought Valère to your attention. And you would never have suffered such torture, such degradation—"

She leaned forward, smoothing her thumb over his lips to halt his anguished recitation. "Had you not deciphered that missive, who knows how many more ships and sailors would have been lost."

A heartbeat of silence passed while he absorbed her reply. His hand clasped the nape of her neck, drawing her close. He rested his forehead against hers, squeezing his eyes shut for three shuddering breaths. In a harsh whisper, he asked, "But what of you?"

"What of me?" she asked gently, tipping his chin up so she could look into his eyes. "Guy, my stay in Valère's dungeon rests squarely on my shoulders and no one else's. I became careless and overconfident. Through a series of poor decisions, I placed my servants and myself in grave danger. As for your intelligence bringing Valère into my circle of attention, that was nothing more than a matter of accelerated timing."

"What do you mean?" he asked.

"As much as I wish it were otherwise, my fate became linked with Valère's the moment I clasped his pendant around my neck. Your intelligence did nothing more than hurry the process along, and for that, I should thank you."

"Don't be ridiculous."

"Be at ease, my love." She kissed his lips. "I grew weary of the search. At times, I wanted nothing more than to take walks in the park or dine in the Tuileries Gardens. But I was determined to find the man who murdered my parents, and you helped me accomplish that goal. For the first time in thirteen years, I'm able to think beyond the nuances of a whispered conversation or the allegiance of my dance partner. I'm able to dream about, to make plans for, a normal life filled with happiness, one devoid of intrigue and lies and death."

"That sounds wonderful." Sincerity and longing laced his words, but his expression alerted her to the fact that he still held himself responsible for her imprisonment.

"Let it go, Guy," she said. "I do not blame you in any way. It is my burden to bear."

"We will bear it together, sweetheart," he said in a ragged whisper.

Tears pricked the backs of her eyes. Giving this man up was going to rip her heart out. "Must you always be so damned noble?"

She startled a snort of laughter from him, lightening the mood in the small chamber by several degrees.

"I could try to tamp it down a bit." The stiffness encasing his body seemed to melt before her eyes. "But you would not love me nearly as much."

Cora could feel heat spreading up her neck. Why had she expressed her deepest feelings? When she had looked back to see him tied to the chair, beaten and murderous, expressing her love seemed a natural conclusion. But now those three words were going to cause her all manner of trouble.

"Guy, I think it best if you forget—"

His fingers tunneled through her hair, tilting her lips

to the perfect feasting angle, and then he kissed her. A ravenous, volatile, we-are-alive kiss, one the recipient would never forget. He continued his assault until her bones melted and her body resurged with new life.

He drew away only so far as to draw breath and speak words that would turn her into a blubbering fool. "I'll not countenance any thoughts on your part of leaving me."

Her eyes widened.

"Just as I thought. Maddening woman," he said with a mixture of amusement and exasperation. "I don't know what odd notions you have skirting around that active— normally intelligent—mind of yours, but I will not allow you to turn your back on our love."

Not allow? She lifted her chin a notch and narrowed her eyes. "I'm afraid you are under a wrong assumption, sir."

"And what might that be?"

"That you have a say in the matter."

His lips twitched. "As your husband, I will have plenty of say. Every piece of your delectable body shall be mine to do with as I please."

A disturbing and wholly inappropriate shiver tracked down her spine. Although his arrogant statement made her want to kick his shin, his possessive reference to her body sent a thrilling sparkle of anticipation straight down to the pit of her stomach.

"I'm sorry," she said in an entirely too-sweet voice. "I seem to have missed the ceremony of my own wedding. I hope I said 'I do' at the proper moment."

"Saying 'I do' won't be the only words whispering from your mouth."

Cora found rational thought nearly impossible when he became quite intent at exploring the long column of her neck. The succulent warmth of his wicked mouth heated her veins into a fiery river. She closed her eyes, not wanting to disrupt his very thorough exploration, but she had to make him understand the gravity of their situation.

She pushed at his chest. "Guy, enough of this nonsense."

He released an aggrieved sigh. "It is not nonsense to me." He swept the knuckle of his index finger down her cheek. "I love you, Cora, and I know you love me. We both want the same things—family, home, a life beyond the Nexus. When I imagine my future, all I see is you." He tapped her nose. "Just you. From the moment your six-year-old feet stumbled upon your brother and me swimming in the lake, and you jumped in to join us, I knew we would be fast friends. And when I found you prancing around Mrs. Lancaster's town house, looking like a damn seductress, I knew our relationship would go far beyond friendship." His voice became raw, rough with emotion. "Destiny entwined our paths, but our future lies within your hands. *Please*, Cora. Please give our love a chance. Give *us* a chance."

"Oh, Guy." She felt the sharp needles of despair closing her throat. His impassioned speech strained her conviction. She wanted nothing more than to live that future with him. But choices she had made years ago now dictated the structure of her happiness, and that structure did not include marriage to an earl. "You must see the impossibility of the situation."

His jaw firmed. "I do not. Pray enlighten me."

Cora could not stop the instinctive contraction of her muscles at his high-and-mighty tone. "Despite your stubborn tendencies, you must realize any association with me would mean social ruin for you. I love you too much to watch the *ton* turn their backs on you, one after the other, because of your poor choice of a bride. I was not exactly discreet while in France, and you know as well as I do that the English Channel will not keep the gossip from reaching British shores. You deserve someone who will bring honor and beauty into your life, not ruination and a dark past that could devastate your good name and destroy your children's chances at respectable marriages."

Much to her chagrin, he seemed more interested in the laces at the top of her nightdress than her proclamation of his social doom.

"My 'good name' has survived five hundred years of politics, war, and scandal, despite the efforts of some incredibly reckless ancestors."

Cool air breezed over her aching breasts. She glanced down at her gaping nightdress, then back up to the sensual lines of his handsome face. Confusion kept her mute for several heartbeats. How could he be so unconcerned about the *ton*'s collective power over his fate? Did he not grasp the number of influential doors that would be closed to him and his offspring?

"Times are different, Guy," she said. "Society is much less tolerant of disgraceful behavior than they were even a decade ago. The *ton* will feed off my past, making it impossible for us to live happily among them."

Slowly, inexorably, he used the sheer mass of his big body to force her into a reclining position. She stared up into his determined dark gaze, and her heart stuttered at what she found there. "Guy, you're not listening to me!"

"Finally we agree on something."

She tried to wriggle out from beneath the cage of his arms. "If you won't consider the repercussions to yourself, think of how it will affect your heir."

He slid his tongue along the valley between her breasts. "I *am* thinking of my heir."

She pressed her lips together, suppressing a laugh despite her irritation with the obstinate man. "You're not. You're thinking of *making* your heir."

"A minor technicality, I assure you."

"Stop!" She clamped her hands around his face and forced him to meet her gaze.

"Yes, love?"

"I don't know how to make you understand what is at stake here," she whispered. "What if my father supplied the French with information? Good God, we won't survive such a scandal."

The smile he sent her was so filled with love that she felt it spill over onto her in soft, calming waves. "What's at stake is *us*, Cora. I will not allow the petty vindictiveness of society to ruin our opportunity at a future together. And whatever Somerton discovers about your father, we will deal with it. Together. No other will do for me but you, Cora Marie deBeau, and I will make the *ton* acutely aware of that fact. Say you will have me."

Cora stared at him in stunned disbelief, her vision blurring with emotion. Could Guy really care so little about what the *ton* thought of his countess? Was his place in society so secure that their opinions held no sway over his activities, or power against his family?

Cora understood society's need to separate its members into two distinct categories—respectable and ruined—and there was little one could do when labeled the latter. It never occurred to her that one could balance a foot on each side of the equation—it simply wasn't done.

At least, not until Guy changed the rules. For her.

He was willing to bear society's ridicule in order to spend the rest of his life in her company. The prospect filled her heart with the sweetest joy she ever felt. Her hold around his face loosened, shifting from shield to caress. "A-are you absolutely sure?"

He nuzzled her nose. "Yes."

"You won't come to resent me when the *ton* turns its back on us?"

"Never."

Cora knew she would forever regret her decision if she did not jump at this miracle chance at love. At having a family, with little Trevelyans calling her Mama.

They would face the dragons together.

Together.

Joyful tears slid down her cheeks. "Yes, I will have you, if you will have me."

His mouth curled up into a teasing angle. "Give me a moment to think on it."

She whacked his shoulder.

"Ow! Yes!" he said on a laugh. Then his voice lowered, "Yes."

"A priceless earl," she murmured against his lips, unable to keep the silly, wobbly smile off her face. "A woman has no need of diamonds with you by her side."

"Does that mean you accept my marriage proposal?"

Her eyes sparkled. "I don't recall receiving such a tempting request."

"No?" His hands curled around her bottom, bringing her into sharp, potent contact with the evidence of his desire. "How remiss of me." He stood abruptly and removed his clothing with preternatural speed. "I shall have to remedy that oversight."

She stretched her arms high above her head, arching her back. "Does a lady not deserve a proper proposal from bended knee?"

He stood naked at the edge of the bed; his broad shoulders and beautifully carved frame blocked out one side of the room. As her gaze raked over the contours of his body, she catalogued each delectable spot she wanted to further investigate.

She finally arrived at his fully aroused staff, and a searing wave of desire struck her with the force of a cannon blast. Her eyes widened farther when his fingers curled around his thick staff, and his hand slid down to the smooth, rounded tip.

"Yes," he hissed between clenched teeth. "A lady would deserve such a paltry show of a man's affection. However, the Raven shall benefit from a proper ravishment from a husband who loves her to distraction."

"Mmm, I like the sound of that," she crooned, flipping back the covers to welcome him inside. He helped her peel off her nightdress, and when bare flesh met bare flesh, they both moaned their delight.

Caught up in the extraordinary sensations soaring through her, Cora carefully placed her body over his and stared into fathomless dark eyes. A lifetime of suppressed hope and forbidden dreams welled up and drenched her world in a watery haze. She tried to blink back tears, but a part of her still could not believe his acceptance of her past. "Say it again."

The half smile he sent her was all predatory male. "I love you, Cora." He kissed the corner of her mouth.

Not to be outdone, she hooked her leg around his hip. "Again."

"I love you." He placed another promissory kiss to the delicate lid of her right eye.

She trailed her hands down the rippling muscles of his back. "Again."

"Love you," he whispered the beautiful words against her lips. "Always."

Yes, she agreed. *Always*.

Much later, when the tempest of their collective heartbeats waned, Cora unwound her quivering limbs from Guy's body, and winced with regret when he slid free and flopped onto his back. Guy's hand sought hers as they both lay there, staring at the ceiling, dazed and depleted of strength.

"I can't believe it's over," she whispered into the silence.

She sensed more than saw his head angle her way. "I will never allow anyone to hurt you again. Not even me."

"Nor I you."

He released a resigned sigh, and she smiled.

"Have we not discussed this bothersome need of yours to protect me?" He rested his arm over his eyes.

"I do recall something of the sort," she mused, glancing over at his partially concealed profile. "But now that we are betrothed, I have an even greater interest in your continued welfare."

His full, luscious mouth curled up into a knowing smile. "Hmm, why is that, my Raven?"

She turned into him, sliding her hand over his chest. "Because ravens mate for life, my lord."

Acknowledgments

As with any debut novel, I have many people to thank. Without the help and encouragement of the following people, *A Lady's Revenge* would still be languishing on my computer—promising, but hopelessly flawed.

First off, a huge hug and thank you to my friends, critique partners, and Romance University blogmates Adrienne Giordano and Kelsey Browning for all your support, wise counsel, and crazy good times. Theresa Stevens, thank you for being the link that bound me to these two wonderful ladies and for always being there to answer my goofy craft and publishing questions. High fives to my other fabulous RU blogmates—Carrie Spencer, Jennifer Tanner, Becke Martin Davis, and Robin Covington. Thank you for all your wonderful work and dedication and for making RU a fun place to learn and hang out! I also owe a debt of gratitude to my marvelous critique partners Victoria Gray and Lucie J. Charles. Thank you, ladies, for all your pearls of wisdom and encouragement.

Of course, Cora and Guy would never have had their fifteen minutes of fame without the extraordinary guidance of my editor, Deb Werksman, and agent, Donald Maass. Thank you both for taking a chance on a historical writer who loves to torture her hero and heroine and for handing me the golden shovel, with the directive, "Dig. Deeper."

A shout out to the Hearts Through History RWA, most especially the Critters group—Kathleen Bittner-Roth, Tessy Grillo, Jenny Ramirez, Eliza Knight, Joan Maze, and Valerie Oakleaf. I really appreciate all your hard work on *A Lady's Revenge*. I also want to thank the Beau Monde RWA ladies for their invaluable Regency-related expertise. And major thanks to my Windy City RWA sisters for helping a shy greenhorn navigate the publishing world. An extra special thanks goes to chaptermates Sherry Weddle, Melody Thomas, Chris Foutris, and Ann Macela for your one-on-one support.

Big hugs to the brilliant Franzeca Drouin, whose indispensable knowledge of all-things-historical made *ALR* a much richer, more accurate read. *Merci, mon amie.* PS—Sorry, z, I couldn't give up the shiv.

No acknowledgement of this novel would be complete without recognizing Brenda Novak for her efforts with the Online Auction for Diabetes Research, where she connects aspiring authors to publishing professionals of every variety while raising funds for an amazing charity. Through Brenda's 2007 auction, I got the chance to work with two incredible and generous authors—Madeline Hunter and Candice Hern. They were the first to read *ALR* in all its raw glory, and I wish to publicly apologize to both authors for putting them through such agony. Thank you, ladies, for your much-needed and much-appreciated feedback.

And to all of my fabulous readers—thank you, thank you, thank you!

About the Author

Tracey Devlyn writes historical romantic thrillers (translation: a slightly more grievous journey toward the heroine's happy ending). She's also a co-founder of Romance University, a group blog dedicated to readers and writers of romance.

An Illinois native, Tracey spends her evenings harassing her once-in-a-lifetime husband and her weekends torturing her characters. For more information on Tracey, including her Internet haunts, contest updates, and details on her upcoming novels, please visit her website at www.TraceyDevlyn.com.

Lord and Lady Spy

by Shana Galen

❧

No man can outsmart him...

Lord Adrian Smythe may appear a perfectly boring gentleman, but he leads a thrilling life as one of England's most preeminent spies, an identity so clandestine even his wife is unaware of it. But he isn't the only one with secrets...

She's been outsmarting him for years...

Now that the Napoleonic wars have come to an end, daring secret agent Lady Sophia Smythe can hardly bear the thought of returning home to her tedious husband. Until she discovers in the dark of night that he's not who she thinks he is after all...

❧

"An excellent book, full of great witty conversation, hot passionate scenes, and tons of action."—BookLoons

"The author's writing style, how this story is built and all of the delicious scenes, and the characters themselves are just so rich, so enjoyable I found myself smiling and absolutely enjoying every single page."—Smexy Books

For more Shana Galen, visit:

www.sourcebooks.com

The Rogue Pirate's Bride

by Shana Galen

— ❧ —

Revenge should be sweet, but it may cost him everything…

Out to avenge the death of his mentor, Bastien discovers himself astonishingly out of his depth when confronted with a beautiful, daring young woman who is out for his blood…

Forgiveness is unthinkable, but it may be her only hope…

British Admiral's daughter Raeven Russell believes Bastien responsible for her fiancé's death. But once the fiery beauty crosses swords with Bastien, she's not so sure she really wants him to change his wicked ways…

— ❧ —

Praise for Shana Galen:

"Lively dialogue, breakneck pace, and great sense of fun."—Publishers Weekly

"Galen strikes the perfect balance between dangerous intrigue and sexy romance."—Booklist

For more Shana Galen, visit:

www.sourcebooks.com

Miss Hillary Schools a Scoundrel

by Samantha Grace

❧

He'll never settle for one woman...

Debonair bachelor Lord Andrew Forest lives for pleasure and offers no apologies. But he receives a dose of his own medicine when his family's entrancing houseguest beds him, then disappears without so much as a by-your-leave. He'd like to teach the little vixen a thing or two about how to love a man... if he can find her...

And she won't settle for heartbreak...

After the dashing man of her dreams is revealed as a lying scoundrel, heiress Lana Hillary is ready to seek a match with a respectable gentleman—if only they weren't so dreadfully boring. Unable to rein in her bold nature for long, Lana flirts with trouble and finds herself entangled with exactly the type of man she's vowed to avoid.

❧

"With heart and humor, Grace delivers a rich and winning Regency debut. Clever and charming, this tale brings in everything Regency fans love..."—Publishers Weekly *Starred Review*

For more Samantha Grace, visit:

www.sourcebooks.com

The Virtuoso

by Grace Burrowes

———— ❦ ————

A genius with a terrible loss...

Gifted pianist Valentine Windham, youngest son of the Duke of Moreland, has little interest in his father's obsession to see his sons married, and instead pours passion into his music. But when Val loses his music, he flees to the country, alone and tormented by wha t has been robbed from him.

A widow with a heartbreaking secret...

Grieving Ellen Markham has hidden herself away, looking for safety in solitude. Her curious new neighbor offers a kindred lonely soul whose desperation is matched only by his desire, but Ellen's devastating secret could be the one thing that destroys them both.

Together they'll find there's no rescue from the past, but sometimes losing everything can help you find what you need most.

———— ❦ ————

"Burrowes's exceptional writing and originality catch the reader and keep the story moving."—Publishers Weekly

For more Grace Burrowes, visit:

www.sourcebooks.com

New York Times and USA Today Bestseller

The Soldier

by Grace Burrowes

———————— ✂ ————————

**Even in the quiet countryside,
he can find no peace…**

His idyllic estate is falling down from neglect and nightmares of war give him no rest. Then Devlin St. Just meets
his new neighbor…

**Until his beautiful neighbor
ignites his imagination…**

With her confident manner hiding a devastating secret, his
lovely neighbor commands all of his attention, and protecting
Emmaline becomes Devlin's most urgent mission.

———————— ✂ ————————

*"Burrowes's straightforward, sensual love story
is intelligent and tender, rising above the crowd
with deft dialogue and delightful characters."*
—Publishers Weekly (starred review)

For more Grace Burrowes, visit:

www.sourcebooks.com

A *Publishers Weekly* Best Book of the Year

The Heir

by Grace Burrowes

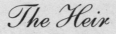

An earl who can't be bribed...

Gayle Windham, Earl of Westhaven, is the first legitimate son and heir to the Duke of Moreland. To escape his father's inexorable pressure to marry, he decides to spend the summer at his townhouse in London, where he finds himself intrigued by the secretive ways of his beautiful housekeeper...

A lady who can't be protected...

Anna Seaton is a beautiful, talented, educated woman, which is why it is so puzzling to Gayle Windham that she works as his housekeeper.

As the two draw closer and begin to lose their hearts to each other, Anna's secrets threaten to bring the earl's orderly life crashing down—and he doesn't know how he's going to protect her from the fallout...

"A luminous and graceful erotic Regency...a captivating love story that will have readers eagerly awaiting the planned sequels."—Publishers Weekly (starred review)

For more Grace Burrowes, visit:

www.sourcebooks.com

A Dash of Scandal

by Amelia Grey

———— ✎ ————

Is she stealing… or just hiding in dark corners…

The Earl of Dunraven is obsessed with catching the thief who stole a priceless heirloom from him. When he keeps running into London newcomer Millicent Blair in places she shouldn't be, his suspicions aren't the only thing aroused…

But Millicent's real secret is a far cry from what the earl thinks—and would horrify him much more if he knew. Yet, every encounter increases the attraction between the powerful earl and the lovely, intelligent, and feisty Miss Blair…

Welcome to the sparkling Regency world of Amelia Grey, where the gossip is fresh and a new scandal is always brewing.

———— ✎ ————

"This is the perfect recipe for a perfect Regency romance novel. A pinch of mystery, a slice of romance, a sliver of gossip, and a dash of scandal. What more could you ask for?"—Royal Reviews

For more Amelia Grey, visit:

www.sourcebooks.com

A Gentleman Never Tells

by Amelia Grey

━━━━━━━ ❧ ━━━━━━━

A stolen kiss from a stranger...

As if from a dream, Lady Gabrielle walked from the mist and into Viscount Brentwood's arms. Within moments, he's embroiled in more scandal than he ever thought possible...

Can sink even a perfect gentleman...

Beautiful, clever, and courageous, Lady Gabrielle needs Brent's help to get out of a seriously bad situation. But the more she gets to know him, the worse she feels about ruining his life...

Enter the unforgettable world of Amelia Grey's sparkling Regency London, where a single encounter may have devastating consequences for a gentleman and a lady...

━━━━━━━ ❧ ━━━━━━━

"A stubborn heroine clashes with an equally determined hero in the latest well-crafted, canine-enhanced addition to Grey's Regency-set Rogues' Dynasty series."—Booklist

"The book is delightful... charming and unforgettable."—Long and Short Review

For more Amelia Grey, visit:

www.sourcebooks.com

Never a Bride

by Amelia Grey

Her name is on everyone's lips...

When he left for America six years ago, the handsome Viscount Camden Brackley never suspected that he would return home to England to find his lovely fiancée embroiled in the scandal of the decade. The woman he planned on making his wife has been kissing every man in London... except him!

But scandal doesn't matter in search of the truth...

Engaged and then abandoned, Lady Mirabella Wittingham is determined to find the man who drove her cousin to suicide, even if it means ruining her reputation and disgracing herself in the process...

When her plans go awry, Mirabella has no choice but to turn to her long-lost fiancé for help. But can she trust the man who deserted her so many years ago, or is he destined to fail her yet again?

"Witty dialogue and clever schemes... Grey's vivid characters will charm readers."—Booklist

For more Amelia Grey, visit:

www.sourcebooks.com